AMERICAN

VOLUME EIGHT

The Best Unpublished Stories by Emerging Writers

GUEST JUDGE

Charles Baxter

EDITORS

Alan Davis & Michael White

New Rivers Press
1996

New Rivers Press is a non-profit literary press dedicated to publishing the very best emerging writers in our region, nation, and world.

The publication of *American Fiction* has been made possible by generous grants from the Elmer L. and Eleanor J. Andersen Foundation, the Beim Foundation, the General Mills Foundation, Liberty State Bank, the McKnight Foundation, the Star Tribune/Cowles Media Company, the Tennant Company Foundation, and contributing members of New Rivers Press. New Rivers Press is a member agency of United Arts.

American Fiction has been manufactured in the United States of America for New Rivers Press, 420 North 5th Street, Suite 910, Minneapolis, MN 55401 in a first edition.

Contents

◆

Alan Davis and Michael White
Editors' Note v

Charles Baxter
Introduction vii

FIRST PRIZE
Cammie McGovern
City Living 1

SECOND PRIZE
Steve Lattimore
Answer Me This 18

THIRD PRIZE
Nancy Reisman
Edie in Winter 32

Jennifer C. Cornell
Wax 48

Nadja Tesich
Crimes of Passion 59

David Mason
Boys' State 68

Tracy Jennison
I Do Not Close My Eyes 87

William Borden
Bear Dances 96

Megan Randall
Majesty Justifies 115

Brock Clarke
The Reasons 128

Misha Hoekstra
The Brother 134

A. A. Hedge Coke
The Sun and Moon Over Jasper 142

Catherine Brady
Rat 149

Garnett Kilbern Cohen
Where You Can't Touch Bottom 161

Michael Beres
Calendars and Clocks 173

Cheryl Pearl Sucher
Kishinev 188

Gordon Johnston
Plight 208

Biographical Notes 229

Editors' Note

◆

The faith we have in fiction at the end of the milennium is no longer a personal luxury, like reading only on the commuter train or in the wee hours when sleep just won't come. The truth of story in a world full of "story" is no longer negotiable. If we don't mark off where we begin and end by finding ourselves in fiction, by voicing the world until it makes sense, then hucksters will do it for us on late-night television, entertainers will delude us into thinking that the pleasures of the page can be found instead at the local video or CD or computer store, politicians and ideologues will fill our heads with slogans. Without fiction, the imagination atrophies and dies and we live a life that becomes less and less interesting with each passing year. A book, Kafka famously said, "must be the axe for the frozen sea inside us."

The stories in this eighth volume of *American Fiction*, chosen from nearly one thousand submissions, are quirky, compelling, sometimes laugh-out-loud funny. They will keep you good company if you read them on the commuter train or at lunch hour or in the wee hours when the neighborhood is quiet. But they also dramatize, as guest judge Charles Baxter points out in his introduction, "a moment when terror has become one of the standard household emotions of common life. Not Holocaust terror, historical and genocidal, but the soul-shocks and ordinary violence of daily existence." We live in a culture where goodwill and human empathy often seem under siege, sometimes by the very people who claim to be defending them. "The future belongs to crowds," Don DeLillo writes in *Mao II*.

These particular stories, each opposed in its way to the logic of crowds, have been chosen through a process similar to the one described in Volume Seven, where a thumbnail history of the series also appears. We refer you to that edition if you are curious. We will say here that *American Fiction* is unique because it is the only annual anthology of previously unpublished fiction by emerging writers ("everyone not yet famous enough to enjoy the certainty of publication elsewhere," according to previous judge Tobias Wolff). The best new work by such writers appears here in book form instead of in literary periodicals and competes for prizes awarded by the guest judge and for the increase in literary reputation that sometimes follows.

We are happiest when we find stories that cannot be paraphrased but must be experienced. As Charles Baxter writes, "I feel like a carnival barker. *Come inside. Wonders galore.*" We hope that your reading experience is as compelling as the one he describes in his introduction.

We thank him for his work, and congratulate the three prizewinners he chose: first prize winner Cammie McGovern for "City Living"; second prize winner Steve Lattimore for "Answer Me This"; and third prize winner Nancy Reisman for "Edie in Winter." Congratulations as well to the other finalists, all of whom appear in this edition. (Two of the stories, Gordon Johnston's "Plight" and Megan Randall's "Majesty Justifies," were selected too late in the process to be considered for prizes.) We also thank Moorhead State University (especially Betty Kucera, Dee Kruger, and honors apprentice Jennifer Moland) and Springfield College (especially Irene Graves) for their assistance and support, including a creative activity grant at Moorhead State and a sabbatical at Springfield College. Thanks as well to everyone who submitted their stories; we appreciate your trust and wish upon you the will and the desire and the stubbornness to bring something new and shapely and memorable into the world. Finally, thanks to New Rivers Press, especially Bill Truesdale, Michelle Woster and Phyllis Jendro; this non-profit literary press established in 1968 publishes each year some of the best new writing available in the country.

Alan Davis
Michael C. White

Charles Baxter

✦

INTRODUCTION

Some time ago I found myself on an airplane, seated next to a mumbling and (I thought) probably grumpy old man. I opened my copy of a book-review magazine and turned to an essay about what was then a new film, *Schindler's List*. My seatmate looked at what I was reading, and then, in a middle-European accent, informed me, "I was one of those."

"You were . . ."

"I was a Schindler Jew," he said.

After I had recovered myself, and we had made our introductions and I had shaken his hand I asked him—I suppose it was a naive question—what the experience of working for Schindler had been like. He said, "What I saw, you don't put into a movie." He then described what he had seen in the camps—a description beyond imagining, which not only convinced me that this man was exactly who he said he was but which also gave me a queasy, vertiginous feeling, as we flew at twenty-five thousand feet over the Rocky Mountains toward Phoenix, Arizona. "Disorientation" is not quite the word for it. I was half in the plane, half somewhere else, floating in time, some place he had taken me, inside his narrative. After giving me a bill of particulars of the horrors he had witnessed, he said, "You know, in that movie, they had some footage of me for the epilogue, but they cut me out of the final version." He leaned back in his seat and peered at me with a sort of distant curiosity. "What are you doing, going to Phoenix?"

I said I was going to a convention.

"You should see the night life," he instructed me. "Ever been to Las Vegas?"

No, I said, I never had.

"You should go. You should see the shows. Every year of our marriage, my wife and I went to Las Vegas. A great place, Las Vegas. You should see it."

Out of deference, I said I would try to get to Las Vegas. I haven't been there yet.

Horror and diversion on the grand scale, Auschwitz and Las Vegas: try to hold these items in your head simultaneously and you become a citizen of the last part of the twentieth century, at least in America.

I thought of the man I met on the plane while I was reading through the stories collected in this anthology. What struck me about so many of them was their interest, actually their insistence, in the yoking of the terrible and the comic-diversionary. And I don't mean "black humor" by this, some sort of recycling of nihilistic, urbane, and (formerly, mostly male) obsessive writing. If these stories are a representative sample, we have come to a moment at the end of our century when the terror and humor switch places so quickly that tone almost begins to take over from action. I found, when I was thinking about these stories after I had read them, that I remembered their sudden turns toward fright or panic as inevitable, as if these darker shocks have become part of the necessary vocabulary in contemporary storytelling.

Perhaps we have come to a moment when terror has become one of the standard household emotions of common life. Not Holocaust terror, historical and genocidal, but the soul-shocks and ordinary violence of daily existence.

In Cammie McGovern's wonderful first-place story, "City Living," for example, the narrator's friend Iona feasts on her crime fantasies. As a New Yorker, she may certainly be entitled to them, but what the narrator (and we) can hardly anticipate is the way in which Iona herself begins to plot her own criminal enterprises. They begin in a petty manner but they do escalate. The narrator herself is not immune to a bit of seemingly harmless personal misrepresentation. The voice in which this particular brand of casual desperation is brought to us is witty, intelligent, and dryly obsessive. All this gives way, in the story's effortlessly brilliant conclusion, to an unforgettable coda in a subway station, where a would-be criminal does something so much worse, and more weirdly truthful, than robbery, that the scene takes on the total clarity of a visible event, almost beyond imagining. But it isn't beyond imagining, and that's the wonder of the story.

Similarly, in Steve Lattimore's "Answer Me This," we are in a world of undifferentiated anger, a contemporary urban setting where Russell, our protagonist, slowly spirals down into the humorously bad-tempered hands of the law. The story's force derives from its high-focus precision and its disconcerting comedy. I felt lucky, reading this story. There's a kind of dazed exactitude and inevitability to it, combined with a perfect pitch for the sentences Americans utter when they're feeling belligerent or impatient. This is the Kafka-of-everyday-life mode, the American Kafka, utilitarian, shiny, and soiled with commodities. Its penultimate scene, with Norma and Russell and the cow in Throc's apartment, has a wild imaginativeness that is beautifully appropriate to the story's themes of procreation and steadfastness. You think: *it's amazing, and it would have happened in just that way.*

And finally, in Nancy Reisman's "Edie in Winter," we are in a wholly different fictional landscape. This story has many secrets, and it withholds them carefully until the last possible moment. Manny, the protagonist's brother, with his bad posture, his hat, his feeling for the proprieties mixed with his desperation—the story takes place in 1948—is a remarkable and heartbreaking character, as is his sister, hopefully and then hopelessly triangulated with him. I knew I had entered a fictional world I would care about when I came upon the moment when Edie, thinking of her brother, reunited with his childhood friend, imagines him "doused in twilight." Yes, exactly: after that moment, I never wanted to abandon this story or this voice. This story, like the first two I have mentioned, takes you away. It creates a world and sustains it from start to finish. I don't want to force my point, but the story also has a snow-blown terror to it, combined with the sadness of everyday life, that leads us to the sense we have when someone we know is about to do the unimaginable and then actually does it.

There. There's that word again. *Imaginable.* I found in all these stories a sense of authority, a power to transport me somewhere that I couldn't have imagined myself but that someone took the trouble to get down, to get mapped, on paper: that water tower in Garnett Kilberg Cohen's "Where You Can't Touch Bottom," or the eerie and weirdly funny north country of William Borden's "Bear Dances." There is a sort of deadpan surrealism here, too, in Misha Hoeckstra's "The Brother," and the odd but logical rituals in A. A. Hedge Coke's "The Sun and Moon Over Jasper" In Cheryl Pearl Sucher's "Kishinev," something happens that you wouldn't believe, something between a mother and her son, but when you read it, you do believe it. And there is, as I've said, the ubiquitous violence and shock of the other stories, often narrated with disarming good-natured humor.

I feel like a carnival barker. *Come inside. Wonders galore. You'll shake your head, but you won't be able to disbelieve the evidence of your senses.*

And now a secret must be imparted. I don't actually believe in contests, not for writing. The world wants them, so we have them. But as Jim Harrison has said somewhere, *Literature is not a sack race.* What you have in this volume are the products of sweat and blood and experience and craft. Truth and beauty are not, strictly speaking, competitive. And it is unseemly to suggest that one manifestation of beauty beats out another. The Trojan War got started with a big mistake. The stories gathered here have been selected from many stories submitted to the editors, and my choices happen to be the record of the ones that made the greatest impression on me. They were the particular fictions that *I* could remember from scene to scene, and whose voices impressed me with their authority and therefore remained in my mind. They broke through to me, but I would resist the temptation to make world-historical pronouncements about why they were better than the others included here.

After all, I can still remember the voice of the man I met on that plane to Phoenix. I didn't like it at first. It was one of those phlegmy and slightly liquid voices, unmusical to a fault. I was sitting in my seat, 23-A, a contemporary American, and like most contemporary Americans I wanted to be left alone. I don't start conversations on airplanes, and I don't expect the people who are sitting next to me to do so and I certainly don't encourage them to make a social effort. Surrounded by other human beings, I expect and hope to be left by myself in my cramped solitude with my beverage and my peanuts. I smile, and I act distant and distracted. On that day, I settled in, I opened my review. That was when he turned to me and began to tell me a story. His name, he said, was Neufeld. We shook hands. He pointed to a sketch of barbed wire fencing in the book reviews and he said he had been there. He told me he had something to say.

You listen, and you never get over it.

Cammie McGovern

◆

CITY LIVING

The September of my first year out of college, I surprised myself by get-ting a real job, with my own desk, a nine-to-five schedule, and a lunch hour dangling like an undeserved reward in the middle of the day. I got the job after a twenty-minute interview with a woman named Aggie who asked gravely if I was a neat person. "I think so," I said.

She nodded. "Fine then."

I filled in the silence. "Do you need someone who's neat?"

"Yes." She studied the resume in her hands with my college extra-cur-riculars in bold font. "It's really the only thing that matters."

The office was a clearing house for information on children's book publishing and children's authors. Every few months, they put out an encyclopedia of author's biographies that went to libraries and, accord-ing to Iona, one of the women I worked with, was not particularly good, nor very widely read. "The children aren't interested. The librarians for-get it's there. Nobody cares," she told me on my first day.

My job was to comb the various trade periodicals, *Publisher's Weekly*, *Kirkus*, cut out any mention of a children's book or author, then glue it with rubber cement to a 3 x 5 index card. This was why they needed a neat person. "Try not to get rubber cement everywhere," Aggie said, pointing to a thin yellow stain of dried glue on one of the cards. "I hate that." As soon as I had rubber-cemented an author's name to seven or more cards, he or she merited an entry in our encyclopedia. When we were alone, Iona pointed out the illogic of such a system: "It doesn't mat-ter if it's the same book mentioned seven times or seven different books."

I

She thunked her head hard. "Like there's not a slight difference?"

It didn't matter to me. Charles Schulz had a stack of cards in our file as long as my forearm and still I scissored out every anniversary edition of a Peanuts cartoon collection. "Right," Iona once said, watching what I was doing. "Great."

There were four women in all—Aggie, Iona, myself and Lynn—working in the same room at four separate desks, our eyes to the wall, our backs to the center. Around us, shelves and shelves of children's books rose up on all sides: collector's copies and first editions with faded titles pressed into the spine. To my right, I had a gold-tipped, leather-embossed *The Tale of Jemima Puddle-Duck*; to my left, I had Iona.

Within the first week, Iona singled me out as the beneficiary of her confidences. "Don't tell anyone I told you this," she whispered, rolling her desk chair over to mine (Iona was overweight and didn't stand up if she didn't have to.) "But this whole operation is pretty much of a joke. It's all a tax write-off. Our salaries, everything." I stared up at her. I was new to the city, a beginner at office work. I never knew what to believe. "We're meant to net a loss. They don't care about this book. They don't even look at it. We could put dirty pictures in it, they wouldn't know." Though we were in New York, we worked for a division of a publisher based in Detroit, and our office was half the third floor of a transient hotel. We shared a bathroom with a woman named Belle who used a walker. She had a foil-covered dinner delivered nightly from Meals on Wheels. We worked without a boss. At the time, it didn't occur to me how odd all of this was.

Iona's great pleasure, second to pointing out the futility of our work, was tracking violent crimes committed around our neighborhood. At lunch every day, she ate two pizza slices and a Coke as she poured over the police blotter column. "Did you all hear this one?" she would say. "Last week, a woman from Queens was raped by two men who cut off the tips of her fingers afterwards. They wanted to keep her fingernails." I would blink, dumb-struck. *What? Her fingernails?* Each time I was stunned. The others listened, shook their heads, and went back to work while I carried the news with me for the rest of the day, hunched over my desk where the rubber cement fumes ate away at my nose hairs.

After work, as I gathered up my purse and coat, Iona would invariably hold a finger up and wave it in my direction. "Wait a second and I'll walk out with you," she'd say. I would waffle for a moment, then linger. Part of my hesitation—though I am embarrassed to say this now—had to do with her size and the way that out on the street her caftan dresses took wind like a set of sails. They would bloom out around her, doubling her sidewalk space, creating a spectacle. I hated the sound of wind whipping through her dresses, the sight of airborne scraps of trash getting lost in her clothing. Invariably, a trip down the stairs with her became a walk to the subway and then a half hour ride from 81st to 14th Street, where, mercifully, we parted for separate lines. If she ever noticed my embarrassment or the wide berth I gave her in public, she never commented on it. Instead, we rode the fifteen stops together in an agonizing silence that she usually ended by saying we had to get together for drinks at some point so she could really give me the dirt.

Then the day before Halloween, Iona told a longer story. "Did you all hear the one about the woman in the laundromat?" She began as if this was going to be a joke. We shook our heads. "It was late, about eleven, and she had no choice, she had to do some laundry. She thought she'd be fine because there were machines in her basement, but then, New York being New York, the dryers don't work. So she has to carry a bag of wet laundry three blocks to Second Avenue where she walks in on a man crow-barring change out of a machine. The only thing she says is, 'Excuse me,' and that does it. Seven blows to the head and dead on arrival." We stared up at her in disbelief. None of us was married. We all carried our laundry long, lonely distances. There was nothing—simply nothing—any of us could say. Lynn cleared her throat and stepped out to the bathroom. The rest of us stared at book spines until the end of the day.

Since the beginning of summer, I had been living with my best friend from college, a woman with whom I shared the same first name. Willa. It was an uncommon name. I have only met one or two others besides us my whole life. For the three years we'd been friends, I loved the peculiarity of calling out to myself and getting an answer, as if fate had paired us in a way more irreversible than marriage. We had had a wonderful summer together, eating dinners off boxes we never unpacked, talking about the life we would have as soon as it started. On weekends we began going out at night, looking for men. Standing barside, holding Rolling Rocks, I spoke about my job as if it was an entry into a publishing career. "It's great," I would say. "I'm learning a lot." Willa was better at the bar scene than I. She managed a nonchalance I could never emulate and eventually, even explaining our shared name seemed a little foolish against the blank stare of a man trying to get the joke. "I'm Willa, too," I'd say, waving over her shoulder, sounding like a sequel.

As opposed to me, Willa had gotten a job that impressed people right away. She worked as a fashion assistant at *Mademoiselle* magazine where her duties included being on photo shoots to organize accessories. She was able to tell stories about the models she worked with and the lemon and lettuce lunches they ate on the set. Men would listen and blink and lean close.

One night, in the middle of October, Willa came home late from work, at midnight or so, and crawled into the double bed I'd made by pushing two twins from home together. I could smell her breath, booze and cigarettes. "I met the most amazing guy today," she whispered. I opened my eyes. "He has these green eyes. I can't describe them exactly. It's like they have yellow in them."

"Where did you meet him?"

"At a party for the crew members of *Saturday Night Live*." Lately she had been opening the mail in her office and pocketing invitations to parties like these.

"What was he like?"

"Really nice. I couldn't believe how nice he was, considering." She hesitated. "He's one of the producers." I could see her eyes, brown, almond-shaped, as dark as my own, in the light from a street lamp outside the window.

I blinked in the darkness. Willa was changing, becoming the sort of person who worked as a fashion assistant at *Mademoiselle*. She spent her day holding earrings and scarves for famous people; I spent mine making rubber cement impressions of my fingerprints.

Fat as she was, Iona wasn't above making mean-spirited generalizations about other people. The next day, when I told her my roommate was going out with a TV producer, she grunted in disgust. "Oh please," she said.

"What do you mean?" I asked.

"They all make me sick—television people, movie people. Let's just put it this way: All the crooks in this world aren't necessarily wearing stocking caps."

Iona's favorite hobby, second to scanning the police blotter pages, was collecting self-defense devices. "Have you seen these?" she'd say, holding a medieval ring with copper-colored finger grips. "Deluxe brass knuckles. They go in his eyes or his groin. Whichever you prefer." Her favorite devices were the less expensive, home-spun ones. All that morning she'd been whistling, bustling about, until finally she showed us the source of her good mood: a plastic bag of cayenne pepper. "A dollar-fifty," she said proudly. "You throw some up his nose and he won't know what hit him."

Lynn looked at the bag, then at Iona. "And what if he's got a bag of cayenne pepper, too?" She was trying to be funny, making light of Iona's obsession. We all wanted to ask these questions, but never did. Now I watched Iona's shoulders heave in the imitation of a laugh, and then I studied her face, as she silently absorbed another fear.

The first night Willa went out with her producer, I told Iona I'd have drinks with her after work. I had no other friends and I wanted to have plans. We went to a bar on the Upper West side that sold Jell-O vodka sliders for $2 apiece. The bar area was packed with people my age drinking beer straight from bottles: boys in their father's suits, girls wearing miniskirts they couldn't sit down in. We sat at a tiny table, hardly large enough to hold our two menus. Iona was uncharacteristically upbeat, studying faces, swiveling around in her seat as if, at any moment, she expected to see someone she knew. "This place is fun," she said. "Have you been here before?"

"Yes. A bunch of times." I tried to look like someone who wasn't embarrassed to be at a good bar with a fat woman. I leaned across the table as if Iona was a funny friend I'd had since childhood. "So what's the real dirt?"

"All right," Iona said, laying her hands flat across her menu. "Are you ready?" I nodded. Her cheeks were flushed, she couldn't wait to tell me. "Aggie and Lynn are—" She wiggled her eyebrows.

I couldn't help but get irritated. "Are *what?*"

She laughed nervously. "You know. Girlfriends."

Everything Iona did and said drew attention to itself and was horribly embarrassing. I wanted to stand up and tell her we had to go. Instead, I flattened my expression. With someone like Iona, you couldn't give an inch. "So? Who cares?"

"Don't you think that's weird?"

"What's so weird about it?"

"They live together. They work all day together and then they go home at night. If you think about it, they spend—what? Twenty-four hours a day together? You don't think that's a little weird?"

"No," I said. I thought of Willa, how in college we spent all of our time together and now I never saw her. "I don't think that's weird." In the office Aggie and Lynn sat behind us, side by side, and spoke almost exclusively to each other. They reminded me of my mother and aunt, their voices overlapping in a chorus of approval for each other's work. They were both older, in their forties, and without turning around, it was hard for me to tell sometimes which one was speaking. I had assumed they were close friends, maybe related somehow to be so intimate. Now I felt naive and stupid to have missed the obvious truth. The next day in the office, I could easily see what had escaped me for two months: Aggie's hand on Lynn's shoulder, the way she leaned in to listen to her.

The next night, Willa came home and described her evening with Leonard, the TV producer. "We rented a car and drove out to Jones Beach. He's about to start filming a show that's set there, so he wanted to scout locations."

"Did you?"

"What?"

"Scout locations?"

She shrugged. "Sort of." A month ago she would have told me everything. Now her expression, flat as a model's, revealed nothing.

After that, she stayed away. For four nights in a row, I didn't see her at all. To avoid the empty apartment, I started walking after work, learning the city by foot, how the sidewalk patterns shifted. I watched the rise and fall of the buildings, how their shadows swallowed each other, how a flat mirrored side could reflect the sky not the street.

One day, as November crept in with its linoleum gray-white skies, Iona slid me a note: *If I cooked dinner this week, would you like to come over?* She had taken to writing notes after telling me about Lynn and Aggie, as if we had secrets we couldn't share out loud now.

This week is kind of hectic, I wrote back.

What about drinks? Or a really quick bite? There's something I have to ask you.

That night I stood next to her at a Papaya King Hot Dog stand. "So here's my idea," she said, eating one of the four fifty-cent hot dogs she had ordered without embarrassment. "You cut and paste index cards, right?"

Outside on the street, a siren howled past us. " Right."

"Seven items cut by you and they're in our book, right? That's what it takes to get a listing? So listen to this—" She put one hand on my arm. "We sell listings in this book. Someone buys a place from us, we make seven phony cards and give them an entry." She stared at me, beaming, for a long time.

"What are you talking about?"

"We sell them for—what? Two hundred apiece? Three hundred with picture?"

"You're kidding, right?"

"We won't get caught. How would someone catch us? Nobody reads the book. And even if they did, what are they going to say—I've never heard of this person? There's thousands of people in here no one's ever heard of."

On this point, she was right. "But who would ever buy a listing in this book?"

"Lots of people. Believe me. This is New York. You haven't lived here long enough. Everyone wants to pretend they're a writer."

The obvious irony of the proposal (a woman terrified of crime suggesting we commit one) was lost on Iona who held a breathless smile on her face awaiting my response. Her cheeks were flushed pink. She'd never looked so happy.

That night I went home and thought about Willa. I saw her now once or twice a week as she hastily repacked an overnight bag with four day's worth of clothes. "Do I have everything?" she'd say, looking around the apartment, but not at me. We hardly talked at all. I saw her so rarely, the stories I had to tell her piled up in my throat and got caught on each other. Whenever I asked about Leonard, she remained evasive. "Oh it's good." We talked about getting together so that I could meet him, but then never set a date. "I really want you two to meet," she said once, shaking her head. "It's so weird. It's like I've got two different lives."

✧

"Okay," I said to Iona the next morning. "Let's try it once. I'm not saying I'll do it, I'm saying I'll try it."

We started small, as an experiment, using a picture of Iona's mother and making up the book titles she might have written: *Too Many Shoes, The Lonesome Bear, Apple Pie in the Sky*. We gave her a story: Emigrated from England at the age of two, she began writing when she was seventeen years old and had her first book published at the age of twenty-three. After a hiatus of rearing four children, she returned to publishing her best work to date: *A River Full of Cupcakes*.

"That's good," Iona said, reading over our work. "That's really good."

Imogen Francis Flynn appeared three weeks later in Volume 28, issue 13, without a hitch. We stayed late and stared down at the picture of her mother staring back at us, a striking woman with clear gray eyes. "What would she say if she saw this?" I asked.

"She's dead," Iona said, and closed the book.

Out on the street, we walked to the subway in our usual silence, more companionable now that we were partners in crime. At times, I even made the effort to shield her from the overt stare of a child or the nervous, thin women who moved away from her on the train.

"She died when I was seven," Iona said, as the train rumbled beneath us. "She committed suicide." I nodded as if this was something I could possibly understand. Six stops later, she leaned over and touched my hand. "It's okay. We don't have to talk about it."

✧

One night Willa came home carrying a small brown bag. "Tonight's entertainment," she said, turning it over on the trunk we'd made into a coffee table. Four packs of cigarettes and a jumbo bag of hot balls fell out. She said nothing of her absence, made no mention of Leonard. "Wow," I said, reaching for a pack of cigarettes and a hot ball, which I didn't really like. I was so happy to have her home I didn't know where to begin. I wanted to tell her all about our crime and see if she wanted to be in the book. If Iona could do her mother, surely I could do someone, too. "So how's everything?" I said.

She flopped down on the only chair in the room. "I don't know," she said and lit a cigarette, looking around the room. "Don't we have a TV?" she asked. I shook my head but she studied the empty wall as if this was a trick. "I thought we got a TV."

After that, Willa stayed away again, but got enough phone calls to fill up the answering machine. "Where are you, Willa dear?" a strange woman said. "I'll die if I don't talk to you. It's about Michael, who can drop dead as far as I'm concerned." I didn't recognize her name when she said it.

"This is for Willa," a male voice said. "My name is Randolph and I met you a couple of days ago at the Lauren show. There's something I need to ask you. If you call me back I'll remind you who I am."

No one used last names or seemed to know there was another Willa here. I wrote down all the messages and then, after five days, I threw away the paper.

Finding people to buy a listing proved to be harder than we originally had thought. "Maybe we should bring our price down to one-fifty," Iona said with some defeat. So far, we hadn't gotten a nibble of interest, even though we'd taken out an ad in a writer's magazine with the heading: "Interested in Publicity?" Iona wrote the copy: "Name recognition is everything in this business. Don't get left behind. Put your name in the book where *names* matter." It was the last sentence that confused people. They thought it was a book for *nom de plumes*. "We had to be cryptic," Iona said, huffing down the street. "We didn't want to get caught."

A few weeks later, I ran into our office neighbor, Belle, coming into the bathroom as I was walking out. She wore a pale pink nightgown and a lacy bed jacket tied at her throat. Her hair, fuzzy gray and thin, had a pink satin ribbon tied around it so that she looked like a ninety-year-old little girl. "Hello, Belle." We all said hello to her, though she rarely answered us. "How are you doing?"

She frowned. "Not good."

"I'm sorry!" I shouted.

Instead of moving, she eyed me suspiciously. "What is it you people do in there anyway?" She tilted her head in the direction of our doorway.

"We put together an encyclopedia of author's biographies."

She nodded. If she had been told this before, she had evidently forgotten. She stared at me for awhile and made no move toward the stall. "What kind of authors?"

"Children's books mostly. Some Young Adult."

She thought about this for awhile. I couldn't figure out if she understood what this meant or if her mind had wandered some place else entirely. To help her along I opened the door further and moved out of her way. Still, she didn't move. I stared down at her sad terry cloth slippers, her tiny blue-veined ankles, thin as hairbrush handles. Finally she said, "What does it take to get in your encyclopedia?"

Back in the office, I passed a note to Iona: *Belle wants to know what it takes to get in our book.* Even as I wrote it, I felt a pinch of guilt. I was so surprised by the request, I hadn't thought of the ramifications: If she was sad and poor, would we actually charge her money?

"It's not for me," she explained when we stopped by her room after work that evening. She lived in a studio, one room with a single bed pushed flush against the wall, a half-refrigerator and hot plate on the floor in the corner. Iona and I sat, side by side, on her mattress. It sank beneath us, soft as a water bed.

"My husband wrote two books." She stood in front of us, leaning on her walker. "They're adventure stories. I don't know if that qualifies for your book or not."

Iona nodded. "It might. What kind of adventure?"

"Sailing in the Pacific. One's based on real life."

Iona looked at me. "Do we do sailing?"

I couldn't say anything. Doing this was awful. Iona turned back to Belle. "Were the books ever published?"

Belle looked down. "Not exactly."

Iona waved her hand. "That's okay. Look Belle, occasionally we do unpublished writers as a favor to friends. The only thing is, there are some costs involved—labor, typesetting, copyright fees, that kind of thing."

"How much would it be?"

I felt my stomach knot. Iona didn't blink: "A hundred and seventy-five dollars. That's our special rate to friends. We'll throw in a picture for free."

Out on the street, I broke down. "We can't make her pay for this."

"Of course we can. These things are symbolic, Willa. She *wants* to pay for it. It's worth only as much as she *does* pay for it. She's probably one of those people who's got a million dollars stuffed into her mattress."

"We sat on that mattress, Iona. It practically sank to the floor." She walked ahead of me and I realized, without thinking, what an unkind reference I'd made to her weight. I ran to catch up with her. "I don't think she had a million dollars stuffed inside it."

"People are weird, Willa. Believe me. New York is a weird place. You haven't lived here long enough yet. Anything is possible."

When I got home that night, the phone machine light pulsed with messages. I thought it was Iona, calling to continue our argument, but when I played the tape, every message was for the other Willa.

"Wil, it's Len. If you're there, pick up." My heart skipped. Until now, I had never heard his voice. He had a British accent.

"Wil, it's me again. Where are you? You must be there. Please pick up."

"All right, Willa, I'm sorry, okay? I'm very, very sorry."

I tried to imagine where she was if she wasn't with him. When the phone rang again, I picked it up. "Hello?"

"Willa, it's me," he said. "Look, I'm sorry, okay. I obviously wasn't thinking clearly."

I waited a long time. The only thing I could think was—she never told me he had an accent. "It's okay," I said. I kept my voice a whisper, like Willa's when she was mad—when she didn't look up and didn't mean what she said.

"Are you all right?"

How could I know? Maybe she wasn't. "Yeah."

"Can I meet you somewhere?"

I hesitated. What was I doing? "Okay."

"We'll just talk, Willa. I promise. I just want to talk to you."

"Okay."

I told him to meet me at the only bar I could think of, the one with Jell-O sliders. After I hung up, I changed into black and put on make-up.

I knew who he was the moment I walked in: sitting at a table by himself, drumming a swizzle stick on his knee, pale, bald, bordering on fat. He looked, if anything, older than thirty-nine, old enough to be our father. He held a book in his lap, open, but his eyes never left the vicinity of the door. For an instant he looked at me, studied my face, and I saw what she meant about his eyes, the pale green of apple candy, yellowed at the center.

In that moment, I knew this was the worst single thing I had ever done. He would sit here half a night, waiting to apologize while she sat someplace else, waiting for him to call. If it wasn't a crime, it was unkind in a way I had never been before. I said nothing, stood by the door, and looked around the bar, above heads quickly, as if I'd only stepped in here in search of a telephone. I stayed three or four minutes, then walked back to the subway and rode home.

That night, after I'd gone to bed and turned out all the lights, Willa came home. For awhile I lay in the dark listening as she moved through the kitchen, opened the refrigerator, closed it, then opened it, then I walked out to our living room, furnished now with two plastic, snap-together bookshelves and a futon folded into the shape of a sofa, lit a cigarette and waited. When she walked in, I told her what I had done. I masqueraded it as a mistake. "I thought it was this guy, Larry, I met last week at work. When I got there I realized it wasn't him." Obviously this made no sense. I couldn't look at her; my voice shook and I stared at the lengthening orange ember of my cigarette. I waited for her to do something: yell at me, cry, take the cigarette from my fingers and keep it for herself.

Instead she shrugged. "It doesn't matter," she said. "It's over."

She flipped on the light. I stared at her as she stared at the room, the spartan furnishings, the eggshell yellow walls that seemed to surprise her each time she came home. "Do you remember that guy at school who used to bring his own salad dressing to the cafeteria and then walk around all day holding the bottle?" I nodded. Her eyes rested on nothing, stared into a thought. She blinked herself out of it. "I saw him today."

"Where?"

"I forget. The subway, I guess."

I asked the obvious question: "Did he have his salad dressing?"

She shook her head, no, and that was all she said before she walked into her room and closed her door behind her.

The next day at work, Iona slid two envelopes onto my desk, responses to our ad. One included a money order made out for a hundred dollars. "Do you believe that?" she whispered. "People are so *dumb*." At lunch, we sat in a plastic booth with slices of pizza. I made my announcement before she could start spinning a plan—branching out, placing more ads: "After we do these three, I don't want to do any more."

She stared at me. "*What?*"

"We're cheating people and I don't want to do it anymore."

"*How?* We're promising a listing in the book and then we're putting them in. How is that cheating?"

"We're selling the idea that being in this book means something which it doesn't."

"Oh please."

I shook my head. "What about Aggie and Lynn? What happens if they find out? We'll get fired." I bit into my pizza while she watched me.

"And you honestly care?" I nodded. "We're finally getting somewhere and you want to stop, just like that?"

"Yes," I said. "And there's another thing, too." She rearranged the folds of her dress around her; for the first time since I'd known her, she showed no interest in the food sitting in front of her. Somewhere along the line, our power balance had shifted; for the first time, I was in control. "We're not going to take any money from Belle."

The next week Willa told me she was going to move out. She'd learned about a rent-controlled studio in a good building near Chelsea, and a chance like this might come once in a lifetime, she explained. On Friday, I came home to find her separating our worthless belongings with careful deliberation: my spatula, her whisk, my dish drainer, her soy sauce. "Just take it," I said, when she held up a roll of aluminum foil. Her breakup with Leonard had held, but now, within a short week, she had a new boyfriend, an assistant photographer she met on a photo shoot, who told her, the first time they spoke, he'd dreamed about her the night before, her face on the body of a skeletal cow. "He's funny," she said.

After that, it felt as though Iona was my only friend. Because going to bars and restaurants with her was awkward, we went to see movies, two or three times a week, taking turns on the selection. She always chose murder thrillers and leaned forward in her seat to concentrate on the plot. She especially loved the ones that focused on the psychopath hunting people down. "Wasn't that *fascinating* how he spelled things in blood?" she'd say afterwards. I made us go to romantic comedies which she yawned her way through, twisting around in her seat to locate all the exit signs.

All through that first winter, sneakering to work, stepping over dirty piles of ash-colored snow, I waited for New York to happen. I bought pepper spray for my purse and a rape whistle. After dark, I walked close to the curb, away from the buildings. I fingered my whistle, imagined the attacks. One day near New Year's, I got to work late after the subway lost electricity between stations. We were stopped in a tunnel and plunged into darkness; everyone asleep woke up with a start. We looked at the shadowy silhouettes of the people around us as if, for the first time, we were seeing each other. I thought I felt a man's reassuring hand on my back only to realize, when the lights came up, it was a woman's cloth tote pressing me from behind. I couldn't help feeling irritated; when I moved to get off, I gave her bag an extra shove. Six months in New York had had its effect. Now on the street I walked past the only people who noticed me, beggars shaking change cups, with a hard shoulder and a grunt.

By March, after nine months on the job, I developed rubber cement headaches that forced me to quit. Both Aggie and Lynn said they were sorry, but only Iona seemed destined to miss me. "I can't believe it," she said, digging into a tin of cookies, a going-away gift. "I feel like you just *got* here." For me, the months had dragged by interminably; I had been doing nothing more than cutting and pasting with rounded-tipped scissors, performing kindergarten work in the slowest start to a career in history. After that last day, Iona and I went out to dinner, her treat, she insisted twice along the way. We went to an Italian restaurant on the Upper West Side that served terrible, gummy pasta sprinkled with disks of sliced garlic. As our main dishes were served, Iona broke down. "So I'll miss you," she said. "It won't be the same."

Why, I had to wonder, did she like me so much? My kindness to her had been so begrudging; our friendship such a stopgap against unpredictable loneliness. As if reading my mind, she explained. "You should have seen some of the lu-lus they got for that job." She mouthed the word *loser*. What could I say? Nothing tangible separated me from my predecessors at the job.

"Thanks, Iona." I said. "You've been a big help to me this year." Suddenly I felt sentimental. "I mean that. I don't know what I would have done without you."

"Oh look." She waved her hand, holding a napkin. There was a ceiling, of course, on how maudlin we could get. "We'll still see each other. It's not like either one of us has anything better to do."

After dinner we walked to the 81st street station, dropped our tokens in the turnstiles and stepped inside to find ourselves on a deserted platform, alone but for a man wearing loose polyester pants roped around his waist and a dirty jean jacket, leaning against a pole, staring right at us. For a moment, it seemed possible he was an average, badly-dressed man, coming home late from work, having an early beer, then he yelled "Hey!" as we walked past him to the only bench in the station, and it was clear, in a single word, he was drunk and crazy. He propelled himself away from his pole, towards us, his head rolling loosely from side to side, one hand rubbing the back of his hip in an oddly feminine gesture. "Hey, you guys got any money?" He tucked one hand in his pocket; if he had a weapon, it would be in there. I touched my rings, my hands, my fingernails. I felt as if I'd been waiting nine months for this.

"No, we don't," Iona said, slipping her hand into her purse.

He stepped closer to us. "Sure you do."

No doubt it was a mistake to have sat down on the bench. We should have stood near the stairs, been ready to run, but now there was some pride at stake in staying where we were, defending this decision. I slipped my hand into my own purse and for a moment that seemed to stretch on forever, we sat side by side, stirring through our purses for our self-defense weapons. The man, so drunk his eyelids sunk down as if weighted, seemed not to notice until Iona pulled out, of all first-line defenses, her bag of cayenne pepper. She clutched it tightly in her fist so that only the bag, not the contents, was visible. Given any other people, this might have been a drug transaction about to take place.

The man lurched toward us. "What's that?" he said, looking down at Iona's fist.

"Nothing." She shook her head and stared ahead of her.

He held out his own hand. "C'mon, fatty, what is it?" She said nothing. "You got something to smoke?"

"No."

"Why don't you give it to me?" I kept thinking: *give it to him, Iona, give it to him*.

Instead, she readjusted her shoulders. "Why don't you be quiet," she said. "Go back to the garbage can you crawled out of." I couldn't help but laugh at Iona's odd bravery. She would rather call someone a name than throw pepper in his face.

"Listen to the fatty," the man said, looking at me.

"Come on, Iona," I whispered. "Show him what you've got."

She shook her head. I knew the fat remarks were making her mad. "No. I don't want to."

I turned to him. "She has a bag full of red pepper that's been treated with hydrochloric acid. If she throws any on you, you'll be maimed for life."

His eyebrows went up as high as they would go. "Is that true, fatso?"

"Shut up," she said.

"Can I see it?"

"No. Absolutely not."

"How come?"

I waited for her to do it, to start playing along. Then she did: "Because if you touch it, it could kill you." She sat back, obviously satisfied with herself.

"No shit," he laughed. "What about *you?*"

She played it with a perfectly straight face. "I'm protected by the bag."

If he had never intended to rob us, what difference did it make? I felt giddy with power, as if our peculiar friendship, with its narrow focus all these months, had existed to prepare us for this single moment: outwitting this drunk. We weren't victims, at last, we were felons meeting a felon. Everything so far had been a rehearsal for this.

Then he sat down. "I had a girlfriend once who was fat like you." Suddenly the mood had shifted. Apparently, he liked us. Now he wasn't going to rob us, he was going to reminisce. He pulled out a pack of gum and folded a stick into his mouth. "God, she almost killed me, all that fat." Iona pressed her lips inward. "I told her, honey you're gonna die with all that blubber. I'm not kidding." He turned and looked at Iona who stared straight ahead as if she was memorizing the poster on the other side of the station. "Yeah. About your size. Fat like you. And you know what happened? She died. Her heart. Twenty-something. Maybe thirty. Shit, was she fat."

There was nothing we could say to this; no story that would help. I prayed for a train, for other people to appear, for Iona to say something. Then, when it looked like he might start talking again, I did the only thing I could think of. I reached into my purse and pulled the red tab on my whistle. The electronic shriek split through the station and bounced off the walls. As I guessed, he was too confused to locate the source. "That sounds like a fire alarm," I said, standing, moving the whistle inside my purse, throwing the noise all around us. "We should get out of here," I said to Iona, who stood up slowly, and straightened out her dress.

"Certainly," she said. And with that we walked away from him, our dignity intact, chased by our own devices. The wailing siren in my purse died as we walked up the stairs, back through the turnstiles, and out onto the street where a light rain had started so we had to work our way through a maze of umbrellas, past a small group of women protesting pornography, before we could think about what had just happened, and by then it was gone, as quickly as it came—the wonder of our improv, the surprise of our strength—and in its place was only everything in the city we had still to be afraid of.

Steve Lattimore

◆

ANSWER ME THIS

The apartment is air conditioned all to hell when Russell gets home. His stomach clenches as the cold hits his sweaty skin. Norma, pregnant nine months, is flat on her back on the floor amidst a spray of sofa cushions. She's chewing her used-up crossword magazine into spit wads and launching them through a fat McDonald's straw at Hairball, their huge gray cat, who's hunched on the kitchen counter, hissing at the sag in the ceiling.

"What are you doing home?" Norma asks. "It's not even midnight."

Russell lies. "The press broke down," he says. "They had to change all the blankets so they sent us home."

"Oh." Norma grimaces. "You're going to be mad at me. I forgot to buy beer."

Russell is already mad, though. No beer just means it'll be longer till he feels better. He hangs his keys on a spindle that says KEYS, leafs through the mail—crap, crap, crap, a letter from the apartment manager. Russell fingers the envelope, knowing what's inside is going to upset him.

"That's okay," he says. Then he says, "I got the day shift. Till the baby comes."

"I thought management said no."

"They didn't say no. They said yes a month ago. I only found out tonight because Glenn says, 'What happened to you working days?' I says, 'They never got back to me.' Glenn says, 'Well, they okayed it. The day shift guy was supposed to tell you.' I says, 'Well, he didn't.' Glenn says, 'I guess he didn't want to work nights.'"

Russell doesn't tell what happened next, that he turned around and walked out, said he was leaving but not why.

"Sorry," Norma says. She shrugs, and the beads of her new cornrow hairdo tic tic like beetles. The hair is Norma's latest offensive in a battle to remain attractive throughout pregnancy.

Russell rips open the letter from the apartment complex. It says the water damage was Throc's fault, and Russell's ceiling will be repaired when either he or Throc pays for it.

Throc is Russell's upstairs neighbor. He's a good guy. Hmong. He farms a few acres of strawberries, has six or seven daughters, a dead wife, one leg, and a sparkling Chrysler New Yorker, a silver beauty usually found under the carport with Throc in it, just sitting there. For about a year now, Throc's been the target of pranksters. He came home several months ago to find his apartment flooded. Someone had broken in, plugged his drains, turned all the faucets on full blast, even wedged a plastic-wrapped bean and cheese burrito into the toilet and flushed. Before that it was strawberry shoots planted in dark mulch in Throc's shoes, in his coat pockets and rice bowls, even in the egg cups of his refrigerator door. Throc transplanted the shoots into his own patch. "Good for me," he said.

Russell figures the jokers are Ag students from the college; the complex is full of them. They see Throc in his New Yorker and on Herndon Avenue selling his berries and get pissed off at the government. During the Gulf war, a guy in the building across the way got bagged and rolled through pig shit for being an Iraqi. Fair enough, except he was from Venezuela, and a nice guy. Russell doesn't have the heart to tell Throc it's the New Yorker.

Since the flood upstairs, the ceiling in the kitchen has been rotting, caving in slowly. A big rust-colored udder of pulpy ceiling stuff threatens to loose itself at any time. Hairball watches it night and day. He sleeps on the counter beneath it and every few minutes bolts awake, hissing. Sometimes Russell sees Norma lingering beneath the sag, sucking a popsicle or just staring into space, and he gets the compulsion to leave, and never come back. It's like when she turns the disposal on and hears it chinking up a spoon or a bottle cap, and reaches for the drain opening instead of the switch. It wears a man down.

"I'm going for beer," Russell says.

"As soon as you walk out that door the baby'll come out," Norma says. "I can feel it."

"I'm just going to the 7-11," Russell says.

"Mark my words," Norma says, straining to look back over her shoulder at the sunflower clock on the wall. "It's nine months at midnight."

"Nine months don't mean nine months to the minute," Russell says. "It's not a contract." He grabs his keys off the KEYS spindle.

"So you're not going to mark my words?"

"I'll only be gone two minutes," Russell says. "I'll mark 'em when I get back."

"Promise?"

"Yeah."

Norma shoots him a face. "Grab my crossword for me first? It's in there." She points to the hospital bag. "Don't go through the bag, though."

Russell unzips the leatherette sack and dumps it out onto the sofa, a violent gesture he immediately regrets.

"Don't go *through* it," Norma insists.

"Christ on a cart horse."

"I said don't look!"

Romance novels, magazines, Game Boy cartridges, a lizard puppet.

"Quit *looking!*" Norma says.

Cashew nuts. Gummi Worms. The camera. Russell looks over at Norma. "A street map? What's that for?" He unfolds the map; the route to the hospital is highlighted. "It's over on Dakota, for crying out loud."

"We might forget when it comes time, 'cause of the pressure."

A Walkman. Her address book. Cheese and cracker snacks.

"Quit looking, Russell, damn it. It's not hurting you for me to pack up my hospital bag. It relaxes me."

Two cans of Pringles. Hair spray. Scotch tape. "You're bringing a thing of Scotch tape?" Russell says.

"Leave it *alone*."

"What are you going to do with Scotch tape?"

"Let it be, I said. You don't know how long I'll have to stay there."

"Your sister was only there a few hours."

"That was her fourth. This is my first. You don't know. Something could happen."

"And you're going to fix it with Scotch tape?"

Norma levels at Russell a chilly-eyed stare. "I could die, you know?"

Russell holds up a children's book, recognizes it at once as another insult from Hannah, Norma's mother. "Oh, The Places You'll Go!" he says in a sing-song. Hannah once asked Norma right in front of Russell how long she thought she could tread water with a rock tied to her leg. Maybe Hannah thought Russell's mind was occupied by the baked potato he was buttering. Russell looked up from his spud and said, "Longer than if she had one up her ass." Now when Hannah calls she greets Russell's hello with silence, and he hands the phone straight to Norma.

"It's not a crack about you," Norma says. "It just means the baby'll be special."

"I'm leaving," Russell says.

Norma's eyes soften. "Don't say it like that."

"I'm venturing forth," Russell says, "into yon night which doth have a twelve-pack calling unto me, 'Russell, I am your destiny. Belly up.'"

"Russell? What'll you do if I die in childbirth?"

"Almost made it," he says. "One foot out the door."

"I'm serious," Norma says. "What if the baby's sick or retarded or something? What if it costs a lot to make him well or I go blind having him and have to buy all special stuff for blind people and have someone stay here with me while you're at work?"

"Your crossword ain't here," Russell says. "I'll pick you one up."

Norma troops out the worried look, the one that says she didn't mean to ask such terrible questions even though she thinks about them all the time, as Russell does.

"Hush," Russell says. "Don't worry about that. It's cheap to be blind, anyway."

"You're coming right back, aren't you?" Norma asks.

"Oh, the places I'll go, Norma."

"Russell? Kiss me."

Russell comes back inside, lowers his face to Norma's but not all the way. She heaves her weight up from the cushions, a full-belly sit-up, and reaches for Russell with her mouth. He pulls back a little, and Norma's brow quivers from the strain. She lunges, and Russell moves just beyond her range, the tiniest bit. She gives up, lowers herself back to the floor and slides a cushion beneath her butt. "Forget it," she says. Russell leans down and kisses her fully and affectionately. He runs his fingers then his lips across her furrowed scalp. It's something he hoped never to see, his wife's scalp. Like the soft spot on a baby's head, it can mean nothing good. Norma and Russell talk a lot about soft spots.

"I'll tell Throc I'm home but I'm leaving," Russell says. Because Throc doesn't have a phone in his apartment (though he has one in his New Yorker), Russell melted a two-pound candle around one end of a mop handle so from the couch Norma can bang on the ceiling, Throc's floor, without having to stand. It's basically a big gong beater. He puts it next to Norma on the floor, realizes it won't reach from there but says nothing. He's not even supposed to be home yet, for crying out loud. He starts out the door then stops, can't help himself. "Norma," he says, "Answer me this: you think people start life doomed and work their way loose, or vice-versa?"

"You're just saying that to be mean," Norma says. "That kind of talk doesn't have anything to do with me and I'm not going to listen."

"I know," Russell says. "Never mind. Just bang on the ceiling if you need anything. But don't bang on the sag."

"I know not to bang on the sag."

"I'm just saying," Russell says.

"Well don't say."

"Fine. Bang on whatever you want to bang on."

"Don't be long," Norma says. "I can tell something's going to happen."

Russell is leaving the 7-11 parking lot when the car in front of him stops and blocks the exit. Russell guns his engine, honks, waits. He pictures Norma beached there on the floor, the too-short mop handle, the ceiling sag. He was wrong to scare her with philosophy stuff. When she hears that kind of talk she thinks he's trying to figure out a way to leave her and feel okay about it. Maybe she'd be better off. Russell makes $6.25 an hour catching advertising inserts as they come inky and stinking off the Goss Community press. He's not really a job man, but this one's okay. The conveyer belt feeds him tab after tab of Save Mart ads and Gottschalk's ads and Mervyn's ads and the motor's whump whump and the tic tic tic of the folder batter his brain with questions. Mostly he keeps them to himself.

"How about it," Russell calls out the window. He inches the van forward and kisses the little car's bumper with his own—a peck, really. But the driver's door opens, and Russell knows it was a mistake. A husky boy-man with a dimpled chin and greasy ball cap, too stout for such a putt-putt car, strides slowly up to Russell's door. He's got mean eyes, and Russell knows he won't easily be turned away.

Russell flashes his palm. "Sorry," he says. "Foot slipped off the clutch."

The guy opens Russell's door, steps back. "C'mon," he says. "Me and you are gonna fight."

Russell rips a Bud from the twelve-pack on the seat next to him and offers it to the guy. "I'm not fighting anybody," Russell says. Then he says, "That's one of those old two-cylinder Honda cars, ain't it?"

"You're not going to talk your way out of it," the guy says.

"Friend," Russell says. "I'm not worth it." The guy backs up from Russell's door, beckons him down, balls his fat fists. Russell looks at the beer warming beside him, shakes his head. "Okay," he says. "Goddamnit."

As he steps down from the van, a ceramic clack chinks in his head, a solid nine-ball break. He feels it in his teeth a little but not much besides, realizes the guy has already landed a quick shot to his chin, not very hard.

"And don't call me friend," the guy says. "I'm about to put a whomp on you."

Russell's mind is calm as crystal, a moment of pure consciousness tinkling in his head. He sees himself from this guy's eyes, imagines how it might feel to drop a quick one onto the chin of a stranger in a buzzing, white-lit 7-11 parking lot in Fresno, California, at midnight, the most unnatural hour of a most unusual day. It occurs to Russell that if this guy saw him the same way they wouldn't have to fight. Russell could go home and drink his beer and Norma would drop the baby spank on time, things would go as they should.

The *clack* of Russell's teeth has him in mind of the Chaffee Zoo, where Norma dragged him to celebrate being pregnant. Maybe he should tell this stranger about that, how he and Norma lingered on the bench by the reptile house, a wobbly happiness in the air, saying baby names out loud—Timothy, Thomas, Tad—when they heard a far-off *clack*, and were for a moment yanked from their reverie. They listened, asked questions with their eyes, then heard it again. "What the hell is that?" Russell asked Norma. She shrugged. They looked around, heard it again—*Clack!* Finally Norma saw; she pointed out to Russell the huge desert tortoises stacked two high behind a bush, humping. It was a moment for Russell and Norma, who could say why? Russell described it on the drive home as a feeling of being suspended in some cosmic solution, not quite liquid or air, outer space maybe. A feeling that he was where he was supposed to be, a star in the constellation. Norma said she felt it too, but Russell already knew that she had. They kissed. Norma asked if a turtle would be an okay pet for the baby, what with the soft spot and all. Russell allowed that it would.

Russell notices the guy's belt buckle, his name in silver letters—Doug. "My wife's having a baby, Doug. Right now." He turns to mount the van and Doug knocks him a crashing blow to the ear that goes off like dynamite inside his head.

Russell wheels around, says, "*That* was uncalled for."

"Fight," Doug says.

Russell looks over at the nose of his van, still in mid-smooch with Doug's bumper. He knows he's going to have to hit him, doesn't want to but what in the goddamn hell is a man expected to do? Circumstances arise, don't they? Things change.

Russell fires a stiff right, and the button of Doug's nose bursts like a ripe tomato. He doubles over, drops to one knee.

It's terrible to have a broken nose. The eyes flood instantly, and a man can't see to defend himself. The palate feels like a hot coal. Whatever shirt you have on, that's ruined.

"See?" Russell says. "If you'd just have some courtesy to begin with."

A police car pulls into the lot, blue lights thrumming a note of cool-headed civic intervention. Most people Russell knows dislike the police, but not him. He drives right, with consideration and restraint, and so doesn't get that sick feeling when he sees lights in his mirror.

Two cops get out, a man and woman. The woman is young, Russell's age. Loose strands of fine black hair dangle about her temples, the rest pinned up beneath her hat. "Evening," he says to her. Without word or ceremony, she takes his arm and pins him face-forward against his van. "You don't have to worry about me," Russell says. "I'm calm."

"Shut your mouth," she says. She pats Russell down, turns him again and points to Doug, who's sitting Indian style on the ground, bleeding into his cupped palm. "You do this?"

"Not happily," Russell says.

"You want to go to jail?"

"No."

"Did you do it?"

"Yeah. But he blocked the exit, then drug me out of my van and hit me. Two times."

"He hit my car on purpose," Doug says.

It occurs to Russell that now would be the time to tell this woman about Norma, about the mop handle that won't reach the ceiling and the baby that damn sure will come at midnight if that's when Norma's of a mind to have it. But he doesn't. Instead, he says, "It's true. I gave him a little nudge."

The cop looks in the window of Russell's van, sees the twelver on the seat. "How much have you had to drink tonight?" she asks him.

"It was just a tap," Russell says. "To get him moving."

"To drink. How much?"

"Why ain't you asking him anything? I'm the victim."

"You're either going to tell me how much you've had to drink or you're going to jail. Choose."

"I haven't had nothing to drink," Russell says. "Zero! What is this, anyway? I was only upholding the law."

"Okay," the cop says, "maybe you're not drunk." She turns Russell around, cuffs him anyway. "But you are disorderly. And you're pissing me off."

Russell waits in the buzzing light, handcuffed. A police van pulls up over the curb—the exit's still blocked—and the cop hands Russell over to its driver. He's tall, with pocked yellow skin and the tired hangdog look of a man expecting the worst. "You going to give me any grief?" he asks Russell.

"I'm not even supposed to be here," Russell says.

The cop nods. "Uh huh." He opens the police van's back door and conducts Russell inside, sits him on a plastic bench against one wall. A black man is slumped at the far end of the seat, asleep against the wire screen separating back from front. He's got on jeans and an American flag button-up shirt, socks but no shoes, and a white straw cowboy hat shrunk to his head like a spooked cat. Kicked back on the bench across from Russell are two Mexican boys, can't be more than fourteen.

"*Hola*," Russell says to the boys.

The smaller of the kids shakes his head, turns to his buddy and says, "Hey man, *hola*."

The other kid laughs. "*Hola*, yeah. Hey, that's Mexican, ain't it? The boy's a home piece."

They all sit for while, the kids laughing and nudging the black guy's feet. "*Hola*," they say to him. "Hey you! *Hola*." He doesn't stir.

The van door opens again, and Doug is shoved in across from Russell, a twist of Kleenex in each nostril. In his broken-nose voice he says to Russell, "What are you lookid ad, screwjack?"

"I didn't want to hit you," Russell says.

"Fuck you."

The police van drives around for a while, doesn't seem to be headed anywhere in particular. "What are they going to do with my van?" Russell asks the hangdog cop.

"Tow it," the cop says.

"That's going to cost something, ain't it?" Russell says.

"Sure is," the cop says.

Doug looks at the roof of the van, screws up his face and says, "I need a smoke!" He bangs his head three times hard against the wall, and his face empties. "Ow."

"That wasn't very smart," Russell says.

"There's no smoking," the cop says. "And shut up."

"I want to smoke," Doug moans. "Now!"

The cop stops the van, turns around in his seat. "How about if I come back there and kick the shit out of you instead," he says.

Doug dishes back an even stare. "Smoke," he says.

The black guy says, "Shut up, motherfuckers. Let a nigger sleep." The cop whacks the metal grill near the guy's head, puts the van in gear and drives.

Doug leans his head back again, blood draining down his throat probably, into his mouth, his stomach. Russell can taste it just looking at him.

"You got cigarettes?" Russell asks. Doug nods at his breast pocket. "Hold on," Russell says. He raises himself off the plastic bench, slips his cuffed hands beneath his ass, behind his legs, bends his knees tight and draws his feet through the hoop of his arms. Doug leans forward and Russell takes out the cigarettes, tosses a few that are soaked with blood and puts a clean one in Doug's mouth.

Doug smiles, thrusts his hip toward Russell, the front pocket of his pants, says, "Lighter."

"Shit," Russell says. He reaches into Doug's pocket with two fingers, finds the lighter, lights him.

"Have one," Doug says.

"Don't smoke," Russell says.

"C'mon," Doug says. "Smoke."

Russell takes out another cigarette, lights it, lets it dangle from his lip but doesn't suck.

A lazy grin spreads over Doug's face, his cigarette glowing in the dark van. "Ah."

As he sighs, the cigarette drops into his shirt front. He snaps forward, stands up and bangs his head on the roof, dances around. "Aaah! Aaah!" He tries to shrink himself in his shirt but the fabric is taut around his fat stomach. The van pulls over, the cop gets out. The overhead light buzzes on when the door opens. Doug's screaming. "Cigarette! Ow! Ow!" The cop slaps Doug's stomach until the cigarette must be smashed up in there. The filter falls out, tobacco sifts to the floor. The cop lifts Doug's shirt and a bright pink eyeball of a blister stares straight at Russell.

"Looks like a pork rind," the cop says. He turns to Russell, sees the cigarette in his mouth, his hands in his lap instead of behind him. Just like Moe from the Three Stooges, he says, "Wise guy, huh? Want to smoke?"

Russell says nothing. The black guy sits up, says, "Yo, smokes, man? Give a nigger a butt."

The cop slaps Doug's belly and pushes him back onto the bench. "Eat a salad once in a while," he says. He grabs Russell by the back of his neck and jerks him out of the van, slams him against the door. "On your knees," he says.

"I can't," Russell says. "The coating on the inside of my patellas is worn off from laying tile. I got bad kneecaps."

"I don't have time for you, funny boy," the cop says. He drills his foot into the back of Russell's leg and Russell goes down onto one knee in the gravelly street. The cop ratchets his knee into Russell's chest until he's bent back nearly flat against the asphalt. He gets behind Russell and unlocks his cuffs, rolls Russell onto his stomach and snaps the cuffs shut again behind his back, this time through his belt loop. Russell tries to move his arms but can't. The pavement is hot and gritty against his cheek.

"Are we going anywhere in particular?" Russell asks. "Or just cruising?"

"Don't worry about it," the cop says. He flicks Russell's ear with the tip of his shoe.

"My wife's having a baby," Russell says. "I'm not supposed to be here."

The cop stands over Russell, grips him by the forearms and lifts until Russell is on his feet. He looks Russell up and down, says, "You think that's smart?" He opens the van door, shoves Russell inside. "If I have to stop this van again," he says, "everyone gets a crack in the head."

When Russell is released at 6:00 A.M., Throc and Norma are in the jail waiting room.

"Hi," Throc says. He wriggles his finger at Russell, squints and grins. "We drive around looking for you. Woman at 7-11 say you arrested. Fighting, hi." He looks Russell over. "Good fighter, hi. Face look good. It's good."

"How was your beer?" Norma asks.

"I never had one," Russell says. "And I wasn't fighting. I was a victim."

Throc says, "Victim, hi? Aha. Aha. Okay."

"I called," Russell says. "There was no answer."

"We were probably in the car," Norma says. "It's got a phone, you know."

"I didn't know the number," Russell says. Then he says, "I thought you were having the baby. It's nine months."

"I was waiting for you," Norma says. "But I'm ready. I can have it any time I want."

"She waiting for you," Throc says. "She strong one, hi."

"Waiting for me?" Russell says.

Norma nods, her beads tic.

The morning sky is pink and blue, baby colors. Throc's kids are all piled into the New Yorker, waiting for Russell. He climbs into the back, fingers the crumpled, heavy-gauge plastic Throc laid down in case the baby comes while Russell's at work and Norma delivers in transit. It occurs to Russell that the highlighted map in her hospital bag may be for Throc. Maybe she expects Russell to be gone.

One of Throc's daughters, five or six, scurries into Russell's lap. He can't remember her name. "Good morning," he says.

"Russell," she says.

A smaller girl up front stands in the seat and looks back at Russell like she might cry. She reaches out and yanks the hair of the girl on Russell's lap. It's clear that he's spoiled some arrangement by not sitting in front. Throc smiles at each girl, laughs in a way that says it's okay, whatever it is. "I want to sit your lap," the girl standing in front says. Then Norma gets in up front and the girl seems satisfied with that. She puts her cheek against Norma's belly and is still.

Throc starts the car, and the engine whispers somewhere beneath them like doves in a cote. "Hi," he smiles. "Hi."

The car phone rings. Norma answers, waits a beat, says, "He's here, sugar. Everything's fine." Norma calls her mother sugar. Ordinarily this steams Russell, coming as it will after he answers the phone and endures Hannah's starchy silence, but now it's somehow a comfort. "It wasn't his fault," Norma says. "He was a victim." She nods, listens. "I have to go, sugar. You'll know when it's time." She listens again, waits. "You'll just know."

It occurs to Russell that he should take Norma straight to Hannah's, or to the hospital maybe, tell her it's okay to have the baby now, then stash himself on a Greyhound bus to anywhere, someplace far. Who could argue she wouldn't be better off?

They're not inside the apartment two seconds when Throc's happy voice upstairs pierces the morning like Fourth of July. "Hi! Oh, hi, hi, hi!" Tiny voices shriek, a dozen footsteps rain down the stairs, small fists flail at the door. "Russell! Russell!"

A terrible noise falls from above, heavy clomps and groaning. Hairball coils up on the kitchen counter, his wild eyes locked on the sag over-head. "What is it?" Norma says. "What's happening?"

Russell opens the door and Throc's girls take his hands, pull him outside. "Russell! Come, come!"

"Don't leave!" Norma says. "Call the police!"

"No," Russell says. "It's okay. Stay here."

He follows the girls upstairs to Throc's apartment, finds Throc nose to nose with a cow in the living room, laughing. The cow's eyes flash to

Russell, wide and nervous, seeing all but understanding nothing. That's how cow eyes are though, aren't they?

"Somebody put me a cow!" Throc says. "Hi!"

"It's okay," Russell says, his heart slowing, finding its normal rhythm. "It's just a prank. Those guys have got your number, Throc."

"This good one," Throc says. "Look! Look her there!" He points to the cow's side. Throc's girls part for Russell and he sees first the pink glare, then the working, pulsing motion of organs behind glass. It's a cow with a window.

Russell kneels down, Throc's carpet still damp from the flood and spongy beneath his bad knees. With the soft pad of his finger, he traces the cow's tight , well-healed stitches, strokes the glass which is some sort of plexi, actually feels the warm coursing of fluids. The animal shifts nervously, but Throc's girls smooth the hair at her flanks, rub her back. Throc picks up his littlest daughter—Bao is her name—and she gently caresses the slope of the cow's nose, between her eyes and across the swell of her frightened brow.

Russell heard of cow windows when he worked a three-day temp job at a dairy once. He didn't see one but he imagined it, and now it's here, in Throc's upstairs apartment. Which reminds him of something stranger yet, that cows can go up stairs but not down. Throc's laughing—he knows—so what the hell, Russell laughs too. What's a man supposed to do?

"Russell?"

Norma's standing in Throc's doorway. Russell waves her over, says, "It's a cow. A cow with a view." Norma comes closer, and Russell shows her.

"This is going to sound weird," Norma says, "but I knew there was going to be a cow up here."

"Good sign," Throc says, nodding. "It's good."

"Did you know it would have a window in it?" Russell asks Norma. He's not cracking wise, he really wants to know.

She thinks for a second. "No," she says. "That part's a surprise."

Russell takes one of the cow's teats, tries to recall his milking grip. He tugs two, three times before a stream piddles onto Throc's carpet.

"Taste it," Norma says.

Russell catches a drop, licks his finger. "It's milk," he says. He takes Norma's hand in his, holds it to the Plexiglas in the cow's side and closes his eyes. "Feel," he says. Norma closes her eyes too. Together they imagine the baby, Norma's nipples, swollen and brown like hazelnuts, a dribble of milk, little lips and gums and foggy blue eyes, a sprinkle of pale hair and the soft pulse beneath it.

"When you didn't come home last night I thought you left," Norma says.

"I know," Russell says. "I was just in jail, though."

Norma squeezes his hand. "I'm glad."

Back in their apartment, Russell spreads the cushions out on the floor and Norma lies down, clicks the TV on and drifts off to sleep. Russell lies beside her, makes a kiss kiss noise to Hairball on the kitchen counter, who merely glances at him, annoyed.

In his head, Russell drives the route to the hospital—the one highlighted on Norma's map—only it's Throc's New Yorker he's driving, not his van, so it's quiet except for the lowing of the air conditioner, smooth. Then a thunderous moo pounds the ceiling. Hairball springs into the air and swipes at the bulb of rot, then falls to the floor in a shower of pulp and dust and ruddy goop. Norma's eyes snap open and she grabs Russell's hand. She says, "Something's happening, Russell. I can feel it."

Nancy Reisman

◆

EDIE IN WINTER

1948

Edie Cole is fourth in line at Mendelsohn's bakery when her heart falls to her feet. No one remarks on the flutter that crosses her face, her sudden loss of breath: Buffalo is frozen and the cold has knocked the wind out of most customers walking in from the street. It's nearly Shabbas, and Mendelsohn's has stayed open longer than usual—everyone's in a hurry. The December sky has already turned pink, shafts of light coloring the bakery air and Edie's coat and boots. "Arthur Blum," Gary Mendelsohn says. "That handsome Arthur," Gloria Mendelsohn says, wistfully. All the married women nod. Ruth Brodsky sighs. Edie swallows hard and feels her throat turn to dust.

Nora Lang swivels her head in Edie's direction. "Wasn't he sweet on you?"

Edie's face reddens and she turns to study the nearly empty dessert case.

"*Nora,*" Gloria says.

"I don't mean anything by it," Nora says. She pats Edie on the shoulder, and Edie offers up a queasy smile. Then she flails in the net of women's voices.

"He was at Normandy. A hero."

"They gave him all the decorations."

"Still not married—Edie, did you know that?"

"Still pining over Judy Shumaker, is he?"

"Oh no, too long ago. I heard he fell for a Catholic girl in New York."

"Really Nora, you shouldn't."

"That's what I heard."

"Well I heard he wanted to marry a French girl, Jewish, out of the camps, but she wouldn't leave Europe."

"After the camps she wouldn't leave?"

"He's been living in New York."

"He must be thirty by now."

"Minnie Abrams is in New York."

"Minnie's married. In Brooklyn."

"He lives in Manhattan?"

"He's staying at his cousin Rita's, off Hertel."

"I heard he was staying at the Statler Hotel."

"You're kidding."

"You know he's a lawyer now. "

"What can I get for you, Edie?"

Edie looks up suddenly and drops her package of smoked fish, her first-graders' papers, her gloves. Her glasses slide down her nose and her woolen scarf drags as she bends down to retrieve them. "My challah," Edie says. Her voice seems clogged and small. She clears her throat. "And that last honeycake."

By the time Edie reaches her block, the neighborhood is turning blue. She hugs her packages and almost runs out of breath. She has to find Manny: if he's not home, she'll call him at the bookstore. She pictures him shuffling between the cluttered stacks and the tilting shelves, sorting boxes from the Martinson estate. How mulish and sad-eyed and shy he is, even with the customers he likes. How calming they find the store's easy quiet. But if Arthur pushes the door open, that calm will scramble, the dust itself will vanish, and Manny's face will revert to the face of a boy. A face Edie hasn't seen for years.

And if, instead, Manny sees Arthur from a distance, on the street? No matter that it's Shabbas, that the houses have hushed, that Manny is due home for dinner. *Arthur, Arthur* he'll call and Arthur will turn to find

Manny doused in twilight. They'll disappear downtown before she can catch either one of them.

Edie pushes the front door open and hurries down the hall to the kitchen. Wet snow slides off her boots and puddles on the floor. The table is set for supper. In the corner, Manny polishes his shoes. He nods hello and returns to buffing the brown leather.

In candlelight Manny is luminous. Even now, after years of their routines, Edie has not stopped noticing the grace of his shoulders, the narrow torso, slim legs, the knob of bone in his wrist. How tentatively he moves. A distant yearning curdles in her belly. He's her brother. But some nights longing rises in her and she is back at the lake, it's summer, a stinging heat, the shock of the water at Crystal Beach. They are diving, floating, while their sisters read novels onshore and braid each other's hair: white fabric in the distance. *Edie! Manny!* Someone is calling. Edie ignores it, but Manny takes a step towards shore, turns his head toward the sound. If she tells him to stop and wait, if she says "two more minutes" he'll stay, patiently, but he will be leaning toward the others. He has always been like that, coming when called.

Manny mumbles the Shabbas prayers and passes her a slice of challah. They chew in silence until he coughs and says, "Edie did you hear? Arthur's back." His eyes flutter. "Can you believe it?"

She takes a hard sip of sweet wine. "Really? I heard a rumor."

"I saw him," Manny says, and he forks up his potatoes, but he is elsewhere, in a private, unreachable country.

Wasn't he sweet on you?

The last time she saw Arthur, he stood in the parlor of the old house on Butler Avenue, biting his lip. Dark, unruly curls fell across his forehead; his eyelashes seemed unusually thick. In the years of Manny's friendship with Arthur, the dozens of Sundays they'd taken her to the pictures, she'd never seen Arthur silenced; that day his chatter evaporated. Edie's mother, still alive, still walking, pressed a tin of mandelbrot into his hands and pinched his cheek and told him to take good care of himself overseas; she retreated to the kitchen, blowing her nose and calling Edie's sisters to come with her. When the others were gone, Arthur stood close to Manny, his hands on Manny's shoulders. Manny wept openly. "Manny?" their mother called. Edie stood a few feet away. She was twenty-two then, wearing a dress of her sister Sylvia's, blue sprinkled with fine white dots, her hair brushed out in long waves. "Pretty Edie," Sylvia had called her. In the shadowy parlor, Arthur glanced at her and pressed his lips against Manny's forehead. Then he stepped back, his hands sliding down Manny's arms, his fingers twining around Manny's.

"Manny, honey, give Edie her time with Arthur," their mother called.

"I'll write every week," Manny said, and backed away, disappearing into the dining room. Her sisters' voices floated from the kitchen. *Manny, you need a handkerchief?* They murmured about the war, about Manny's bad knee, about being a man. *There's plenty you can do here.*

Arthur's hands trembled, he turned to Edie, giving her a look she couldn't fully comprehend, a begging for mercy sort of look. He hugged her hard, wept into her waved hair. No man had ever held her like this, pulled her so close she might lose her breath; she could feel his muscle and bones and skin beneath the layers of clothes. Her body seemed too light, too fragile for the yearning rushing through it. Arthur whispered to her, " Look out for Manny, okay?" Then he pulled back and kissed her on the cheek, the way she kissed her mother, and left her bewildered.

For a few days, Edie's left hand was an object of discussion in the neighborhood; had Arthur transformed it, or was it as ordinary as ever? "Maybe he's saving up," Nora said. "Maybe he's afraid something will happen to him," Ruth Brodsky said. *Absence makes the heart grow fonder,* her older sisters repeated. In the months that followed, Edie and Manny wrote letters to Arthur and clenched their jaws during news broadcasts. For a time, Manny barely spoke, and when he did it was privately, to Edie. "Do you think he'll come back?" That year, Manny fell into the first of his bad spells, weeks when he couldn't get out of bed. It was then that Edie grasped what looking out for Manny might mean.

Now it's as if the moment of the blue and white dress never occurred. Manny's spells have become routine. Edie's grown plump, and she still doesn't know how to date. The awkward ones ask her out, or the older, fat ones she can never bring herself to kiss. No one she would press close against the way she did saying good-bye to Arthur. A few times a year she puts on her good maroon dress, clips on gold earrings, applies matching lipstick and sits in a dim kosher restaurant, dabbing her lips with her napkin and listening to someone's bachelor cousin or someone's friend's brother chew lake whitefish. Her body is rigid; there's no feeling in her legs. She's receded to a knot of muscle in her ribcage. Later, he takes her for a walk in the neighborhood. He holds her limp hand. In front of her building he kisses her on the cheek. Hope pours out of his lips. Her skin crawls. She smiles. *Thanks for the lovely evening.*

Manny falls asleep early, on the couch, to the sounds of jazz combos aired over the radio. Dating seems utterly beyond him: each year he becomes more reclusive. When she returns from these evenings and finds him, sprawled out like a beautiful animal, waves of tenderness leave her in tears.

On Saturday afternoon when the doorbell rings, Edie is aproned and dowdy. Out the window she spots Arthur, the same strong jaw, the same broad lips, the same chocolate drop eyes. His hair is cropped closely, tiny darts of gray creeping in. *That handsome Arthur.* Edie rushes to her bedroom, throws her apron on the floor and fumbles through her handbag for a lipstick. She snaps on her gold earrings and reddens her lips while the bell rings again and Manny calls from the bathroom "Edie, would you get that?"

When she opens the front door, the reality of Arthur surprises her: the smoothness of his face, his slightly chipped tooth, the lush weave of his camel coat, the tang of his skin when he rushes in to kiss her.

"Edie. How wonderful you look." For several seconds she's wrapped in his bear hug; she closes her eyes and feels her muscles loosen, as if she had slipped into a bath. "I've brought you something," he says. Beyond him, light snow has begun to fall. He tucks her fingers around a box of chocolate-covered cherries.

"So nice of you," she says.

In the foyer he squeezes her hands and a warm flush races through her. "It's been much too long," he says, but before she has time to take his coat, Manny is there, cutting past her, embracing Arthur.

"Told you I'd be here," Arthur whispers.

Edie furrows her brow and tugs at Manny's sleeve. "Let Arthur take his coat off."

"Of course," Manny says, and awkwardly backs away.

She waves the box of chocolates like a shield. "Look what he brought."

"Open them," Arthur says, "They're lovely."

When she offers the box to Manny, Arthur kisses her hand.

She sets out the English teacups, slices the honeycake, arranges and rearranges the tray. When she enters the parlor, Manny and Arthur are side by side on the sofa—Manny leaning slightly forward, glancing at the floor as she nears, Arthur's arms spread across the sofa back. With a face like that, Arthur could be in Hollywood, she thinks, he could be a leading man. She pours the tea and serves the cake and pulls up the heavy rocking chair. "How long are you in town?" she says.

Arthur shifts his body forward and shrugs. "I don't know yet." He sips tea and samples the honeycake. "A beautiful tea set," he says and leans far enough in her direction to touch her hand. "Tell me about you, Edie." Manny rolls a spoon back and forth across his palms.

"Did Manny tell you I'm a teacher now?" She stumbles over the details. "Reading, yes. And math. And oh, we do projects, we decorate the room."

Arthur picks up the conversation and carries her with it. "First graders? I bet you're great with children. Have you been to Manhattan? Really, Edie, you should visit. And how are your sisters?"

Edie answers and blushes and smiles at him. She starts to regain her composure. There are things she wants to know: why he stopped writing and what went on in England and France, why he stayed away from Buffalo for so long. He seems untouched by the war, more self-possessed than ever. "What happened?" she asks, but his attention has begun to stray.

Let's not talk about the war. Let's talk about Manny. Manny, have a chocolate. Really, you'll love them. Edie? No? Manny savor it—wonderful, yes? What about this bookstore of yours? You're not giving everything away, are you? Is he, Edie? Manny, you have to charge enough to make a profit, you know. You have to pay the rent. How like you, Manny. What do you make of Henry Wallace, Manny? He's more than a spoiler, I think. More chocolate, Manny? Manny. Manny.

Manny's face is soft, he looks almost tipsy, but Edie forces her smile and finally excuses herself, walks down the hall to the bathroom. It smells of shaving tonic, a spill in the sink. Flat shaving lather films over the shelf top; Manny's unrinsed razor and brush lie between the taps. He never leaves things this way. She stays in the bathroom an extra five minutes to clean up the mess, refold the towels, redo her lipstick.

When she returns to the parlor, the sofa is empty and the men are pulling on their coats and hats.

"We're going to Arthur's cousin Rita's," Manny says and fingers the buttons on his coat; when he glances at Edie, his voice weakens. "Tonight Arthur's taking me out to dinner."

"We should go to Oliver's," Arthur says, "We should have prime rib." He brushes off his hat and beams at Edie. "Thank you," he says, as if she's offered him a Chevrolet.

She gives him a tight smile and takes a step back. "Nice to see you, Arthur."

Manny's already at the door. "Oh Edie." Arthur says, his voice intimate. He strides toward her and runs his palm along her cheek. His scent rushes over her again.

She bites her lip, then nods. "Have a good time," she finally says.

Edie skips dinner and eats tinned olives while she plans lessons for the week. At school she's been reading fairy tales. "Rapunzel." "The Frog King." "Briar Rose." All of them have saviors, all undergo transformations. Evil lurks in certain women and certain animals. The stories are like warnings—she isn't sure of what—but enchantment still draws her. She plans through Wednesday and gives up, paces the flat, finishes the olives without tasting them. In the bathroom she spreads cold cream over her face and becomes a mask, big eyes peeping out from a layer of white stucco, eyebrows thick above them. The pink of her lips and tongue jumps out against the whiteness. Below the stiff suits of weekdays and the frumpy dresses of home, the rest of her is also white and pink, but she fears the pink will seep out of her; she can feel herself fading into potato paleness. She's nearly thirty, and everyone in the neighborhood knows it. When Edie rinses off the cold cream, her face in the mirror seems non-descript, almost absent, and the small hope, *Pretty Edie*, eludes her. She undresses, pulls on a prim flannel nightgown, and returns her reflection; her broad shoulders and heavy breasts make the nightgown float down like a tent. She buttons the collar to keep the ruffle along the neckline from swelling too much.

Manny returns late at night. In the morning, there's a new fedora on the hat rack, Manny's name sewn in gold thread on the inner lining. Expensive. She whisks eggs and milk, drops the broken shells into the garbage pail, and pours the mixture into a hot skillet. Manny takes his time washing and dressing, but from the kitchen Edie can hear him whistling. Whistling. He sounds vaguely like Benny Goodman. And when he comes into the kitchen he is smiling. From a few feet away she can smell his best aftershave.

"Nice hat," Edie says.

"Uh huh. A beauty. Arthur got it."

She peppers the eggs and keeps her eyes on the skillet.

His voice wavers slightly. "A late birthday present."

Only after the waver does Edie smile. "That's nice." She gestures at the counter. "Jam on your toast?"

Her class is full of round-faced Polish children and dark-eyed Italians, the girls wearing thick braids and gold crosses, the boys practicing curse words in the coat room. All day they pinch and push and clamor. Miss Cole, they say, tell one about a king. Miss Cole, tell about a princess.

"First tell me again what we read Friday," Edie says, "Why did Briar Rose fall asleep?"

"She's under a spell," Teresa says.

"She was cursed," Joey Csznowski says.

"By the wise woman," Angela says, "the one who didn't get invited to the party."

"The one who lost her shoe," Paul says.

"No," Mary says.

"That's another one," Anthony says.

"What will save her?" Edie says.

"The soldiers," Joey Santora says.

"The prince," Lucille says.

"How?" Edie says.

The boys elbow each other and snicker. A few of the girls cover their mouths.

"What happens next?" Edie says.

"They live contented to the end of their days," Angela says.

"Yes," Teresa sighs, "that's how it ends."

All week, Manny skips supper and stays out late. Edie doesn't sleep until she hears him come in—eleven, midnight, later. He's abandoned his early morning walks, his seven o'clock coffee and newspaper. She leaves for school without seeing him. Late Thursday afternoon, she stops by the bookstore. The sign on the door is handwritten in someone else's script. *Closed for the day.*

Edie visits her sisters: she reads to Sylvia's little ones, diapers Dora's baby, drinks tea in their kitchens and says nothing about Manny, or Arthur. She spends Shabbas at Marilyn's, but otherwise eats alone, leaving plates in the icebox for Manny. Some nights she falls into a heavy blank sleep; some nights she's awake until she hears the key in the lock, Manny's footsteps in the hall. One night she waits until Manny's movements have stopped; at two o'clock she stands in his doorway, gauging the depth of his breathing. Then she enters his room. He's asleep in his clothes—his best trousers, an unfamiliar shirt. The room smells faintly of whiskey and aftershave and something sharper than either. It's almost intoxicating, that smell. She wants to lie down on the bed next to him, to wake him up and remind him who she is. But he'd be shocked to find her there, he'd push her away, and the shame of simply watching him overwhelms her. She does not cover him with a blanket; she closes the door and in the kitchen makes herself a cup of tea. She sweeps and mops the floor and dusts the living room furniture until half past three.

"Where did you get that shirt?"

"What shirt?"

"The one on top of the laundry basket. It's linen."

"It's Arthur's."

"Why doesn't he wash his own?"

"He lent it to me."

"You wear linen shirts to the bookstore?"

"I'll wash it myself." Manny picks up the newspaper and fortresses himself in the reading chair.

Edie tucks the shirt more deeply into the laundry basket. Later, when she loads the wash, she sniffs at it. Manny's scent, riddled with smoke.

The day of the snowstorm, school closes early and there is bedlam in the coat room. The boys push each other and trample stray mittens, Mary's forgotten to use the bathroom before pulling on her woolens, Joey Csznowski keeps pulling Lucille's hat off, and Matthew repeatedly shouts "snowball war, snowball war." How enormous and slow Edie is in this swarm of small, restless bodies. Why should this make her tear up? She buttons them into their coats and watches them depart in noisy clumps, led away by harried mothers. In her boots and coat and hat, Edie returns to the classroom and erases the board.

The streetcar is slow to arrive and already the snow falls heavily. An inch or more an hour, the driver says. Cars skid as they turn onto residential streets, and the sidewalks are already emptying. No one is bothering to shovel; cleared paths will vanish in minutes. Edie wraps an extra scarf around her head before she gets off at her stop, so only her glasses peek out. Snowflakes on the lenses melt in small patches.

Manny isn't home yet, and she telephones the store: no answer. She fills pitchers with water and lays out candles and matches, in case the power goes out. She puts on a pot of soup, boils noodles and layers them with egg and raisins and apples for kugel, waits. Through the window the city air seems pearly and opaque, even though it's only two o'clock. She turns on the radio news, crochets, watches the minute hand on the living room clock. Finally she dials Arthur's cousin.

"Rita? It's Edie Cole."

"Edie, how are you? Such a storm."

"Terrible. I wondered if Manny was there."

"Manny? No. He's not out in this, is he?"

"He must be checking the store. You know he worries about floods."

"All those books."

"Can I speak to Arthur?"

"*Arthur.* If he'd just listen to me. I told him, I said I heard about a storm. He drove to Toronto for the day and now he's stuck. He called from a hotel, thank God."

"Toronto?"

"Oh Edie, you know Arthur. Friends everywhere, and he always has to say hello."

"Sure," Edie says, "I know how he is."

Manny is not at Marilyn's or Dora's. When Edie dials Sylvia's house, she hears the click that means Marta Block has picked up on the party line they share: she'll have to watch what she says.

"Sylvia, are you all home safe?"

"We're fine. Eli got in a couple of hours ago."

"And the children? Did Manny help you get them home?"

"Oh, I didn't ask. He's got his hands full with that store. Emily Eisenberg helped me out."

"All right then."

"By the way Edie, have you seen Arthur Blum?"

"He visited." Edie hesitates. "And brought chocolates. He sends his best."

When the kugel is out of the oven, she layers on her woolens, pulls on her overcoat and fake fur hat. The snow is stinging, blinding, already drifting to mid-calf. She doesn't know where she's going, and she can barely see across the street. Parked cars have metamorphosed into mounds of snow. When she reaches the intersection a few blocks over, the red glow of the traffic signal seems to hover by itself. One plow drives by. Edie tries to wipe her glasses but the snow smears and freezes on the outside while the inside fogs from her breath. She pictures them, Manny and Arthur, laughing in the lounge of Buffalo's Statler Hotel, the only hotel she knows: they are beyond the snow, far beyond Edie. For a mile she lumbers through drifts, her fingers and toes numbing, her legs heavy and unsteady.

Manneee Manneee. A few blocks from the store she starts calling, but the wind swallows up her voice. The store is dark, locked: she takes off her gloves and rummages in her coat pocket for keys. Inside the book-store, the deafening gusts are muted to a soft whoosh. *Mannee?* She walks the perimeter of the store, takes the flashlight from the desk, checks the basement. It's dry but cold, musty, and empty of Manny.

Stacks of Latin and Greek textbooks form a barricade on the far side of Manny's desk; the front shelf displays *The Settlement Cookbook, Visiting Scotland,* and *The Great American West.* From Manny's phone she dials the flat, tightens a fist around the receiver and counts a dozen rings. Finally she hangs up.

The brother she knows would never go off to Toronto without telling. Edie's Manny always leaves notes. He calls her, he leaves messages in the school office. She paces up and down the wood floor, a wet trail melting from her coat and boots, water rolling down her ankles, seeping into her socks. If she calls her sisters back, she'll have to tell about Arthur.

The cash register is locked, but the desk drawers are open. Receipts. Letters from other used book dealers. Queries from professors. A pint bottle of scotch whisky, a chocolate bar, stamps. A cigar box of other letters, some from Arthur. Recent postmarks. She can't help but touch them, open them. *My dear Manny* the letters all begin, and mostly tell where Arthur is living, where he is working, name his Army friends and Manhattan friends. She skims along the lines. *Thank you for the wonder-ful books,* she reads. *When did you start reading plays? I am finally myself again, no longer sad. The very idea of Buffalo wears me out, a coffin of a city. But you are there, Manny, and I'll try.* The latest, from September says, *I mean it, come to New York.*

Come to New York? I mean it. He sounded like he meant it when he told Edie, *Really, you should visit.* That's what people say. And of course they've stayed in touch, they are best friends, why shouldn't they? For an instant Edie's lips quiver, and then she staunches the impulse, stills, feel-ing her spine become rigid, her face stiff. She replaces the letters in the cigar box, wraps herself up again, enters the storm. The visibility is only a few feet.

Not long after Edie arrives home, the electricity goes out. She spends the night upright on the couch, watching the ghostly streets, crocheting socks for Dora's baby, lighting candle after candle.

By morning Edie is red-eyed and frayed, and it isn't until noon that the storm settles into light snow and the city begins to dig out. Early in the afternoon Manny calls on a line steeped in static.

"Terrible storm," he says.

Edie bursts into tears. "Why didn't you call me?"

"I tried. You didn't answer. Then there was a problem with the phone."

"The electricity, not the phone. Where are you?"

"Rita's."

"You didn't call here."

"I did, Edie, I swear, Marta picked up to dial."

"Manny—"

"Marta, are you listening? Tell Edie."

"I was here."

"Maybe you were in the bathroom."

"I would have heard the phone ring."

"Not if you were running water, Edie. Maybe you were running water."

At the beginning of February Edie redecorates the classroom, hanging red hearts edged with paper doilies. The children make cards for their mothers, writing *I love you* or *My Valentine* and writing their names, the letters blocky and awkward.

Manny is home when she gets there; for three days he stays home, lying in bed, the lights out. The first night he comes to the table for supper, then returns to his room. After that Edie takes him trays. She brings the radio to his room and she sits in the parlor, reading, until ten o'clock; these nights, her sleep is deep and uninterrupted.

On Thursday evening, Arthur rings the bell.

"He's not feeling well," Edie says.

"I know. I'm here to see him."

"Leave him alone."

"Edie," Arthur says. He takes her hands. He squeezes her fingers and rubs his thumb across her skin. "Let me see him."

She relents. She busies herself in the kitchen and lets Arthur go to Manny's bedroom. But she creeps back toward the hallway as she hears their voices rise. Only a few clear words *the only way, I can't, stubborn, you don't know.*

Then Manny bursts out of the door and heads for the bathroom. She can tell by the flush on his skin, his pursed lips and drooping neck that he's crying. Arthur follows to the bathroom but Manny's already shut the door. Edie hurries down the hall and pulls Arthur away, out into the parlor.

"Why is he crying?"

"Edie —"

"I want to know why he's crying."

"We had a disagreement, that's all."

"He hasn't cried for months. He was fine before."

"I don't want him to cry."

"Well, stop it. You started it, you stop it."

"That's what I'm trying to do here, Edie."

They stand in the parlor, glaring and silent, until Manny opens the door and shuffles down the hallway, holding his head. "I've got a headache," he says, "I've got a real headache." When he reaches the parlor, he gazes at the two of them. "Edie, stay out of it."

"Why are you so upset?"

"It isn't your business."

"What do you mean?"

"Just leave me alone. You never leave me alone."

Edie's eyes narrow and her voice goes cold. "I see." She starts toward the kitchen and calls back, "Arthur, you can show yourself out."

Then she is burning, clanging skillets against saucepans. He'll leave again and what will she have? Manny, broken, months of his headaches and sleeping and crying, months of leaning on her, months of resenting her for being there to lean on. No one to shore her up, to kiss her on the lips, no bed of tenderness.

She hears the door close, the lock click as they walk out of the flat. From the window, she can see their bodies melt into the dark, first Arthur, then Manny. Once again, Manny resumes his late night routine, while Edie's silence extends like lake ice.

Edie knows that it's only a matter of time before Arthur returns to New York; he's seen too much, he doesn't belong in Buffalo. *A coffin of a city.* She watches for signs, and in a week they become clear to her. Manny has begun to drip humility again, he's jittery, solicitous: the way he acts when he is afraid.

"What are you teaching now, Edie? I brought you some books, for the kids, this one has trains." "Edie? Do we need anything at the market?" "Edie I can get those shoes repaired for you, you want them repaired?"

Finally he tells her. It's Sunday afternoon. He shuffles and stares at his feet. "Arthur's going back to New York."

"Oh?"

They sit down at the kitchen table, the pause between them like a live thing.

"He asked me to go with him," Manny mumbles.

"I see."

With effort, he looks her in the face. "I need . . ."

"What?"

"You're the only one who knows."

"What?" Edie says.

"You know."

"I don't know anything."

"Edie, don't do this."

"I'm not doing anything."

"*Please,*" Manny begs.

He's waiting for her to fill the gap she always fills, to say it will be fine, to say: *You'll love Manhattan, I'll visit you there.* To tell him he can always come back. "What is it, Manny?" Edie says.

"Help me," he says.

"I help you all the time."

Without Edie, Manny takes the suitcases from the storage closet, launders his boxers, undershirts, socks, picks out towels and linens. Without her he makes arrangements for the store. Without her, he counts his money and visits Sylvia, Marilyn, and Dora. Edie pretends to ignore every act, every gesture: she teaches her classes, shops on her regular shopping days, cooks the usual suppers.

On the morning of the departure, Manny paces the flat and sweats through his shirt. His suitcases stand in neat rows at the door. His store files are in the bedroom for Sylvia's Eli to pick up. Edie rocks in their mother's rocker, making no attempt at conversation. Blue yarn spills over her lap and her knitting needles click; she concentrates on the baby blanket as if it were the child.

When the yellow taxi cab honks in front of the house, Edie rises and kisses Manny on the cheek and hands him a packed lunch for the train. Then she returns to the rocking chair and takes up her needles. Manny hesitates, nervous, at the door, as if waiting for something else.

"Take care of yourself, Edie," he says.

"I will." She steals a glance at the window; she can see Arthur emerge from the cab and approach the front door. He knocks but does not come in.

"Just a minute," Manny says. He hands one suitcase out to Arthur and turns back to Edie again. "Well," he says, "Good-bye then."

Edie doesn't drop a stitch. "Good-bye Manny," she says, and peers at the blanket.

It isn't until the door closes that Edie looks up, then moves to the window. The neighborhood seems grayer than ever against the brightness of the taxi. The driver and Arthur lift the suitcases into the trunk, while Manny takes quick glances back at the house. He has always had a graceful silhouette. For the briefest instant, Edie moves into the lamp light near the window, so Manny can see her looking out. There is too much of her and not enough beauty, she thinks, and she quickly retreats. In the parlor's shadows the radiator hisses, the clock ticks. The slam of car doors echoes over the ice outside, and Edie drops back into the rocker, crosses her arms over her chest, and rocks, rocks, rocks.

Jennifer C. Cornell

◆

WAX

Barry Sinclaire could hypnotise anyone, and he didn't need crystals, or a gold watch and chain. He'd been a child in Draperstown when a traveling showman so entranced a local woman that she sat on display in a shop window for fifty-two hours, before Barry stepped forward and broke the spell. At seventeen he'd cured a woman with a riot of symptoms who had labeled the painful parts of her body with the names of the medical men and women who had treated her previously, without success. But his most famous case was that of a man who'd not crossed a road in sixty-four years; even a few of the English papers had printed a photo of the man and Barry, walking together through an open field.

Signs led us through the hotel lobby and up the stairs to the second floor till we reached a long table flanked by easels displaying posters of Barry on either side. Behind the table sat two girls with clipboards. "Symptoms?" one of them asked my father, while the other one counted our money and recorded the sum before pulling two tickets from the deck in her hand. My father described how he had trouble sleeping, how he'd tried requesting additional hours in the hope that exhaustion would help him rest undisturbed, but with orders way down and nothing new coming in, he'd been cut back to three days a week instead. At home he'd start books he wouldn't finish and cook us large meals he barely touched. There was more to it, too, that he didn't tell her. Though by now I'd begun to accept the fact that apart from keeping a blanket ready there was little I could do, the first time it happened I panicked: I snapped my fingers and waved my hands, called his name loudly, even shook his arm

48

though the doctor I'd rung had advised against it, but he hadn't noticed. For over an hour we'd stood together in the open doorway, until my father turned without warning and went back up to bed of his own accord.

"Stress, maybe?" the first girl offered, consulting a list of available options.

"You tell me," my father answered. The girl stopped her pencil just short of the page and eyed him without humor. "Aye, alright," he added dryly. "That'll do."

We were put into groups according to malady. There were seven each of smokers and addicts, nine overeaters and six who drank too much. Those with arthritis went in early while a party of people suffering from migraine who'd been held up at roadblocks outside Cultra were still checking in with the cloakroom attendant in the lobby downstairs. Bed-wetters and nail-biters went in with their parents just as the pregnant women came out, talking of buckets of cold and hot water, induced anesthesia, and quick, painless birth. The one individual with constipation emerged with a look of relief on his face. In fact, only those troubled by low self-esteem or a lack of self-confidence reappeared looking much the same as before.

One of the men in our group had a dog with him the size of a hen. When they called us in finally the dog hurried after, but the man at the entrance collecting tickets halted the queue and reached back to seize the other man's sleeve.

"Hold on, mate," he said. "You can't bring him in there."

The other man shrugged. "What can I do? He won't leave me alone. I put up fences and he digs out under them. He jumps out the windows if he's locked in the house. He's like bloody Houdini. I've tried to get rid of him, but he won't stay away."

"I don't make the rules," the ticket man told him. "But he's not get-tin' in."

Again the man shrugged. "I've given up," he answered. "If you think you can stop him, go right ahead."

"Just grab'm for us, will youse?" said the ticket man wearily, so the man caught the dog by its scruff and handed it over. Someone else fetched a bin and between the three of them got the dog underneath it. He'll be alright, the ticket man told me crossly as we filed past him, though I hadn't protested. If you've got a problem with it, ring the SPCA.

Though he'd led the way into the auditorium, my father left the choice of seating to me. From what was left I selected a place near the front, well away from the exits, but still I disliked the distance between us enforced by the wide, outstretched arms of our chairs, so I got up from mine and stood next to my father's.

"Now don't start, luv," he said. "Go on, now, sit down. I'm here, amn't I? I won't run away."

I knew he wouldn't. He was a man who honored commitments, and I'd made him promise he'd attend in good faith. All the same, it hadn't been easy. If his condition was worsening, as everyone said, it was largely because he'd relinquished concern for it and no longer bothered to fill prescriptions or show up when scheduled for further tests. At my insistence he had seen a specialist, but two days later he was halfway to Poleglass again in his nightshirt and slippers, with no explanation whatsoever to offer the occupants of the official Landrover which had been his escort for nearly a mile. They brought him home discreetly enough, but still the curious had come to their windows and rumors began that the two were related, my mother's absence and his arrest. Only then would he look at the newspaper clippings I'd saved for him, praising Barry. "Why not, eh?" he'd said, after weeks of resistance, "There's no reason not to. It can't do any harm."

"What time d'you have, luv?" my father asked the woman beside him. When she told him he grunted and turned away.

"He's worth the wait," the woman assured him. "I've come eight times now and I always enjoy it."

My father cast me a look of gloomy triumph, as if he'd just won a point that no longer mattered. "Where have you brought me, wee girl," he muttered. "Eight times, for God's sake, and he's not cured her yet?"

Yet when Barry did step from behind the curtain onto the stage my father sat up and straightened himself like a schoolboy. To save time he'd lost in earlier sessions, Barry dispensed with his introduction and instead moved at once to what he predicted were our most likely fears: that he would abuse his power over us to entertain others, and in the end, hypnosis would prove an ineffectual cure. While it was true, he admitted, that the treatment could work only if we did not resist it, even so he could make us do nothing that would cause us embarrassment, or was opposed in any way to our moral sense—nothing, in short, that we'd not freely agree to when conscious and in full control. The ordeal would be painless, he promised, and there was no chance that having gone under we would not wake up. The rest was a question of self-empowerment, and our own willingness to abandon ideas that had no foundation, no matter how fiercely we might believe them.

Are youse ready? he asked with sudden energy, and the whole room nodded. When he gave the signal, we placed our right elbows on the arms of our chairs and, as instructed, thought about things that weren't in the room while he spoke quietly to our open palms—Fingers, rise up now, he was saying, Muscles, contract—until I saw arms everywhere lift off their cushions, and thought about Gulliver waking from slumber, how even the locks of his hair were secured. I closed my eyes then to picture him rising, but I could not stay focused on Barry's voice. Once, as part of a cross-community venture, I'd attended a service at which Catholics and Protestants had gathered together to share their experience of a common God. When they bent their heads to enter a prayer I too closed my eyes and folded my hands and opened my heart to the same Holy Spirit I could sense communing with the others there, but still I remained outside the experience, alone among the genuine many with a faith in each other and in Heaven as palpable as steam. Now the same failure opened my eyes to the faces around me, expecting to see that private conviction from which I'd always been shut out before. Instead, their expressions were as I knew mine had been, pinched with the effort of concentration, distracted by appetite, incomplete conversations, worrisome footsteps in the room overhead—the difference being, however, that unlike me, they weren't giving in. The previous year I'd had a teacher who had read aloud from Virgil's *Aeneid* while a bat induced chaos all over the room. Its evasive arcs and sudden diagonals had produced such hysteria that another instructor from the classroom next door had stepped in finally to protest the noise, and even then he'd kept on reading. Only when the caretaker arrived with a broom and murdered the beast did his eyes leave the page. He closed the book then, collected his things from the desk in front of him, went straight to the headmaster's office, but he did not resign, and the next day was back as if nothing had happened. "Jobs are scarce, luv," my father said when I told him the story. "The way things are these days if you give one up you'll not find another." I had no sympathy then for that explanation, siding instead with my mother's argument that the meagre security of the familiar should not be the reason we stay in a place where we're no longer happy. But later, after she'd left us, and the drawers in the kitchen filled up with boxes with a single match in them and the cupboards grew cluttered with weightless tins that rattled when shaken, for he would not use the last of anything, and he would not let anyone throw them out—after weeks during which he boiled no water so as not to empty the kettle she'd filled, I began to think it might be more admirable to take on discontent, however sure a contender, if that were the only way left to shield another, to protect them from its hammering blows.

When I looked to Barry for the guidance he'd promised I couldn't find him; at first I didn't realise that he'd left the room. Sounding so much like the man himself that no one had noticed he'd made the switch, a tape of his voice was slowly winding from one spool to the other in full view of those whose eyes fluttered gently behind their closed lids, their uplifted faces, even my father's, oblivious and serene.

I stood up myself then. I'd just pulled the door shut on the people behind me when I saw Barry step out of a lift across the hall.

"Hullo," he said. "What're you out here for?"

I shook my head dumbly. I had expected him to be apologetic, a little embarrassed, to offer some explanation, at least, as to where he'd been, but instead his expression was that of a man called away from enjoying a short-lived pleasure to attend to some inconsequential matter which anyone else could have handled just as well.

"Who is it you're with? The big fella, isn't it? Is that your daddy?"

I nodded. We looked at each other in silence for a moment, then he thrust his hand in his pocket and rattled his change.

"I'm not a magician," he said, as if refuting an accusation. "There's only so much a person can do."

I didn't deny it. I'd tried everything with my father and it had made no difference.

"How old are you?" he demanded abruptly, then complained, when I told him, that I didn't look twelve. I began to explain I was tall for my age when he said just as suddenly, "Give us your hand—and keep those eyes closed, too, till I tell you to open them." An awkward movement tugged me toward him and again I heard the tinkle of coins. "I'm going to give you a penny," he continued, readjusting his grip, "and I want you to close your fist over it; tight, now; that's it. Now don't let go of it till I give you the signal."

I felt the hot press of that coin, could feel its two faces imprinting my skin, and thought again of the opportunities I'd wasted, knowing at once I'd miss this one, too. On a school trip to Paris with Protestant children I'd seen an American carve her name into the Arc de Triomphe. She'd been with two others who'd watched her do it and held her things for her while she gouged at the stone. I'd wanted at least to register protest, but a boy I fancied had threatened to leave me, to pretend not to know me if I made a scene. I'd done nothing either the time I'd been a witness in the company of others headed up Botanic Avenue toward University Street—middle-aged men in professional attire, bakery girls in their pinnies and caps, a gaggle of students whose jackets and cardigans, too warm for the season, had been tied round their waists, and a boy with long hair directly in front of me, a large, lazy dog on a lead by his side—all ambling past a man who wore boots that had seen lots of action, lounging with three others like him on the broken front step of a derelict house. He'd pushed off from the wall with the unhurried thrust of a swimmer reversing, and then kicked the boy's dog so hard its ribs cracked. The boy clutched the lead close to the collar, crossed the street at a trot and hurried back toward Donegal Pass while the animal screamed and I kept on walking, we all kept on walking, past the uniformed guard at the gate to the Gardens, past the landrover vehicle parked just inside, and there was no reason for it, we would have risked nothing, no one need ever have known we'd informed.

"You can open your eyes now," Barry said finally, then he placed his hands on my shoulders as I stood in front of him, blocking the way, and not ungently moved me aside. "Keep the penny," he added lightly. "A wee souvenir, so you don't forget me. Of course, if you don't want to keep it, you could give it back."

My eyes fell to my palm and its contents, still tightly scrolled, but like other watched things it remained unresponsive, though I used all my strength to will its release. "Yours it is, then," Barry said. As he slipped back into the room behind me, I heard the door just brush the carpet, twice, like a breath. Across the hallway a lift split open and a cleaner appeared, wheeling a barrow whose stock of towels wobbled deliciously, the mischievous spring of the laundered fabric barely containable under her hand. "Won't be long now, luv," she called when she saw me. "They'll be comin' out there any minute, you'll see."

There was a boy beside him when my father emerged. His arms were thin above the elbow, and his cheeks and chin looked unused to razors.

"You'll do it, then?" he was saying. "You promise?"

"Right away," my father answered.

"Thanks a lot," the boy said earnestly, and gave my father a set of keys. We crossed the courtyard together to the security gates and stepped out onto the street, where taxis had queued to collect the departing. The boy looked both ways as though expecting an ambush, then took off at a run away from the town.

"What did he want?" I asked my father.

"Just a wee favor, luv. He doesn't have time to do it himself."

The boy was a joyrider who'd ignored several warnings. When he was finally forced out of Twinbrook, he'd had every intention of keeping the promise extracted from him to give up the habit and settle down, but after three months the boredom had gotten to him. He'd stolen a Jetta and driven clear to Lough Swilly, where, on an impulse, he drove the car in. He slammed his foot down as it entered the water and hung onto the wheel, casting a broad plume of surf in his wake like a cheer. He'd done the same with a Clio, an Audi, a couple of Escorts, amused, for a while, by feigning sympathy when the thefts were discussed the following day. This time, however, he'd heard they were on to him. A friend of his mother's, whose own son had been kneecapped, said they'd shoot him dead this time around, but still his mother had gone to appeal. Because of her he'd been granted twenty-four hours to get out of the country. He was catching the ferry to Scotland that night.

"But what's he want you for?"

"He keeps bees," my father explained, as if the incredibility of it still made some part of him widen with awe. "He's got a hive on the roof of Unity Flats."

I'd walked through there once, out of necessity, detoured by partitions the police had erected to block out the sight of a Loyalist protest marching down from the Shankill to the City Hall. Processions were coming from many directions, and there had been fearful talk of the consequences if those with opposing aspirations were to spot each other along the way. Inside the complex the concrete facades had towered above me and I'd had the impression of walls caving in. The Executive was tearing it down now, however, and erecting two- and three-bedroom houses in its place; only a few of the original buildings were still inhabited. Most of the curtains had been pulled from their windows, the naked panes torn by objects that left neat holes upon entry, as if the glass had been soft and silent when it broke. Disused balconies on the lower floors were filling with rubbish from passing pedestrians, and the stairwells had the fugitive look of abandoned campsites. Even the murals were outdated now and beginning to fade.

On the roof of the building the boy had specified sat the hive, raised on cinder blocks and facing south, near a faucet that swelled and dripped and a paddock containing the boy's tools and brushes. On a nail by the paddock hung a muslin jumpsuit, which my father ignored. He'd been stung so often, he could approach any colony, managed or wild, without protection, even open a hive ungloved and bare-chested while their bright, humming bodies settled on his. I hadn't his courage. An acquaintance of his, having heard of his talent, asked him once to dispose of a nest he'd found in a tree on his property, from which large numbers of bees set out each day to enter the house through a drainpipe or flue. When I joined my father on that inspection I insisted the insects be well sedated before I drew close. Now, squatting comfortably to one side of the hive, he called me over.

"It's alright," he insisted when I shook my head. "C'mere till you see."

The boy had told him the queen might be failing and he suspected the colony was preparing to swarm. My father confirmed that the signs were evident: workers were clustering at the hive entrance but hardly any were taking flight, and despite the presence of dome-shaped cappings there was queen cup construction along the bottom edge of the frames. To prove they were gentle in this condition he scooped up a handful. I watched from a distance as they whirred and huddled, trying to summon what I knew about bees—that through an intricate, mathematical language they communicate distance and direction, and yet are myopic, confused by the movement of branches and leaves; that the queen bee, once mated, returns to the hive and never leaves it; that some fifty thousand of her children, working together, perform the life functions of a single being, the survival of each depending on all. My father and I had begun reading books about their behaviour during the twenty-eight months he worked for a farmer transporting honey and beeswax candles to health food groceries throughout the North. The farmer, whose business was small but successful, had approved of my father's undesigning enthusiasm and enlisted his help in the run up to harvest. But then the man's son was murdered in Derry and he sold the business. He sold his house, too, and moved to New Zealand, and my father, who could not afford to buy it from him, was forced to give up the van he'd been driving and find work in a factory, away from bees.

With no trees nearby for the swarm to land on, the boy had provided a short wooden scaffold in a bucket of sand. A few scouts moved busily along its crossed beams, relaying their signal to the rest of the colony; already a slender column had struck out from the hive. "Leave her," my father said when one of their number stopped on my sleeve and argued furiously with the threads that delayed her before flying on. Of the short films on nature we'd been shown in school recently, the best was a slow-motion sequence which revealed the demanding contortions that various species of flight involve. Observing the thickening spout of bodies in motion and wondering how such complex choreographies failed to collide, I almost forgot the unyielding knob of my fist and the coin inside it, out of sight beneath my arm.

"You tired, luv?" my father asked softly. "C'mon lean against me. Close your eyes. I'd've been sleeping myself, to tell you the truth," he continued, "if that wee lad hadn't been such a bundle of nerves. You should've seen it. I reckoned if I didn't talk to him he was going to explode."

"What is going to happen to him?"

"He'll come back," my father said simply, then shook his head. "Maybe he won't. God knows I've been wrong before."

"I know," he said finally. "I'll tell you the story. To help pass the time."

"What story?" I said.

"The one Barry told us, when he got back. Do you want to hear it?"

I lay back in his arms as he spoke of a woman, blind from birth, whose sight returned soon after she married. When her husband, a gamekeeper's son, claimed he could draw illness out of the sick like a splinter, the most distinguished of the world's physicians assembled to see him proven a fake. And indeed he was discredited, his entire practice collapsed in disgrace, people who'd spent large sums of money to receive the treatment lamented the ease with which they'd been duped—until one of his most tenacious supporters stepped to the front of the amphitheater and put this question to the crowd: if a man had no better weapon against pain and affliction than the medicine of his imagination, would he not still have a marvelous thing? The speaker was heckled, expelled from every professional body to which he belonged, later he even broke with his mentor, but no amount of medical evidence could disprove the fact that that woman could see.

At length the flow from the hive abated, and my father released me for a closer look. When the spherical mass at the knot of the cross, shimmering delicately, took to the air, I thought of the perfect rows of hexagonal entries they'd left behind and would build again when they resettled: how good it would be, surrounded by sisters, deep in a place where I fit precisely, where all would defend me if I were threatened, where everything I touched was a part of myself. Then the queen fell like soot at my father's feet and he knelt with a cry that turned me toward him.

The handful of cohorts that had fallen with her clung to his fingers when he picked her up. He stepped back with his arm upraised and the swarm surged after him like a crowd of revelers reentering a world where the time is significant to see the last bus of the evening about to depart. When they were first married, a friend of my parents acquired a second-hand home movie recorder, which he brought 'round one evening to ask them to help him test it out. In that brief film, they clasp each other 'round the waist and shoulders and beam at the camera, their faces pressed close. At the time the house they lived in was empty of furniture apart from a kitchen table and their bed upstairs; in such a space they could waltz or fandango with nothing to hinder them, no obstacle to negotiate or avoid. Now my father moved with the same clean momentum, dipping and spinning, leading the swarm. With the queen imprisoned between his hands, wherever he went he could make them follow.

"C'mon, wee woman!" he called to me finally, while they churned and swirled round him like a liquid stirred. "C'mon," he said. "You have a go."

I gave him my wrists and he uncurled my fingers, cupped my hands for me and eased the queen in. I could feel her exploring the crevices there with slow curiosity before the others found her, before my arms were immersed in velvet and cellophane except for the place just above my right elbow where I could still feel my father's sure grip, steering me gently. When we arrived at the far edge of the roof, I turned my palms over so they faced the ground, so that anything left there would surely fall out, and then marked their progress until my father, still taller than I then, and with better vision, told me finally that they'd disappeared.

Nadja Tesich

◆

CRIMES OF PASSION

It was an ordinary day in a small beauty shop that had known better times. I never go there on Tuesdays because the boss is there, a heavy set woman who makes me think of Kapos in the movies. She can kill you with a never-ending lament about how the neighborhood has changed, how romance is gone, and how women shouldn't wear pants. But here I was on a Tuesday because the holidays were coming and I wanted something drastic done to my head. Something really different I decided in the morning as the radio announced wind, rain, the flu season. I thought about the tropics.

I noticed right away that the atmosphere was different and saw immediately why: the boss was not out for lunch the way I assumed; no, Hilda was gone on a two week skiing trip to Austria. Maria's movements were slow, leisurely, she did a manicure as if making love. Chatting all along. A sign on the wall that said "don't put your feet on the wall" was openly ignored. They drank coffee, nibbled on cake. They gave me some. Soon Jimmy switched on the radio and merengued around an old lady who was getting a special perm for her son's wedding. She said she still didn't believe it.

Her son's wedding got everybody interested in Princess Di, if she'll divorce or not. Maria was sure that yes, because Di had a lover, someone more passionate than Charles. Jimmy claimed that no, it's the other way around because he knows someone who knows for sure. "The world is coming to an end," said the woman getting the manicure, "if royalty is behaving like trash." "They always did," said Jimmy, for my benefit, and winked. Maria laughed, moving her whole body. "Yes, but nothing is good anymore," continued the woman, "just take a look at this." She pointed to the paper and the major news for a week—the horrible death of a little girl in The Village and the subsequent miracle—a teenage mother finds the baby son she had given up for adoption in the same apartment with the same couple who killed the little girl. All thanks to the media. FORGIVEN BY HER PARENTS, one headline said. REAL FATHER STEPS UP, said another.

"I don't understand," said the same lady with long nails. "Primo, she shouldn't have been pregant at sixteen, right? Secundo, why did she give the baby to him if she herself was a Catholic? They have Catholic charities, couples who'd kill for a kid. How come she didn't think? Nobody thinks anymore."

Maria came to the girl's rescue: "A paper says a doctor recommended him—how's a poor girl to know? He wasn't supposed to steal a child, he told her he would find her a Catholic family. He just turned out to be a crook. Look what he did to his wife—did you see her eye? It has nothing to do with religion. Trust me. I know, Mrs. Mintz."

The old lady, blue, permed and looking like a thin chicken, got up and left. She paid in cash because a sign in front of the desk said "Positively no checks," in Hilda's handwriting. My turn next. I said, "Jimmy, I don't want a cut this time. Could you dye it, maybe black?" He was surprised. "Nobody ever dies blond hair black. It won't look good on you, hon . . . but I don't do color anyway. Maria, you've finished one hand, why don't you do her now if Mrs. Mintz doesn't mind." Mrs. Mintz gave her permission, Maria hesitated then said she'd do a temporary brown so I won't regret it later. I realized it was a good solution but if Hilda had been there she would have made sure I got permanently hooked. And my first experience started with only a slight sting, a sensation of cold. I'll walk out a brunette, I thought.

Jimmy looked bored. We gossiped for a while about Elizabeth Taylor, if she did or didn't, and both of us decided yes because not only did she lose all that weight, she seemed to have lost every wrinkle too. Just as we started on Cher and her improvements, a woman appeared in the door, with a baby stroller and a baby inside, asleep. She said she wanted something different, she is so tired of her old self too, but it had better be practical because she has no money for fancy upkeep. She spoke miles an hour in a breathless, husky voice about how she came from Virginia and how much she loves New York. She even volunteered she had two more kids over there, with her husband. "We just separated," she said casually. She looked very young to have had three.

Jimmy did wonders on her head—a short pretty cut transformed her into a slim adolescent boy. He was truly happy, she thought he was a genius, he raved about her cheekbones. Getting up to pay, she raised her voice: "Oh my God, I've got nothing to pay with. I'd better rush over to the bank. Do you mind keeping my little angel for a minute?"

"Why not," Jimmy said, and I silently agreed. And she was gone.

"Isn't it funny," Jimmy said, cheerful again, "you can always tell when someone is not from New York. No pure New Yorker would leave the baby with us. People here are so cold and cynical . . . I can never . . ." Jimmy was from Puerto Rico, he still had a lovely soft accent, something soft about his whole person.

"There's a reason for it," I said, trying to defend New Yorkers and myself. "You can't imagine what happened to me last week."

"Yes?" he asked, and I told:

A well-dressed woman had stopped me on Broadway and wanted to know where I had bought my black coat. She said it was exactly what she needed to stay warm. I told her carefully the site of the store; she said I had the most interesting voice. Then she said she had a very peculiar problem because she had just found a package and wondered what to do with it. Someone must have forgotten it inside the telephone booth, she said. "Try calling information," I said. "I've thought of it," she said, "but look, there is no address, just his name and how many Smiths do you have?" "You have to open it then, maybe his address is inside," I suggested. "Good idea," she said, and ripped open the manila envelope, then exclaimed "Oh my God!" I saw what looked like thousands of dollars inside a cellophane bag. A note attached to it said "here it is, but you'd better keep your mouth shut." There was no address. "Now what?" she said. "Something fishy about this." "I would hand it over to the police," I said. "You're kidding!" she exclaimed. "Those crooks will just divide it up. Why are they any better than . . ." She looked at me with what seemed like embarrassment and suggested we go to her place and split it. She felt she couldn't take it all. At this point another woman appeared on cue and got interested as well. She was rougher, not as well dressed.

And I knew they had picked me because I must look like a sap.

"So, Jimmy," I concluded, "how can you trust anyone here?"

"I still do," he said. "Nothing will change that."

Maria got interested in my story because of the money. The thought I had stupidly lost thousands of dollars and could be rich now bothered her. She played the lottery every week and sometimes asked me to give her magic numbers. She kept shaking her head, "You made a mistake. I would've gone, just in case." Maria wanted to open her own beauty shop in Puerto Rico and will do it when she wins big.

Warmed up by my story, Jimmy started on his: "This very beautiful young man, well-dressed and everything, appears right here in this store and says, 'Are you Jimmy? Carmen sent me. The garage doesn't accept checks and I can't get my car out. Carmen said you could help me until tomorrow. Can you?' See, I know Carmen, but I know not one but many Carmens and I am so busy cutting hair so I say to Hilda to give him a hundred from my pay. And I never saw him again," Jimmy concluded without bitterness or anger. He was laughing at his foolishness and Maria laughed too and then they spoke in Spanish. "I never change," he said. "My nature."

"Mine too, Jimmy," I said and whispered to him what I haven't told anyone. I had let this young man from Texas stay in my place and he ran away with my TV set.

"No!" Jimmy said, then, after thinking, continued in a low voice: "Was he handsome?"

"Yes, he was, very. He told me he danced."

"We pay for things. That's how it is," Jimmy said, looking nostalgic. I didn't tell him I was only putting the guy up. It seemed better that way.

Mrs. Mintz, whose nails had been done long ago, suddenly said, "didn't she say she was coming right away?"

"The lines are getting big at Chemical," I said. "True, true," she said, "they are. Everything is coming apart, you wait in the bank and in the post office and you never know what's lurking about and who'll steal your television set." Her hearing was remarkably good for her age.

The little girl woke up. She had beautiful green eyes with long lashes, curly brown hair. Jimmy cooed at her. Maria said you could get hungry for a new baby. I thought she was the most beautiful baby ever.

"I don't think she is coming. Mark my words," Mintz said.

"Well, she knew who to pick," Jimmy said and nudged me.

"Which one of you will keep her?" Maria laughed. Jimmy looked nervous all of a sudden. "She'll come back." I said.

The baby laughed for no reason, and we laughed too, looking toward the door. "She probably went to shop," Maria said.

"It's been more than half an hour," Jimmy said, biting his nails.

"What did I tell you?" Mrs. Mintz said. "Didn't she say she was divorced?"

"Yes, she was," Jimmy said, "she has two more kids in the South."

"Of course, "Mintz explained, "he kicked her out because she had this one with a young lover. They always say bastards are prettier than the other ones."

"All that love!" Jimmy sighed.

"How do you know he was young, maybe she had this one with a wealthy older man," said Maria and revealed as always her weakness.

"No," Mintz said, "she's not the kind. You have to have a certain style to catch a wealthy man. I know. I was married to one, may he rest in peace."

"What else did she say," Maria asked, lighting up a cigarette.

"Something practical," Jimmy remembered, "because she didn't have money for . . ."

"There you have it," Mrs. Mintz concluded, victorious. "The new man left her too and now with a new haircut she left us her brat."

Maria had to wash my hair and then put me under the dryer. I didn't stay long because others had gathered around the stroller looking concerned. They wondered if she had left some important instruction or the child's name, if the whole thing had been premeditated. We found a change of diapers, a full bottle, and the sweetest furry book. Mrs. Mintz was now convinced that everything was well planned, just look at the evidence. Jimmy and I argued that the furry book and bottle only showed she loved the baby, and it was obvious if you looked at her clothes, her beautiful cheeks.

The telephone rang but it was only a customer changing her appointment to next week. Mrs. Mintz made clicking sounds with her tongue then said, "You have work to do. We'd better find out what's what. I'll go out and investigate." She put her old fur coat on, applied some red lipstick. Exiting, she looked like Joan Crawford.

I looked for the first time at my temporary brown hair. Did it transform me, is this how I wanted to look? I wasn't sure. I had time to think, she said it will fade. The clock said three-thirty. Maria was going to close earlier since there were no more appointments and a storm was coming, she said.

Mrs. Mintz marched in, huffing and puffing, but otherwise happy. "She is not anywhere near the bank. I've checked the supermarket and the cleaners and the pharmacy. But I could swear I saw her get into a cab with a man just now." We were silent at first, then we argued what to do. We decided against the police for now. It wouldn't be good for the baby to sit in the police station. It would get her scared. Maria lived in the Bronx and that was too far for the baby and besides her husband wouldn't like it. He was a jealous man, he might get ideas. Mrs. Mintz said her hands shook and she was too old to handle such a young body with care. Before Jimmy could open his mouth I said, "I'll take her." After all, I lived nearby, was single, and physically fit. They seemed relieved. Everyone laughed. I left my telephone number just in case and, with the stroller, the two of us stepped out on Broadway.

Outside it was the most beautiful autumn day, blue-gold, not a single cloud left. The weatherman was wrong again; he never imagined that the winds would chase away the rain. We stopped at Cake Masters for eclairs and bread.

"What a beauty," the manager said and gave her a special cookie to chew on. Then we bought daisies at a flower store. An old lady stopped to admire her and pinch her cheeks and parents everywhere with babies and strollers smiled at us with complicity: another young mother and child. The world on the street fitted as never before. There was nothing vague or needing explanation about my person. Was this the beginning of what took place or did it exist before, that very morning, months and years before?

In front of my building the super, always in a bad mood, was cleaning the steps. He looked at me in consternation but said nothing. A young loud kid from upstairs with whom I'd had a fight over his stereo and he had called me names, now beamed like a Buddha and lifted the stroller up. Through the glass door, both men looked at me, surprised. I saw it suddenly: they thought the baby was mine! They had decided that I either hid my pregnancy or just adopted. Nobody really paid attention to my hair, or is it that it blended so well with hers, and because of it appeared less noticeable.

I wondered where to put her and finally settled on a corner near the living room window so she could have all the light and watch the plants. I worried about Basho, my cat. What if he scratched her? I'd have to lock him up somewhere or give him away, I thought. For now he was asleep in the kitchen. Then I emptied a drawer, lined it with a blue cotton sheet: her bed, a bit small. I'll have to figure out something about the food, one bottle wasn't enough. Was it regular milk or something special? Who could I ask? Fortunately, she was a happy child, fascinated by small things. She examined my face in a way that you could tell she was very bright. She looked at the cactus and laughed; I noticed it had turned dark out. The days are so short. She had her bottle, I sang to her and patted her hair, then she fell asleep as if she had done this before.

Watching her breathe, I thought I'd have to call the police soon. But if I do that, they'll take her away from me because that's what they do. There is no husband, just lies. And if her mother had disappeared (probably gone to Florida or maybe not . . . after all you can get permanently lost in Manhattan too) they'll put her up in a foster home, and eventually for adoption. I imagined a dim ugly place, dirty, look what happened to those two kids in the Village. They'll never let me adopt her because I'm single, as if being married provided an immunity against cruelty. I saw her mistreated, suffering, slapped around, when with me she would be happy. I should call a lawyer but then I realized it might be better if fewer people knew about it. I will tell Jimmy when I see him that I gave her to a cop immediately and have no idea what happened since. Still . . . if I want to make it legal I have to report her. Maybe I could call Jimmy and ask him to marry me, just like that, the way you get immigration papers . . . he might say yes, even though he would be shocked. But he might be afraid of the whole legal mess and there I'd be—with one extra person who knew my real intentions.

No, the best is to keep silent, I decided, having fallen madly in love. Slowly, over a drink, plans formed—take the money out of the bank early in the morning then head for Chicago for a while and surprise my mother. She'll forgive me when she sees her, the way that other mother forgave her teenage daughter in the paper. And we'll finally have something real to talk about—my pregnancy, birth pains, (oh how happy she'd be) and she'll agree with me that it was best I didn't marry the bastard since he drank so much. Then six months later, when everything is over, and the baby bigger, I'll come back. Donna will take care of the apartment, Basho, and the plants.

My plans were interrupted by the phone. Jimmy. "How are you?" he asked. "Fine," I said, feeling like someone else. "We've cleaned up and are going to close. She never showed up." His voice sounded like something from the grave.

"Such is life," I said.

"I'm sorry," he said. "My fault. I shouldn't have said yes. I always do."

"Don't worry, Jimmy," I consoled him, "everything is fine."

"Do you need anything?" He sounded real guilty.

"Nothing at all. I'm coping marvelously."

"What are you going to do?" he asked.

"Well . . . probably call the police as soon as she wakes up. What else could you imagine?"

"We'll tape your name and number on the door. Is that okay?"

"Sure." I said. "I'm sorry," he said again, then hung up. She moved in her sleep. I decided to call her Laura, a pretty name. Another call interrupted my thoughts. A doctoral student from Columbia who had always depended on me said, "It's all finally done," as if I had been intimately involved with his misery. He wanted his thesis typed and edited, the way only I knew how to do. Three hundred pages on the drinking patterns of American males, good fast money, but I declined because I was relocating, I told him. He seemed really shocked, hurt, he wanted to argue even. So, before another call wakes her up I took it off the hook, and continued my interrupted dreams of flight to Chicago. I was marking my top priorities on a pad—call Donna, bank, call mother, pack—when there was a loud knock on the door.

There they were—the super, a middle-aged Irish cop, and the mother, red from crying. "Is this who you want?" the super said, and she whispered yes. Then she screamed, "Is she here?"

"Don't shout," I said, "you'll wake her up." The super looked at me the way you look at dangerous criminals and moved away.

"We've been calling and calling," she said. "Thank God we found your address in the directory."

"You could've come alone," I said, looking at the cop. "And come on time."

"I panicked," she said, and started crying again. "I'm sorry . . . it's been a hard day. Where is she?"

Both of them saw my makeshift bed by the plants, the stroller next to it, the little snow suit on the chair. She pulled her out, all limp and hot, then dressed her with amazing speed.

"Lady," the cop started, "I know you aren't from the city and all that but you're damned lucky to fall on this nice decent lady instead of . . . heaven knows who. . . ."

"I know, I know," she cried. "I told you I had all those complications. He had come back looking for us and it got to be real messy. It was really lucky Ginny was somewhere else."

I wanted to know who had come back to look for her. Was it her husband or her young lover? There was no way to tell. They were out. I closed the door. She had forgotten to take the bottle and the little furry book. Both sat on the table, the remnants of my brief love affair with Laura. Basho moved in the kitchen. He probably wanted to eat. Stretching and yawning, he slinked over then rubbed himself against my shin. He wanted to be caressed. His beautiful face repelled me for no reason. I wanted to kick him, to push him away, to scream, to do something violent. I ignored him instead.

David Mason

◆

BOYS' STATE

I was looking right at the podium when Will bolted from the bleachers and assassinated the Governor. It took everybody by surprise—even me, though I knew it was coming. I looked at the far end of the gymnasium, where the clock hung on the wall beyond the basketball hoop. Mr. Anderson leaned against the wall with his arms folded, watching, and Mr. Hood straightened and stepped into the room as if there were something he should do to stop us, and even the aged Legionnaires in their uniforms seemed aware that something was wrong with this picture.

The Governor was shocked. He was a good-looking black kid from Seattle, and I felt nauseated because of what we had done to him. Not that it was serious. Nothing was real at Boys' State. He just stood there, watching Will run out under the clock waving his pistol and shouting something about anarchy. The Governor wore a coat and tie, and as I walked up to him I couldn't help feeling sorry for him. He had trusted me, big mistake, and when I stepped up to the podium he gave me a hurt look. He said, "What are you doing?"

By now there was considerable din in the gymnasium, confusion from the bleachers, the kind that pull out from the walls. I couldn't see or hear clearly—the bleachers filled with boys, the hollow rustling and the echo of disbelief—but I saw the Governor, Eric, step back and look at me as if he wasn't sure whose side I was on. "It's okay," I said. "You've just been assassinated."

"What?"

"This is an assassination." My voice surprised me, cutting through the din. "We're seceding from the state."

"You can't be!"

I had to admit I was almost as disappointed as he was. I nudged him aside, unfolding the envelope on which I had written my speech.

There were teachers who thought I was a screwed-up kid from a broken home, who thought my long hair, which grew like a blond bush, meant that I was on drugs or something. But that was the year they sent me to Boys' State, this educational program run by the Legion, and I thought my mother would feel honored if I went. I don't remember whether I even told my father about it. He lived in Seattle. I'm not even sure my mom realized what I was saying to her about a week in Spokane and the model state government. She didn't tell me not to go.

I thought Will Cass was the second coming, but when Will ran out with his pistol in the air I almost hated him. I did hate him, because he couldn't see how wrong we were to shoot this kid from a poor neighborhood who was all dressed up for his inauguration. Will thought it was cool, something to sneer about, the way he sneered with admiration when I was elected Mayor of our town. Our wing of the dorm was supposed to be a town called Spruce. There were two political parties in Evergreen State, the Blues and the Reds; I was a local chairman of the Blues, Will a mere plebeian of the Reds. At our first party caucus the boys were impressed that I knew the Rules of Order—Mr. Hood had given me a copy to study on our first night in Spokane—and they nominated me for Mayor. I ran on the promise that I would not use victory as a stepping stone to higher office. What the hell. I remember a gathering in Will's room that night with some of the guys. Will's roommate was a nerd from Twisp, one of those kids you can't really place at first because you can't see his eyes through his glasses. We'd been in Spokane twenty-four hours, and already this kid worshipped Will. I think I was sort of wary. Will had a cynical air

I admired and the sort of good looks I thought girls would go crazy for.

He was taller than me, to begin with, and enough to matter. His hair was stringy, blond like mine, but thinner, so it didn't look like a bush, and when he smoked his unfiltered Camels—smoking was against the rules— you could see he had strong hands with good bones, thick knuckles. He looked like a guy who'd been places, and I guess he had. In his faded jean-jacket, ripped jeans and tennis shoes, he looked like a hood without the self-reproachful stoop. Maybe it was his eyes, blue eyes that mocked everything they saw and then took you in, accepted you as if you were in on a secret, or maybe it was the way he lounged on his bunk and smoked, but the clincher, the way he really snagged you, was the fact that he was experienced. He knew women, had known women, in the Biblical sense, had seen the inside of a jail cell and a whorehouse. You might wonder how a kid who'd done all that, who'd been busted for possession and had spent a night puffing over the fat tits of a Vancouver madam, had ever been selected for Boys' State, the reward of young leaders. But how could I wonder about Will when I didn't even know why I'd been selected myself? The whole thing was a farce. I was there to bring honor to my mother, who wouldn't even remember I was gone.

There were half a dozen of us in Will's room, one of those generic dorm rooms you see all over the country, with dressers, covered radiators and yellow walls. He offered us cigarettes and I took one and felt like an idiot. I smoked and hated myself for it. Will nodded from his bunk. "I voted for you," he said.

Some of the guys nodded, like they voted for me too.

"Crossed party lines."

"So did I," said the nerd from Twisp. I didn't even know there was a town called Twisp till I met this kid.

Will said, "I thought you were bullshit, Ryan, but you were less bull-shit than the jack-ass from our party."

"Thanks," I said.

"Yeah, thanks." Will looked at me like this was a test. For a moment I thought I should leave.

"It's okay," Will said. He was letting us all know it was okay for one of us, one of the loose Sprucers, to have power of the sort I had won that day. Without a word, we had all known from the first night who our real leader was. He didn't need to run for office to confirm it. He picked

tobacco leaves from his tongue with those fine fingers, rolled his head
back against the wall. "I thought you were a jerk to run, you know?
Taking this bullshit seriously. I mean, the American fucking Legion."

Everyone laughed. It was 1972.

"I mean, who the hell are these guys to teach us about government?
These are the guys who want us bombing Cambodia. Fucking Cambodia,
man."

"I know," I said. "I felt weird running."

"You were weird, Ryan."

Everybody laughed again. Everybody except me and Will, who
watched and seemed to soak in all this approval from the others. "I had
ideas about you, man, but you were good at that meeting. They'll want
you for Governor now."

"I won't run."

"Why not? They like you. Hood likes you. He's Ivy League, man. You
got the Ivy League on your side."

That made me uneasy. Mr. Hood had already asked me about my
plans for college. I made some vague reply and he mentioned Williams
College in Massachusetts. He said he was a Seattle Alumni Representative for Williams, and he could arrange a meeting for me with
somebody from the college. I thanked him for it, gave him back his copy
of the Rules of Order, and got out of there. Mr. Hood was an advisor for
Pine, another town in our dorm, but for some reason he took an interest in me. The advisor for Spruce was Mr. Anderson, who was more like
us; he thought the Legion sponsorship was weird like we did, because of
the war.

"Fucking Ivy League," Will said.

I tasted the smoke on my tongue.

Will wanted to know how many of the guys had tried dope. The nerd
from Twisp hadn't tried it, nor had the kid from Yakima, the apple capi-
tal of the world. I had tried it at my girlfriend's sister's apartment, but it
was a total bummer. I didn't know how to hold smoke in my lungs without coughing. I fumbled the bong.

Will talked about bongs like a pro. When they busted him for possession, he spent a night in jail because his old man wouldn't come down
and pick him up. He told us all about crossing from Oregon, getting
pulled over this side of the border. I hadn't even been to Oregon. I

couldn't describe the way we smoked from the bong, afraid I might get a detail wrong, so I said nothing except that I'd tried it once.

Will laughed. "Not you, man. You're Ivy League material." We all thought Ivy League meant squeaky clean. It meant New England and boys with pink, healthy-looking cheeks—choir boys who could play hockey. "Hood likes you," Will said. "That fucking L.L. Bean shit he wears." He took in the others, with his eyes, with his whole posture, legs crossed casually on the bunk. "You can't talk about bucking the system if you haven't smoked. When they caught me I just held out my wrists like this." He held out his wrists. The cigarette clamped in his lips bobbed when he talked. "I just laughed, man. I was stoned. I just didn't give a shit. Cops couldn't believe it. There was this one skinny-assed guy said he wanted to beat the tar out of me cause my hair was long. I had real long hair then, down to my shoulders. I knew he was bluffing. I got one phone call, and I didn't even call my old man. He wouldn't come, anyway. I called Lisa."

He told us about Lisa. An older woman. College-age, easy, dope-happy, a good supplier and an amazing lay. There was also Jackie who loved his ass and took to a back seat like a beaver to water and had a way of fighting when she fucked. By then he was into his stories, and I was just like the rest of them, listening to Will's stories with a mind full of gratitude and fear.

Boys' State was held on the campus of this big university in Spokane. Each dorm housed a make-believe town or two. Our advisors were people who had lives of their own in Seattle, Vancouver or Olympia. I think Mr. Anderson was a teacher, Mr. Hood a lawyer. I didn't know much about them. Mr. Anderson came to Will's room that night when we were all there, saw us smoking and didn't bawl us out. He told us he had been coming to Boys' State for twelve years, but he was beginning to see it for the farce it was. Will had used the same word. Farce. We all knew the system was corrupt to its core, we knew Kissinger was a liar and Nixon was worse and there were boys not much older than us fighting in Nam. People used to talk about the system in those days. Mr. Anderson lit a cigarette, walked over by the window and turned toward us as if he wanted to blend in and be one of us. "You should show them," he said, "what a farce it all is."

"Like how?" said Will. "Ryan here's about to go Ivy League on us."

Mr. Anderson smiled at me through his smoke. He had a gray, kindly face and a build that was simultaneously tough and dumpy, which made me think he drank. He held his face in a smile like a carved mask. "Ryan's okay," he said. "You're all okay. There's nothing wrong with working in the system, and there's nothing wrong with hating it. I'm beginning to hate it myself." He paused. "So maybe you could show them what you feel about it."

Will laughed. "Yeah, we should legalize dope."

"Why not?" Mr. Anderson looked at each of us. "Why not do what you want? Legalize marijuana. Show them what freedom means. It means they can't limit you, but they don't seem to know that. They want you to learn about government and responsibility, but that's not what I want you to learn." His face was puffy and kind and gray, and his voice had a feminine lilt. "I think you should learn what freedom is. How you make your own freedom, and how they can't stop you from doing what you want."

After Mr. Anderson's speech there was talk about politics, and later a dry thunderstorm passed over the university and we all ran outside to watch lightning touch the flat land beyond Spokane. I had never seen lightning without rain before, or the kind of dry, soulful clouds you get east of the mountains. In Nooksack it always rains, and the clouds are the same color as the bay. They're just there, like dirty gin in a bottled world.

I didn't know anyone on the bus to Spokane, except one kid named Kirk who was assigned to another dorm so I hardly saw him the entire week. He was elected Attorney General later on, and seemed to have made a good thing out of the experience. He had a withered arm, and I think people admired a kid with a withered arm who could do the right thing all the time. I ran into him once when I was walking to dinner with Will. We were smoking unfiltered Camels, and when I saw Kirk I tried to act as if I wasn't really inhaling, but he had seen me blowing smoke and he gave me a righteous look. What are you doing to yourself? his look said.

Your mom know you do that? Is this the sort of example you intend to set back home? And I felt half-sick with smoke and guilty butterflies in my gut, and kept looking for Kirk in the dining hall, hoping he didn't see me with the others grouped around Will. We were laughing at Will's stories about prison food, which was just like college food, only better.

But that bus ride over had been nice, much nicer than the ride back. We crossed the Cascades at Snoqualmie Pass, dropped down into the dry apple country on the other side. When we crossed the Columbia River gorge, I remember thinking it looked like a desert in the movies, and I thought about riding across that desert alone on a horse. It became a place from a John Wayne movie with Apaches hidden behind every rock or tuft of scrub. I imagined little battles, little cavalry charges, the dry wind in my hair, hair no longer bushy, but slicked back under the sweaty brim of my cavalry hat, and when my hat flew off in the wind I felt my hair blowing, and I dodged arrows and Winchester bullets. Then I remembered I was a pacifist. I don't know how I forgot, I just got carried away. My mother was a pacifist in Nooksack and my father was a pacifist in Seattle, and I thought what a dumb kid thing it was to make cowboy movies in the Greyhound window.

I liked the dry air of Spokane, the dry lightning at night. We were given strict instructions not to leave campus, but one night I followed the dry, oily railroad tracks into town, walked up and down a street where cars were cruising and girls rode by. I wanted to meet them, but they went cruising by in the bright lights of the strip while lightning flashed in the distance.

Will had gone to town that night with some of the guys. He said he would show them how to get laid. I wanted to join them, but I'd been held up at a Blue Party meeting, and by the time I got back to the dorm Will and the others were gone. We could have been suspended for leaving campus. I didn't care. I did, I didn't. I looked at girls cruising by, feared the next car would be full of Legionnaires, returned to the campus alone by way of the railroad tracks.

After the Blue Party meeting, Mr. Hood had asked me to come to his room. That was why I missed the others. We went down the hall with its sickly yellow walls into a room not much bigger than mine. Mr. Hood was quick, all business when he walked, and spoke with that clipped, forward confidence that seems to come from the east, from having been there and seen all the big cities and met all the right people. "Have a seat," he said, and closed the door. "I've been meaning to talk to you."

He had his leather luggage in one corner, a stack of books about elections on his dresser. The room smelled like aftershave. I knew Hood approved of me so I just sat there and hoped he wouldn't hold me long. He wore wing-tip shoes and black socks, and probably this was a vacation for him—he looked like a man who would usually wear a tie. "You've been handling yourself very well," he said. "I think you should know that. You're a good speaker, and you did well with the mayoral race."

I thanked him, but there was something strange about his confidence in me. It seemed misplaced, as if he should have been able to see I wasn't Ivy League material. I wanted to find Will and escape into town and meet some girls, preferably easy girls who were no good at remembering names. There was Nancy, of course, my girlfriend back in Nooksack, but everything with Nancy was respectable, though we had had a few close calls.

"I've had my eye on you," Mr. Hood said. "You should take that as a compliment."

I said I realized it was quite a compliment.

"I've been to some pretty good schools," he said, "and I know ability when I see it. It's not a thing I take lightly, and I don't think you should take it lightly either."

I said I didn't take it lightly.

"Coming from some of these towns, say a town like Nooksack, sometimes you don't think you should raise your sights. Sometimes you don't think you deserve to know what the world is like. But there are people with native ability, and I think you show what I call native ability."

I didn't ask what native ability meant.

"Ryan," he said, "I think the kids here respect you. Maybe more than you know. They respect the way you handle the town meetings. What I'm trying to say is, you should consider running for higher office. You have the native ability to make Governor here, and after that it's Boys' Nation. Washington D.C. The Legion would pay your way and everything."

I took a deep breath.

"Is something wrong?"

"My promise," I said. "I promised I wouldn't run for higher office."

Mr. Hood gave me an exasperated look, ran the fingers of one hand through his hair and then rubbed the hand on his shirt as if he weren't aware of the motion.

"That's commmendable," he said. "I don't mean to diminish the value of promises. I value promises. I value integrity. But I also value native ability."

"I can't break my promise," I said, and I suppose there really was some native integrity I clung to, but there was also the fact that I knew my limits. I knew I'd never win another election. Maybe I didn't want to win one. I could see Hood's mind planning to use my integrity to my advantage, and I didn't have the courage to tell him to leave me alone, leave me out of it, leave me out of his plans.

"Fine," he said. "That's a good move. It will only stand you in good stead. My problem is . . ." He breathed through his nose. "I'm thinking ahead, you see. I'm thinking of the Governor's race, Boys' Nation, scholarships for college. I'm trying to make you see the larger picture. This isn't just a game we play here, bringing boys to this place. This is the way government really works, and you could be a player." He watched me as he talked, and when I started to respond, he held up a hand to prevent me. "But I understand your choice. I understand where you're coming from. I want you to know that. I want you to know I have some power in this organization, with the Executive Council, and I'll keep an eye out for you. You should know that Ken Anderson . . ."

I stiffened.

"He's a good guy," said Mr. Hood, "but a lot of people are disappointed in him, and frankly, I don't think he's setting a good example for you guys. He's cynical. Things aren't working out for him in his life. He's going through a divorce, and there are other problems. I want you to be very careful how you deal with him, okay? In many ways, I don't think they should have let him come back this year. Teachers get cynical; they spend too much time in the trenches. They see too many problems and stop caring." He saw that I didn't want to hear any more, paused, and tried a new tack. "Ryan, at least consider another office. State Party Chairman. How about that? It's a temporary responsibility. Wouldn't require leaving the Mayor's office. In fact, all you really do is deliver the keynote address at the party convention. Would you consider it?"

I said I would think about it.

"You have to make up your mind by tomorrow night. I'll lobby for you, okay? I'll even help you with your speech."

"Okay," I said. I glanced at the door. "I kind of have to be somewhere right now."

"Where? There aren't any meetings tonight."

"I told some guys I'd meet them."

"Don't do anything wild, okay? These are crazy times. We've got to hold this thing together."

He told me to remember my native ability and let me go. I went back to Spruce, saw that I'd missed the guys and felt like an old beach ball shot full of holes. I had to climb over a Cyclone fence behind the dorm to get to the railroad tracks, and all the way into town I kept looking back over my shoulder.

People said I made a good Party Chairman. Though I'd written my speech in a hurry and hadn't shown it to Mr. Hood, he said it did what a keynote address was supposed to do, got people hyped up. Will came to our party convention because he didn't like the guys in the Red Party. He smirked all the way through my performance, but he knew I hated it as much as he did. He had come back late from Spokane, and when I saw him at breakfast the next morning I told him about my meeting with Mr. Hood. "Pure Ivy League," he said. Then he told me to play along. He had a plan, and even Anderson knew about it, and he would let me in on it too. The first step was to get the legalization of marijuana on the Blue Party platform, since the Reds were all narcs from hick towns, and anyway he had more friends among the Blues. We would shock the pants off the Legionnaires.

I asked him if he'd had any success in Spokane, and he smiled. "Spokane's the biggest one-horse town I ever saw, man. All you can do here is cruise and fuck, cruise and fuck, and I didn't have a car."

In the end, the Blue Party went way beyond our expectations for social reform. Not only did we put legalization of marijuana on the platform,

but we also nominated a black kid for Governor. Anderson was ecstatic
by the time we finished. Hood kept watching me, trying to read my
expression, which I kept as neutral as I could. I let him think whatever
he wanted to think about me, just in case.

Eric Marcus, our candidate, was a quiet, well-spoken guy. He held
himself very carefully in a crowd. He dressed carefully, held his shoulders
back when he stood and let his arms drop at his sides, as if he were standing at attention. It was hard to read him. I knew he was from an inner
city school and I thought he must know a lot I didn't know. I thought
maybe he'd be angry at whites, but Eric's acceptance speech surprised me.
He spoke about justice and the memory of Martin Luther King. He spoke
about low-income housing and economic aid for students. His voice was
sometimes so quiet I had a hard time hearing him, had to lean forward
and cup a hand to my ear.

Mr. Hood watched me carefully through the whole event, and afterwards he took me aside. He didn't touch me, but stood so he had me
against the wall and I couldn't escape him. I could smell his aftershave.
"You're doing well, very well. Marcus is a good candidate. He appeals to
conscience. That's good. Nobody would dare vote against him, except
the worst sort of red-neck, and we've got plenty of those. You should get
close to him. Get in his inner circle. Introduce yourself to him as Party
Chairman. Tell him you want to help with his campaign."

I stood there like an idiot, nodding and trying to break away. Will and
Twisp and some of the others had their eyes on me, and I tried to look
like I didn't give a damn what Hood was saying. I had learned to see
Twisp's eyes through his lenses now. They didn't seem to care what they
focused on, unless it was Will. When I came up to them later I saw they
had been talking about me.

"What's Hood want?" Will asked.

"He thinks I should get into Marcus's circle."

"Do it. Let us know what's going on there."

"What are you going to do?"

"Nothing. We can't do anything until somebody wins the election.
The Reds have nominated a twerp named Stoltz, so it looks like Marcus
is the man. I like it. He's got dope on his platform. It's cool."

Twisp nodded and hung on Will's every word as if Will were Robert F.
Kennedy back from the dead. Will lit up a cigarette, right there in front

of everybody, and nobody told him not to. He threw back his head and laughed as he blew out smoke.

Marcus won the election by a landslide. I was right there in the middle of it, and I felt glad for him. I saw pride and disbelief trade places on his face, saw him blink back tears of happiness as his handlers slapped him on the back. For a moment his shoulders slumped, his thin hands rose to his temples as if to keep the top of his head from floating off. We had set up headquarters in a lounge in his dorm, the town of Hemlock, and held strategy sessions, advised and bickered. Rumor had it that the Legion was furious over our platform. One kid from a ritzy school in Bellevue said we should make public charges of racism against the Legion. Marcus said no, we had no evidence and it would only interfere with the election. He wore his coat and tie all the time, carried a plastic-covered writing case and sported a Cross ball-point pen an advisor had given him. I wondered if the whole business was going to his head. Evergreen State was not really Washington State, and nothing he said really mattered except on campus. He would never be Governor in the real world beyond the railroad tracks where cars went cruising on the main drags of a thousand towns. Maybe he felt some grave responsibility in his new position. That was exactly what Mr. Hood wanted me to feel, and I felt nothing at all. I felt numb.

Between Will and Mr. Hood, I didn't know which way to turn. The week was nearly over. Our little political world would disintegrate, and all its citizens would return to houses in those towns. We would be children again, for a while. And then I would have to decide what to do with the rest of my rotten life.

It was after the election, sitting with the Governor-elect and his handlers, that I heard about Will's plan. Some poor goon from Hemlock gained an audience with us because he had heard something important and had to tell us. I was standing at the edge of our little circle, too far from the entrance to the lounge to be comfortable, and this kid blocked the only exit I had. Eric Marcus sat at the low table in the middle of the room, toying with his ball-point pen. Some of his handlers had taken to wearing coats and ties, so I suppose we looked like a fairly serious group, and the kid was nervous. "I was over in Spruce," he said to the Governor. "Will Cass and a bunch of guys are plotting to assassinate you at your inauguration."

I felt all eyes turning toward me, the Mayor of loose Spruce. I had to keep my eyes from losing focus, and for a moment I just stammered at the air. "A rumor," I said. "Nothing to it." Inside I was thinking things with no words for them, or maybe just the word, assassination. It had the flat dead sound of all my growing up. I was scared the people in the room might hear my heart pounding. If they decided to accuse me of con-spiracy, I might not get out of there undamaged.

Governor Marcus—he already looked formal and grown up—set his pen on the table, looking over one shoulder at the informer. "What exactly do you mean by assassination?"

"I don't know," said the kid from Hemlock. "There was a meeting in one of the rooms. I heard about it."

"It's just a rumor," I said.

"Are you sure?"

"I heard about it yesterday," I lied. "Cass was kidding around. And it wasn't you he meant. It was Stoltz, if Stoltz got elected. Cass is on our side, he wants our platform."

One of the handlers leaned at Marcus across the table. "I think we should look into this."

Marcus looked at me. He was no good at disguising his disappoint-ment. He knew damned well what it was like to be betrayed, but maybe he thought being Governor would put an end to all that.

"It's nothing," I told them. "Just Cass sounding off. He thinks he's being funny. And it wasn't even you he was talking about. He wants our platform. It was Stoltz he was talking about."

"I just heard it," said the kid from Hemlock. "I was just over there." But his voice cracked, and I knew he felt like an idiot for bringing nega-tive news to the victor's camp. I stood my ground. I looked Eric Marcus in the eyes, and saw that he had decided to trust me.

When I got back to Spruce I didn't go straight to Will's room as I usual-ly did. I went to my room first, but it was small and I felt claustrophobic.

It was pointless to sit in there by myself, nursing my nerves. So I walked the halls, careful to avoid Pine, where Mr. Hood might find me.

In the lounge where the two towns bordered, where I had run my first Party caucus and town-meeting what seemed like weeks ago, Mr. Anderson sat by himself, watching daytime television. I felt as if I were seeing a too-private moment in a stranger's life. He was slumped down in a big armchair with tattered upholstery, like a soft lump of gray clay that had fallen on something very hard. I wondered if he knew everything about Will's plan. I wondered if he cared. But I backed away without calling attention to myself.

Will's room was number 110 in the west wing. I heard voices behind the closed door, and when I opened it I saw the room was full of smoke struck by afternoon sunlight. So this was what they meant by smoke-filled rooms. Will said he was glad to see me, but the other guys, Twisp and a few others, were silent. I told them what I had heard at Party Headquarters. I said Governor Marcus had been worried, but I thought he would forget about it.

"Good," said Will. He was stretched out as usual on his bunk, half a six-pack of Rainier on the nightstand and an open beer in one hand. The place smelled like a tavern. "You did good, man. We're okay." He looked at the others. "No problem. We're okay."

Somebody closed the door behind me.

"Have a beer, Ryan."

I said no thanks.

"Have a beer, Twisp."

"Sure," Twisp said. He flipped the pull-tab and guzzled beer like a cormorant downing a fish. He even had the long neck for it.

"I was going to tell you," Will said. "We had to wait for the right time." He opened the night-stand drawer and pulled out a cap-gun with a red tongue of caps. "Got it in town the other night."

He had been planning it for days.

"Does Anderson know about this?" I asked.

"Course he does. We're all in on it. And we want you to give the speech."

"What speech?"

"Like we're seceding from the State. We blow the whole thing open, man. I run out shooting. You step up there and call the government a fraud, the Legion, the whole mess. We'll give them fucking heart attacks."

Twisp laughed. He wore a jean-jacket like Will's, I guess he'd bought it the other night in town.

"Okay?"

I bit my lip.

"Okay, Ryan? Loose Spruce, okay?"

"Okay," I said.

He shot the Governor that night after dinner. State of the State Address. The whole gym was full, not only of boys but of Legionnaires and people from the local papers. I remember walking in and seeing Anderson by the door. He seemed to have packed himself back into the image of an upright man. Hood was not far away, but not talking to Anderson, looking at me with encouragement.

I considered walking out on the whole fiasco.

My speech, written on an envelope, spoke of justice and hypocrisy, and I had struggled to keep it from sounding like Eric Marcus's nomination speech. My palms sweated. The hollow clatter and rattle of voices inside the gym filled my skull and made me weak-kneed. I sat on a lower bench, surrounded by my townspeople. I didn't know if Will was among them, because I couldn't focus my eyes, and I certainly couldn't bring myself to look over at Mr. Hood.

It was Kirk, the Attorney General from Nooksack, who introduced the new Governor. His introduction was full of platitudes about duty. He even thanked God for giving him this opportunity to learn about our great government. The Legionaires liked the God bit. The crowd responded with enthusiastic hoots. Feet stomped on the bleachers. Hands clapped. There were more faces than I had ever noticed before, Blues and Reds brought together for the first time all week, more faces than I remembered even in the dining hall.

Kirk stepped away from the podium, flushed and awed by the moment, holding his withered arm as if it might take off in a Hitler salute and embarrass him, and Eric Marcus took his place. He held the ball-point pen over his speech as if he intended to revise it then and there for posterity. He seemed steady. He was wearing the same brown slacks and blue jacket and red tie that he had worn that afternoon, and I heard someone shout behind me: "Hey, Ivy League!"

The Governor raised his hands for quiet and the crowd went wild. They loved him, or maybe loved themselves for electing him. Maybe they were just seven hundred boys with too many hormones who were happy to see the whole experience come to an end. A group of aged Legionnaires in peaked caps, seated before the podium, were also glad to see this young man get his opportunity to speak. It was a free country, one they had fought for, and I was about to secede from it. What in hell did I think I was doing? Who did I think I was? I was wrecking the best thing I'd ever done. My heart felt like a fat jumping bean; I had to swallow hard to control it.

Eric spoke about growing up in the inner city, wondering whether he would ever have the opportunity to better himself, grateful that he lived in a country of opportunity. When he came to the Martin Luther King part there was a deep silence in the gym. I began to feel sick. I reached for my envelope, took a deep breath.

That was when Will stomped down the bleachers, smashing the reverent silence with each deliberate leap, jumping all the way down, step by step, each reverberation swallowed whole by the gym's high-walled silence. He yelled like a TV Apache: "Loose Spruce! Long live anarchy!" The sound of the exploding caps was so faint many people probably never heard it and wanted to know what all the fuss was about. But I saw the gun, a silver glint in his hand. Saw his blond hair wave as he ran out to the podium, pointed the pistol at Eric and made little tap-tapping noises in his direction. For good measure, he shot a couple of front-row Legionnaires, then ran out. I was at the podium.

"What are you doing?" Eric said.

He saw it all, but he couldn't quite believe it. I wanted to apologize for abusing his trust, couldn't look him in the eyes. On the other hand, I could hear loose Sprucers and a few other people cheering me on. So I gave my speech. I announced that the town of Spruce had seceded from Evergreen State and the United States of America, and formed a union of its own dedicated to freedom and anarchy and truth and the end of violence everywhere—a statement which, as I spoke it, sounded pretty crazy.

I don't know what I expected. It wasn't real. It wasn't as if there was any apparatus for our arrest and imprisonment. The aged faces arrayed before me were outraged and disgusted. More even than that, I saw Mr. Hood within thirty feet or so from the podium. He stared at me. He had his hands on his hips.

When I left the podium, I was not attacked. In fact, I don't remember much of anything, except a few confused words from Mr. Hood and a smart salute from Mr. Anderson. "Hey kid, don't give any information but your name, rank and serial number." He had blurred eyes and his face was puffy, and I could tell he was out of it. He was gone, stoned, stinko, blotto, boiled, three sheets to the wind. It was pretty familiar from home.

I went outside alone. As the bleachers emptied, the whole gymnasium sounded like a giant snare drum. Will stood on the grass outside, smoking a cigarette. He smiled at me, tucked his pistol in his pants and shook my hand. "We showed those bastards, didn't we? I loved it, man. Did you see the look on that guy's face? I loved it."

We stood there until Twisp and Mr. Anderson and the Sprucers joined us. "Bet they've never seen that before," Mr. Anderson said. He smiled, but his face looked gray and puffy. "I'm glad you did it, boys. You showed them. Whole thing's a farce. It doesn't mean anything."

The crowd at the gymnasium doors seemed to stick there, as if people had forgotten how to move. I noticed that my townspeople had started off toward Spruce, and I ran to catch up with them.

That night I looked for Will in his room. Twisp was there alone, packing because his bus would come early in the morning. He said he didn't know where Will was. I could see by the dull look behind his lenses that he felt betrayed.

Some people in the halls congratulated me, said it was a good gag and we really showed those Legionnaires. Mr. Hood came and stood at my door while I packed. He breathed slowly, as if collecting himself. He rattled change in his pocket, shifted his weight on his wing-tips. "Ryan, why did you do it?"

I was getting pretty good at avoiding people's eyes.

"I wish you'd talked to me first. I was trying to help you. I'd mentioned your name to the Executive Council and they were interested. They were really interested."

"I just had to."

"But why? I don't think you realize what you've done. It may look like a joke to you, but we take this experiment very seriously."

"Sorry."

"No sorrier than I am, Ryan, I assure you." He squeezed each word out between pressed lips. "I don't see how I can recommend you after this."

I didn't have it in me to tell him how relieved I was.

At breakfast the next morning a guy told me I was a fucking asshole. He tried to keep me from getting any food. "What are you taking our food for? You seceded from the State!" I stepped out of line with a doughnut and a cup of coffee. I saw Twisp and said, "Thought you were leaving early."

"Me too. The bus got a flat. Somebody let the air out of a tire."

"Seen Will?"

"He left last night," Twisp said. "Told me he had business in town and then he was hitching back home."

Everything felt flat. I couldn't believe he had done that, left without saying a word of good-bye, without any acknowledgment of what we had done together. I betrayed the Governor for him, just like that, and he took off. It didn't mean a damned thing to him.

When I boarded my bus later that day, I noticed that Kirk had made sure there was somebody else in the seat next to him. I had hurt his feelings and I didn't like doing that to a kid with a withered arm. I went for an empty seat, but the kid in the next row called me a fucking anarchist, so I went on to the back of the bus and had a row to myself. So that's what I was, a fucking anarchist. I couldn't believe Will took off without saying good-bye. I mean, why had we done it? What was the purpose of the whole thing if we only disappeared like this and never saw each other again? Who did he think he was? And why was I such a nobody, such a piece of crap?

I remember how hot the air was, how I couldn't get the window open. I hadn't slept the night before, and I couldn't sleep now. When I had said good-bye to Mr. Anderson, I smelled the booze on his breath. I didn't like that. It was like the booze I smelled in my mother's house. It made me think the whole adult world was screwed up, something you had to bear for a few years and then escape. But what would I escape to? I couldn't believe I actually had to get off this bus and go home.

Outside the window there were miles and miles of dry grass, then the gorge like a jagged scar in the earth's crust, then orchards and white farm-houses. Twisp was out there somewhere to the north. Will was out there, hitching a ride. We crossed the mountains, came down into the world of green woods and drizzle, the scurry of Seattle. Turning north, we passed through the farmlands of the Skagit Valley. Here at least was something familiar. It had nothing to do with people, really. The weather was dependable. It was the weak light, the smell of diesel and salt air, seagulls cruising the muddy ploughing.

When the bus left me off in Nooksack I found myself standing next to Kirk. He wasn't angry any more. Maybe he was just worn out. He seemed like a kid again, kind of shy about his arm. When his parents came to pick him up, he noticed I didn't have a ride and offered me one. I thought about staying in town, maybe walking to my girlfriend's place, but all the sudden I knew I wanted to be home, even if it was the emptiest house in the world, and I thanked him for his kindness.

Tracy A. Jennison

◆

I DO NOT CLOSE MY EYES

The Crusaders came by today. They took Yun-Chin, a fifteen-year-old girl who is going to marry an important man in the military. At least, that's what others have told me.

Sometimes early in the morning, when we bathe and brush each other's hair, we whisper stories about ourselves, stories that could have us beaten if Master found out. He doesn't want us to reveal any truths to each other. We are to be pretty girls with pretty names that we never would have chosen. He has named me after the flower Hyacinth, the only name that customers know me by. But in those early mornings I return to the name Alia, the name my mother blessed, and I whisper it to myself over and over, letting the hushed sounds caress the paper walls of our room like fingers over satin.

Fen-Nu says that last week the military man came here requesting Yun-Chin. It is said that he had seen her before on an earlier visit and had fallen in love with her beauty. Yun-Chin has almond-shaped eyes and one which is blue, causing her whole look to change, depending upon which direction you look at her from. If a man were to walk in on her left, he would see her brown eye, a smoldering feature that calms its fires beneath the cool flutter of eyelashes. From her right, the man would see a crystal blue eye, so clear that it's empty. From that side, Yun-Chin looks almost American, and her price was higher because of it. I once heard her whisper that sometimes men demanded that she close her left eye, allowing them to believe that their forty dollars was going to more than a mere Thai girl. But I preferred Yun-Chin's darker eye, because I

87

knew how she felt whenever I looked into it. In her darker eye I saw the same fury that I felt, and more than once I've had to look away, for it is not good for anger that strong to run into itself. It was in that eye that she gave away her true feelings; every other part of her face smiled, even when she hissed curses at Master under her breath.

It is whispered that Yun-Chin's blue eye is the result of an American grandfather. Missionaries used to come and challenge our beliefs, showing us a man that they exalted as God, a God whose body hung on a miniature cross around each of their necks. Their God's wings of glory came from dying and coming back to life again; a God who promised a heavenly bliss when our bodies die and our spirits rise up to meet him. It sounded like a nice story to me, one that even now sometimes gets whispered when hope becomes invisible and our spirits sink.

But my people had rejected the missionaries. They said that they could not abide words of men who wore their God dead around their necks. They held tight to images of Buddha and refused to turn to a foreign God. So the missionaries damned the people in the villages. Their men grew bold and let lust overtake them. They raped the village girls and claimed that it wasn't a sin since they considered the girls heathens. They stole the treasures and heirlooms of our ancestors, they taught us what greed and hatred were and then damned us to rot in its belly. The people of the village had nothing after the missionaries left. Their crops were destroyed, their money gone. It came as no surprise then when the fathers of the village began to sell their daughters to the Masters. The girls were considered worthless anyway. They had been deflowered, and no man's family would accept a dowry for an unclean bride. Knowing this, the Masters offered little money, and what scant offerings they did give were eagerly accepted by the the fathers. For with these offerings came drugs, syringes, and heroin. There never seemed to be enough to go around, though the Masters made sure there was just enough of the drug to clamp on to the souls of the fathers and begin to feed. After that, they had little trouble getting new girls. For less than one spoonful of heroin, the fathers would kidnap and sell just about any girl to the Masters. They would have even gone themselves had the Masters let them, for they weren't fathers any more. They had become caretakers of the Demon within them, a Demon that ate them out from the inside and danced along the paths of purple veins on their arms.

Yun-Chin had grown up in this house. Her mother had been sold here before her and Yun-Chin was the result of what sometimes happens when men get drunk and forget to withdraw. She grew up upon these soiled mats full of cum. She watched her mother grow hard and shriveled, until she at last succumbed to one of the many diseases that men expose here. Yun-Chin told us once that she used to wash her mother's skin with rosewater, a scented luxury that we are to only use on our faces. She described how she used to lovingly pat the fragrant water on her mother's body, careful not to open the sores that caked her mother's legs and buttocks. "She died in agony and in shame," Yun-Chin had said. "But she made me promise one thing before she passed on."

"What?" we whispered as the brushes swish-swooshed through our hair.

Yun-Chin lay down her brush and placed her hand upon the head she'd been brushing. "She made me promise that I would break the chain. She told me that it would be better to die with honor than to live on in shame. She made me promise to get out of this place."

We all stared at her, wide-eyed and afraid. "How will you do it?" I asked.

Yun-Chin pursed her small red lips. "I will use the very tool that is meant to destroy us." She pointed to her crotch. "Men come in here and poke us with the one thing that makes them feel superior. They come, they take what we are forced to give, and offer not even the slightest caress of love. With that tool they brought life to me and death to my mother. They whisper hot words of longing, and yet there is no love in them." Yun-Chin's eyes narrowed and I saw fire ignite the black in her eye. "It is that very same tool that will get me out of here. I will choose a man of power and teach him to love. I will take my hand and reach into his empty soul and fill it up with himself. I will mirror the majesty that every man hungers for and do it in such a way that he won't be able to live without me. My kisses will taste like honey and my juices like milk. *He* will be the key to my freedom."

"You will still be a whore!" Pon spat, showering Yun-Chin's face with her rage. "He will own you as Master does and you won't get away. He will know that you do not love him, and he will destroy you then as Master destroys you now."

I nodded my head in agreement. *Where there is no love, there is no freedom.*

"Ah , but I will open my eyes and let him look inside," Yun-Chin said, "and in my eyes, there will only be a reflection. And when he looks he will see himself there, peering in and seeing nothing." She began to laugh. "Men are vain, stupid creatures, and he's sure to mistake that image of himself for feelings of love, since man is only capable of loving himself. He will think I exist just for him, and he will trust me because of it. And it is in that very thing which my freedom lies."

Pon crossed her arms defiantly. "How? What will you do?"

Yun-Chin smiled and rubbed her hand tenderly across her crotch. "I will lull him to sleep after he uses his tool. He will be satisfied from see-ing his face in my eyes. And when I at last hear the steady snore of sleep, I plan to take that tool away from him and feed it to the gulls."

Yun-Chin's bitter smile met our own, and we all prayed for the plan's fulfillment.

Some of the girls hope to be freed by the Crusaders. The Crusaders are a group of village men who have plotted together to sneak into the whorehouses and steal back their daughters. These are men whose chil-dren have been taken by force or have been stolen away in the night. Most people in Thailand are very poor and cannot get help from the police, for even the police are poor and will accept large bribes from the Masters to protect their domains. But I have seen how the Crusaders work. The men come in and pretend to be customers. Agreeing to find a particular girl, they search every whorehouse until they find her. Most of the time they aren't very lucky. The Masters know of these plots and often hide the girls who have been stolen from their families. But most of us here have been willingly sold, so our Master isn't afraid of us being taken away. But I hope. I dream.

My mother was sick when my father sold me away. She was curled up like a dog on the mat and shaking, unable to even sip water when offered. Father, though I loved him dearly, had the Demon in him, and he was not the same man as the one who had picked rice from the marshes and had made dolls for me out of grass and cord. The Masters had sneaked into our village not long before, buying girls from the poorest of us and leav-ing behind tastes of heroin as gifts for the remaining villagers. I like to think that my father accepted the Demon to escape from the pain of

watching Mother suffer. They had married as children and seeing her
dying must have been more than he could bear. I never saw him tie the
band around his arm like the other village men did. He didn't sit in the
square and wait impatiently for the needle. He must have done it in
secret in hopes of not scaring my mother. How could he have known that
one little prick to his arm would ignite such a hunger that he would sell
his family to satisfy it?

He told me that it would be for only a little while; that because I was
his child I must obey, and he would use the money to get medicine for
Mother. His eyes looked yellow. I knew it was not Father speaking to me,
only a prisoner disguised as him, peering out from those desperate, glazed
eyes. Mother had begged him to let her die. I watched as she clung to his
leg, crying for him to let me stay. The Master came closer then and put
something in Father's hand. I watched my father sigh with relief before
pushing my mother back down to the mat. I was crying when he told the
Master to take me away.

One time one of the girls, Pon, ran away. She did it by knocking out
one of her customers and wearing his hat and trenchcoat to escape. She
made it about four blocks down the streets of Bangkok before Master
caught up with her. He cut off her nipples for running away and threw
them at the rest of us, warning us that this would happen to us as well.
We shuddered as Pon shrieked and sobbed behind him.

I think that is why Pon was so angry when the Crusaders came for
Yun-Chin this morning. It is whispered that Pon's family knows she is
here and yet they haven't tried to come for her. The Crusaders have come
here once before, about three years ago, when I was brand new and didn't
yet understand what was happening. The morning had started out as routine, each of us dressing in the silk kimonos that Master provides and
whispering stories to one another as we bathed and brushed each other's
hair. It was said that a tour group had come in from South Korea, about
sixty men with their young sons to indulge in the promiscuity that
Bangkok offers. These "rites of passage" groups were nothing new to us,
but in the past we found that the South Korean men tipped more than
their Thai counterparts. I've kept my meager tips hidden under a loose
floorboard under my mat. Sometimes when the men enter me, I think
about the money and try to imagine where I'd go if I'm ever freed.

We heard the call about an hour after dressing. When prestigious customers come through the door, Master pushes a little doorbell that sounds like a telephone in our back room. When we heard it, Yun-Chin, Pon, myself, and fourteen other girls lined up in single file and entered the Parlor Room, a plush, velvety area that provides a sensual atmosphere for the customer to choose a mate. The men we saw were moderately dressed, not wearing any of the rings or suits that promise little extras to be slipped under our bottoms before the customers leave. I watched the two men scan the faces of the girls. This was odd, because a real customer will look at our breasts and hips first, faces later. After some talking amongst themselves, the two men then turned to Master and offered a high price for Maharii, a skinny, shapeless girl who was brought in a few months before. She didn't look older than twelve, which was something that could get Master in trouble if caught. Master squinted at the men and stayed silent. If he doesn't agree on a price he will stand and glare at the customer, weakening his will until the customer shrugs and grins apology before raising his initial offer.

The men glared back at Master. "It's a fair price," they had said. "She's skinny and ugly and hardly worth the cost."

"She's young, so she's more."

The men looked at Maharii and then at the rest of us. "She looks no younger than the rest of them. She must be at least fifteen."

"She's not fifteen," Master said.

"We want someone young. We will pay double to have her together."

Master's eyebrow arched. I could see him softening. "She's young. Worth more than you offer."

One of the men approached Maharii and touched her breast. "Is she thirteen? I'll pay more if she's thirteen."

"She's twelve," Master replied. "Hardly touched by man."

Suddenly the other man blew a whistle and the room exploded with enraged, determined men. Master tried desperately to exit out the back, but a police officer grabbed his jacket and yanked him back into the room. "You know it's illegal to have any girl under thirteen," he said.

Smiling, Master shrugged his shoulders in bewilderment. "I did not know she was so young. She told me she was fourteen."

The man who touched Maharii's breast snorted contempt. "You said she was twelve!"

"I lied."

The policeman looked at Maharii. "How old are you, girl?"

She stood trembling, darting her eyes from the policeman to Master. I saw how he glared at her. I knew she was thinking about how he had cut off Pon's nipples.

"Well?"

She licked her lips and ducked her head. "I'm fourteen."

Master smiled triumphantly and reached for Maharii's arm.

"She's not fourteen!"

Master's hand froze in mid-air. He turned, seeking the voice that dared contradict him. His eyes locked on to a peasant boy, who stood with his back rigid, legs staunchly spread in the wake of his confrontation.

Master's smiled stretched into a tight line. "Who are you?" he asked. "And why do you challenge me?"

"I am Maharii's brother. She is not fourteen. She's twelve."

"If she says she is fourteen," Master replied, "then she is fourteen."

The brother glared at Master. "We have come for Maharii. She will leave with us today."

"She is here on her own free will. She won't go away, will you, Maharii?" Master's grip tightened on Maharii's arm, a silent threat that made her shudder. She shook her head and shifted her teary eyes away from her brother.

Master's grin widened. "See? What did I tell you?"

But the boy would not give up so easily. "She is afraid of you, that's why she lies."

"I take good care of her. This is where she'll stay."

"No she won't," the boy insisted, "for I have brought someone here who'll confirm she is twelve."

The boy stepped aside and waited as a small, weathered man pushed himself through the crowd. He stopped alongside the boy and peered out from underneath a tanglement of dirty white hair. Maharii's eyes widened when she saw him. A faint trace of a smile played around the corners of her mouth, and we all held our breaths in excitement and hope.

The man nodded at his girl. "Daughter," he whispered. Maharii flew into his arms.

For that incident Master was charged with a minimal fine and warned not to do it again. As the room started clearing of people, I watched as

Pon ran up to one of the men and begged that he save her too. I remember how he touched her face and shook his head. Pon was beaten severely afterward. Master had bloodied her up so much that she couldn't work for a week. She wasn't allowed to eat then, either. "If you don't work, you don't eat," Master had told us in the beginning. Pon had proven to us that Master meant what he said.

I know that the Crusaders will never come for me. There is no one who wants me saved. I have been here over three years and I still don't know what's become of my parents. Sometimes I like to think about my mother getting well. I pretend that she has recovered from the sickness that ravaged her and has begun to look for me. I picture my father being freed from the Demon. I see his forearms brown and flawless and his eyes winking at me. Sometimes I look for their faces in the crowds on the street. When I go to sleep at night I can hear my mother whispering Alia, sweet Alia, over and over again.

I was still sleeping when the Crusaders came for Yun-Chin. They say it was different this time. For Yun-Chin, there were no sneaky plots or entrapments. Apparently the military man has enough pull to take her at will. It is whispered that Master himself came and woke up Yun-Chin to take her. He led her to the Parlor Room where the Crusaders and the military man were waiting. Pon claims to have seen it all. She says the man who took Yun-Chin looked at least fifty. She says he handed Master more money than she has seen in a lifetime. There was no arguing or defeat. Both men at the end of the exchange were happy. We were brushing our hair when Pon fell to the floor weeping. She said that the worst part was when Yun-Chin caught her eye before leaving. Through tears of rage and frustration, Pon demonstrated how Yun-Chin had narrowed her eyes and grabbed at her crotch, smiling knowingly at Pon before taking her man's arm to be led away.

Freedom.

That word haunts me now as heavily as the whispers of Mother, cooings that bring me to tears and make me ache as if I'm rotting inside. I think about Yun-Chin and wonder where she is. I imagine her opening her strange almond eyes wide for her lover, letting him peer inside to become intoxicated by himself. I hope she makes it to the Andaman Sea. The gulls will be very happy if she does.

The floorboards creak as my customer kneels down beside me. I watch him look hungrily at my breasts and he instructs me to lie on my back. In my mind I hear the whispers of Mother. *Alia, sweet Alia.* I think of Yun-Chin, and her ghost spins around and around me, its small red lips chanting.

Freedom.

I usually clamp my eyes tight when a customer first enters me. But this time, as I open my legs and let the customer in, I do not close my eyes.

William Borden

♦

BEAR DANCES

WHAT A BEAR DOES IN THE WOODS

They walk on the entire foot, as does man.
—*A Field Guide to the Mammals*

Lyle Gustafson leads us through the woods, over downed trees, through tangled brush, the grass brown, the autumn leaves underfoot, everything soggy from the recent cold rain. We're strung out behind him, three of us, the young guy from the TV station with the video camera, the good-looking woman producer with him, and me. We're bundled up in coats against the sharp autumn wind, but I'm sweating with the movement over the uneven ground, and my gimpy leg is giving me trouble, and Lyle is out in front, hurrying, excited, holding the antenna out in front of him, the earphones clamped to his ears, he might be getting messages from outer space but they're really only beeps from the radio collar Rudy is wearing. Lyle seems to think we're getting close because he's almost running, and now he's calling, "*Rudy! Rudy!*" eagerly, calling an old friend he hasn't seen in days or weeks, and we're having trouble keeping up, Lyle's out of sight now over the hill and we're climbing, trying to catch up.

Lyle's in the clearing, dancing. Dancing with Rudy. It's a kind of waltz, and they're waving their arms. Rudy's up on his hind legs, and we watch in amazement, and the guy from the TV station is going nuts trying to get his camera squared away to catch this moment of Lyle dancing with Rudy, the black bear he raised from a cub.

Rudy's almost as tall as Lyle, and Rudy's beating a rhythm with his feet, moving his hind paws in little steps, easily balancing himself, and Lyle mimicks the little steps, only Lyle lifts his feet higher, Lyle sort of prances, he does a kind of bear jig, and they both wave their arms in front of them, flapping their arms like wings, and I wish I could hear the music they're dancing to.

The young guy with the video camera is running to get closer, he's slipping in the wet leaves, he's flailing his arms, camera in one hand, he's loaded with equipment, he's sliding, he catches his balance, and now he's up close and he's getting this dance on tape, but the woman producer is hanging back, as if she can't quite believe what's happening, or else she doesn't want to get too close and spoil it.

Now she's calling the young guy back, "Get a long shot," she advises, "it looks great from here, you get the woods, the context, the sun through the leaves." So he backs up slowly, he trips, he falls on his back, but he holds the camera high and scrambles up again, mud all over his Banana Republic pants and safari coat and he's lost his Tilley hat somewhere.

So he shoots the long shots then moves in closer and she walks closer with him but now both Rudy and Lyle seem tired of dancing so Rudy's on all fours again rummaging around and Lyle's squatting nearby talking soft-ly to him, reassuring him, it sounds like, and telling him softly how much he's missed him and he's a hell of a good bear and how's he been making out did he find enough grubs and things?

The woman producer's found the Tilley hat and she wants to put it on Rudy's head but Lyle says, "No, Rudy's not a circus animal, he's not even a tame animal, despite all appearances, and bears don't like to be touched," he says, just as she's putting out her hand to pet Rudy.

She lets her hand hang in the air, petting empty space a moment, or maybe imagining Rudy's there anyway. "He'd look cute," she says. "That's the trouble," Lyle says. So she hands the hat back to the camera guy. He looks at it skeptically because it's muddy but finally he puts it on anyway, but it doesn't look cute on him.

"I've tried petting them," Lyle says, still hunkered near Rudy but not touching him, not petting him, "but they see it as an infringement on their personal space."

She's standing next to Lyle, who's hunkered on the ground, her knees by his head, her boots near his, and she looks wistfully at Rudy, who's found some fat white grubs under a rotting log and is chewing them up.

"Petting a bear," Lyle goes on, "would be like me putting my hand between your legs." She doesn't move her hand. It's a nice hand, thin, freckles, no rings, no nail polish, nails trimmed. "Without an invitation," Lyle adds.

Lyle stands up. Rudy moves off to another log. Lyle goes after him.

LYLE GUSTAFSON

When the Ainu find a young bear, they bring it home, and the wife suckles it. . . .
—*The Golden Bough*

Rudy was tiny when I found him. His mother, Cary, was one of my sub-jects. I knew where she was hibernating, and I'd go out in my snowmo-bile every few weeks during the winter, temperature below zero, snow a meter deep, and crawl beneath those logs where she'd hollowed out a den, take blood samples—she'd wake up, bears don't go sound asleep when they hibernate, they wake a little, doze, dream, like you and me—and I caught Rudy on camera just after he was born, tiny and naked, crawling up her chest to grab her nipple—so in the spring, I was going out to check on them because I figured she'd be up and about now—I was tromping through the brush—snow had melted, couldn't use the snow-cat anymore—when I heard the shot, then a second and a third, and I knew some bastard had nailed her, still sleepy maybe, and maybe she was too trusting of humans because she was used to me. By the time I got there all that was left was tire tracks in the muddy road. He'd cut off the radio collar, of course. Otherwise I could've tracked the sonofabitch and nailed him.

It was Ben Cresswell, I'm sure of that. He poaches deer, elk, bear, lives in a shack way back in the woods, a nasty guy, killed one game warden, got off claiming it was an accident, but since then nobody wants to go in and confront him without a SWAT team and we don't have a SWAT team up here in the woods of northern Minnesota.

Anyway, I went back to the den then, found the little fellow in there, crying, hungry, and gathered him up, fitted him inside my coat, next to my flannel shirt, next to my heart, and brought him home and fed him.

I wasn't going to make a pet of him, of course. He's a wild bear. As wild as he can be, anyway.

Trouble is, see, he imprinted on me, not his mother. He thinks I'm his mother. He thinks we're all bears, like him. So it's a problem during hunting season. According to the rules, the Division of Forestry rules, which, as a Forestry researcher, I'm obliged to adhere to, Rudy has to stay out in the woods and take his chances like every other bear. But the rules don't cover every contingency. That's the trouble with rules. So, during hunting season, Rudy lives with me.

LYLE'S WIFE

In Navajo the bear is called atco naxeti, *which means "it may change into anything."*

I leave during hunting season. I visit my mother in Saskatoon. This time I may just stay.

I was Lyle's student when he was teaching animal management at the university. Back then no one had heard of sexual harrassment. Back then faculty-student affairs were just part of the curriculum, like finals and dissertations. Heck, Lyle was a good lover. Patient, as he is with his bears. Which is good for me, because I'm a little slow sometimes.

I was assisting Lyle out in the woods. We were following Number 24. Back then the bears just had numbers. It was Lyle who started naming the bears. The other Forestry people disapproved.

We were following 24, following her trail, rather, we were about a day behind her, and we were recording where she went, and what she ate. My job was to pick up her scat—find her turds, in other words—and put them in a plastic bag and label it and record where and when I found it and then later, back at the lab, I'd weigh it and examine it, you know, to see if she'd eaten berries or nuts or beetles or ants or larvae or whatever. Not a glamorous job, but that's science.

It was summer. It was a hot day. Lyle took off his shirt. Lyle doesn't have a great physique, but it's not bad. He's lean and muscular. He usually wore a shirt—Forestry regs—so he was all white except his neck and hands and the top of his forehead where his cap came. It reminded me of my father, who was a farmer in Saskatchewan—wheat—when he'd come in at night all dusty and sweaty and take off his cap and shirt to wash up for supper and his white skin, set off by the burnished brown of his face and neck and hands, always had a strange effect on me. I felt like I shouldn't be watching him. I felt like I was seeing him totally naked. Yet I couldn't take my eyes off him. He'd ask for the towel and I'd hand it to him. I'd watch him dry himself. It was the only time he looked as if things could hurt him.

I wasn't thinking about my father when Lyle took off his shirt in the woods. I was scooping up bear shit. When I stood up, Lyle was bare-chested, wiping the sweat from his face with his wadded-up shirt. There must have been sweat in my eyes, too. You know how it is sometimes on hot days—you see things that aren't there. I looked up from scooping the bear shit—well, I was thinking about bears all the time, of course, it was my research topic—so when I looked up, I saw, I don't know, a thing in front of me, moving, upright, Lyle's face was the wadded up shirt and the white chest surprised me, somehow I thought the bear was there, the bear we'd been following, and Lyle somehow had walked off and the bear was there before me, and I felt guilty because I was stealing her shit. I know that doesn't make sense, the bear didn't want it anymore, she'd left that behind her like yesterday's faint regrets, but you get odd thoughts in the summer on a hot afternoon when you've been tracking a bear looking for her shit for six hours and you're not really thinking straight and you haven't been quite human yourself for awhile, I mean it's not like sitting in a classroom, and it's not like waiting tables, which I did to make money, and Lyle and I never talked in the woods because we didn't want to apprise the bear of our presence in case she was near and anyway Lyle had this Indian thing about being in the woods, you didn't talk, you tried to blend in, you "become what you're looking for," he'd say, which I took to mean I should become a bear not I should become bear shit.

I guess I gave a little gasp when I saw the bear, I mean Lyle, bare-chested, because he looked at me funny. He gave a little quizzical grin, which was the way we communicated, silently, in the woods, and after a moment I realized I was staring at his chest, which was white and hairless and not like a bear's chest at all, and he looked down at his chest as if to check if anything was wrong and then looked back at me as if to ask what *was* wrong—"I thought you were a bear," I said.

He smiled a big grin. He wiped the sweat off his white chest. His dark brown hair hung over his forehead. His face had a day's growth of whiskers. His eyes were cobalt blue. A slight breeze wafted through the leaves of the trees. The sun dappled through the trees above. Odors of earth and leaves and grass and a hundred organic entities hung in my nostrils. Insects sang in the background.

Lyle fell to the earth. On hands and feet, legs bent, like a bear he charged me.

Now black bears are really pretty harmless. They bluff. And the way a black bear bluffs is he charges, and when he gets right in front of you, he stomps his front paws and he gives a loud *Whoof* noise, very sudden, which scares you if you're not expecting it.

"*Whoof!*"

I jumped.

He was smiling.

Since then, I've seen bears smile like that. It's a subtle smile, but it's there if you look for it.

"*Whoof!*" Lyle said again.

This time I didn't jump. I kneeled. We breathed each other's breath, the way bears do to recognize each other. His breath smelled like summer and danger and like the gum he'd been chewing a little earlier and like aspen leaves and the wild raspberries we'd eaten, the few the bear had left. I imagined he could smell my breath, too, breathing it in and then out so I smelled my breath coming back at me only now it was mixed with his breath. I put the palms of my hands on the sides of his face, on his whiskery jaw, like holding a head in a lab for inspection. I looked into his eyes. Cobalt eyes. Like diving into the sea. Into a mountain pool under a waterfall. Diving in, never coming up, just following the pool to the bottom into an underground passageway into the earth, another world you never have to leave.

His chest was so white it needed to be protected. I pulled it into my chest, my shirt, wet with my sweat, and I protected it there, wrapping my arms around his back to hold him there, and he held me to him as if he knew he needed my protection.

It was hot and it was summer and we had been alone together for days and hadn't spoken in hours so everything was strange and I believed that there was no world outside us, no Minneapolis, no United States, no other people ever anywhere, and he released his arms and leaned back a little and I let go a little to see maybe I was holding him too tight, was trying to protect him too much, but he was just leaning back so he could unbutton my shirt so I could be a bear too and he did and I was.

DINNER CHEZ LYLE

Lyle's invited us all to spend the night, me and the TV documentary team who're doing the story on Lyle and his research, even though I'm not part of the TV documentary team. It's going to be an hour-long show, for Minnesota Public Broadcasting. There's plenty of room in the old log lodge Lyle uses as his research station, he says, and he has extra sleeping bags and cots, and he's pulling venison out of the freezer while the camera guy follows him with the camera. He's a young guy, the camera guy, new to the job, I think, and he's getting a kick out of it, imagining he's Robert Altman or Oliver Stone at the beginning of their careers and he's going to be them someday.

The woman producer, who's older than the TV guy but not so old, follows Lyle around asking him questions, holding the mike, and she has her hair braided and wrapped around her head so I guess when it's down it's long. She wears jeans and boots and a plaid shirt and a cap and it's as if she's trying to look butch and outdoorsy but isn't fooling anyone, certainly not Lyle, who always has a little smile on his face behind the bushy beard that's streaked with gray. His brown hair's streaked with gray, too, and falls into his eyes and he wipes it away with a boyish gesture as he throws the chunks of venison into the pot and talks about how sometimes you can't tell who's human and who's a bear. "Native cultures all over the world have stories of people turning into bears and bears turning into people," he says, uncorking a bottle of wine.

The camera guy circles them with the camera. She tells the guy to stay still, for chrisake, it's a documentary not a Kenneth Branagh film, so the guy makes one more circle, and then stays planted while Lyle pops another cork. "There's a story about a bear who becomes a woman," Lyle says, "and she wants to marry the fellow, only secretly she's still wild, you see, still untamed." He twists the corkscrew into another cork and looks closely at the woman, as if this part is especially for her. "She has teeth in her vagina," Lyle says, "and she wants the fellow to fuck her." Lyle squeezes the bottle between his thighs, grasps the corkscrew, and gives a quick jerk. "'Fuck me,' she keeps saying. 'Fuck me.'"

The woman glances at the camera guy, but he's taping away, so she just holds the mike, and I can tell she's editing all of this in her head, trying to decide whether to *beep* or just cut the whole story.

"But his grandmother, who knows the score, says, 'Watch out, Grandson.' So he makes a clay pecker, and the next night, when the bear in the form of a woman grabs him and says, 'Fuck me, fuck me'"—by now we all know she's not going to use this but the guy still tapes and she still holds the mike—"she wants him to stick it to her, but he sticks that clay pecker in her instead of his own. Well, she grinds that clay pecker up into dust." Lyle pops another cork.

"The next night she's hot for him again. But tonight, with his grandmother's advice, he makes a stone pecker, and he gives it to her with the stone pecker. Well, he breaks off all her teeth in there with the stone pecker, and so then she has to become a normal woman, she can't be a bear anymore. He tames the wildness of woman."

Lyle looks slyly at her. She lets her arm fall, as if it's tired. The mike hangs pointing to the floor.

"It's a fear that goes back millenia," he says. "The notion that women have teeth in their vagina."

"Shit, I never knew that," the young guy says. He lowers the camera.

"Little teeth," Lyle says, "like on a northern pike, I'd guess. Many rows of little teeth, each sharp as a razor." Lyle bares his teeth, a little crooked and yellowed, in a broad grin.

"Jesus," the camera guy says, quivering in a strange sort of fearful anticipation.

The woman keeps her eyes on Lyle. She smiles. She shows her white teeth between her red lips.

EATING AND DRINKING WITH BEARS

Autumn . . . is the period of hyperphagia, excessive eating,
necessary to lay on enough fat to survive the winter. . . .
—*The Great American Bear*

Lyle's a wine connoisseur. He's stashed an extensive cellar in the cabin's root cellar, which he has nicely remodeled, and he has half a dozen bottles breathing on the table as the venison stew bubbles on the stove. He says he likes a California Barbera with the venison, but he's uncorked a couple of Cabernets and an Australian Shiraz for variety, as well as a California Syrah, just to taste the difference, and a Muscadet for dessert, which will be the lemon soufflé he's whipping up now. The TV guy is recording the soufflé, but the woman producer, whose name for sure is Diane, is telling the camera guy to cool it, he'll run out of tape, the documentary isn't for the Julia Child show, but the camera guy—is his name Ted?—thinks he's Frederick Wiseman and he's got to capture every damn fly on the wall—now he's focusing on my snifter of single malt, for Chrissake—Lyle's drinking Lagavulin, which is too smokey for me—we had a little taste test—so I've got the Cragganmore, and the producer— Diane—is drinking the Talisker, drinking it maybe a little too fast on an empty stomach because she's unbraided her hair now and it falls to her ass, it bounces down her back as if it had been restrained by those tight braids so long it's really a wild beast let loose now to roam.

Diane takes another swig of her Talisker—the only single malt made on the Isle of Skye, Lyle informs us, where the distillery faces the sea on the west, on the shores of Loch Harport. Robert Louis Stevenson, he adds, favored Talisker.

Diane grabs the camera from the camera guy, tells him to sit down, damn it, drink his beer—Sam Adams Autumn Wheat—she's taking over, she's the producer—she's aiming the camera, panning the room, taking us all in—the bubbling stew, the biscuits rising, the paintings of bears on the walls, the photos of bears on the walls, the photos of statues of bears from all times and places on the walls, the moosehead on the wall above the mantle—she's down on her knees, going after fancy shots—the snifters of single malt, the fire crackling and leaping in the stone fireplace, Lyle coming towards her now with the bottle to refresh her drink, and she's crouching on the polished wood floor pointing the camera at Lyle's crotch.

LYLE'S WIFE'S LETTER

Saskatoon, Saskachewan

Dear Lyle,
I don't need the clothes right now. I'll stay the winter with mother. Her arthri-
tis is worse, and she's missing Dad a lot. You're busy with your research any-
way and won't miss me I'm sure. I know we talked about a separation. I'm not
sure if this is it or not. Anyway, we can see how things are with us in the spring.
Things look better in the spring. But then again, some springs they seem worse,
and it seems like the snow will never melt. I'm sorry to hear about the investi-
gation. I'm sure nothing will come of it. After all, that was your money, those
advances, and to say that it belongs to the Forestry Dept. just because you
work for the Forestry Dept. and the books are based on your research with
them, well, that's ridiculous. I don't care what the lawyers say. But I'm stay-
ing with mother anyway. See you in the spring.

Your wife

P.S. Lyle, I hope you're eating all right. I know you like to try those inventive
dishes of yours but really they're the strangest combinations.

NOT SHOOTING AT BEARS

The female knows from the scents on marked trees that . . .
males in the area are on the prowl.

We're all pretty happy now. We're outside, under the stars, and Lyle has
lined up the empty wine bottles and the empty single malt bottles on the
fence a hundred feet away, and he's put a candle in each bottle and lit the
candles, so we can see where the bottles are, and he's loading his deer rifle
and we're going to take turns trying to shoot the bottles. If you miss, you
have to take off an article of clothing.

Rudy, the bear, who's in seclusion here from the evil hunters, is in the
pen Lyle built for him, next to the lodge, eating the rest of the venison
stew. We ate all of the soufflé, but Lyle says that's all right, Rudy doesn't
need sweets. Diane was surprised that Rudy would eat venison, she
thought bears were vegetarians, but Lyle says, hell no, each spring he finds

pieces of fawn in the bear scat he collects, bits of fur. Bears, Lyle says, are omnivores, just like us.

Rudy makes little grunting noises as he eats. He seems to like the stew a lot. One of the bottles of Cabernet wasn't quite finished—it was half full, actually—but Lyle wanted the bottle, so he poured the rest of the Cab into the stew before he gave the stew to Rudy. I think he poured another bottle into the stew as it was cooking. Lyle says he's writing a gourmet hunter's cookbook. He's already got a contract for it and an advance from a major publisher and a contract and advance for his book on bears he's writing, and he's negotiating, or rather his agent is negotiating, the possibility of a TV show for one of the cable networks. He won't say which one, it's too early in the negotiations, Lyle says, everything's very delicate at this point, but it would be a kind of post-modern Wild Kingdom, a kind of deconstruction of the old Frank Buck's *Bring 'Em Back Alive* series, which only Lyle and I are old enough to remember. Lyle says the theme would be one world, we're all in it together, we're all related. He'd maybe have a Native American sidekick to give it that earthy feel—but it wouldn't be a Lone Ranger and Tonto thing, he assures us, especially Diane, who has missed the bottles for the third time and seems to prefer to remove her shirt and bra and belt rather than her boots, I guess because the grass is wet and the ground is pretty cold to one's bare feet, because I took my shoes and socks off after missing four times.

Actually no one has hit any bottles yet and the candles are burning down as the little flames flicker and dance in the soft autumn air. Ted is down to his undershorts and hopping around in the cold but he keeps insisting he'll hit the next one and he hangs on to the rifle and shoots again. For some reason Lyle hasn't shot at all and has all his clothes on but no one has mentioned that, I guess because he's the host and he's letting his guests have all the fun.

Ted has a small circumcised penis and blond pubic hair but no one is paying much attention. Ted is hopping around trying to get warm—we're practically in Canada, after all, and it's damn near freezing even if it is only September—but Lyle says Ted can't put his clothes on, it's against the lumberjacks' rules as laid down in legendary, mythic time by Paul Bunyan, the father of all lumberjacks, which Ted seems to believe.

Lyle is helping Diane, he's talking confidentially in her ear, telling her how to sight and everything. All ten bottles are still standing, but one candle has gone out from the breeze. Lyle's fitting the stock of the rifle into the hollow of her bare shoulder and arranging her hands on the rifle and then putting his big hand lightly into the small of her naked back, into her hair flowing down her naked back, like a dark river full of danger and mystery, and his other hand is positioning her elbow and brushing one breast, and her nipples are small and pink. She misses again.

Ted hops faster, his penis flopping and flapping, trying to get warm, but Lyle says real woodsmen bear the cold without complaint, and I think now Diane's going to take off a boot, which she does, but she takes off the other boot, too, which she is not required to do, even by the mythic and legendary rules set down in time immemorial by Mr. Bunyan, but apparently she just doesn't want to get her feet cold because she took her boots off only so that she could get her jeans off, which she does, and then she pulls her boots back on. So she's standing in the dark, in the light thrown weakly from the windows of the cabin, she's standing there with her breasts pouting and her nipples stiff in the cool night air, her boots coming up to her knees. She wants to shoot again.

It's like she's mad now and hardly even aims but squeezes one off like she's done this every night of her life and the Talisker bottle explodes and the candle falls to the earth still burning.

She puts her bra on.

"What are you doing?" Lyle asks.

"Paul Bunyan rules," Diane answers. "When you hit, you get to put something back on."

Lyle starts to argue, but Ted, suddenly seeing some hope for his hypothermia, dances in and grabs the rifle and starts shooting. We can't stop him until the rifle's empty, and still he's naked.

Ted gives up and heads inside, his clothes wadded in his arms, dancing over the cold earth and the occasional rock, fuck the Paul Bunyan rules.

Now Lyle gets down to business. He wants to wind this up before Diane puts all her clothes back on. He loads the rifle, aims, and hits a bottle. He hits another. Another. Another. He seems to have forgotten about me. He doesn't care what I do. He doesn't care whether I take my clothes off or not. He hits the bottles, one after the other. He's deadeye Lyle.

There are three bottles left and he has to reload. When he does, Diane takes the rifle. Now she gets down to business. She aims. She fires. She snuffs out a candle—leaving the bottle untouched, although it wobbles a little.

She takes off her bra.

She picks up the rifle and shoots out the second candle.

She slips off her bikini panties.

Now I realize what's she's doing. She's showing Lyle she can hit any damn thing she pleases, and she pleases to take her clothes off.

She's naked, except for her socks and boots. And her long wild dark honey hair.

She hugs the stock of the rifle into her shoulder once more. She sights. She takes a little longer this time.

She squeezes off a round. The last candle flickers, flares up, then dies.

DIANE

Bears do not make love like other quadrupeds but can
embrace each other mutually, like human beings.
—Vincent of Beauvais, thirteenth century

Lyle's bedroom is large and crowded with books. He has a king-size bed. The sheets are Bill Blass. The walk-in closet is half full of a woman's clothes.

I didn't like this assignment from the start. It was too much like a Disney shoot. Guy befriends bears. Northern woods downhome story. From the sound of his voice over the phone, when I was arranging the visit, I pictured an old guy in overalls and a Smokey hat, Andy Griffith in the woods.

Driving makes me horny. I can't help it. It's that constant vibration.

I started fantasizing about bears. I was seeing, as with my third eye, bears, bears grinning at me, and I was doing it with the bears, a real group thing we all were enjoying, black bears, brown bears, Kodiak bears, polar bears—in the water with the polar bears, and then on the ice, on the ice floes. I wondered if white people could belong to clans, if maybe we did already but didn't know it, if it was in the blood but undiscovered because it's not in our totemless culture, and if maybe, unknown to myself, the bear was my totem, if I belonged to the bear clan.

Lyle makes love slowly. He's tired. It's the second time. I rushed the first one, but I was cold and I was high from the shooting. It had been years since I had practiced with my dad, his old rifle kicking my shoulder until my shoulder was bruised, and it was a Zen thing, like archery, where sometimes I could kick my mind into a different place and everything was clear and together and one, and I knew just what to do and the candles were a last-minute thought it just seemed so fucking cool and they went one two three like that and Lyle, bless his heart, didn't know what to think he thought he was so sharp so cool with his stupid version of strip poker-Russian roulette, I just laid him there on the ground, jerked his pants to his ankles so he couldn't get away—I had to work a little to get him ready, what with the cold and all he'd drunk, but once there he stayed the course and I got on top and I rode him to the finish line. I don't know what happened to the other guy, so quiet, just watching us but nice enough, a beard like Lyle's, a writer, I think, maybe writing it all down who knows I don't care I run with the bears I fuck bears I am a bear.

ANOTHER LETTER FROM LYLE'S WIFE
Saskatoon

Dear Lyle,

I thought I would miss you, Lyle, and I do sometimes, but I'm also learning to live without you, and I'm finding that it's not so much different than living with you, because you're gone so much, tracking and studying your bears, and even when you're home you seem away, mentally, I mean, writing or thinking or whatever you do in your study. Even when we're having dinner or when I'm talking to you, or even when you're talking to me, I think you're someplace else, in the woods maybe or even in some other dimension I don't know it's hard to explain.

And now you have these whole entourages of amateur bear watchers you're like a rock star with groupies and I know you like it but I'm left out in the cold even if literally it's you out in the cold with your fans watching your bears hibernate and I'm in the warm kitchen, being Lyle's wife, a nonentity.

I know you encourage me to get involved with research again now that the kids are grown, but, Lyle, you're the bear expert, where would I fit in there? I'd just be your assistant again or co-author, and that's where I started out. I didn't mind writing all those articles for you, both technical and popular, because I knew I was better at writing than you, that your heart and mind were really in the research, in the field work, and I could organize all those fragments of notes and scribblings and meandering audio tapes, and I didn't mind not getting any credit, putting your name under the title of each one, because I knew that that's how a reputation is made, and I knew that you knew that I had written them and that you appreciated it, and I know that you still appreciate it, and I don't expect you now to go out and tell everybody it was I who wrote everything, I just wish—I don't know what I wish.

I don't think I ever really wanted to be an animal researcher, Lyle. I just wanted to be with you.

Do you know what I really wanted to be?

I wanted to be a forest ranger and spend my days alone high in a tower looking for something.

Your wife

DIANE: SOFT BEARS

And I'm afraid that I'll lose him, I'll lose him for good.
—*Waltzing with Bears*

Since he's become famous, people send Lyle bear things. He's got ceramic bears, bear cookie jars, bear T shirts, bears carved out of logs with a chainsaw, and stuffed bears. The stuffed bears are cute, and I think it's a tribute to Lyle's acceptance of his soft, feminine side that he keeps these stuffed bears in his large bedroom, on the king size bed, and we have to move them off when we go to sleep at night or make love in the afternoon. The stuffed bears are white, brown, black, tan, and there's even a blue bear. One wears a cap. One wears a vest. One wears a cowboy hat.

I don't think getting fired has hurt Lyle's popularity. My documentary was picked up by National Public Broadcasting and the video is available now at Blockbuster and Mr. Movie and the other video stores. "Lyle's Bears" it's called, and it does very well for a documentary.

LYLE'S WIFE WRITES AGAIN

Saskatoon

Relationships are easier with animals than with men.
—Franz Kafka

Dear Lyle,

I was watching TV and it was Hollywood stars pretending to be circus people, and I remembered years ago when we took the kids to the circus in Winnipeg, it was a little circus, but they had some bears dressed in clothes and the bears rode bicycles and rolled balls around and I don't remember what else, but I remember watching you, and you looked so sad.

I thought the documentary made you a bit bigger than life and those shots of people in our living room getting drunk and the stew bubbling—was that supposed to be Fellini or something? Some people said it wasn't really a documentary but a profile of you, which I guess is great for you and it was great seeing you on TV, but I felt left out again I guess that's why I feel like those circus bears, I just ride a bike in circles while you're there at the center of things.

I got a letter from Babette who said she visited you recently (she's changing majors again, did she tell you? That's her fourth, I think—first nursing, then dental hygiene, then civil engineering, and now medieval literature—I think wide interests are fine but frankly, Lyle, I'm afraid these are signs of her losing her way.). Why is it it always seems to be me who worries about our children? I know you always say you're just giving them freedom and you have confidence they can work everything out and mostly they have, once Bernadette went into treatment, and she seems pretty satisfied working at the food co-op in St. Paul although it has no future but at least she's eating healthy foods, anyway, Babette said you have a bunch of stuffed bears on our bed.

Lyle, you always hated stuffed bears.

Would you explain the stuffed bears on our bed, Lyle?

Mother's looking at maps saying she wants to go to China. Is this how Alzheimer's starts? I mean with mother not me.

You know who, I hope

DIANE: WHAT SHE WEARS

I tell Lyle this indefinite suspension is definitely illegal, and they've postponed the hearing four times now. I'm sure it's because they have no evidence against him but they can't admit they're wrong. Just like the TV station. Bureaucracies are the same everywhere.

Even after I resigned from the station, they sued me, arguing that the money we received for the video rights belongs to them, but I didn't see them spend their money flying to New York and L.A. and taking meetings and lunches and every meal in the book and getting stiffed half the time by charlatans until I finally found an honest distributor.

And if that woman in St. Cloud thinks she can get anywhere with that paternity suit, a woman who spent one day with Lyle, out in the field, with a dozen other researchers—and has only now remembered, under hypnosis, it was Lyle—she'd better think again. And come up with the blood sample she's reluctant to send for the supposed DNA match.

And the Forestry Service wants Lyle to move out of his cabin, says it belongs to them and they need it now for their own research station, never mind that Lyle has increased the value of the property threefold. Fortunately the judge used to go ice fishing with Lyle and was quick to issue the restraining order, so we're safe until the fall, it looks like.

And it's spring, everything is greening up, it's that beautiful moment after the snow melts and the ice goes out on the lakes and leaves pop out on the trees but the mosquitoes haven't hatched yet or the gnats.

Lyle's been unusually quiet recently. The Service continued their suspension—the judge can't do anything about that—and Lyle isn't supposed to even observe the bears, but they haven't sent anybody else to observe them, so Lyle goes out anyway and videotapes them. We have a good shot at a cable slot for a "Lyle's Bears Part Two" or maybe we'll call it "More of Lyle's Bears," or possibly "Lyle's Bears: Return of the Wild."

When Lyle comes in from visiting his bears, he dictates his recipes to me, and I enter them into the computer and fax them to the publisher. It's boring, but not every moment of life can be a peak experience. Besides, when it gets really boring, I wear the pink garter belt and pink stockings Lyle bought me, and I put Etta James on the CD player.

ONE MORE LETTER FROM LYLE'S WIFE

Duluth, MN

The bear will devour all your flesh and make you a skeleton,
and you will die. But you will recover your flesh, you will awaken,
and your clothes will come rushing to you.
—Inuit

Dear Lyle,

Thanks for sending the clothes. UPS did a good job, but who packed them? It couldn't have been you, everything is neatly folded. I know how you pack so I can only surmise that a female person is in my closet and no doubt now has her lovely frocks hanging where mine used to be. Well it's only fitting I guess or ironic or poignant—there are so many ways of looking at things and I seem to be looking at everything a hundred different ways at once.

I got the papers and signed them I guess you're happy but you're not very articulate, about as verbal as your bears. I was sorry to hear about Rudy how they're going to take him away from you saying he isn't yours but who's is he if he isn't yours? He was like your son—Bjorn by the way got into Harvard I guess he told you—and they're going to send Rudy to Michigan to the woods where he'll surely be killed he has no woods sense but it wasn't his fault or yours maybe, there are so many ways of looking at something is that the relativism the right wing is complaining about these days? But that's the way it is! There are hundreds of ways of looking at anything! God knows I know because one minute I want to come back to you and love your white bare chest and the next I'm in bed here with Dr. Raymond Goetz, veterinarian of small animals, and while he's different than you are, Lyle, I think he can make me happy anyway I'm giving it a trial we're not committing ourselves to anything and I know ultimately or basically or essentially or tentatively you want me to be happy as I do you what's her name anyway?

Anyway, Dr. Ray and I are just trying things out, a day at a time and so on, because I don't really like these little yappy animals, Lyle, I like big animals, furry ones, bears, like you.

Love,
Ursula

LYLE: HONEY BEARS

Rudy gets into the Volvo—he loves to ride—and we drive as far as we can, to the end of the road. We cut off his radio collar. Diane wants to leave the tag on him, so if and when someone comes upon him, or kills him, we might know about it, but I say ignorance is occasionally, well, not bliss, exactly, but why should we ask for bad news?

He scratches his neck. Diane says maybe we should have left it on him, maybe he'll feel unnatural without it, he's worn it all his life, but I say he'll forget about it, he'll feel free he just won't know why. I tell her I know what I'm talking about.

He doesn't want to get into the flat-bottomed boat, but Diane entices him in with a gob of honey she's brought along in case of just such a contingency, and he bounds in—it's all I can do to keep the boat from turning over—and I push off while Rudy goes nuts licking the honey off Diane's hands until it's all over her, over her face and clothes, and by the time we get across the lake to the island where I don't think any human has ever been and I hope will never go, she's laughing and taking off her clothes and smearing honey all over her body, so white and creamy after the winter, and I take my clothes off and she smears honey all over me, on my pecker and in my hair, and Rudy's licking both of us and we're licking each other and laughing and it's afternoon and a bald eagle is gliding overhead and the water is sniffing at the rocks on the shore and finally Rudy wanders off into the woods, into his new home, and Diane and I lie in the cool grass slowly licking each other all over, all over, and then we come together, holding each other tight, and we're sticking together.

Megan Randall

◆

MAJESTY JUSTIFIES

The moment they step from the bus the sound of rushing water fills the air. The parking lot lies in filtered shade from tall trees, their leaves large and strange, like houseplants at home. Loud cries of unfamiliar birds weave through the jungle over the bass note of the falls. In the constant noise, Eva feels more than ever as if she were drifting off, not in a real place at all.

"You don't have to do this," Michael says with a quick, solicitous look. Eva feels a familiar sting of guilt. How often since they discovered the lump has she intercepted that look?

"Oh, I'll see. Maybe I will," she says. "Everyone says it's so much *fun.*" He snorts, gives her an ironic look. They share dry little jokes now, the way as new lovers they'd shared a secret language of desire.

They follow the young social director from the resort where they are vacationing. "One ting we gotta do, we gotta stick together," he says. "You got to stay wit the group."

He looks very natty, very colonial in his pressed whites. Eva naturally thinks of his mother, ironing his clothes, fussing over and admiring him, and a wave of grief rises from her belly.

Giddy children are running ahead and back like dogs at the start of a hike. They jump up and down and shout "C'mon! C'mon!" Even the adults act silly, joking, throwing their arms around one another. Everyone has told them the falls will be great. The group that came back last week were as exuberant as drunks, Eva thought, but stragglers coming up the hill now from the opposite direction are drenched, carrying mashed hats and sodden sneakers. They look battered, wrecked.

They must be getting close. Strangely, the shouts and calls of the others seem to recede to a distance as the sound of water swells and fills her ears. Drowned, Eva thinks, with a shudder. But isn't it more like deafness?

The path turns and there is the waterfall, crashing angelic white against foaming rocks. Following the park guides, the people form human chains to pick their way across the rocks and up the falls. They cling to one another; they waver and pull each other off balance. To Eva, it seems a malevolent version of "The Golden Goose." Where is the goose leading them? Not astray, exactly, but she thinks of the plague lurking behind the nursery rhyme. Ashes, ashes, we all fall down.

Her group joins hands. She looks into Michael's warm eyes; he raises his eyebrows in that way of his, a clever, quizzical monkey look. She laughs in spite of herself and reaches out for his hand. His grasp is sure, his whole palm flush with hers, fingers tight. And if she would rather pick her own way across? Still, she does like the feel of his muscled palm. But his balance depends on hers, and hers on the next person's, and so on down the line. On her other side a man grips her, and from the tremor in his cold hand she senses he is frightened. He is a man of sixty or so, she guesses, probably a hotshot executive. Even nearly stripped, in nothing but a bathing suit and hat, he has the best, is accustomed to power. So that the current of fear from his hand up her arm is all the more real for being so unexpected.

The force of the falls is immense. It could knock you over and send you sprawling down the rocks. "Over here, right dere," the guides shout, telling her where to put each foot. The rocks are more slippery than they looked from below. The current runs fast and treacherous; a cleft in the rock streams with slick green weed. Eva takes a deep breath and steps across the channel after Michael. She strains, Michael pulls, and she jerks the executive. There is a dizzy moment, a flash of falling, and then she is across. She turns to help the man and for an instant encounters a small, terrified boy. She looks away, ashamed.

The nurse practitioner in the obstetrician's office discovered the lump, and the first chemotherapy sessions started the day the Navy Seals swam ashore to begin Desert Storm. To Eva and Michael it had felt like the world was about to end. It would have been a grim ending, to go out in a fog of black petroleum smoke and chemotherapy nausea. And then the radiation: her fear of it so pervasive, so gritty, that the fear of death began to seem simple and clean. When the treatment was over, one of her breasts was tattooed with a sickle of tiny blue-black dots where they had pinpointed the radiation.

The waterfall rushes down in steps, a milky blue-green that makes Eva wonder if there is something—iron, copper?—that gives the water all around this island its magical, jeweled color. She can hardly believe this color could be so common. To her it represents something precious, lost. When she was pregnant, she dreamed a song that haunted, though sweetly. "Many deepest blues are passing by . . ." When she awoke, all she remembered was a scrap of tune, the single line, and the jewel image of the deepest blues, which was exactly the color of the sea here.

When Eva pulls herself over a boulder to the next level, her heart jumps in surprise. In a flash, she almost imagines two manatees on the rocks in front of her. Two enormous women loll against the stones. They are both a smooth coffee-with-cream color, wearing wet sarongs that cling to monumental thighs, their pendulous breasts there for all the world to see, pressed flat against great bellies, every detail distinct. The nipples are dark, slightly distorted by the fabric. One of the woman has small fierce eyes and a large jaw, but the other is remarkably seductive, Eva thinks. A wide moon face, a face full of curves.

How amazing they are, with their ferocious looks. Eva, proud of her strong, slim figure cannot imagine what brings them to this public display of their tremendous curves. At a waterfall, a tourist attraction?

"*Puta*," she hears the executive say behind her, with an ugly laugh. Puta, that's a whore. But it's difficult to imagine what kind of business hookers would do at a waterfall. It doesn't strike Eva as convenient. As if reading her thoughts, the beautiful one calls out to her. The words, her Caribbean patois, are lost in the roar of the waterfall. Puzzled, Eva brings herself to say, "Excuse me?"

"You!" the woman calls across to her. "You gotta be justified." At Eva's confused look she shouts each syllable distinctly, "Jus-ti-fied." There is no mistaking her words. She is not angry, the meaning of the message is not an insult. Eva smiles apologetically and turns away. The woman's companion lets out a belly laugh.

There are people who think red hair marks you, sets you apart. These people choose Eva. They choose her for the wrong reasons, for her red hair, but maybe they are right? Because Eva does listen to them. Especially since the cancer, she has been alert to signs and portents.

Stricken with one of those intense flashes of imagination, Eva sees the waterfall without all the wobbly whites, their instamatics and neon plastic sunglasses, their flip flops and water shoes that will get lost and float off down the falls. Without the shrieking tourists and hallooing guides, would this be a sacred place? By moonlight, at daybreak?

"Did you see those women?" she asks Michael when they stop to rest.

"I think maybe they pose for tourists . . . for money," he says, looking uncertain.

"Oh lovely. We should've brought the camera," she says. But her sarcasm gives her no satisfaction. After the surgery she had seen so clearly how small and mean and critical she had often been, how habitually immoral it was. Too soon the habit crept back. It makes her sad that she is helpless to change something so important.

Around her, people laugh and laugh, even the executive, laughing with relief. It's as if they speak another language, one she can't remember. But the constant sibilance of the falls, so fresh and sweet-smelling, is insistent in the way it works on her body, calms her. She would like to sit here for awhile and study the bright flowers, the strange vines and tiny ferns growing near the water. Here and there are trees like the ones that grow right out of swamps—mangroves. Trees with great elephant roots reaching into the water.

That evening, back in the resort, she is very tired. She wanders to the outdoor bar and orders a strawberry daiquiri; she has been living on these like food since they came here. She sips the sweet fruited slush and walks to a chaise lounge on the beach. From here, she stares into the pink and blue pattern of the sunset on the surface of the water, a pattern like fish scales, or a variable liquid net. Settling her drink in the sand, she lies back to rest her arms at her side. The sea shushes softly against the jetty. The tension in her body releases with almost audible ticks, and with the letting go her grief rises. She allows the tears to flow out of the corners of her shut eyes until they trickle into her ears. Taking a deep breath, she thinks of the huge women at the falls.

How would she explain her decision to women like that? What would she say? She sets it to herself as a problem of rhetoric: if you had to convince this woman, what would you say? About the cancer—start there? Is cancer the unspeakable terror to these people too, or do simpler diseases of poverty take them first? No, better start with the pregnancy, how they were already painting the study yellow to be the baby's room. Then the lump that same week, just at four months. The biopsy. All the small, ineluctable steps toward her loss. The doctor explaining to her that the hormones of pregnancy were stimulating the cancer to grow, just as they did the baby. Progesterone, estrogen, the whole litany of delicate chemical signals that had been keeping her on a roller coaster of moods and morning sickness, the longing for vinegary foods, the desperate need to nap. Those powerful, comical hormones had suddenly turned against her. The doctor said, "I have to recommend termination of the pregnancy."

Eva read what she could find and asked frantic questions of her friends, but there wasn't time. At her next visit a few days later, the doctor said, yes, some women tried to tough it out and keep their babies. He had no statistics, only his disapproval, his ridicule of those women. He called them "earth cookies." But every day since then Eva had faced the truth: she did not have their courage. Not in the face of cancer, no. She would have wanted to be a lioness for her child. Instead, she and Michael signed the papers and the surgeons took the baby from her womb.

Afterwards, while she lay groggy and cocooned in the recovery room, they told Michael it had been a boy.

"Justified." Of course! Eva sits upright. The woman had said "justified," the very word calculated to bring Eva back to explain herself. She knows something about me, Eva thinks. I have to go back and talk to that woman.

In the morning, she waits for Michael to go off snorkeling. At the front desk they give her a car and a driver. Another handsome young man— these are handsome people. She has seen him by the boats on the beach;

he tells her his name, Lon. He drives too fast along the narrow, sandy roads.

"You like reggae?" Lon asks, and shoves in a tape, at shattering volume.

They pass a shack built entirely of silvered driftwood, like a child's fort. Eva recognizes all of it from yesterday: the jerk pork place called "Aunt Sallie's," the roadside lean-tos selling pink conchs and carvings (the same carvings over and over), the house where she had seen the man in dreadlocks. People live in these scrap-and-driftwood shacks.

Everywhere outside of the fortressed resorts is poverty. Shacks and lean-tos no bigger than a closet crowd together on thin strips of land far away from the beaches. Dusty palm trees, vultures circling over a hidden garbage heap or dead dog. Goats and chickens, even lean brown pigs. Lon pounds on the horn, tearing past skinny children as if they are dispensable. People walk along the edge of the road—there are no sidewalks— or ride dilapidated bikes right on the verge. Now and then Lon swerves to avoid an emaciated dog.

At the falls, Eva rushes from the car. The boom of the waterfall fills her ears again. She hurries down the walkway, watching for side paths, trying to judge which one will lead her to the women. Lon trots beside her, keeping up easily. She chooses a side route and follows its damp, mossy windings toward the noise.

Roots trip her until she slows. She has taken the right way, she knows it. She can imagine the women ducking past these branches with the swaying lightness fat people sometimes have. Sure enough, she comes to the little gravelly beach and the rocks where she had seen them yesterday. They are not there.

"Oh!" she cries. A nearby guide, standing on the rocks and calling up a string of tourists, turns at the sound of her voice.

"What you lookin' for lady?" he smiles. "You lose someone?"

"I'm looking for two women who were here yesterday," she says.

"Two fat women?" he asks, his grin broadening.

"Yes," she admits, blushing.

"Dat's Majesty an' Victoria," he says. "They don' show today. Maybe later, maybe not. Dey don' come every day."

"Oh," Eva says again. Her eyes sting with tears. Ever since the baby, the smallest things make her cry. "Oh well," she says.

"Dey don live far," he volunteers. "Dey probably home. Right over in Ocho Rios. You got a car?"

"Yes! Yes, I do. Ocho Rios! That's on the way back, that's great. Can you draw us a map?" She lifts her bag from her shoulder and scrabbles for a pen.

Lon steps out of the woods.

"Lon, this man can tell us where they live. It's Majesty? and Victoria, right? They live in Ocho Rios, on the way back. Can we stop? Here," she proffers pen and paper, but the guide speaks quick patois to Lon and ignores the scrap of paper in her hand.

They nod and laugh—the broad laughter and white teeth of these people. "No problem, mon, no problem," Lon says several times. "Sure, mon, sure." Eva finds herself humbled and grateful at how easily they go along with her wishes.

"Majesty. What's her last name, in case we can't find her?" she asks the guide.

"Don't know, lady. She call herself Majesty Seraphim. Everybody know her."

Majesty Seraphim. That had to be the one who spoke to her. Eva imagines her putting a broad finger at random on a page of the Bible. Does she know seraphim is plural? Eva remembers that from her brief time at Hebrew school. Maybe Majesty believes several angels inhabit her body, an indwelling host?

Ocho Rios is mud-colored and decrepit. The streets are crowded with people, especially at the tourist market in the center of town. Here the spirit is a little ugly. Even though she's in a car, the vendors yell at her, "Here lady, look at this, only two dollar lady." Behind her back they turn sullen; she can see it as she cranes her head to look back at a stand of brightly colored baskets.

Away from the market it's worse, dirty and grim. Lon turns and turns again and Eva loses all bearings. Now they are in the heart of a slum of rickety shacks like those seen from the road. Eva can no longer guess the way out. All around her are black faces: thin, thin people with beautiful eyes. Everyone on this island has beautiful eyes, as beautiful as

Ethiopians. People shout after the car, their teeth gleam, they seem more fierce in here. Never has Eva felt so conspicuous. Lon stops to ask a question of a street vendor, and when he rolls down the window, the scent of rancid cooking oil makes Eva retch, like chemotherapy or morning sickness. The vendor is very tall and thin like a Masai, and when she points, her long, black finger resembles a tree root.

Lon yanks the wheel and screeches up the road. Eva cowers, terrified he will hit a child. After a long minute and more turns, he halts outside a shack. "Dis is it," he says.

Eva stays in the car for a minute, trembling. When she looks out she sees a sign, a crude hand with an eye in the palm and the words, "Majesty Seraphim Reader." Eva has had to work hard not to imagine Lon taking her somewhere to rob and kill her. The words on the sign seem miraculous. She steps out of the car. The smells are unbelievably worse. Urine drying in the hot sun where someone has pissed against a wall. Raw sewage. More cooking smells. But there is Victoria sitting in the doorway, her buttocks bulging over the sides of an orange crate. She wears little more today than yesterday: a loosely belted yellow housecoat open to reveal her black bra.

"Victoria," Eva calls to her. Still shaky, she clutches her purse. Lon joins her.

"Is Majesty in today?" Eva is conscious that saying these words makes her feel like a needy courtier.

"Yeah, she's in," Victoria says, unsmiling. She shows no surprise at seeing Eva.

"I was at the falls yesterday," Eva begins.

"Majesty," Victoria speaks into the darkness behind her. "Customer."

Majesty appears in the doorway, robed in a long blue mumu. Her face brightens when she sees Eva, and Eva begins to feel less out of place.

"Hullo, it's you." Majesty is actually smiling. "Come in, come on in," she says, beckoning with her broad golden hand.

Inside, a bed made up like a couch, with pillows and a thin orange cover, is pushed against the wall. A table with two chairs takes up the little space left. For a floor, a scrap of linoleum covers packed dirt. Red lace curtains frame the window and a cheap pink scarf flung over a single lightbulb above the table softens the light. Eva sees a pan sputtering on the cook stove against one wall. Majesty goes over to it and turns off the flame.

"You want some ackee?" she asks Eva. Eva shakes her head, a mute no. She wouldn't dare eat anything here. And yet it smells awfully good. Majesty dishes up two plates of ackee and fried plantains and takes them outside. Outside, Lon laughs.

She looks about her while Majesty is gone. The tiny room is scrupulously clean. Religious prints hang on each wall, but also paintings of the beach, idyllic villages in the mountains, a church on a hill.

"Who did these?" she asks Majesty, pointing at the pictures.

"Victoria is the artist," Majesty says.

Eva nods. "She's good."

"Sit, sit," Majesty says, pulling out a chair for Eva. Sitting down opposite her, she says, "Now den, why are you so worried in mind?"

Eva's eyes fill with tears; she can say nothing through her tight throat. Majesty lets her cry. A tarot deck materializes from her copious pockets.

"I'm sorry. This is silly," Eva sobs.

"No problem, no problem," Majesty puts in.

At last Eva brings out, "How much for a reading?"

"Ten dollar, US." Majesty cuts the cards into three stacks. She begins to deal them out. Both she and Eva look hard at each card.

"You been sick," Majesty states.

Eva nods and cries some more.

"You been havin' a bad time. I see a death here," she points. "So what you want to ask the cards? If you still sick?"

Eva nods.

Majesty frowns. She lays her hands flat on the table and says, "Look, there's nothing in here about that. I don't like to look for that stuff. That's not the way I work."

Eva's heart lurches, then rights itself as Majesty says this. At first she is frightened: maybe the woman has seen something bad in store for her? Then she is relieved; she wouldn't really want to hear anything but true good news, and how would she know it was true? She knows prophecy isn't the deeper purpose of the Tarot. Guessing the future is for fools, no matter how desperately you want to know.

"OK," she nods. "I understand." She takes a deep breath and then asks, "I—what did you mean 'justified?' I have to talk about that."

"Justified," Majesty nods, and points to a card. "Sometimes either way you choose is gonna be bad." She looks at Eva searchingly. "You were trying hard to do right?"

Eva is crying again. "Yes, but I was so scared. Fear makes you so . . . crazy." She makes a grasping motion with her fists.

Majesty sweeps the cards sideways, they stay in their place, but skewed. "You gotta see one ting only," says Majesty. "You gonna look in Romans 1:17, that gonna be your verse to think on."

Eva blushes. "Romans? Is that in your Bible? I—I'm Jewish. Anyway, I don't know the Bible at all."

Majesty shakes her head. "Don't matter. You justified because you want to be. That's what it says: 'all are justified freely.'" She closes her eyes and says, "'Blessed are they that hunger and thirst after righteousness.' Amen. That's all it's about. That's all. No more to it than that, though they tell all them lies in church." She opens her eyes and looks hard at Eva. "No more cryin', no more thinkin' about that now," she says, quite fiercely.

"I can't help it," Eva says with a wobbly laugh. "Thinking is what I have to do."

"Tell me what happened," Majesty demands.

So Eva explains about the pregnancy, discovering the lump at four months, the baby already quick within her. She explains what the doctor said, she leaves nothing out. How some women defy the doctors and carry their babies and wait to have the chemotherapy after. How some die and some survive. How Michael cried, he had wanted her to live more than anything else, although he was as heartbroken as she about the baby.

"And now nobody wants to listen, they all say, 'Of course you did the right thing, don't be silly,' but it's not like that, it's just that I . . ."

"Uhn," says Majesty. "You havin' a hard time." She looks around the room as if searching for something. "Don't know what I'd do," she says, shaking her head slowly.

"And I have these marks on my breast, and it's firmer than the other, so I think about it all the time, too much . . . I can't stop . . ."

"Let me see," says Majesty.

Eva lifts her shirt and pulls up her bra. Standing before Majesty like this, she is surprised that it seems so natural.

"A tattoo," Majesty says, touching the line of dots. "You got a tattoo." She laughs and teases, "One tittie like a girl, one like a woman." She hefts her own breast as she says this and Eva laughs too, because it's true, the chemotherapy breast is firm as a girl's.

Majesty looks her up and down.

"You need a real tattoo. Why don't you get Victoria to make it pretty?"

"A tattoo? Victoria does tattoos?"

"Sure she does. Here, look in this book."

Majesty takes down a looseleaf binder full of samples: rampant tigers, bleeding hearts, roses, snakes, voluptuous girls, swords, lightening, skulls. Eva leafs through slowly. Some are quite pretty, if a little insipid. She can't quite picture herself with a butterfly on her breast. Then she spots the ship, a tiny thing in full sail, with a high pointed prow rising over a line or two of waves. It seems just the thing and she loves it immediately.

"I wouldn't mind that one," she says, to her own surprise.

Majesty looks over her shoulder. "Hmm," she nods. "Nice, not too fussy. That's cheap too, 'cause it's simple. "Victoria!" she calls.

Victoria comes in, with Lon behind her.

"She's thinkin' about a tattoo," Majesty says.

"Hey great," Lon says, with a laugh. "You'll be flash."

"But does it hurt? I don't want to hurt."

"It ain't too bad. Victoria's good," Majesty says.

"It hurts a little. Just a little prick, then I stop, then another little prick. Like a mosquito," Victoria says. Her voice is husky, soothing.

"But does it take a long time? Does it hurt after?"

"One that small only take maybe half hour. It don't hurt when the needle ain't in."

And so Eva finds herself draped in another of Victoria's housecoats, a satiny red one, and settled on the orange crate, while Majesty and Lon sit at the table and drink Red Stripe beer, talk and tease and feed her bites of ackee. It is wonderful stuff, salty, full of onions and a hot pepper they tell her is called Scotch Bonnet.

First Victoria takes out a stamp of the ship and shows it to Eva. She stamps it in a pad of permanent ink, then carefully presses it to Eva's breast, one hand holding the skin taut. "Now I just fill in a little color, see," she says. Then she sets to work.

The tattooing does prick and then burn as the color goes in, a stinging, surface pain. Victoria is silent except for whistling a tune under her breath, a constant little sing-song that shows she is absorbed. Eva is happy to sit and listen.

Now and then Victoria's wrist or hand brushes against Eva's breast. It is pleasant to feel her skin prickle in response. Victoria is gentle, she takes Eva's hair in her hand and moves it aside, smoothing it behind her ear.

"Beautiful hair," she says, stroking it back. Majesty turns and says, "Mmm, beau-ti-ful." Her eyes meet Victoria's, they exchange a secret smile.

Eva wonders how they touch each other, these two. How would it feel, the great breasts rubbing against one another, the hands so deft and strong?

"There," says Victoria at last. She stands back to look, and smiles. "Nice," she says.

Majesty and Lon come over to look. Majesty puts her arm around Victoria's ample waist. "Dat's very pretty," she says. "You done good."

"Very, very pretty," Lon says. Everyone laughs. Victoria brings a mirror and Eva looks. It seems wonderful to her.

On the way home she imagines what Michael will say. "A tattoo? You had a what? A tattoo? You never told me you wanted a tattoo."

And then, "Are you sure it's safe? On your breast? So soon after—I don't get it. You're the one who worries about every little thing you put in your body."

Every little thing; she knows he thinks that. She knows he finds it unbearable, sometimes, the way she focuses the laser of her attention on minute cellular interactions in her body, as if by knowing about it she can arrest the course of the disease. But no more thinking! No more thinking. Eva strokes the talisman of freedom, her brand, starting down the gentle swell of her right breast, moving jauntily toward the trough of her sternum. It is natural to think nautically about her breasts now that she has the tiny sailing ship.

Maybe it will turn him on? She is thrilled with it. It's better than a new piece of jewelry.

She sighs. "God, I hope my husband doesn't think I've gone nuts."

Lon looks at her and laughs. "Nuts? What for? He's gonna love it. It looks good." He shakes his head at her. "No problem, he's gonna love it."

Eva laughs, "You think so?"

"Sure, mon."

"Maybe he'll think it cost too much."

"Nah, he don' care about that. He loves you. He'll do anything for you."

Instead of resenting his presumption or mistrusting him for flattering her, Eva knows what he says is true. It's a different way of knowing, when an outsider sees it and tells you so. And it comes to her that all these people that she watches from her seat by the pool, all the staff in the resort, yes and Majesty and Victoria too, they have been watching her. They have thought things about her and Michael, have imagined entire worlds from a single touch. They have formed conclusions too, and invented possibilities. And if they imagined them rich and happy, well? Hasn't Eva wished that she could laugh like these people? And look how they live. She thinks of Michael, floating over the reefs, absorbed in the silent kingdom below. She knows she will greet him in a warm and loving mood, though he will be grumpy and disconcerted by the tattoo. She laughs to herself. Michael will get used to it, she thinks. She strokes the ship and smiles.

Brock Clarke

✦

THE REASONS

Mr. Millingford stands against the bookcase making sucking noises with his tongue and his cheeks.

"I always thought you were a drunk," I tell him. I have heard that this is the case. It is a well-loved story around school that Mr. Millingford passes out in the back seat of his Chevy Nova each Friday by midnight. The rumor maintains that large, demanding crowds gather to watch our librarian turn the glass of his car windows into a dense, bewitching fog, the steam of alcohol battling against night's unrelenting and oppositional cold as he sleeps it off.

"Yessir," I go on. "I was convinced you were the most obvious drunk around."

"I am a drunk," he says, his voice barely audible over the sound of his mouth preying upon itself. "I wish I were drunk right now."

"So it's all true then?" I ask, trying not sound too surprised. "Every Friday. In your car."

"Yes," Mr. Millingford says. "All of it's true. There is even more, if you'd like to hear it."

"That's just great," I say. "It's nice to know you can count on something."

For the last four years I have believed in Mr. Millingford's inebriation like a novice priest longing for the truth of God, a desire that dares not have faith in itself but rather strives to trick belief into actual existence. Mr. Millingford's mythic alcoholism has always had great meaning for me, has always given my schooling some immediate sense of purpose. A routine. I feel a daily need to remind him of all his alleged problems. For instance, it is my habit to skip study hall with my friends just to tell Mr. Millingford every morning that he looks tired. We like to ask if he has been out late the night before, boozing it up with all the drunks we know or pretend to know or people we think have the potential to be drunks. My friends and I enjoy naming names, even if we have to make them up. We even form drinking motions with our pinky fingers and thumbs cocked, lifted, spout-like, articulating gurgling sounds in our throats as if we've been shot and are busy swallowing our own blood.

Mr. Millingford never says a word. He gives us looks that says he wants to slap us, knock our teeth loose and pick them up and store them in a box with overdue notices and misplaced file cards and other signs of abused property. But he never does. He straightens his glasses and goes about his awful, encyclopedic work with a patience that suggests there is a greater purpose to all things.

Now I know that he is in fact a drunk. That information turns out to be more insignificant than I could have imagined. This saddens me and then doesn't. The things that should matter don't. There, it's out where I can see it. I am now that much smarter.

"You're always waiting," I tell him. "What are you always waiting for?"

He shrugs, a movement full of apology. But I already know. I know Mr. Millingford has been waiting for that moment when I finally get what's coming to me. Well, I've got it. What I do with it now is the issue of the moment.

"Where did you get that gun?" he asks.

"It's a .38," I tell him, a meaningful caliber.

"But where did you get it?"

"At the gittin' place."

"That sounds familiar," he says. "I know that phrase."

"Mrs. Caprice," I say. "Senior honors English."

He nods, his head moving like some fatalistic, wrong-way metronome. "Flannery O'Connor. A Good Man is Hard to Find. PS 347. O 33." The librarian recites the call numbers sadly, as if his awareness of them, his general knowledge confirms his own helplessness.

"No, that's not it," I tell him. "You aren't as smart as I thought. To be honest, I can't remember exactly where it's from. I do remember, though, that the boy who said it killed three men before he was killed himself. He didn't mind dying, although I'm sure the men he killed did. There was a big deal made over their suffering. I remember that much."

"Are you sure this is what you want?" Mr. Millingford asks. He moves forward slowly, pulling his reasonable-adult routine.

"None of that," I say, waving my gun like it's some bony, Ichabod Crane index finger in full scold. Mr. Millingford beats a quick two-step back to the bookshelf.

"You're a tough kid, aren't you?" he says, a world-class suck-up.

"I am a tough kid," I tell him. "I also have a horrible life at home. You know what that means, don't you? Good kids, bad environments."

This said, I cock my hip and try to look like a killer and he strikes and maintains a slouch, looking like a victimized still life and we stand there.

Mr. Millingford's mouth keeps pulling and pushing on its various parts, drawing and exhaling loudly as if it is trying to resuscitate itself. I have a never seen him do this before today. I have never seen anyone do it. It must be a nervous habit that comes with the threat of death or the promise of certain types of large-scale change. It is not a comforting thing to watch.

I find myself pulling my own cheeks inward with my tongue and then I stop.

Finally, I waggle my gun at him. He stops his breathing exercises and puts his arms up without me telling him to. His cheap shirt is stuck to his skin, a translucent cotton-blend seal skin. The shirt looks like it was man-ufactured wet, more a texture than a color or a condition. I wave the gun again and he puts his arms down, as if there is a string between him and me and I am pulling it.

"But you're not only a drunk," I say. "What else are you?"

"I'm a librarian," he says, not without pride.

"Yes, you are a librarian. And you're something else too. You're at least one more thing."

We stare at each other for a long time. Mr. Millingford looks at the gun and I look at his hair, which is blonde, retreating in double-time over his forehead. He looks at my white basketball sneakers and I look through the window behind him, into the hallway. It is empty because of the fire alarm I've just pulled, and I know that it won't be that way for much longer. He looks at the red dye on my hands from where I grabbed the alarm, looks at the red transferred from my hand to the gun's grip and I stare him in the eyes, willing him to do the same. Mr. Millingford finally raises his eyes, all vague and teary and nearly unable to focus, and through our looks we come to the understanding that I will shoot him if he doesn't tell me at least one more thing about himself, and it is possible that I will shoot him anyway.

"I'm your mother's boyfriend," Mr. Millingford says finally. The heels of his wing tip shoes click nervously against the red spine of the World Book: A-H on the bottom shelf.

"'My mother's boyfriend,'" I repeat. "That's an interesting way of putting it, especially since my mother is married to my father. Technically, then, I'm not sure you can be my mother's boyfriend. Her lover, maybe. Does that sound better to you? Lover?"

"That sounds fine," he says.

"She's very pretty, isn't she?" I ask him.

"Yes."

"Much better looking than you are. Wouldn't you say that? You wouldn't say you were better looking than she is, would you?"

"I'm not sure what difference that makes," he says, not all the pride sucked out of him yet. "This is a very strange conversation."

"That's not what I'm asking you."

"No," he says. "It's not even close. She's very beautiful."

"I'm just trying to understand," I tell him.

He nods slowly, like he knows his head might pop off at any moment, that his spine is a thin, frayed chord. "I realize that," he says.

"I saw you the other night," I say. "I saw you outside the bar, the two of you in your car. I bet you're a shitty kisser. That's the one thing I could tell from where I was standing across the street. Your mouth is all wrong. It's like it isn't even attached to your face, like it is somebody else's mouth and you can't control it."

This is an insult he can't swallow. There is always something.

"I saw you there," he tells me, the sweat pouring out of his scalp now, down the thin, flat sides of his face and into the corners of his mouth. I watch as Mr. Millingford attempts a grin through his body's own deluge. "I saw you looking at us."

"I know you did," I tell him and then I shoot him in the left ankle, right where there is bone and tendon and not much else. Nothing that he really needs to live. Mr. Millingford falls to the ground and his mouth takes on a crazy O-shape, like he's preparing to swallow the world. Then out of it comes this fierce rumbling noise, like he is a cow giving birth and dying at the same time. This goes on. I wait for him to stop yelling at me, at his own disabled foot, for him to get accustomed to the pain before I make him get up again. There is a quiet in the library, something in and around us that has made me deaf to the sound of the gunshot, of the fire alarm ringing, of Mr. Millingford bellowing even though I know they are all real, all things that I am directly responsible for.

"I have shot him," I think, wondering what else I might be now capable of. My school motto says: "There are no impossibilities, only weak imaginations."

Mr. Millingford stops yelling. He is trying to act like a quick healer, someone tough on the inside, and who knows, maybe he actually is. The librarian makes a move to get back on his feet. I tell him to grab onto the bookcase for support and he does, holding it like it is the mast of a wounded sailboat.

"When you were in the car," I tell him, "you looked like you were enjoying me being there. You looked like you never wanted me to leave."

"I was enjoying myself," Mr. Millingford says. He voice is thick, ragged, like his teeth have embedded themselves in his tongue and in his throat. "I was happy you were there to see it."

"How happy?" I ask him. He looks down at his foot and sees that there is blood on the carpet and on the World Book: A–H. The blood drips cautiously and steadily out of his body like water from some snowpile caught out of season. He looks back at me. Mr. Millingford knows I am not a bad kid, despite my having shot him and he guesses that there are ways out of this that even I can't see. He closes his eyes and tries to think of them. He wonders about all the right things to say. He imagines himself limping away from all this. I know that's what Mr. Millingford is thinking because his good leg shakes like there is a bee caught in the inside of his pants.

"Not that happy, in retrospect," he finally admits. In this case, lying is the best policy.

"That makes sense," I answer. "It seems like the logical thing to say. I think we're going places."

"I hope so," he says. "I really hope so."

"There is just one thing I want to know before we go on," I say, switching the gun to my left hand so I can give my right hand a rest. My wrist hurts from the tightness of my grip, throbs like it is another heart, but I don't rub it.

"I can't help thinking about my parents," I explain. "My parents are on my mind. They locked themselves in their bedroom last night, killing each other for five hours straight. It seems like a relevant phrase, 'killing themselves.' They were pretty quiet about the whole thing, considering. I stood outside and listened to them talk. Not yell, but talk about how things go wrong, who was at fault, what could have been done differently. They talked like we're talking. Calmly. Under control. They decided that they couldn't have done anything at all, couldn't come up with one thing they might have changed if they had the chance. Not one damn thing. Can you imagine that? My mother called my father a fatalist and he said that she was one to talk and they both agreed with what the other had said. It was finished like that. But I could tell. I could tell that they were dying. There were breaking sounds coming out of their mouths, if that makes any sense. I don't expect you to know. But there is just one thing I need to understand."

"What is it?" Mr. Millingford asks. He seems attentive. He wants me to know that he will help me if he can. That is his job, after all.

"I need to know why. I know what you did and what my mother did and I know where you did it. Now I need to know why you did it. And even better, I need to know why my mother did it."

Mr. Millingford falls back against the bookcase, as if I have shot him again and he knows that he is dead already.

"You want reasons," he says, his librarian's voice quietly pleading with me to tell him that he has misunderstood, that I want something else entirely. But Mr. Millingford's powers of interpretation are just fine. I nod and we stand there while the school refills and crowds against the doors of the library and we stand there still like two poorly made statues in full combat, cracking and crumbling in full view of each other as we wait for what comes next, the part that might tell us about all the things we can't know and how there is nothing in them for us to learn.

Misha Hoekstra

◆

THE BROTHER

A brother is like one's shoulder.
—Somali proverb

I am playing in the sandbox when my mother calls me in. Opening the screen door, I see a dozen spirit and seltzer bottles on the floor where my mother, whose head is in the cupboard underneath the sink, has been setting them behind her. They clank as she makes room for each new bottle by using it to push the others back. Finally her head emerges and she stands up with a squat celadon jar of unusual brilliance, cradled in the crook of her left arm. She pops off the wire bail that holds it shut, tipping it forward to disclose the gray cottony growth inside. —Take off your shirt, my mother says, —and turn around. She plunges two long fingers deep into the jar and spreads a stinky green matrix on my right shoulderblade. It is cold and it smarts, and I protest. She bends to the spot and, clearing her throat, hawks on it. Very soon it develops into a boil, but she will not lance it. When I pick at it, she laughs at me and binds my wrists to my beltbuckle with a length of twine from the toolbox on the table. The pressure in my shoulder increases and I feel something begin to pinch and gnaw at the bone, it is swollen to the size of a songbird's egg, it grows heavy and painful. I snap at the lump but only succeed in losing my balance, falling to my knees and then my left side. —Be careful with that, she says to me over the noise of what she replaces under the sink, —be kind, you might as well start now. But the growth asks to be smashed, it hurts like nothing I have known, it is now the size of a fist.

With my hands bound I cannot rise, I can only roll about and grind my shoulder into the floor. She shuts the door after the last bottle but one, which she brings over with the toolbox, to set gently on the linoleum next to my head. From the toolbox she extracts a chrome lighter, a clean folded pair of cotton panties, and an exacto knife; a tender, bemused smile lights her face. She places these items on the floor so that they are equidistant from and parallel to the length of the toolbox and then, grunting as she strains her small frame to do so, she pulls me over onto my stomach, so that my horizon is dominated by the brushed steel face of the gaping toolbox. I twist so that I can see her and then I do my best to bellow, trying to register my discomfort on her face. She brushes a strand of hair back from her forehead. The pain is excruciating and general, something moves violently in my shoulder the size now of a softball, or a gravy boat, and the skin there is stretched as tight as a teakettle. — Hold still, she says, introducing the panties into my mouth. —Bite down on this. It is almost a relief to do so. With her left knee in the small of my back, I can no longer move anything but my eyes. When she lays her hand on the hump, it stops its furious quivering, though it retains the shoulderbone in its fierce grip. The world slides in and out of focus. — Hold *still*. I feel the knife score my skin in a great curving ex that slices through the center of the blister, I see the knife returned to its place. My mother takes up the bottle and unstoppers it with her perfect white teeth, pours from it into the palm of her left hand. She sets the bottle down and, dipping her index finger again and again in the pool of spirits, daubs the alcohol onto the beading red ex, so that her stinging signature grows strangely cool. After wiping both hands on her jeans, she lifts the bottle to receive the stopper from her wry lips and replaces it on the floor. She picks up the lighter and, in one smooth rebounding wristsnap, flips the top off and rolls the flint with her thumb. With this ignition am I suddenly suspended eighteen inches above some boy's grossly distended shoulder, am I concentrated to a point. With this ignition am I shorn from pain's immediacy, and able to see forth in every direction. My mother raises the flame with her left thumbnail until it is three inches high, and then, her mouth cracking into a full dimpled grin, she brings the flame over to where the base of a bloody cross commences in the middle of the boy's side. A blue flame runs quickly up the line, splitting into three directions at its bellied center. It soon settles down, a flickering swath of yellow above an invisible base. The line of blood crackles and blackens, the taut triangles of flesh brown at the edges. As the heat rises, the tumor starts to stir and then to thrash, and with each new spasm the flaps of skin separate a little bit more, revealing a milky blue membrane that begins to bubble as the flames lick over it. My mother unlocks the parlor door and returns with a bulky square, which she folds out into a cage the size of an upright piano: bamboo, with a wicker weave bound to the cross-pieces of the roof. She lights a menthol and goes through the pantry to the meatroom, where I hear her tear off a piece of butcher paper from the roll next to the bandsaw. She comes back with a large rectangle that she sets down on the floor, tucking one white edge neatly under the boy's disturbed side. His eyes have closed and the flame gone out but the hump continues to struggle, rocking his body back and forth. My mother stands up. She ashes in her breastpocket. She walks over to the stove, dons a canvas apron, and pours sesame oil into her largest frying pan. With an old dishtowel draped over her arm, she sets the pan next to the toolbox, from which she takes a lilliput flensing knife. When she has stropped it to satisfaction on the heel of her palm, she peels back the lowest flap of the boy's skin; its charred point hangs over his side and just touches the paper, revealing, beneath a throbbing oblate sphere the size of a large cantaloupe, or a small medicine ball, the raw meat and bone of the boy's shoulder. After stubbing the cigarette out on the side of the frying pan and rolling up her flannel sleeve, my mother plunges an arm under the base of the trembling membrane and tries to dislodge it; but it grips the bone fast. She gets a hatpin from the top tooltray and pokes the creature with the tip, gently at first and then an inch, two, causing the thing to relax a moment and then convulse ever more violently. She notices the pause. When she jabs it twice in rapid succession, the blind mass all comes free at once, flopping wetly down next to the frying pan and taking with it the center of my distant pain. A sigh escapes my mother. She wedges the thing between her aproned knees and then, gently, firmly, makes an incision with the knife. Pulling up on the cut membrane, she passes the keen edge of the blade lightly back and forth against the line of attachment, so that the glistening tissue falls slowly away from the creature like a shroud as she rotates it, to reveal a pale hairless eyeshut head. The head is large and almost human except for its coloring, which grows purplish, indigo, blue. When the mouth and nose have been cleared, she sets the knife down and begins to tickle the creature through the rest of its quaking caul until at last the mouth gapes and twists in a fit of sneezing, sneeze after sneeze that make the complexion redden, the body bend and release like a bow. My mother picks up the spasmodic beast and returns to her flensing, humming a tuneless phrase under her breath until, without warning, it chomps down on her pinkie and she gasps —Bastard!, almost drops it, has to go for the hatpin again, this time with less mercy. At last the membrane lies still on the floor. The creature has a fatty fishlike tail where I expect a neck; the whole thing is shaped like a giant slug. My mother towels it off and, holding it gingerly with the cloth like a hot casserole, brings it to the door of the cage and gently rolls it inside. With a length of red silk string from the hank in her pocket, she ties the bamboo door to with a single bowknot. The creature is trembling, and my mother drags the cage over to the window where there is still some late morning sun. She stands in front of the cage a long time, look-ing down. —Forget I said that, she says very quietly. And she turns, and comes back. She takes up the wet casing and, holding it over the frying pan, lops it into bitesize pieces with the flenser until the pan is nearly full. A toothbrush scours out the last bit of membrane from under the boy's skinflaps, a roofing knife trims a tab of asphalt shingle to size; a hand fits it into place beneath the flaps. Then, with a sailor's needle and some twelve-pound test, my mother begins to draw the skin back together with large looping overhand stitches. —Misha, she says, and at the sound of my name am I back in my body once more. —This is only temporary; we don't want it to grow back together, not yet. . . . My whole shoulder is on fire, and all the muscles in my body are clenched. As she begins wiping the various implements clean and returning them to their proper trays, I try to relax my muscles group by group, letting the pain wash through me. She lights another cigarette and, humming once more, puts the apron in the hamper, the paper in the burn barrel, the full frypan on the back burner, low heat. The bottle goes back under the sink, though I see that the celadon jar, with its foul matrix, gets reached up to the top of the fridge. The twine that binds my wrists is cut with a switchblade from her boot. And then my mother bends over me, and she takes the wet panties from my mouth. —Misha, she says, tousling my crewcut hair, —go and say hello to your brother.

✧

It is feeding time but the iron ship's bell by the back door does not ring
and I know something is wrong. I grow agitated in the sand and finally I
dash into the kitchen of my own accord. She is feeding him, usurper, her
fingers laced around his caudal appendage, supporting him, she is gazing
down at his noisy suction with a look of tenderness such as I cannot recall
ever having seen before. She does not look up, even when I throw my
bright yellow saw and green screwdriver against the fridge and rush over
to her. I reach up for the free grease nipple even as I am raising my arm
to shove him away from the other fitting, but the concussion of her *No!*
knocks me to the side with such force that I am driven head over heels
into the pantry against the lower shelves, cans and bottles rolling heavily down onto my splay limbs, torso, head.

—Backhand, she chuckles, —did you know that a squash racket is a
special kind of hammer? Same as a bat or golf club, piano key or plec-
trum. Listen, she says to me through the rising waves of my sobs, —listen boy, even if it weren't time, I've converted the fittings and made the
mix richer. Even if you could attach without too much spillage, I'm afraid
this new mix would only make you sick. And it *is* time.

I look over to the table where I now notice, next to the toolbox and
arrayed neatly in a line, the worn gas fittings, the bottles of witch hazel
and acetone, the glass cutter and skinning knife, the majolica jar, the
needlenose pliers; I notice the carpet stapler, the emery cloth and rubber
tubing, the gouges both vee and trough, the two conoid sponges dripping
red. My curiosity is roused but I show nothing, I pretend her technique
holds no interest for me. I do not stop crying.

—He was ravening, she explains, —I'll put the things away as soon
as he's burped.

Thinking I hear a note of apology in her voice, I say, —What about
me? My hunger is so *strong!*

—Hold on a minute, and I'll grind you up some supper in the quern.
I'm graduating you to more solid food, starting with some waste eighty-
weight and sawdust and old macerated leather. Over the next few weeks
I'll start folding in iron filings, corks and spokeshavings, and then, when
you've adapted to that, grommets and glazing points and woodscrews, a

few veneer peelings and assorted essential oils, and finally, if at the end of the year you've taken to this like I think you will, brickbats and worm-gears, fanbelts and stripped bolts and perhaps the odd churchkey.

I grunt, I scowl, even as the muriatic acid begins to flow from my paratid glands. I'm not about to let on how enticing this sounds, treated only to the occasional lightgrade oil as I have been.

—He's a lot rougher, she says, —than you ever were, though I imagine it's always worse than one remembers. Yet the pleasure for me seems all out of scale to the mechanical simplicity of it all. . . . She pauses as if holding something underwater, and then finally she looks up at me. —Any ideas for a name?

—Yeah sure, I say,—Drossbelly. Shopsweepings. Salamander Pissabed Metalwaste, Pigiron Marlinbait Stripslot Poprivet Slagtail.

—Hmmm. I see this is going to take longer than I'd hoped. Am I going to have to take you out behind the shop for some ad hoc soldering?

—Bentspoke Dirtoil Kerfpowder, I say, almost spitting out the words,—Unsquare Meltfuse Featheredge. Factorybevel, Distemper Gaptooth Leakseal, Stretchbelt Rustspot Burnbearing Overgrind, Offsize Untrue Imbalance Catchspur Bindblade—surging now for the door—Misdressed Crossthread Fatiguecracked Gumsprung Undershot Inlubricate Roundoff Parasite Pressureloss! I pull at the screendoor as if to take it from the hinges, run blindly through my tears for the sandbox, screaming— Splinterjoint! Overswaged Warpface! Chiploose Misgaged Outofround Dulledge Lacklimb!

My brother is in his beautiful cage on the grass, sitting in an inverted cone, brilliant and silver, suspended two feet up by a bungee cord that passes over a crossmember. The slingshot is ineffectual, it just hurts my wrist, and so I am forced to fling the sand between the wicker wattles with a shovel. He beams at me with the full set of his serrated teeth, whose points mesh perfectly. When I get down to wet sand the weight is too much for the faded orange plastic handle, and throwing the busted shovel weakly against the cage I take up an old rusty pail and rain sand through the bars until, blind and exhausted, I hurl the whole pail

against the side of the cage and fall onto the sand. When I raise myself
to look, he is swinging back and forth slightly, and there is sand sprinkled on the surface of his outstretched expectant tongue. I am banging
my head against one of the railroad ties that impound the sand when I
feel a gentle thock on my good shoulder. I stop my forehead against the
creosote-scented tie and rotate my eyes upward, so that I can just distinguish my mother's bib overalls in the thin stripe of visible yard.
—Listen, she says, —*what* are you doing? You want to get your shoulder infected and imperil the graft? And Misha, you know he's not on
solid food yet. If it's your own digestion you're trying to improve, let me
suggest a #10 stonescreen or even a light gravel rather than this fine
sand, which will only scour the pipes and clog the lower fitting. And
then she walks off, her channel locks, trident, and seed mill all chiming against each other in her bib as she moves across the lawn to where
she's been retrofitting the wellhead. I spring up furious, run my good
shoulder up against the door of the cage but it will not give way, run
over to the picnic table where I pick up the pruning shears and run
back, slipping but once on the grass. My idiot brother still has his
tongue outthrust, and drool begins to spill from the corner of his mouth.
The shears are no good on the bamboo, it's tougher than it looks; I
throw them onto the top of the cage and try to climb it but it's more
slippery than it seems too. I look wildly about, see my Radio Flyer and
drag it over next to the cage, use it to boost myself up, onto the top. I
push the shears in front of me but the crosspieces hurt my kneecaps and
I keep slipping into the wicker interstices. The handles I find are for
someone with much longer and stronger arms, and I have the worst
time getting a blade under the bungee loop without it slipping free.
And when at last I get the shears to close around the cord, the swing
slips down only a couple inches, for though most of the cord has been
cut, the center strands of elastic are only pinched sideways between the
blades. My brother gazes up at me with curiosity, bobbing up and down,
his tongue still stuck out. Then the final strands ravel and I crow out
my triumph as the little warhead hits ground, I raise my arms on top of
the swaying cage and whoop while my knees keep their tricky balance.
From below me comes a strange burbling sound, and I press my face to
the wickerwork. I cannot actually see the cone but from the pixeled tilt
of his round head I can tell that it has stuck in the soft ground, tipping

a couple inches to the back. I see the limp tentacles of cord snaking out to either side. I see the sand-speckled lozenge of my brother's tongue on the grass, bright red where his perfect incisors have done their work. And I see how he quivers in his cone, in the center of the frame, in time to the bubbling music I cannot believe is laughter.

A. A. Hedge Coke

◆

THE
SUN AND MOON
OVER JASPER
(Lucy)

Like two coins laid on the eyes of a dead cowboy, Sun and Moon hang bleached and white at the same moment in the sky. Jasper rises and pulls the cloth shade further down until it snaps up toward the ceiling with a flutter and kick.

I watch him. His lean back and boney hips barely outline his character. I wonder why he sleeps with arms pulled in like sparrows' wings, knees drawn so tight to his chest he looks like a tangle of fleshy wood.

These days summer rolls by in a fury. The smell of dirt from the road blows hot through the window by nine. The sky is sealed in field clouds and mist even though I know it's blue just a short drive away.

Jasper reaches out to take his white cotton t-shirt down from the wall hook. He has a habit of hanging up clothes normal people usually fold in drawers, and leaving hanging clothes in piles all around the house. I gave up trying to keep them in place a long time ago.

His eyes slope with weariness. Crows call on the jays in feathered altercation. They rush to battle with such vengeance even the cats flee the grounds. Jasper's thin arms poke through the shirt sleeves and his face pops the top slot like a jack-in-a-box. There's a hint of worry knotted somewhere behind center rim of forehead above his nose.

I hate his mother. I hate the way she bulldozes him down like a sapling in the way of planting field rows. She has the spirit of a ghost gone wild.

The spirit wrapped forever in iron-fisted punishments only she has the right to bestow. Her image conjures putrid tastes in the back of my tongue and bitter smells intruding my nostrils. Evil. She smells like Evil.

I snort like a horse blowing sour grain and call Jasper back to my side. He tries to refuse my affection but is so starved, he surrenders into the folds of the bed. We hold one another, but it is more like a sick pup clinging to teats for safety.

I want more. I'm angry. I don't understand how this man can give so little and suck so much emotion while masquerading indifference.

It's her fault. His mother. And there's no way she's going to do anything to him ever again. I know he's fixing to walk the road down to her place this morning. Probably he'll expect to eat a second breakfast. She always pouts if he's eaten before she sees him. He'll expect to see her wrinkled hands stir clumps of oats with milk until it's all a gray gruel. He'll expect to hear her baby-talk him, once again, beg her to take her shots. Yeah, he'll expect the same as every day. But, I've fixed everything. I've got her tied down in the old yard—the one back of the horse corrals down in the hollow. No one goes down there. She's going to stay tied down there until her mouth is sweet. She's so full of cursing, Evil glides along her gums and roots between her corn-yellow teeth.

See, she puts this sugar in her words, curls baby language to her full-grown son. Just to coerce and control him. Shoots her blood sky high but she don't care. If he pays me—or his job—any mind, then she starts in complaining and threatening until he caters to her every wish again.

You know what? She even has him sleep with her when she's sick. She does. She says, "Jasper, come warm me up. I'm freezing." He's so ignorant he slides in and holds her like she's his baby. Gives her more comfort than he can muster up toward me, for sure.

I used a bridle rein to tie her. I put her on a loading shoot and strapped her up like a fresh filly from the mustang rounds. She can't get away. I made sure.

Soon as Jasper heads down toward her house, I'll take her down some water and let her piss in a tin can. But I am not letting her go.

Tying her mouth was the hard part. I had to use a bandanna and she kept spitting at me. Foul as she is, I thought I'd catch something before I got her gagged good. Now she can't say a thing to no one. Ha! This is my day now. If my name's not Lucy Snake.

I reach down and scratch Jasper low on his back. He winces and turns away.

"I already ate your biscuits, now I gotta go down to Mama's." He puts on his belt and looks out the window saying, "She'll be waiting for me."

The screen door swings on rusted hinges billowing dry dust into whirlpools following behind him up the path.

I don't care if she rots, I think and step into my slippers slowly, then slip on the golden chain and cross my mother gave me just before she died of consumption. I drag out a duster to wear over my scrawny shoulders and down to my knees. Then I take down a canteen to fill and make my way through the thorny briars on the old path. Sun and Moon glare at me. I want to strike them with an open hand until they spin like pocket watches, but I spit on the ground to get the dust out of my swill. I find her tied-up like I left her in the hollow. She's limp. Head down and forward. *Hope she's gone*, I think and bang the canteen with my fist. She raises one eyebrow at me and narrows her eyes. I know she hasn't had enough yet. I kick her feet apart and slide the can underneath. She goes in a flood of ammonia-smelling pee. When I toss the fluid out past the gates, it hits the ground with a sinking sizzle.

"Old Woman," I say, my hands on my hips. "Old Woman. You have got to learn a lesson. One you should have learned way before your husband left you. Probably should've learned it before you married even. Probably why he left."

She sneers at me, gagged and all. She wrinkles up her nose like a rabbit and leers deep into the meat around my throat.

"So, you want to choke me, huh? Well, Old Woman, you're not in any position to do the punishing anymore. Might as well give it up. If you want some of this." I hold the canteen up high and spill some water on the ground right in front of her. She looks pitiful all tied up and sweaty, but I know she's anything but. *Her mouth is her mind*. Evil bottled up in female disguise. I can't believe she ever gave birth she's so full of anger and meanness. Maybe it explains why Jasper is the way he is in bed. Maybe the blood itself won't let him reproduce another like her. Nature has a way of rubbing out the unholy.

I reach down and untie the cloth at the nape of her neck. She wiggles and glares. *I guess she can't help her meanness*. I wonder how I am going to get it out of her. But, I know I will.

Her lips are curled around the tin mouth piece, her jaws clenched and pulling. "Enough," I say and put the cap on.

She starts to say something, then has to spit to clear her throat. Again she opens her mouth. "If you don't cut me loose I'll kill you! If something happens to me, my son will kill you for me!"

I slap her face and tie the gag on. "That's it. No more water and you can piss on yourself for all I care." I pour the rest of the water on the ground real slow just to bother her and say, "If you don't say something sweet the next time I come down, you will die of thirst. You will." I leave her without looking back even once. On the way back to the house, I pick purple and orange flowers. I put the handfuls in the crook of my arm until I have a whole bunch. Once I step into the kitchen I shake the dust off of them and run cold water over the blooms and stems. Tiny aphids scurry away and fall down the drain. I run the water harder to chase them down the sink hole.

Jasper comes in. He looks funny, says, "Mama's not home. She's not anywhere around the house. You hear her say anything about taking off today?" His voice is quavery, the vowels spread out and choppy. Kinda like when she's told him off real bad.

I shake my head, "She don't tell me nothing about where she goes. She didn't say nothing about going nowhere. Not today. Not any day."

He sits at the table like he's lost without her bossing him around for the morning. I feel sorry for him so I ask, "Jasper why don't we take a drive somewhere?"

"What? What would we want to do that for?"

"For fun," I say, opening my eyes real wide and smiling.

He scratches his head, says, "Alright. Maybe we could look for Mama on the way. I gotta find her before I go to work tonight."

"Look here, Jasper. Look at these flowers I brung in." I take the bunch and hold them right in front of his face, "Don't they look like the ones you used to pick me?"

He just sits there.

I lean in closer, "Well, don't they?"

"I don't recall." He fishes around in the table basket for his keys, finds them and jingles the set like they're bells. "Let's go," he says and grabs my hand.

"Wait a minute. Look here, Jasper. These flowers look exactly like the ones you picked me when you proposed. Don't you remember?" I set them down again and make my lips poke out a little.

"Oh yeah, "he says, "back when I was breaking horses down below."

"Yeah, back then. You do remember. I am glad, Jasper. Because sometimes you get so caught up with your mother and your factory job you just forget all about me all together."

We take a long drive up the state road. On the way, Jasper starts smiling and pulls over by the long creek to pull some more flowers. He stands there smiling like a little kid. Tucks his chin into his collar bone and hands me half the bunch, says, "These are for you." Fingers the rest and says, "These are for Mama. Wonder where in tarnation she is." We head back down the road again. When we get back home I fix some soup and bread. Jasper eats it up so fast I'm startled. "Guess I missed my second breakfast," he says. After, he even offers to help me with the dishes. I'm so used to fending for myself I almost insult him with my fear of him near the sink and underfoot. He laughs though. Laughs like I never heard him laugh like for years. Like he feels the joy inside somewhere. Then he heads for work and leaves me with a sweet little kiss. I don't even want to see his mama's dry, old face. So, I stay inside and read Harlequins all night long. Come morning, Jasper's getting up before I even know he's home.

"Where to so early?" I ask.

"Going down to look for Mama. Her light was on all night again."

"Maybe she ran off with the junk man," I say and get up out of bed behind him. "Why don't you come to the table and let me fix you something to eat."

"No, that's alright. I gotta go. She's my mama, Lucy."

His face is all pitiful looking like his mom's, but on him it's real. He is pitiful. She's beat him down so much there's not much left to beat. Some other woman might just think he's spineless. Me, I think his spine's just choked out by his mother's weedy fingers.

Jasper heads out the door and down the road toward his mother's place.

Canteen full again, I head down to the hollow. His ma, she's looking weathered as an old scarecrow out to the cornfield. *I should've brought a straw hat to hang on her*, I think as I get closer to where she's tied. This time she don't glare at me. She's too tired and parched to see good by now. I pull the bandanna off and pour some water over her cracked-up lips. Her eyes look like they grew full cataracts overnight. It's kinda hard to believe they'd grey that much.

"Old woman, you had enough yet?"

"Old woman, I'm talking to you. I said, you had enough yet? I'm getting pretty tired of this."

She looks up and says, "I can't see, Lucy. I can't see." Real quiet like she's feeling funny.

"What about your tongue? Can you still curse? Because if you can I'm not cutting you loose."

"I can't see." She says.

Then I remember. She hasn't had no insulin in more than two days. "Alright. Alright. I'm going to cut you loose. But, you listen to me. You're not ever going to boss around my man like he's a boy again or I'll keep you down here till you wither up and blow away. You hear me? I said, you let him be a man. No more of complaining and cussing around to get your way. I don't want Evil interfering in our lives again. You keep Evil away from Jasper."

I reach down and untie the reins. Her hands are shaky and veins are bulging blue. She crumbles up like scorched paper.

"I'm taking you back to the house. If you ever get with Evil again I'm bringing you back here and leaving you till you're gone. You are never, ever, going to hurt Jasper with your ways again. You will keep your distance and mind your manners. You hear me? You're going to talk sweet and good and say nothing about none of this. I have had it and I am not going to have it again. You are going to learn, once and for all!"

Her eyes look like Moon and Sun yesterday. I look up and notice they're both still sharing the sky. I tell her it's a sign and that's why she's gone blind just like those ghostly bodies above. She's gone blind as Sun and Moon from seeing too much Evil in the world. I tell her she's to tell Jasper she got lost when her eyes went. I tell her everything's going to be alright now since Evil shot out of her eyes in the night and she's free of it at last. When I stand her up straight, she falls over. I have to lock my arms around her to hold her up. Her gray head falls on my shoulder and I see she's turned into a woman I can deal with.

She starts to cry a bit and asks, "Why did you do this? I'm blind. Why did you do this to me?"

I hold her tight and say, "I didn't blind you. The power of right blinded you. It was for Jasper's sake. He needs to be a man now. Jasper needs to be a man." I hold her cheek right next to my own and say, "Evil was so deep in you I thought you were one and the same. Now I see Evil escaped through your eyes and we are never going to let it come back again. I don't want to have to go through this trouble ever again. You just keep this a secret and we won't have to."

She reaches out in her blindness and says, "I won't tell him. I won't say nothing. I won't. Please don't tie me up. I won't ever interfere in my baby's life ever again. I've learned, Lucy. I've learned."

Jasper sees us and comes running. I hold the nape of her neck and remind her, "Not a word." No need to though, she's so beat from the heat and blindness she's practically comatose.

"Mama, what happened to you?" Jasper cries, grabbing her limp shoulders.

"She wandered off, lost her vision—both eyes. I told you she was ready for an old folks' home. I found her down by the draw." I let go of her and let him hug her up. She doesn't say anything, just cries. Jasper takes her inside and pours cool water in a pan to sponge her off. She falls asleep in her chair at the table.

Jasper carries her like a small, wounded child, lays her on the divan and comes over to me whispering, "Lucy, she's blind." He's all teary-eyed and wrinkled up on his brow. "She's blind."

I pull him toward me and kiss him fully on the mouth. The tears river his cheeks and he holds on to me. She doesn't say a word, but lies on the couch exactly like an old woman should—stiff, quiet. *The half bunch of flowers Jasper picked her will look just fine in the vase with mine. She can't see them anyway. I'm sure she won't mind now.*

I kiss him again soft and long. Even though his lips are dry and closed, his eyes are wet and soft.

"Don't worry, Jasper. Everything's going to be just fine," I say. "Everything's gonna be alright from now on. I'm always gonna be here with you, just like Sun and Moon. You hear me? Just like Sun and Moon."

Catherine Brady

✦

RAT

My grandmother comes sniffing into the kitchen, dragging the lump of herself on legs that look brittle and slender as sticks. Her jet-black hair is drawn back into a tight bun, though I know that when she takes her hair down at night it forms a long, oily, snaky string, with a kink at the end like a mean question mark.

I look up from my drawing to watch her. She stares at the kettle hissing on the stove. Her tiny black eyes, hard to see behind the glint of her glasses, narrow and sharpen like her nose as it reads what's in the air. She can learn through her skin, her nose always tells her when there's food out in the kitchen, her tiny eyes find the cookie tin, the whiskers on her chin shiver as they tell her that what's here is worth her greed.

She calls for my mother. "Molly," she says, "where's my tea?"

My mother comes in the back door with the empty laundry basket, the bag of clothespins hooked over the crook of her arm. My mother's softness is sleek all over; even the muscles that stand out on her arms as she grips the laundry basket have full, pleasing curves.

"I'm just putting the clothes on the line, Mommy," my mother says. "What is it you want?"

"My tea," my grandmother says. Her voice is tiny and helpless, like her hands against her swelling belly.

My mother scoots the laundry basket into the corner with her foot, wipes a loose, sweat-damp strand of hair back from her face. "It's coming," she says. "I've the kettle ready. It'll just be a minute."

My grandmother stands by the stove watching every gesture of my mother's as she puts together her tea. She looks as if she might moan. My grandmother eats all day long, breakfast of eggs and sausage, midmorning bowl of porridge, lunch, this tea, dinner, and another tea before bed. My father says she is eating him out of house and home. This is possible, I think, because she has been growing ever since she arrived from Ireland last year. My mother says she had to come to us in Chicago after my grandfather died because Auntie Audrey is here too, and Grandma's other children are scattered all over the *globe*. When my mother says globe, I see the world, a big glass Christmas ornament that you can shatter simply by pressing hard with your thumb.

My mother piles cookies out of a box kept specially for my grandmother and serves tea in a cup and saucer. My grandmother says it doesn't taste in a mug.

My grandmother follows the plate to the table and sits down beside me. I can smell pee on her, and I inch away.

"Would you have a bit of toast and jam, Molly?" Grandma says. "I've a powerful appetite, I'm in need of something substantial."

My mother, lifting a bag of potatoes from under the sink so she can wash and peel them for dinner, sighs and makes the toast for my grandmother.

"You won't eat your dinner," I say. That's what my mother says to us when we ask for food too close to dinner time.

My grandmother regards me with suspicion. "I've a good appetite, thank God," she says. "Even when my back is very bad, I can still eat."

My mother's face goes soft, the way it always does for one of us girls if we come to her with a skinned knee or hurt feelings. "Is your back bad again today?"

"Oh, you've no idea," Grandma says. "I can't turn my neck, it pinches so bad. It's terrible uncomfortable to sit."

But she sits all day before the TV, while my mother is at work. She is supposed to watch the five of us now that we're home from school for the summer, but all she does is eat and make us turn the channel to the station she wants.

I hold up my drawing for my mother, and she admires it.

"Mommy, will you look at that? She's talent, she has, like Alfie."

"Your brother could draw something wonderful. He'd draw your portrait and you'd swear at the likeness, you would."

"She takes after him. Kit's quick like him too. She didn't get that from me."

"Ah, well," my grandmother says. When she chews, her lips make moist, sucking noises against her gums. "You were a good girl, and that's the thing." My grandmother turns her narrow face toward me and fixes me with a stare. "I worked two shifts at the hotel, didn't I, supporting us all. On my feet till nine at night. And your mother'd have my tea for me when I came in the door."

My grandmother is always telling me what a good girl my mother was.

My mother hefts the pot of potatoes onto the stove. "I looked after my younger brothers and sisters. I bathed them and fed them and got the supper, didn't I, Mommy? I had to stand on a chair to reach the pots on the stove."

"It's Daddy," Grandma says. "Drinking away his earnings from the barber shop. I've no choice, y'see, but to leave you children."

"That's a long time ago now," my mother says. Sometimes she has to remind my grandmother what happened when. My mother says my grandmother has trouble with her blood, and sometimes it doesn't get to her brain the right way, and then she has her moments. My mother smiles at her now. "But you were good to us, Mommy. You gave us all an education. You made sure I'd the two years of secretarial college."

My grandmother lifts her legs to the side of her chair with her hands and slips her feet out of her slippers. Her ankles puff over her slender feet, with their corns hard as nails. "Molly, would you bring me a basin and some epsom salts? I've to soak my feet or they'll be the death of me."

My mother turns from hacking at a head of cabbage. "Could it wait a bit, Mommy? George'll be home any minute, and he wants his dinner when he walks in the door."

"I hate to be any trouble, but the pain is fierce."

"Kit," my mother says, "go and fetch the basin from the bathroom for me."

I unwrap my legs slowly from the legs of my chair. I cap my pen carefully.

Grandma leans across the table and raps me sharply on the arm. "Go now, like your mother said. You see your mother's killed making the dinner, don't you?"

Grandma doesn't care if I can hear her tattle as I leave the room.

"That one doesn't mind. I caught her climbing up the rain spout, trying to get up on the roof after a ball. She wouldn't come down when I told her, the saucy thing. She says her father lets her, bold as you please."

"Ah, she's only nine."

"He shouldn't be encouraging her."

When my father comes home, I will tell him I went up on the roof and he will say, "Pity you didn't fall and crack your skull. Would have knocked some sense into you." He is teaching me to ride my bike as if it's a circus horse, standing on one foot on the pedal and lifting the other leg out behind me and pointing my toes. My grandmother makes messes in her bed, and last week, lighting the pilot on the stove, she set a dishtowel on fire and I had to drop it in the sink to let it burn.

I sing to myself as I go to get the basin. Rat, rat, rat.

I am in our basement, puncturing empty tin cans and stringing them on an old jump rope. I knot the string so the cans will be spaced a foot apart. When I'm finished, I'll take this to the field across the street from our house. The four streets that make up our neighborhood have been cut out of the field in the shape of a rectangle, and our house on the corner is the last tiny box you can see before you enter the field. The farmer who sold the land for our houses no longer works the field, so it belongs to us kids. The field is as big as the sky, and its tall grasses in summer hum all day long in the wind. Once you are in it, in the grasses that are above your head, the field is forever, you can't see where you came in unless you've matted down the grass to make a path, and you cannot see to the end of it.

Somewhere in the heart of the field the bogeyman lives; the big boys on our street say they've seen him. They say they've been to the clearing, where he has built a hut of reeds, grass, and mud, left the scattered bones of the children he's caught. But my sisters and I never go far enough into the field to find the bogeyman. We stick to the edges, or go as far as the pond, where the cat-tail reeds grow, or walk the paths we've made. We have cat-tail reed wars with the boys, and the reeds' velvety brown, sausage-shaped tips shed their stuffing when you smack them hard and sharp on your enemy's back.

I have made a path of my own, careful not to tramp very much grass so that the path will be overlooked by the other kids. I have a nest there in the grasses, and in it I have a crate of supplies. I am saving up what I'll need: string, matches, a knife I've been sharpening on a stone, an old blanket from our basement, a can of tuna fish, a can of beans, a rusted church key that will be good enough for opening the cans when I need it. I am going to go there if I have to. I can live there, and I can always sneak back to the house to steal food when I run out.

I'll string up these cans around my nest to make a booby trap, so that when the bogeyman comes, I'll be warned. I am testing a knot when my father calls down to me from the top of the stairs. "Come out," he says. "We need you."

I don't want to interrupt my work, but he'll ground me if I don't do as he says. Out in our back yard my father has organized a Saturday game of kickball, the four older ones—Anna's too little to play—and him against the boys next door and the three Heibein kids. In Ireland where my father grew up, they don't have baseball and so he isn't good at it. But he played soccer, and he's good at that, so we have kickball. My father always spots the other team ten points.

Our team is up first. My father coaches Peggy as she waits for the pitcher to roll the ball toward her, and then after she kicks the ball, he runs along the baseline yelling encouragement. When she's tagged out, he thumps her on the head. "I told you, Fred, you've got to slide when you see the first baseman has the ball."

My father has nicknames for us—Fred, Billy, Shorty, and Peewee for Marybeth, who's the oldest and the tallest. But my name is already a boy's name—Kit like Kit Carson—so he only calls me Kit or K.T.

When it's my turn, I kick the ball hard and it flies over the hedge into the neighbor's yard, automatic home run, since the fielders have to go around my father's hedge. My father picks me up and whirls me in the air after I cross the plate. He reminds Peggy that it would be two runs scored if she'd hustled her fanny. And we all laugh, because he sounds so funny when he tries to talk American.

Because I've done well, my father lets me play first base when we take the field. When I tag out a runner, the runner steps on my toes, but I don't cry and I don't let go of the ball. Lynnie Heibein always cries when she gets hurt, but my father doesn't make her stand on the side the way he makes Peggy or me if we cry.

We are winning when my mother comes out with Anna and interrupts the game.

"I'm wondering could youse be quieter or play across the street for a bit while Mommy has her afternoon sleep," my mother says. "She's complaining of the noise."

We stay at our positions as my father dribbles the ball toward my mother. "Your mother's supposed to be at your sister's the weekend," he says.

"Well," my mother says. "Audrey'd a church picnic to go to this Sunday—"

"That was the agreement," my father says. The ball glides smoothly between his feet, as if it took commands. "We'd keep her during the week, and Audrey'd take her the weekend. How many times is it now she's been here the whole week?"

"She'll hear you," my mother says.

"I won't be told to keep quiet in my own yard," my father says.

"For an hour." My mother bends to Anna, who hangs onto her leg.

"She nearly burned my house down last week. And I'm working ten hours a day just to feed her. And she's got to have Guinness every night for her blood, and sausages for her breakfast. And you peeling her orange for her, for Chrissake."

"I'll make you sausages, if you like."

"You've no idea where money comes from, do you? You'll have us in the poorhouse with your sausages and bloody Carr's biscuits for her."

My mother sniffs back tears. "It's like I'm between a rock and a hard place."

My father looks at her as if she ought to understand she has it coming, the way we deserve a thump on the skull when we boot the ball. And if you cry, you have another thump coming.

Marybeth pulls at my father's hand. "Dad, I hear the Good Humor truck."

And then the rest of us hear it too, the tinkling bell that announces ice cream is on its way. All the kids converge on my father, pulling on his hands. "Please, please, please," we chant. Sometimes he will treat the lot of us.

My father grins, swipes at us with his hands. But he's grinning. So we ball up around him—even Anna lets go of my mother—and we pull at his arms, and with pretend reluctance he lets us drag him around to the front yard. The Good Humor truck moves slowly down the street, its bell chiming. It pulls to a stop before our house and the driver in his white uniform steps out of the truck and opens the little door to the refrigerated compartment in the back. Cool air billows out, visible as smoke. My father says we can have whatever we want, all of us, and while we study the pictures on the side of the truck, making up our minds, he takes his wallet from his pocket and fingers bills, his tongue between his teeth. I look at the cracked leather of his wallet and worry that there won't be enough dollar bills in there.

But he pulls out enough to satisfy the driver and orders an ice cream for Peggy after she says she doesn't want any. "Ah, come on," he says, "quit your sulking."

I don't want to go to the poorhouse. I wish my mother could understand about that. I wish we were rid of the rat.

Grandma is supposed to be watching us while my mother is at work. My sisters and I are out at the pond. We have a bucket with us, to take tadpoles home in. We like to watch them lose their tails and grow legs. Their tails shrink as the nubs of their legs grow, and when they finally become tiny frogs, there's still a v-shaped tip left at the base of their spines. But most of them die before they make it.

I wade into the water, dipping in a jelly jar so I can scoop up a gooey mass of frog eggs, so transparent you can see the eyes of the wormy pellets inside. The mud smeared on my legs feels smooth as cream. Because I'm busy searching, I don't hear the boys when they come. Usually I am our best scout.

Mitchell Blaisik and two other boys jump out of the grass, waving cattail reeds. They chase Marybeth and Peggy into the water, but they don't bother with Anna, because she's too little. Bridie has the bucket and she freezes. She is usually off-limits too, because she won't fight. But Mitchell forgets about Bridie and gives her a great thwack. She screams and drops the bucket, spilling tadpoles that squirm like tiny eyebrows in the soft mud on the pond's banks. I want to kick Bridie.

I go after Mitch, but he's ready for me. As he brings down the cat-tail reed on my arm, I grab it, snapping it in half. Then I land my fist in his stomach. He looks so surprised. We've never fought with our fists, only with the reeds that leave a lozenge-shaped welt on your arms and legs. He punches me back, in the face. Nobody's ever punched me in the face before, and it hurts, so much I can't get my breath. Now I'm surprised too. We stare at each other, and then he turns and runs, because you're not supposed to punch a girl. And we go home to tell on him.

Grandma looks up from the sofa when we come in, all talking at once. Everybody wants to be the one to tell her about Mitchell Blaisik punching me.

She frowns at me. "So it's you. Acting like a savage again."

I step back from her, thinking she'll slap me. But instead she starts to laugh. "You're the bold one, aren't you? I'll bet you gave as good as you got."

Bold means bad in Irish. She pulls me toward her. I can smell her smell, all the odors of the bathroom gone sour and mixed with sweat and sweet face powder.

"I was a bold one myself, you know. I ran off with Daddy. Climbed out my window and met him in the lane, and we ran off, we did. Eloped."

She keeps her grip on me, but she talks at the air. I think maybe she's having one of her moments. "I got myself a bicycle. My mother said we'd not the money for it, but I got one. The day of the Easter Uprising. They were fighting the black-and-tans, the bloody British, in the street. And everyone who could ran from the fighting. All over Dublin, they left their bicycles lying in the street. And I went out that night—I'd plenty of practice climbing out my window, you see—and I had my pick of the lot. I'd good use of that bicycle. I was a bold one, all right."

She could never have been bold. Not like me. Blood throbs in the bone below my eye. "I want steak," I say.

She stares at me funny.

"For my eye," I say. I've seen this cure on TV. Cold, raw meat pressed to the swelling bruise.

"But how am I to cook it? I'm not allowed to use the stove. Your father's mad at me over that dishtowel. He's going to send me packing if I don't behave."

I see that I will have to wait for my mother to come home from work.

I sit on the floor with my sisters to watch *As the World Turns*, and every now and then I get up and go to the mirror to see how my eye is doing. It blooms blue and green and purple. By the time my mother comes home, I'm feeling impressed by how it looks.

My mother puts a hand over her mouth when she sees me. She drops a grocery bag on the table and takes me by the shoulders and stares into my face. Her attention is so much like a question, one I can't avoid, and I would like to give her the answer she wants. But my face answers for me.

"Honey," she says, "honey."

Peggy comes to tell her how I got my black eye, and Bridie shows her the welt on her arm, but my mother doesn't seem to be listening. She roots around in the fridge and pulls out a bag of frozen peas. "Press this to your eye."

Grandma, slump, slump, slumping, comes around the corner into the kitchen.

"Mommy, what happened?" my mother says.

Grandma's eyes dart back and forth like little fish. "They'd gone off to play in that field, is all I know. They tell me she's been fighting with a boy."

"Mitchell Blaisik," Bridie says.

"Kit," my mother says. "You can't be fighting with boys. You'll end up getting the worst of it every time."

"I hit him first," I say.

"They could be hurt out there, and I'd never know. I'd never get to them," Grandma says. "God knows who might be out in that field, lay-ing for them."

My mother taps a finger against her mouth. "I'm hearing there are teenagers sneaking out there. Smoking."

"We've got to keep them home," Grandma says. "There's no know-ing what could happen to them."

"It'll be none too soon when the farmer sells off that field," my mother says. "I've seen the surveyors out there, marking off plots."

I have seen the stakes planted in the rich mud of the field, strips of plastic stapled to them like tiny tongues. But I did not know why those stakes were there.

My mother slaps the kettle on the burner for Grandma's tea and then hauls potatoes up from under the sink to start dinner. But then she stares at what she sees in the sink. "Mommy," she says softly.

My grandmother has fished cookies out of the grocery bag and torn open the package. But her hand pauses over the box at the sound of my mother's voice.

My mother lifts a nightgown of my grandmother's out of the sink. The foul odor of diarrhea comes up with it. The gown is wet, flecked with stains.

"I'd an accident," my grandmother says. "But I washed it out good, Molly."

My mother drops the gown back in the sink, braces her arms on the counter. "It's all right, Mommy. You sit down and I'll have your tea soon's I clean up here."

"Mom," I say. "We always go to the field."

"You're to keep out of there!" my mother says. "Just once do as I tell you."

I walk Grandma up and down our street. This is her constitutional. The doctor says she must have it. With every step, she claps her cane, another skinny leg, on the pavement with such force that I know she doesn't really need it. She doesn't need me either, but she grips my elbow. I wish she would let go.

"There's a man in the field," I say. "If we go too far in, he comes after us."

"He comes after you? What man is this? One of these teenagers? You're to show me. Show me this instant." My grandmother gives my arm a shake. "You were told not to go there anymore. You should be locked in the house, you should."

I lead my grandmother into the grasses, parting them for her. Her breath comes heavier now; she hunches over the cane after every step. I don't know if she can make it all the way. But I am going to lead her to the place I've made ready. I will leave her there. Maybe I will leave her there for a long time. She can use the blanket, she can eat the can of beans. I won't let her die.

"If this is some shenanigans of yours, you'll get the back of my hand," she warns.

"He's there," I promise. This, at least, might not be a lie. I think he's there. Curled in the heart of the field, hiding in the grasses that cloak us from the rest of the world when we play. I think the bogeyman watches us when we are at war out there, waiting for the chance to reach out with his clawed hands and take one of us. But he won't harm my grandmother, not her, with her own fierce tiny hands and her stealth that, in spite of her bulk, enables her to sneak 'round corners on us, give us a pinch for whispering in church before we know she's in striking range.

I mean to take her where I'll leave her, but instead I follow the path that leads deeper into the field. Where he lives. I have to bend back the grasses so Grandma can maneuver her swollen self through the narrow channel.

Last night my mother got up to fetch my grandmother and lead her back to bed. My father caught her. I heard them. You can always hear my father, even when he's trying to be quiet. I heard the snipped bits of their fight. *Getting up in the middle of the night after her—She doesn't know she's doing it, she's disoriented—Can't manage, look at you—Where? She's nowhere to go—She's got to go.* I thought I heard my mother crying, but sometimes I only dream that I do.

I have never come this far into the field, into the maze of narrow, crisscrossing paths. I think I might not find the way back. Ahead of us the grass begins to thin. Through the chinks of it, I can see light, bright as a coin, reflecting off metal. I crouch, I creep forward. My grandmother nudges my back with her knuckled cane. I make myself smaller as the shield of the grass thins. Finally we come out into the clearing: there's a broken washing machine, its guts scattered in the dirt, an old mattress, broken bottles.

My grandmother inches upright, then cuffs my ear. "There's nobody here."

The washing machine looks sad, like something lost. Cigarette butts litter the ground, so many they're pressed like tiny tiles into the earth. There's no hut. No pile of picked bones. He's not here. He doesn't live here.

I turn to face my grandmother, trying to think of some excuse. Her face has gone funny. Her mouth is open as if it's been twisted out of shape, her eyes look as if they have been thumbed by some giant hand.

I run all the way home, the snapping grasses stinging my face. My mother is at the house. When I see her, I'm ashamed of running. I never get scared of things.

She doesn't speak to me. She only takes my hand, and I understand I have to take her back to my grandmother.

By the time we reach the clearing, my mother has pushed ahead of me as if she knows just where we are going. Grandma sits there crying, her legs stuck out in front of her, her skirt hiked up over the onion bulbs of her knees. Her glasses have been knocked half off. With her glasses like that she does not look so much like a rat.

My mother kneels beside my grandmother and heaves her to her feet. She tells me to pick up my grandmother's cane. When I lean down to fit the cane into Grandma's curled hand, her hand, rigid, comes up and hits my jaw.

"She-got-me-out-here," she says, in a voice gone stiff and crooked like her face.

My lips lift from my teeth, a snarl to match hers.

My mother looks at me as if she wants to ask me for something. "She doesn't mean it," she says. "It's not her fault."

Sweating, she gets my grandmother's arm over her neck, where it settles like a fleshy collar.

I am free. This field is mine and now I know I won't even need the tin cans on a string to warn me if the bogeyman comes. I will be the only fierce creature here. But my mother keeps her eyes on me, asking. I see the slender, tagged stakes that mark off the field in measured rectangles. I see how much I have to lose. And how it can be taken from me, piece by piece.

My grandmother who used to steal bicycles raises a futile, curled fist and tries to knock her glasses back into place. I reach up and tuck the earpiece over her ear where it should be. I move close enough to her that I am within the reach of her sour smell and put my arm under hers. I help my mother.

Garnett Kilberg Cohen

$\blacklozenge$

WHERE YOU CAN'T
TOUCH BOTTOM

Crouched on the floor by her bedroom window, Libby watched the glow of her cigarette as she waited. A bead of amber radiated between the white cylinder and the growing band of ash—the only light in the room. She knew she didn't have to wait. She didn't have to go with them. She could go back to bed, pretend not to hear them when they appeared beneath her window. She didn't want to go with them. She was afraid.

Libby carefully rolled the ash against the window sill so it separated from the cigarette. A perfect unbroken band of gray and white flakes, still holding the shape of its former self.

"Libby, Libby," a hushed voice rose from below, then a chorus of whispers. "Lib-bee, Lib-bee, Lib-bee."

She crushed the stub out in the well of the sill. Yes. She had to go with them. She had no choice.

"Quiet, I'm coming," Libby called down. She gathered her tennis shoes and tossed them out the window so that they sailed above and beyond the attached garage roof.

"Catch," she called after them.

A seasoned night crawler, Libby slipped deftly over her windowsill onto the garage. The shingles felt gritty under her bare feet. Steadying herself, she walked sideways down the slope to the edge. She sank to her knees, then holding tight to the gutter, pushed away from the roof so that she swung a story above ground. Swinging from her clasped hands, she hesitated. Her hips felt as weighted as a heavy belt, her belly as stretched as Turkish Taffy. The summer before, this part—the dropping—had been no more difficult than climbing over the sill. But now that her breasts and hips had swollen in disproportion to her thin legs and arms, she felt awkward. Adjusting to an adult body, a body that seemed to belong to someone else, restricted the flexibility she had grown to expect. She dreaded the hard drop to earth, her tiny feet having to balance such a grown-up body.

"Let go, Libby, come on!" she recognized her best friend Maudie's voice.

Libby closed her eyes and released her fingers. She felt a rush in her belly, then the solid earth, the sting in her heels. She didn't care; at least she didn't topple. She became aware of the moist grass between her toes, and looked around, just enough moon to make out five or six forms. Someone handed her her shoes. She sat down to slip them on. The forms towered over her. As soon as her eyes adjusted, the moonlight would be sufficient for her to distinguish faces.

"Hurry," said Maudie. "Your parents' light is still on."

Libby tied quick sloppy bows and stood up.

"Come on," said a raspy male voice that Libby recognized as Casey McIntyre's. He ran across the street. They all followed, across the black asphalt, shining like a river in the moonlight. They ran around the corner, ducking under bushes, into the backyards of Elm Street, to the far back where they formed a running line along the borders of yards. The night air clung, cool and moist, to Libby's forearms. Except for an occasional whisper, only the rustle of cotton summer clothing could be heard as they ran. Libby felt the crotch of the one-piece bathing suit she wore beneath her clothes ride up her crack. She wished she could stop to pull it down. But a pause could be dangerous; someone might see them and call their parents before they reached their destination. They were going to the field far behind the high school to swim in the old water tower standing sentry at the edge of East Hubbard Woods.

When Libby thought of it, her underarms prickled in fear and adrenalin shot from the pit of her stomach like a geyser. The boys had made this excursion before, but not the girls.

"It's easy," Casey assured them the day before in Hubbard's Drug Store. "Nothing to it. We drop a rope in so if you get cramps or something, you can hang on until you feel better. Besides, someone will stay outside on the scaffolding in case anything goes wrong."

Libby had sipped her cherry phosphate and spun around on her foun-
tain stool.

"So, what if something does go wrong?" Susan demanded, hands on
her hips. By tacit agreement, she was the leader of the girls, the strongest
of them, the prettiest. "Is that somebody going to run all the way back to
downtown Hubbard and get an ambulance?"

"Nothing is gonna go that wrong," retorted Casey. "Besides the rest
of us will be right there."

"I don't know," said Susan, shaking her head softly so that the ropes
of her lustrous brown hair swung slightly.

Libby also didn't know, but she was too timid to speak up. Lately, their
regular weekend nocturnal jaunts seemed to grow progressively less cau-
tious. At first being outside without permission while the rest of the town
slept was enough. They simply roamed Hubbard, the small Illinois village
where they lived. When Libby grew up and moved away, people would
find her allusions to the village where she grew up curious, parochial. But
her portrayal was accurate. It really was a village. A town square with a
circle of park benches, a flagpole, and an old clock tower was protected
from time, as with obsidian glass, by a layer of shops, then by tall white
Victorian houses standing proper inside wrought-iron fences, and finally
by sprawling farmland that kept Hubbard safe from the city and
encroaching suburbs.

Walking through Hubbard late at night, a pack of adolescents, they
felt like the only survivors in an abandoned land, as if they had taken
possession. Libby liked the feeling of owning, of belonging, so much in
fact that sometimes it bothered her in the light of day to see so many
people freely roaming her town. But now, claiming the village wasn't
enough. They wanted more, particularly the boys. And the more they
took, the more Libby felt they were losing. She wasn't brave like Susan.
She couldn't openly protest—not that it would matter. She knew she
couldn't yet articulate what she felt, couldn't put it into words.

A few weeks before, Libby and four other girls had walked all the way
out to meet the boys at the old cemetery, the one with ancient grave
stones with quaint sayings that the elderly women of Hubbard used to
make grave rubbings. Some of the stones were so worn that the relief
letters appeared to be in the final stages of melting. All the stones, from
years of rain and wind, slanted backward like hairs combed in the wrong

direction. While waiting for the boys, the girls had tiptoed between the huge tombstones, reading the epigraphs to each other by the beam of a single flashlight. They made up stories about the people buried beneath their feet. Libby was filled with desire for things she would never feel, people she would never know, a desire that suggested there was too much to feel, too much she couldn't have. But when the boys arrived, the mood changed. They wanted to play "ghost," running from headstone to head-stone. The raucousness threatened to destroy the evening. But when the horizon glowed pink, the girls left the boys in order to be home before their parents awoke. They hitched a ride on a milk truck. Many years later, when Libby saw an etching of multi-armed Shiva, Hindu god of war and reproduction, she would recall the ride and imagine the truck, all the girls on the running boards, their pale arms waving against the sky. The etching would help her understand why she was forever reining in: how even as a woman, in control, she would sometimes delay understanding the layout of a city to preserve the mystery of place, and no matter how many times she made love with the same man she would return to the study of her hand in his, would trace his veins with her index finger. It was a way to prevent the power of sexual intimacy from betraying the wonder of first touch. She would remember the water tower. But that night as she ran, Libby could only feel dread at the thought of what awaited her, fear of being sealed off inside the enormous drum.

Breathless from running, she was relieved when they reached the field. The houses were behind them and they could walk. She was almost happy until she saw the tower in the distance. Silhouetted against the sky, it rose above the woods on soaring stilt-like legs. On top sat a gigan-tic ball covered by a peaked roof. It looked like a big-bellied monster wearing a Chinese coolie's hat. Libby remembered trolls and giants from childhood reading. Was she really going to climb inside voluntarily? Libby looked at the others. In the open field, the moonlight bathed their features. Libby could make out faces: Casey, Randy Foster, Sam Woods, and—Lucy sighed—Dusty Walker.

"Are we the only girls?" Libby whispered to Maudie.

Maudie shrugged. "Everyone else chickened out." Libby took a deep breath. She knew the opposite was true. The others had been brave enough to say no. But she couldn't say this to Maudie. Now that they were in, Libby knew she would have to play it the other way, that they were adventurers. But even though Maudie was her best friend, she wished that if she had to be one of the only two girls, that Susan was the other girl.

The boys were talking among themselves, laughing and boasting of their feats the last time they'd gone swimming in the tower. How Casey had saved Sam by grabbing his hair when he swallowed a mouthful of filthy water. How Dusty had almost scaled a wall—would have, in fact, if he hadn't been cut by a jutting scrap of metal. How Randy had treaded in place, his hands above his head, singing six rounds of "Yellow Submarine."

Randy flipped on the portable radio he always carried. A static-ridden "Johnny B. Goode" blared; the boys whipped out their invisible guitars. Most guys her age were never without their air guitars. Casey squatted, closed his eyes, and threw his head back, never losing his grip on the instrument. Everyone laughed. Randy joined Casey in the exaggerated pose, extending his feet out in front of his body in quick jerks so that his knees followed and his belly became a table on which to strum the guitar. They all laughed harder. For a moment Libby forgot the purpose of their mission. She closed her eyes in laughter. The night air hugged her, permeating her clothing, thick and tangible like cool smoke rising, billowing, enclosing her. She was caught in laughter and freedom and the smell of summer grass. Then she opened her eyes. Dusty was looking at her, his eyes slits. She shuddered and tugged Maudie's sleeve.

"Come on," she whispered. "We better go ahead to undress."

"See you guys at the water tower!" Maudie said, her voice too cheerful, too solicitous, as if she was afraid the boys might not follow.

Had she known she and Maudie would be alone in a group of boys that included Dusty, Libby would have been able to say no without qualms. In the spring she had thought he was her friend. Even though he was going with Susan, the prettiest girl, Dusty seemed to like to talk to Libby. Sometimes they walked home from school together. She thought he told her things that he never told anyone else. Yes, she was sure, they were friends. So she had taken him to her favorite place, a vast but private stretch of land behind the oldest barn outside Hubbard, the one with the little steeple and the date, "1834," stenciled on the roof.

They had walked against the sun. Libby loved the heat spreading across her cheeks, the long yellow grass brushing her bare legs. She felt wonderful, clean and happy. So when Dusty turned to her and said "Can I ask you something?" she had thought it could only be something wonderful. She said "yes" quickly. He looked her in the face. Libby was surprised by the glassy look in his eyes. His face was red and grimy from the heat, his lips almost swollen, and a single drop of sweat cut a path down his brow. She was about to ask if something were wrong when he spoke. "Can I touch your breasts?" Even at fifteen, with no experience besides a hurried kiss behind the bleachers, she was stunned that he could pose such a question without thinking to kiss her first, to touch her hair. She knew she was weak enough that she would have surrendered had the request followed a moment of physical tenderness. But he had framed it so she would have had to have been worse than weak to comply. So she said "no," feeling hurt, yet also pleased by the calm in her voice, "I don't think that would be a good idea." Though her knees were wobbly, she managed to resume the conversation right where they left off.

It was one of those rare moments that Libby felt she had handled well. But when she came to school the next day, Libby realized that her reasonable reply had been exactly the wrong thing. Dusty spent the entire day making fun of her. Obviously his strategy was to prevent her from revealing his weakness by discrediting her first. She hadn't planned to tell anyone, but now she knew she couldn't; the truth was trapped inside her; no one would believe her and even if they did, she would be humiliated. When Dusty became particularly nasty, Susan had pulled Libby aside, against the lockers, and apologized: "I don't know what's gotten into him today; sometimes he just needs to pick on someone. It's nothing personal. I know he likes you." For the first time, Libby had known the true nature of a secret, the pain of needing to tell.

What she could not know either that day as they stood by the rows of straight military gray lockers or now—as she and Maudie left the boys behind to walk ahead to the water tower—was that her favorite field was not permanently ruined for her. Because in a year, when she became sixteen, a boy she loved would take Libby, in a special flowered sundress she had borrowed from Maudie, to that very field. The purple clover would be the thickest she would ever see it, so frothy that it looked like the flowers were bubbling over. Together they would lie down, the fragrance of clover and rich New Hampshire earth so overwhelming that they would almost become dizzy from the smell, the steady hum of insects, the buzz of bees. As dusk descended, they would make first love, their bodies adjusting to one another, allowing them to unravel again and again, flattening the matted weeds, reshaping the earth. When finally they rose, they saw that the borrowed dress was ruined, stained with grass and blood.

"Don't worry," the boy said, for he was a farm boy, different from village kids. "It'll come out. I'll give you a solution we use." Then, wrapping his shirt around her waist, bending to knot it in the front, he would add, "for now, take this." Together they walked up the slope, around to the front of the barn, across the gravel road to his car, an old Chevy with fins. He opened the door for her and kissed each of her fingers before she climbed inside, a sweet gesture because it was both contrived and natural. After he turned on the radio, they sat and listened, the boy holding her tight to his side. When "Love Me Do" came on, the boy took out an invisible harmonica and she asked, "What happened to your guitar?" Without acting like it was an unusual question, the boy said, "I prefer a harmonica to a guitar. It takes more care. Did you know you have to keep it by your bed in a glass of water overnight to keep the reeds moist?" She loved the way he said guitar, "gee-tar," so different from the village boys. And she found the information about harmonica reeds the greatest wisdom ever imparted. She would be the happiest she had ever been as she watched his dancing fingers slide the invisible instrument against his lips.

But since Libby could know none of this on her way to the water tower, she simply said, "God, I can't stand Dusty Walker."

"Oh, I think he's kinda cute," said Maudie. "You just don't like him cause of that one time, you know, that day by the lockers last spring."

"Maybe," said Libby. She considered telling Maudie, then decided against it. Though she was Libby's best friend, Maudie wasn't great with secrets.

They were almost to the closest leg of the tower. "Do you want to smoke a cigarette before we change?"

"Sure," said Maudie, pulling a crushed pack from her hip pocket, and handing Libby a flattened cigarette.

They leaned against the enormous steel leg of the tower, quietly smoking. Holding the cigarette between her ring and middle fingers, Libby gently waved her hand. The burning tip became a supernatural jeweled ring that shed trails—brilliant amber streamers—when it moved.

She was transfixed for only a moment before shifting to her haunches to take a long drag. As the smoke filled her lungs, she was imbued with a strange mixture of longing and dread. She knew it was foolish to swim inside the tower. She knew but couldn't turn back. Libby looked up and saw the dim shape of the boys coming toward them. They had finished cavorting and were ready for the tower. Libby crushed her butt out in the dirt.

"Let's step into the woods to change," she said.

"Uh-huh," said Maudie, as she flicked the stub of her cigarette in an arc across the night sky. Casey McIntyre clapped hollowly at the brief light show. The ember sizzled and blinked in the grass before dying.

In the woods, the girls lifted their blouses over their heads.

"Hey Maudie, hurry it up!" called Casey.

"I think he likes you," whispered Libby.

"Me too," said Maudie and they both giggled.

When they stripped, Libby was surprised that Maudie wasn't wearing her suit under her clothing. Instead she wore just bra and panties. In Hubbard's Drug Store, Casey had tried to convince them that underwear was as good as a swimsuit. Obviously he had succeeded with Maudie. To Libby, it felt odd to be standing in a suit at night on a matted forest bed of old leaves and broken twigs. She wondered if Maudie felt uncomfortable now that it was actually time to leave the woods. But as with so many of the things she couldn't know that night, she couldn't know that in just a few years she and Maudie would no longer be friends. And Maudie, who had always squatted inches above toilet seats to avoid germs, would have slept with close to fifty boys. Libby would be one of the only ones in their crowd who hadn't, as the parents said, "gone bad," drinking, drugs, or worse. But that night, as Libby and Maudie emerged from the woods, Dusty said, out of the corner of his mouth, "figures she's wearing a suit, and a one-piece at that." Libby pretended not to hear him. At least she didn't have to fold her arms across her breasts the way Maudie did. Besides, the boys looked less threatening in their underpants than she would have guessed. Gleaming in the moon-light, their legs looked long and chalky, like the stick legs of awkward young colts. Libby glanced away.

"Well?" asked Casey. He shot his cigarette in the air—a sparkling arc—as Maudie had just moments before, and gestured to Maudie, a footman's exaggerated bow, for her to begin her ascent. Such gallantry seemed silly coming from a boy wearing nothing but short white briefs. It didn't matter. Maudie was clearly charmed. She started up the ladder, Casey right beneath her. Once they were six feet off the ground, Casey looked back over his shoulder, the right side of his face illuminated by the moon, his eye crystal, yet as blue-white as his cheek. "So?" he said. "What are you guys waiting for?"

Like gold fish drawn to a single crumb, the group converged at the ladder's base, Dusty and Libby at precisely the same moment, his arm brushing hers as he grasped the side railing. She shivered.

"Oh, excuse me, you go ahead," she said, glancing away.

"No, I wouldn't dream of it," he said sarcastically. She felt his warm breath on her hair, her pounding heart. She stepped in front of him onto the first rung. Libby was startled to see how straight the ladder was, perfectly vertical. She had to turn slightly sideways to climb in order to allow room for her knees not to scrap the rungs. Dusty followed her. She felt uneasy with him immediately beneath her, almost touching, his arms encircling her calves. But what could she do? Besides, it was better than having no one to cushion the fall. She looked up at the ladder rising above her in a straight line and felt dizzy. She paused. She wanted to back down. But she knew the line of boys beneath her wouldn't descend to make way for her.

"Don't stop," commanded Dusty, and then, in a gentler voice. "And don't look up or down."

He was right. If she stared straight ahead, the rush in her belly subsided. She climbed until she felt Maudie reaching down to help pull her up the rest of the way.

The group crowded onto the scaffolding hugging the tank. While Casey gave instructions, the rest stood at attention, a solemn ceremony. Afterwards, Casey removed the door to the tank, causing a great scraping noise that sent shivers down Libby's spine. Randy tied a rope end around the railing and tossed the tail into the dark hole. A plopping noise soon followed.

"It's really full tonight," he said.

"Uh-huh," agreed Casey. "They must have just filled it."

"Who first?" asked Maudie.

"I'll go," said Randy. He shifted his long exposed legs onto the ledge, squatted, then dove, making a wonderfully hollow splashing noise.

"I'll be the first lookout," said Sam.

"Maudie, you and Libby go next," said Casey.

Maudie climbed up, then pushed away, holding her knees, cannon-ball-style. Libby took her spot on the ledge and looked down. Except for a circle of rippling moonlight on the dark water, the interior was pitch-black.

"You guys outta the way?" she shouted into the hole.

"Yeah, come on," Maudie called back, her words echoing.

"Is it better to dive or jump?" asked Libby, knowing she couldn't stall forever.

"It doesn't matter," said Randy, another echo from the darkness. "It's really deep. You couldn't touch bottom if you wanted to."

Without thinking, Libby pushed forward with her feet. Her stomach soared. Diving was like plunging into a void. Hitting water was a surprise, yet her outstretched arms opened quickly, automatically, dividing the liquid, drawing her deeper. She kicked to propel herself to the surface. Her right arm swept against a floating object—a flake of rust, she imagined, drifting aimlessly like an industrial lily pad. Never had she felt so suspended. Except for the single shaft of light illuminating the dangling rope, she was in utter blackness. Her feet could not touch bottom and there were no railings or edges to cling to, only huge curving walls. Holding her hand an inch from her face, she could not see it. A big splash was followed by another burst, then another, then nothing but the rippling sounds of the other swimmers, their reverberating voices.

"This is so weird," said Maudie. "I can't see a thing; the air blends right into the water—you can't tell where one ends."

"Hey," said Randy. "Who wants to play blindman's bluff?"

"I'm it," shouted Dusty. "No one's allowed to go into the light."

"Roll call first," said Casey. Everyone called their names.

"Okay," said Randy. "Go!"

"Blindman's!" cried Dusty.

What sounded like a dozen "bluffs" answered, resounding off the curved walls. Everyone dispersed, sending a series of waves, purling out, slapping the walls. Libby swam as hard as she could against the tide, but she seemed not to move at all. When she finally felt safe enough to pause, she was weak. If only she had some support for a moment, anything to clutch.

"I got you; I got someone," said Dusty.

"My ankle," said Maudie.

"You're it."

"Blindman's!"

"Bluff!" shouted the others. Again, it was difficult to tell where the voices originated. Libby saw her fingers flash momentarily in the light, like touching fire, then swam in the opposite direction, toward the blackness, an odd sensation, like swimming in India ink, solid pigment, from nothing, to nothing.

The water surged in all different directions like a pot being stirred. Libby was tossed one way, then another.

"I can't get anyone," sighed Maudie. "I'm confused."

"Over here, I'm to your left," said Casey.

"Libby, where are you?" asked Maudie.

Libby opened her mouth to answer, but no words came out. She found she was weaker, her arms and legs drained. She attempted to move in the direction of Maudie's voice, but her limbs were powerless, empty. She was afraid to speak, couldn't speak, as if it would exhaust her breath, take the last of it. She wiggled her feet, but her legs wouldn't follow. No matter how hard she tried to reach Maudie, she remained almost stationary, unable to close any space. She realized her error; with what little strength she had she should have tried to reach the rope instead of Maudie. Now she didn't have the energy for either. Regardless of how hard she tried to kick, her legs sank. The water seemed as thick as mud, like it was sucking her under.

"Libby?" Maudie called again, panic rising in her voice.

"We better do a roll call," said Casey. Libby could hear the water lapping softly as everyone treaded in place, responding to their names, everyone except Libby. She couldn't afford the breath. There was no way to signal; words would not come.

"Oh God, where's Libby?" asked Maudie, near hysteria. "Lib-bee, Lib-bee, answer, right this minute, Lib-beeee."

"What's the matter down there?" called Sam. Libby could see the silhouette of his head and shoulders against the night sky.

"We can't find Libb," said Randy, his voice weak.

Their voices faded. Libby was completely vertical now, her body trailing from her head like weighted ribbon, her feet barely swaying, her head thrown back, face turned upward, a small island above the surface. She knew if she called out she would forfeit the last of her strength and drown; if, instead, she saved her breath, she couldn't be found and rescued. There was nothing to do.

"Libbbeee, Libbbeee," Maudie was shouting.

The others joined in, a chorus singing her name: strung together over and over, it sounded like a strange word.

Libby's feet dangled like dumbbells. She hadn't known she could be so removed from her body while so controlled by it. Water trickled into her mouth, then rushed down her throat. Her head sank and was swallowed. She gurgled and followed the pull of her feet.

Something—a hand—touched her arm, then grabbed it.

"I've got her!" called Casey. "Quick! Over here!"

In a flurry of splashes, it seemed like a million hands were on her— the hands of her past, her present, and her future. She was an infant sleeping in a dresser drawer at the end of her parents' bed, a girl sipping a soda in Hubbard's Drug Store, a girl-woman making love with the farm boy, a woman leaving home for college, making decisions, going places, a woman marrying, bearing children, divorcing, finding fresh love, mature love, all without ever touching bottom. She knew she could hold on while letting go. Though it would never happen again, it was all right— for all the moments of her life came together in that one moment, in a single swirling second, when mystery and wonder were no longer outgrowths of fear and weakness, but entities she could own, even while surrendering herself to the churning water and the multitude of hands.

Michael Beres

◆

CALENDARS
AND CLOCKS

Denny, whom I hadn't seen in almost thirty years, arrived at my house in a mint-condition 1959 Chevy convertible. His return to Illinois on that first day of spring was not a total surprise. Two nights earlier his wife Polly had called from Boston and told me about the trip back to the old home-town, and about the reason for it.

"He's dying, Mike."

"Dying?"

"Yes. Two months ago he had surgery for a brain tumor. It was malig-nant. The radiation treatments slowed it down but it's spread into other organs."

"I'm sorry, Polly."

"I know you are."

"Why is he coming here?"

"He wants to recapture his high school days. He wants to imagine he's starting over again."

Polly and I had gone steady for a year before she began dating Denny. When the inevitable triangle faded, Polly belonged to Denny.

That was before my wife Eve, before our daughter Jill, before Jill grew up and went to college. Polly's call that night to tell me Denny was on his way to see me made the intervening three decades seem like a board game running out of steam.

"Why aren't you coming with him, Polly?"

"He wants to do it alone. He says when he returns to Boston we'll start over again because he'll be cured."

"Is he seeing a specialist in Chicago?"

"No."

"How will he be cured?"

"He won't, Mike. The operation did something. He's not—he's not exactly the same person he was. He used to be so quiet, now he's outspoken, says whatever comes into his mind, a lot of it about work at the lab before his disability, a lot of it about when we were kids."

"Why did he pick you to visit?" asked Eve after Polly's call. "He had other friends in high school."

"Because I'm the only one who stuck around here and Polly says he wants to come home."

Eve comforted me that night after the call, said she didn't envy my position, seeing an old friend after all those years and knowing he's dying. The next night Eve cleaned the guest room and, before leaving for work the morning of the first day of spring, said I should insist that Denny stay with us.

I was in the front yard trimming dead branches from the budding forsythia bushes along the drive when Denny arrived. The top was down on the Chevy even though it was cloudy and in the fifties. Denny wore a Red Sox baseball cap and jacket. Instead of immediately shutting off the engine, he gunned it a few times and grinned at me while the Chevy roared through its chrome side pipes. The Chevy was an exact replica of the one he bought after high school—black, red interior, fender skirts. He gunned the engine once more before I got to the car.

Denny was heavier than I expected, his face puffy, perhaps from chemotherapy. When he got out of the car, we shook hands, then hugged. Touched, his flesh seemed to ooze aside beneath his skin, allowing me to feel the bony kid I once knew. On the way into the house he walked slowly, occasionally reaching out and touching my arm for balance. Once inside the house, when he took the baseball cap off, I could see his grey crewcut and, while he stared at me and I stared at him, the calendars and clocks chalked up the thirty years since high school and we were suddenly two sad men in our late forties.

Denny brushed his crewcut with his palm. "The haircut wasn't my idea, Mike. Last year it fell out from chemo. This year they had to shave it for the operation and this is as far as it's grown back." He turned around, pointed out a longitudinal scar above his hairline. The scar had stitch-mark legs and held very still, hiding in its mist of thin grey hair.

We drank beer at the kitchen table that afternoon and talked.

About his wife Polly, he said, "I've done the basic scientific research and concluded she hasn't changed much, not even since you and she were making your way around and around one another."

About my wife Eve, he said, "Eve of Adam and Eve. The forbidden fruit is what she wanted and what she got. Well-rounded fruit, forbidden pleasures. Skin to skin in those days."

About my daughter Jill, he said, "I bet she's pretty. A nucleus with boys running round and round her. Guess she's lucky being born into this nuclear age with all this nuclear medicine."

About the state of affairs in the world, he said, "These nuclear power plants of ours are getting so old I'm beginning to wonder if the end of the cold war and all those missiles left erect after Moscow went to bed with Washington is as big a problem as they make it out to be."

About his job, he said, "It's all gone. Nothing left upstairs to give to science because the surgeon's knife took it. No more research for this birdbrain because they took out a hunk the size of a sparrow. But I should consider myself lucky."

"Why?"

He pointed to his scar. "Because there was a chance they could have blinded me. They had to get around the occipital lobe to get at the tumor. I might not have been able to make this trip."

"Why did you make the trip, Denny?"

"Because I wanted to go cruising in the old hometown. The Chevy cost five figures. Guy I bought it from didn't want to part with it until I gave him a price he couldn't refuse. I want to cruise the town in a car just like my old car. I want to get some answers."

"To what?"

Denny looked out the kitchen window where the sun had come out from behind clouds and the maple tree in the yard was bright with buds. He touched his scar with an open hand, a feminine gesture as if cupping upswept curls. "I want to find out if there's a way to turn back the atomic clock and undo what caused my dick to go limp."

✧

Denny was too tired to go out cruising that night. He was quiet at dinner, staring at Eve occasionally, but saying nothing strange or upsetting. When Denny retired early, saying he needed to rest because of the long drive, I called my boss at home, explained the situation, told him I'd be out the next day, but mentioned neither the blue glow I imagined seeing beneath the door to the guest room nor the absurd thoughts of critical mass and explosion.

After breakfast the next morning, we cruised. Denny wore his Red Sox cap and I wore an old White Sox cap I'd found in the basement. We drove all over town, which wasn't much driving because in an hour we were repeating streets as well as stories.

After lunch at the A & W drive-in, Denny drove to the high school. He parked in the student lot. Through a row of classroom windows, we could see the bent heads of students taking an exam.

"I wonder which of those heads has a time bomb ticking inside it," said Denny. "I wonder which one's already gotten the dose that'll make the whole goddamn panel of docs agree, when he's in his forties, that he'll never make it to fifty. I wonder which swinging dick in there is out to get himself a widow."

When I didn't comment, Denny drove around to the shop entrance where a dozen boys gawked at the Chevy. One boy gave us the victory sign when Denny gunned the engine. Then we took off on the road along the football and track field where grass was just beginning to green up from winter.

Denny did a couple of runs on the unofficial quarter-mile dragstrip—still marked with paint and layered with rubber like in the old days. The strip was on a dead end section of the interstate frontage road. Back on the main road, Denny got on the interstate and headed south.

"Where are we going?" I shouted to be heard over the rush of wind and the roar of side pipes.

"Seneca!" shouted Denny.

"The nuclear plant?"

"Yeah! Remember when we were in science club and went on a tour?"

"I remember!"

"I'd like to see the place again!"

The guard at the gate said there were no tours that day. But Denny insisted, saying we were scientists from out east. After a phone call, the guard told us another guard would meet us at the visitors' center.

The guard at the visitors' center took our names. Denny had the guard prefix his with "Dr." while he winked at me. We were told to wait and sat in flimsy orange plastic chairs in a room with a chalkboard in front. The furniture and tile floor were old and worn and I imagined thousands of visitors being told, over the years, how wonderful and beneficial and safe nuclear power was and how its critics were simpletons who wanted to freeze in the dark.

"You didn't tell me you'd gone on for your doctorate, Denny."

"I don't have a doctorate," he said.

"That's what I thought. Last night I remember you mentioning Seneca, something about it being the cause of all your problems."

"Did I say that?"

"Yes. Is it true?"

Before Denny could answer, a man dressed in a cheap suit came in and told us we'd have to come back the following week if we wanted a tour. The man was our age but the photograph on his badge looked like it was taken in high school. He smiled and apologized, saying we could look around at the displays and photographs in the visitors' center and that he'd be happy to explain any of them. Then, without warning, Denny began shouting.

"If you've got time to tell us all this crap, why not take us around? I'll tell you why! Because you're hiding something! Exactly the way you hid the facts thirty years ago when you irradiated me and gave me cancer!"

Denny raised his fist and backed the man in the cheap suit up to the door he'd come through. "I wonder how many other poor bastards you've already killed! Innocent science club nerds coming here to see your goddamn atoms for peace! Wise-asses thinking you're Fermi or Einstein! Taking chances and nothing stopping you unless it stops you dead instead of some poor sap kid who might just as well have stayed home and brought in a note from Mom the next day saying he was sick instead of being here at the fucking wrong place at the fucking wrong time!"

Two guards escorted him to the car. I followed, trying to explain to the man in the cheap suit how the cancer had affected Denny, but the man did not acknowledge me. He simply gave instructions to the guards, words spoken softly but firmly like bones beneath weakened flesh, words of caution and safety and guardianship repeated over and over as if on a loop of tape.

Once we were at the car Denny was quiet. I tried to get in the driver's seat but Denny slid over and glared at me.

The guards followed us to the gate in a van. Once outside the gate Denny stopped and got out of the car. I thought there would be more trouble. Within the fence the two guards were out of their van watching Denny. But all Denny did was turn toward the containment dome and stare at it. Then, after a few seconds, he clasped the back of his head with both hands and wept, the tears on his cheeks aglow in the bright afternoon sun.

Back in town we went to the Iroquois bar on Main Street. The bar was dark, the only other patrons two men in their sixties watching a television game show. We sat at a corner table and, after beginning the first of several beers, Denny told me his Seneca theory.

"They had a release there while we were touring the place, Mike."

"How do you know?"

"I was doing some work at Brookhaven a few years ago and an old-timer from the Atomic Energy Commission said a lot of accidents occurred at power plants in the early sixties and were kept quiet. He mentioned Seneca as one of the plants. He said at Seneca it happened in nineteen sixty-three on the March equinox. The first day of spring, Mike. The first day of spring in our sophomore year. Does that date ring a bell?"

"Was that when we toured Seneca with the science club?"

"Now you've got it."

"But Denny, it couldn't have been much of a release. Someone would have found out, or more of us would have been affected. Hell, the wind would have carried it all over the place."

Denny smiled and shook his head. "No, Mike. It wasn't in the air. It was a surface spill. It was on the floor and we walked through it. We got it on the bottoms of our shoes. And then, when they gave us lunch in the cafeteria—"

"I don't remember any cafeteria."

Denny looked quite angry then. "There was a cafeteria, Mike! They fed us lousy little sandwiches in clear plastic. I had ham and swiss. The ham and swiss that proved to be my undoing, because I was foolish enough to drop half the sandwich on the floor, then pick it up and eat it. Ham and swiss. Imagine it. Ham and swiss with gamma emitter on rye. A gamma emitter that got into my bloodstream and lodged in my brain and irradiated me from the inside for thirty years so I'd come back to the old hometown and visit the Iroquois bar and drink to my demise."

I ordered another round, waited for Denny to calm down a little, then asked if he had really heard about an accident at Seneca.

"Why are you questioning me, Mike?"

"Because if it's true you should sue the pants off the utility company. Bring it out in the open in case anyone else might have been affected."

But Denny said nothing more about an accident at Seneca and I wondered if the episode had been nothing more than an elaborate game to help him cope with the unfairness of being forty-seven and dying.

Just before our final beer, Denny asked if I would try to comfort Polly after he was gone.

"Come on, Denny. Don't talk like that."

"I mean it, Mike. Tell me you'll comfort her."

"I'll do whatever I can."

"You knew her, Mike. You went out with her before I did. If I hadn't come along you might even have married her." Denny grabbed my wrist and squeezed it. "Take her, Mike."

"What?"

"When I die you can have her."

"Jesus, Denny. This is crazy!"

"It would be a comfort to her."

I tried to pull away but Denny held my arm with both hands.

"Mike! Mike, you don't understand. I'm dying. My time is nothing. My life is nothing. Polly'll need help, at least during those first few weeks."

The game show had ended on television and the two men at the bar glanced toward us. Denny saw them and we continued more quietly.

"Look," I said. "I know this must be very hard for you."

"You can't know."

"Okay, I don't know. But what you're saying now won't even make sense to you later when you've had time to think about it."

"I've already had plenty of time to think, Mike. In fact thinking is all I do. I know Polly. She'll need help."

"But you're talking about something I can't give her."

"Why not?"

"Look, Denny, you know Eve and I are happily married."

"Yes. You must love her very much."

"I do. That's why this conversation is insane."

At dinner that night, during a lull in a conversation Eve and I had tried to steer toward things light and cheerful and boring, Denny turned toward Eve and said, "Your husband loves you very much. I just thought you should know."

Denny died four months later near the end of summer. I knew when to expect it because Polly had written several times, keeping me informed of the final stages. The night Denny died Polly called me and I booked a flight.

Because both sets of parents were still alive, and because there were a lot of siblings, the funeral was quite crowded. I spoke briefly with Polly at the wake and at the funeral, giving my condolences and assuring her that the spring trip back home had been a pleasant experience for Denny.

At the wake and the funeral Polly wore a black loose-fitting dress. Because I didn't know the other relatives and friends, I had a lot of time to think and recall the year or so Polly and I dated. And I had a lot of time to watch her.

There were certain familiar movements—the way she turned her head when another mourner arrived, the way she shifted her weight from one leg to the other when she grew impatient with someone who had gone on too long about how peaceful Denny looked. These were movements from our youth, movements that caused me not only to recall the past, but to fantasize.

Polly was a bit heavier than the girl I knew, but I could tell, by the cling of the dress here and there, that she had maintained her figure quite well through the years. Once, when she bent to retrieve a tissue she had dropped, I saw the dimpled backs of her knees and remembered a long day at the Indiana Dunes. It was a day that ended in a remote part of the dunes on a blanket beneath the stars.

"It was thoughtful of you to come all this way, Mike."

"It was the least I could do."

We were at the cemetery. It was a sunny, warm day. Beyond the crowd of mourners, birds in the trees in an older part of the cemetery chirped excitedly for us to scatter and get on with our lives. Polly's hands, both of them in mine, were soft and small, unchanged. Holding her hands made other things about her also seem the same. Her eyes still reminded me of a green-eyed swimmer just surfaced. Her lips were still full like a woman's lips on a little girl. Her neck was still slender and graceful as she looked up with tears beginning to form. We embraced in mourning, and there, in front of Denny's coffin suspended above the hole, I was aware of the press of Polly's breasts and hips and thighs against me as they had been that night at the Indiana Dunes.

We said goodbye after the funeral meal at her house. We did not embrace but she kissed me lightly on the cheek.

When I called Eve from the hotel that evening she told me she had gotten a letter from Denny.

"From Denny?"

"Yes. He explains in the letter that he gave it to an orderly he'd made friends with at the hospital. The orderly was to mail it the day he died and the letter just arrived here today."

"What does it say?"

"It says that you love me very much."

"I do love you."

"It also says he asked you to comfort Polly while you're there. It says that I should know what that means and that I should be sympathetic."

"My God!"

"That's what I said when I read it."

"I didn't tell you, Eve, but he asked me the same thing when he was at our place in the spring."

"What did you tell him?"

"I told him I couldn't do what he was asking. I told him I loved you."

"And he repeated it that night at dinner."

"Yes."

"Your flight arrives at noon tomorrow?"

"Yes."

"Call me when you get in."

"I will, Eve."

Later that night, shortly after I got into bed, the phone rang. It was Polly calling from the hotel lobby. I told her to come up.

She was still wearing the black dress. Her makeup was smeared and her eyes were red. She took a letter from her purse and handed it to me.

"A nurse who got to know Denny at the hospital gave it to me at the funeral," said Polly, wiping her eyes. "I didn't open it until tonight with the other cards."

The letter was from Denny. In it Denny said that he loved Polly and that he was doing this for her. He said his trip home helped him very much in dealing with his grief and that a nostalgic trip, coupled with the comfort an old friend can give, would be the best thing for her. He said she should seek me out on the night of the funeral and that both Eve and I knew all about it.

I sat on the bed. Polly sat in a chair across from me. We sat for a long time. Polly wept and talked about Denny. At exactly midnight the phone rang.

"Yes?"

"Mike, it's me."

"Eve. Is everything okay?"

"Everything's fine here. Is Polly there? No, don't answer. I shouldn't put you in that kind of spot. I know she's there."

"You do?"

"Yes. There's another part of the letter I didn't tell you about. He said not to tell you and he was so convincing."

"What is it, Eve?"

"Let me speak with Polly."

I handed the phone to Polly and went into the bathroom for a glass of water. I left the door open. The half of the conversation I heard went like this:

"Yes."

"Thank you."

"Thank you for thinking of me."

"I showed it to him."

"No. Nothing."

"It's not right, Eve."

"I don't know. I suppose it might help, but this is crazy."

"Goodnight, Eve."

When I came out of the bathroom, Polly sat staring at me.

"What did Eve say?"

"She said she'll pick you up at the airport tomorrow and that you needn't take a cab."

The following spring, after Eve and I returned from delivering Jill and a U-Haul trailer full of "necessities" back to the university, I had a series of phone conversations with the attorney Polly had hired for her lawsuit against the utility operating the Seneca Nuclear Power Plant. The conversations with the attorney were like worm holes through layers of time.

I began to remember details of the Seneca plant tour. I could see the shine of new steel machined to sharp edges like the points of a triangle. I could smell the odors of fresh concrete and ozone. And, although I hadn't recalled the cafeteria when Denny mentioned it to me the previous spring, I began to remember the bustle of kids at tables, the scrape of chairs, the sounds of dozens of sandwiches in clear crisp plastic being unwrapped, the smell and taste of ham, swiss and mayo.

The excavation of these memories put me in a nostalgic mood. I began listening to a golden-oldies station on my car radio and reliving memorable events from my youth. Many of those events were times Eve and I shared together. But one very special event that returned again and again and became more and more vivid was the clear, moonless night beneath the stars with Polly at the Indiana Dunes.

We had been going steady for a year. It was one of our last dates before she went out with Denny and I met Eve. We lay side by side, bathing suit to bathing suit, skin to skin. We petted and touched and prodded as far as Polly's mother's oft-repeated advice would allow. We kept our suits on and clung to one another. We talked and talked about stars and possible futures and atoms as universes and how much sand was in a dune.

In a way the night at the Indiana Dunes was very much like the night in the hotel room after Denny's funeral. In the hotel room we kept our clothes on, me in my slacks and wrinkled white shirt, Polly in her black dress. We spent the night weeping, talking, hugging, catnapping. We spent the night honoring Denny's memory and Eve's understanding. I remember once during that night having an insane desire to tear Polly's black dress apart, spread suntan lotion over her body, sprinkle sand on her, and drop through a hole in time.

In the fall, a year-and-a-half after Denny's death, I was called to Boston to be a key witness for the plaintiff. Eve drove me to the airport, parked the car instead of dropping me off, and accompanied me to the gate. We sat in a row of seats facing the floor-to-ceiling windows overlooking ground crew preparations for the flight. Directly ahead of us a wing tip light flashed on and off, on and off.

"Will you tell them you remember the lunch in the cafeteria?" asked Eve.

"Yes, I'll tell them because I really think I do remember it."

"Are you sure you haven't simply sold yourself on the idea that it happened?"

"How could I sell myself on something as vivid as that?"

"So you really remember eating in the cafeteria? And you really remember Denny dropping his sandwich, then picking it up and eating it?"

When I didn't answer immediately, Eve looked out the window where, in the distance, above the wing of my plane, a wide-bodied jet settled with feminine grace on the runway. Then she looked back to me.

"What I'm getting at, Mike, is that the story seems to have been born last spring. And since that night you spent with Polly you're like the atheist who changes into a creationist."

"Eve, I told you nothing happened that night. You said you believed me. Why the hell do you keep bringing it up?"

We both looked out the window again, watched another jet settle down. This one dropped more quickly, its wings flexing like the legs of a woman doing splits.

"I'm sorry, Mike. But I can't help thinking Denny used you and is still using you from his grave. He needed someone to believe his crazy story about a lousy ham and swiss sandwich that fell on the cafeteria floor, and I think he found him."

"Maybe thinking about things makes them true. Maybe that's the best-kept secret in the world."

"What will you tell them?"

"I'll say that, to the best of my recollection, I think I do remember that day in the cafeteria. I'll say it because I'm afraid if I don't, I'll regret it someday when we're old."

Eve reached out, held my arm. "Why when we're old?"

"Because by then, when our short-term memories have gone to hell, all we'll have left are old memories in which something as insignificant as a mayo stain on a tile floor becomes crystal clear."

"Will the memory of past lovers also become crystal clear?"

"I don't know."

As the plane climbed, the haze of the city closed in like a fade-out in an old movie. The sun was brighter up here, the banking plane allowing it to shine on my arm. I wondered if plexiglass—or whatever the hell scratchy plane windows are made of—stopped ultraviolet rays or let them pass through and get down into my poor old genes and chromosomes.

Drowsy, I pulled down the shade and tried to imagine what my exact words would be when Polly's attorney asked me to recall the Seneca visit. I even tried to visualize the cafeteria—Denny sitting next to me, cracking jokes and goofing off and blowing bubbles in his milk and saying it's radioactive milk and hearing someone else make a wisecrack and turning in his chair and knocking the sandwich off the long tippy folding table with his elbow.

I dreamed Denny's '59 Chevy convertible, Polly's hair flying in the wind all that summer, me starting to date Eve, the two of us in the back seat where the backdraft pounds the backs of our heads so that we slouch down low hanging on to one another as Denny drives the four of us to the Indiana Dunes where we spend the day hugging in the sun while I catch Denny glimpsing me and Eve when I try to glimpse him and Polly.

The four of us sharing lunch on a cooler top, ham and cheese sandwiches, Denny dropping his in the sand and complaining like mad. Then later, at dusk, the splitting apart and joining back together as covalent pairs on remote dune tops beneath the same moon. And beneath me, pressing upward as if to fly, bathing suit to bathing suit, skin to skin, is Eve tempting me with loose straps and drooping shoulders. Sandy shoulders, skin oiled with lotion, the smell of lotion and lake, the fabric of Eve's damp suit cool against my chest, Eve kissing me and saying, "I'll always remember this night, Mike. Tell me you'll remember it too."

"I will remember it, Eve. I'll remember it as long as I live."

The rattle of the beverage cart awakened me. When I opened my eyes the stewardess leaned across the unoccupied seat smiling, her eyes sexy—like a surfaced swimmer—as she asked if I wanted something to drink. I shook my head "no" and watched as she eased the cart forward a row at a time.

I opened the shade and looked down at the overcast that blotted out the world. I wasn't sure anymore. I didn't know if the fatal sandwich was a construct of Denny's brain—minus a bird-sized tumor—or not. When a sandwich wrapped in plastic was handed to me, I told the stewardess I thought it was a dinner flight.

She smiled and said, "No, just a snack today."

The plane banked slightly and when I looked out the window I saw a break in the clouds. Far below the plane, on the glistening banks of a river, I could see the twin cooling towers of a nuclear plant. The plant was across the river from a small town, the steam from the cooling towers floating above the town. It seemed a peaceful scene until the plane straightened and the sun, lighting up a series of scratches on the window, created a glowing row of stitch marks like those on the back of Denny's head.

The image of the scar reminded me of Denny's arrival in the driveway in his '59 Chevy. Then, suddenly, Denny and I were back at Seneca where we watched as a man in a cheap suit wearing a badge stood before a group of crewcut science club nerds saying that the atom had ended World War II at Hiroshima and Nagasaki and that not only would the atom protect us from the commies, but by the end of the century its power would make our land into a Garden of Eden and we'd all have wives like Brigitte Bardot. This made all us nerds laugh like hell, including Denny who picked his teeth with a toothpick he'd pocketed in the cafeteria.

Just as quickly as the break in the clouds had appeared, it was gone and I took another bite of sandwich. The clouds rushed past.

Cheryl Pearl Sucher

◆

KISHINEV

It was a bad summer in Kishinev. Yetta Gesundt's favorite cow, Malka, would not be milked from one teat and Channah Esther, the feather woman with one bald eye and flecked cheeks, swore to all who would listen that the sky was razed by halibut-shaped demons. And Yitzhak Chayim Gesundt, the grandfather I would never know, was thirteen years old and started growing things in strange places.

At first, my grandfather attributed his ringing ears and swollen glands to the endless rains. Rivers ran where paths had been and pontoon planks were erected as pedestrian crossings. Horsecarts waded through flooded ditches bearing mosquito infestations. Termites ate through tree trunks and Shabbos candles refused to light, their wicks were so sodden. When Zevulun the Barber said the town's name should be changed from Kishinev to Lake Kishinev, the elders turned to Reb Hitchkeh of Berdichev for an explanation.

"God is weeping!" Reb Hitchkeh proclaimed, tugging his lemon white beard with fingernails long as rams' horns. Reb Hitchkeh had seen Nicholas' coronation cape turn into a blood river long before the catastrophe of Khodynka meadow. Ever since that premonitory sighting, he was known as the province's great visionary.

"Man is not good enough for life, that's why God is crying so hard. He's asking, as he has for centuries, 'Why have I made man out of my own temptation?'" The Reb sipped the blackberry wine presented to him by the Kishinev Women's Auxiliary and proclaimed, "Another test is coming, so watch out!"

The elders, who could not swim, shook so hard their blouses came out of their pants. They begged the Great One to tell them what the test would be, but Reb Hitchkeh only said, "If I knew the answer to that question, I wouldn't need to dream for I would be master of the universe."

The visionary offered the elders biscuits and black bread before sending them home, more confused than ever.

Gradually Kishinev forgot there was ever such a thing as a day without precipitation. By August, the elders were interpreting the rains as an overly prodigious gift from God.

"*Nu*," Reb Schwartz appraised, "It could be worse. There could be no water at all."

"And the tomatoes!" Reb Heilum evaluated, "they're so big, they could be meals in themselves."

"Have you seen the cows?" whispered Reb Moishe Rabinowicz, the last member of this trio (the three had been singled out while still students at the great Yeshiva of Memel), "They have so much milk they could pish all day and still be full up. At least this year no one will die from hunger, thank the Holy One, blessed be He."

Even as boys, this trio displayed a unique capacity for philosophical reasoning and feeling compassion.

"There's a saying that says if a man has enough, he wants more; and if he has nothing, all he wants is enough. So let's be content with more than enough."

"I agree." Reb Schwartz nodded, his eyes buried in time's locks.

"But what is this test of Hitchkeh's?" Reb Heilum uttered, raising his finger in the air before eating a herring in cream sauce.

"A test like any other. When does the Holy One not test us? We are his flock, he is our shepherd, he leads us to fields of flowers. Sometimes, there are so many flowers we can't see the fields, but just because we can't see the fields, do we fail to believe we are standing on the earth?"

The Rebs nodded in enthusiastic unison.

"Without tests, we would not know our own image," Reb Rabinowicz whispered for he could not speak out loud. His voice had flown from his voice box to follow his only daughter, Channah Esther, on the journey of her elopement.

Channah Esther had fled Kishinev in the middle of the night to escape an arranged marriage with an arthritic mortician so she could pursue a young Jewish radical whose only purpose in life was to free all the oppressed people of the world. The Reb Rabinowicz knew the young man's vision was as doomed as his daughter's romantic pursuit for both were constructs facile as air, seductive only when ensconced in the imaginative realm. The real, he knew, was never as gorgeous and intoxicating as its promise. The realization of promise, he had learned, was even more crushing than the impossibility of its attainment. Beauty was a tacit mystery. No perfection ever conformed to any other. Each singularity diminished upon revelation, mocked by the commonality of desire. Unknowable as God's form; ideals were sustained by faith, compromise and the occasional miracle.

"When will man realize he can never be free?" said the Reb to himself, his own private litany, "He's a slave to his body, a prisoner to his family and most of all a plaything put on earth to act out the big dramas of an angry God. Man is a slave, forget all this talk of enlightenment; the freedom my Channaleh left home for is an idiot's illusion."

If the Reb remembered the political radical at all, it was as a long slab of wood with eyes like a peeling bark's rotten whorls.

"Those who can't bend will break," the Reb told himself. Time would do its work and he would wait. Yet, as he waited, he cried in his sleep with hope. "Wasn't a man meant to be taken care of by his children in his old age?"

Inside himself, Reb Rabinowicz saw the endless rains as God's infinite compassion for his small but great sorrow. Urging his fellow elders not to panic, he told them to be patient and to wait for a sign, believing the sign would be the return of his voice. But because he could not speak out loud, he could not tell anyone his secret, and the entire town of Kishinev waited.

In the interim, the townspeople took joy in their increased crops. Fodders filled with cooked fruit and smoked flesh. Yeasted bread doubled over bowls and the Women's Auxilliary's blackberry wine fermented in tubs. Girls and plants ripened to bursting, turning men's eyes inside out, away from God and in search of naked earlobes.

Only the Gesundts could not sleep. They feared the harvest was God's way of apologizing in advance. Reb Gesundt had seen a gaggle of geese floating tails up in a barrel of horses will. Yetta (my grandfather's mother) saw cowheads on haystacks and developed a low-grade fever that would not diminish, not even when cooled by Zevulun the Barber's miracle mustard plasters. And Yitzhak Chayim Gesundt, the grandfather I would never know, started to feel his body give way beneath him.

Hair sprouted on his knuckles and above his thighs. His voice dropped from a cantorial soprano to a dusky baritone and dreams of stallions and mares dancing upright startled him awake. Sparklers raged through his veins, emitting strange fluids. He was frightened but he did not cry out for he knew no one would listen. Reb Gesundt was preoccupied with dread. Night after night he sat before his Mishnah, shouting at the Almighty by speaking all the inversions of his name.

"Creator, Master, Maker of the Universe, oh Holy, Holy, Holy One! Help me understand your ways for I am afraid!"

Sometimes the wind replied by blowing out the Reb's candles, sometimes the rain answered by trickling through a gap in the ceiling; but God did not respond to the Reb's pleas by coming to earth dressed in beggar's clothing, wasting his days sitting in the Kishinev marketplace whistling folk melodies.

Yetta wasn't keeping her monthly mikvah appointments either. Zevulun said her menstrual omissions were symptomatic of fever, but Yetta, like the Almighty, was playing dumb. She sewed patches into blankets, knitted noodles into booties, massaged Malka's barren teat and placed pebbles on her ancestors' gravestones, praying to be blessed with a girl child. Sound moved within her, yearning enshrouded her like a tight fist. Yitzhak felt her distended pelvis but pulled his hand away. His fingertips had started to burn.

When he soothed his scorched hands in the benediction bowl, he looked at his reflection in the water's mirror. There he saw a boy with chalk-colored eyes and skin covered in down. He was staring at his own face but he could not recognize it. Though his soul was bursting through his pants, butter-colored hair curled over his *yarmulke's* lip.

"How can this be?" Yitzhak thought, "Inside, everything's different, yet outside everything's the same."

But the routine of events that comprised the seasons had changed. Not once that summer had Reb Gesundt described to his son the

mysteries of the Zohar. In the past, he would place him on his lap and
speak of God's spheres, the heavenly coordinates, Hebraic inversions and
the body's numerological motifs. Over time, my grandfather trained himself to concentrate by twirling his forelocks round his fingers and making
braids out of his prayer fringes. Watching his father's eyes, Yitzhak, the
Pitzkelah, saw their pupils whirl like the runaway wheels of a collapsed
milkwagon.

"Is it candlelight that causes his eyes to spin and dance?" he asked
himself as his father's words galloped beyond his grasp, pursuing the spiral
of their ineluctable reason.

The evolution of ideas obeyed the physical laws of discourse, he had
learned while still a young boy in *heder*. His torah masters had whipped
his palms to incline him toward mastery. While other children played
football with rotten potatoes, he had been learning prophets' wisdoms
and visionary riddles in rhyming couplets and nursery rhymes.

The effect was like seeing without touching. The words made no
sense in his mouth. They were sensations embedding themselves on the
template that would become his memory. My grandfather had been
taught, as so many before him had been taught, to never fear apprehen-
sion, no matter how complex, for it was all part of the great messianic
plan.

One day, he was told, he would understand. One day, he sang day after
day in prayers which caused his eyes to mist over and his throat to chafe
with tears, his people would be redeemed. What he could not see, he was
taught to believe. What was not yet real, he yearned for with a singular and
unmovable purpose. Hope and belief were entwined, together they kindled
miracles. Hope was his God just as chance would be the God for those who
would later survive the terrors. But during the days of Reb Gesundt's solil-
oquies, the world was innocent of terror and brimming with poetry.

My grandfather Yitzhak heard each of his father's words yet never
paused to attempt comprehension. He was saving the words for later.
Though these talks delighted him, they also made his bowels foam.
Knowledge, he knew, was not only a gift but a burden. The sublimity of
wisdom was God's way of choosing. It was easier to know than to live by
what one knew, or to influence others to live by that knowledge.
Somehow he understood that the Reb Gesundt was not just speaking to
him, his son, but through time for time immemorial.

"Revelations will appear," the Reb whispered, "but only when you can see shadows in the night and hear sounds in the silence. What God sees is not meant for man to hear. The secret of vision is to try to do what one sees, for even when God is bad he is good. To do good is to know God, only then will darkness come alive with meaning."

When the Reb talked of mysteries, his hands danced, spanning the shadows of God's emanations. My grandfather Yitzhak believed during these times that his Tateh was not just his Tateh but a manifestation of *Elohim HaMelech*, the king of all light and master of the sunrise.

Since the rains, however, the Reb's lap had been empty. He looked through Yitzhak as he looked through walls. When the Holy One did not respond to 378 inversions of his name, the Reb went on a starvation diet. His organs boiled down to a soup and he ranted about stacked wishbones and the scent of burning hair oil. Yetta didn't pay any attention. Hallucination ran in her family since the days of the Chelmnitski massacres. She believed visions were caused by hormonal imbalances.

"Men's problems," she called them, speaking to Yitzhak as she undressed him for bed, "When desire goes to their brains instead of *you know where*," she said, caressing the inside of her son's thighs, "They scream so loud they think it's God. Let them think it's God," she said, tucking her son into bed but kissing his penis first, a habit she developed when Yitzhak was a newborn, for it was the only salve that soothed his colicky cries. "Does God represent pleasure or the denial of pleasure?" she asked as she moved to taste the milky tear crowning her son's member. "Nothing tastes as sweet as the forbidden fruit," she thought as she melted into the pleasure of giving pleasure. Nothing was so sure or successful as her nightly applications and as she became the beat bringing her son toward wonderment, her thoughts turned away from sin and toward awe.

"Perhaps God is the forbidden fruit," she asked herself as she caressed the alabaster of her son's thighs, innocent of sun, hidden the length of his days by woolen leggings and dark, baggy pantaloons. The knowledge that she alone knew the beauty of her son's skin excited her and impelled her work. Though a voice inside her screamed, she chose to ignore its alarm and succumb to the patter of her son's voice before it dissipated into an ecstatic murmur.

MAMA

"For him, it is only part of nighttime," she told herself as she kneaded his testes, "Little sacs of immortal dust, like the spice satchels you get at market. I wonder if he talks about the way he falls asleep with his friends." An icy frost surged through her, causing her first to shiver then to draw away in fear.

Pausing to breathe, she felt her heart cry out. The room was dark yet incandescent, illuminated by shards of moonlight. Like fireflies, the light swayed and danced, describing galaxies in the night shadows. Yetta believed the incandescence was life itself, that it endowed objects with eyes that could see into her soul. Covering her face, she peeked through her fingers. Her son was groping himself. Even at a distance, she felt the tugging at her scalp, a sensation akin to his infant suckling. Yetta remembered how it felt as if he had been drinking not her milk but her marrow. But when she had closed her eyes, moisture had flooded her body. The agony which had ruled her long labor eased, giving way. Smiling, she realized that feeding was part of God's plan. The baby had ravenously taken, but not without giving back some and then more.

"God help me!" she cried as she removed her kerchief and bowed to her son's fevered hand, "I am just taking back what I have given," she shouted, not so much to herself as to the demons she believed inhabited the incandescent sparks. As she worked, she imagined these demons as men with boar's snouts dancing a wild, snorting arabesque. Their voices came to her as the men's chorus saluting the *moël* during Yitzhak's circumcision.

It was happening again, the beginning of it all, all over again, as if time existed only with the shadow of its moving circle.

For Yetta, ritual *brisim* had always been occasions for great merriment. Feuding neighbors settled disputes, *schnapps* flowed, delicacies abounded and *tsoris* abated in celebration of the new future. But Yetta had always been an onlooker, never a participant. When she realized that the child being placed on the coin-covered silver platter was her son, she felt the barbarous edge of the *moël*'s sharpened blade.

"Why torture a life whose eyes are still shut to the world?" she asked herself, trying to close herself to her own rebellion. But her child had not yet learned this art of transcendence and continued his sobbing, winding his cries tighter and tighter into themselves until they were taut as watch-maker's coils; forcing her, as was the custom, into prayer. The pain entered, becoming her. When she opened her eyes, she heard the stag-gering voices of men stinking of sweet brandy and confession. Staring at the coins decorating her son's belly, she wondered how the rubles glim-mered, catching the *minyan's* dark light.

When the deed was done and the table laid with delicacies, she forced herself into conversation. For others, she fantasized her hopes for her son's future. Yet as she brewed tea in cracked glasses and laid out poppy seed and raisin cookies, she was flayed by the unending cries. Trembling, she hid her fingers in her apron pockets.

After the guests left, she asked her husband to move the baby from the bier to his cradle. She could not bear the thought of touching her child's raw wound. Though the Reb Gesundt had never changed a dia-per before, he replaced the cloth soaked with genital blood. It was he and not Yetta who doused the infant's gums with blackberry brandy. Though his loving applications were thorough and ceaseless, the baby did not stop howling into the night.

Remarkably, this shrieking did not disrupt the Rebbe's sleep. He dreamed of heaven, a place where men who were never hungry sat in golden chairs as naked women rubbed the corns out of their feet, asking eternal questions whose answers they could watch unfold over the progress of millenia.

Yetta, however, did not sleep for a moment. Her husband's hand lay unconscious on her breast, kneading her nipple as if it was the *tefillin* he rubbed during prayer. Her body leaked like a cut flower.

"This was motherhood," she thought, or so the married women had told her from the moment of her first menstruation to the agony of her first labour, "This is what I've been waiting all my life for," or so she had been told. The older women had warned her that the *bris* would be a torture, but they had also cautioned her against attempting to ease the baby's suffering. Untoward compassion could create a perverse bond between mother and son leading to unclean acts. Such a bond could never be broken.

"I beg you" they cried, one voice, watching Yetta yield to the agony of helplessness, "Remember Picha Yitka? How her teeth fell out before she was forty years old? Well, she comforted her Shmuel the night of his bris and look what happened to him! He lost all religion and became an athlete and moved so far away from home that she heard from him only when he sent her money from his boxing so she could buy a pair of false teeth that she never bought because she did not want to give away the money he had touched with his own hands. So she she sat all day, a widow, unable to chew, eating only soup. It will happen to you, Yetta, if you don't listen!"

Yetta didn't listen. She couldn't help herself. Even as a child, she could never ignore suffering. Despite her mother's assignation, she brought wounded birds home in her skirts, nursing them to health on her own concoction of nuts and flowers.

"The dirty birds will foul my Kosher home!" her mother yelled, pulling strands of grey hair out of her head whenever she discovered the checkered powder of ancient droppings, "Get rid of them or else!" Yetta never got rid of the birds, she only hid them in boxes in the family's vegetable garden. If anyone asked, she said she was growing cabbages. No one questioned her. Yetta was not only inclined toward compassion, she was a gifted liar.

Thus began the greatest secret of her life: the fellatic ritual inaugurated the night of Yitzhak's circumcision. Whenever she tasted the sour-sweet of her son's emissions, her ears filled with that mechanical wailing. She told herself that all she was doing was taking on her son's pain, but she started to hang amulets over his bed to ward away the evil eye. Still, nothing could draw her away from the sublimity of her son's face as he fell asleep to the rhythms of her mouth. This was her lullaby. She could not stop her lips from speaking their song of solace.

The night curled in around her, suffocating her in a blackness which extinguished the sparks.

"I'll stop when the next child is delivered to my belly!" she cried, even though it had been thirteen years since she first offered The Holy Name this great bargain. Life, however, had stubbornly refused to stir within her, ignoring all her plant concoctions, extra prayers and husband's erotic imagination.

"I promise you!" she urged, knowing God did not listen to the promises of the disobedient. Still, she prayed for His compassion.

Water moved within her as she moved her head beneath her son's hand. Kissing his palm then the white flesh at the top of his thighs, she grasped the starving muscle, dark with blood. Rubbing the vein deep at the shaft, she needed all her power to withhold her strength. Her eyes moved from his prayer fringes to his nipples. In the past, she would loosen her shift and put his free hand to her breast. Sometimes she would rock him in her arms; but tonight, she was one with the rain rising in her ears; the slurring, splashing, drowning water. Everywhere it rained, it would never stop.

Yetta became the rain of afterbirth, the water drowning Kishinev, the black pool where Yitzhak fell blissfully, over and over, to dream.

"Water!" she cried as the first stickiness inked her palm. Her son trembled. She closed her eyes.

"Bring me a girl child!" she wept without end. Her mouth was sore, afraid. Yitzhak cried out.

"Please!"

Meanwhile, in the marketplace, the *narodniks* in peeling pants and greasy caps, denounced Kishinev's poor people. Marching between barrels of shelled peas and sacks of new potatoes, they distributed copies of Leo Pinsker's "Auto-Emancipation."

"Arise!" they shouted, in need of haircuts and hot meals. Channah Esther tossed geese necks at their mouths.

"We are the dead walking among the living!"

The Hasids turned their heads, licking their lips with God's thoughts while stealing apples from fruit carts.

"Specters inhabit our muscle!" they shouted, waving photographs of clay huts and sand mountains above their heads. "We must reclaim the land God gave us!"

Babushkas, children strumming their skirts, moved closer to the radicals in order to see the picture of a land where the sun stood still. They tried to imagine this place where it never rained in the summertime. Was it as far away as Saint Petersburg or was it part of a past captured only in prayer?"

"Anti-Semitism is a two-thousand-year-old disease!" the *narodniks* proclaimed, "Do you want to wait around and get infected? Do you want to subject your children to such a plague?"

The women clutched their children's hair, drawing them into the folds of their skirts and putting their hands in their pockets. "Do you want to be ghosts forever, wandering unseen in the land of the living?"

Cheeks drained of light, the hooded-eyed men of *Hoveve Zion* scanned the crowd for alabaster earlobes and hair the color of wheat. For one moment, the entire village of Kishinev moved toward a single plea.

That night Yetta Gesundt gave birth to death.

Cries awakened my grandfather Yitzhak from his sleep. It had been weeks since his father had started his fast and Yitzhak had grown accustomed to starvation's somatic rages. The flat, gray plain of slumber where time had been a field devoid of wildflowers and carrion, had become a landscape blocked by horror. Not even his mother's nightly kiss could still the harrowing voices.

Often he tried to shut his eyes to the sounds by covering his face with his prayer shawl and binding the straps of his phylacteries so tightly around his hands, he forced them to bleed. Other times, he stood in front of his parents' locked bedroom door until he grew tired of his fear or became frightened by the memory of his father's haunted possession.

Desire became his secret conflagration. When he was supposed to be studying, his mind moved towards the flood of sensation inspired by his mother's lullaby kiss, a feeling so deep even its imagining set him on fire.

"God help me!" he cried.

When he confessed his clandestine conflagration to Reb Heilum, his bar mitzvah *haftorah* master, the Reb scratched his beard and said, "Don't worry, before you know it, you'll be married. Then your feelings will find their resolution. Once a man becomes aware of his manhood, he is incomplete without his bride. What do we call our day of rest but 'our bride?' Don't we sing to her? Without a day of rest we would not be men but animals."

But Yitzhak could not help but worry. Marriage seemed the calm hearth, the place where one knew where one's meals came from and where one's laundry would be washed. It did not seem the extinguisher capable of dousing the fire of howling animals. Human passion was inspired by man's passion for God. But was God an animal?

His life started to move toward the rhythms of these accustomed terrors. However, one night he was wakened by neither his own emissions nor his father's ravings. The sound which startled him was a cry similar to the voice of his congregation as it approached the *Kol Nidre Aliya*, the prayer which heralded the rising of ablutions as songs to God's ears. The wail in Yitzhak's ears lilted, pattered then howled. Walking toward his window, he searched the grounds for a dying animal.

"Water, bring me water!" a voice rasped.

His heart gasped. The voice was inside, not outside. He held his breath, waiting for the night shadows to come into focus.

"Water, icebergs, skating on a pond! Water from my womb, pull it out, pull it out!"

My grandfather Yitzhak wondered why the voice was screaming for water when there were floods everywhere. A throbbing struck his belly with a heat which devoured him the more he willed it away.

"Water!" one voice cried.

"I am water!" the other answered.

My grandfather followed the voices across the cold foyer. Strangely, the door to his parents' room was ajar. He moved into the opening. A breeze had parted the curtains. Moonlight was falling in slips onto the rumpled bedsheets. He saw a crescent of silver rise and fall with the rhythm of the water cry.

"I am death!" a voice cried before expiring.

Silence swallowed the Pitzkeleh Yitzhak until he was one with the respiration moving him and toward the crescent hiding in the darkness.

The next morning, the Pitzkeleh Yitzhak refused to look at his mother.

"Nu, boychickle," Yetta asked, resting her hand on his, "Did you sleep well?" Yitzhak nodded, mesmerized by the sight of butter melting into his warm black bread.

"Look at me, Pitzkeleh," Yetta demanded, turning him toward her by the chin, "Are you the son I put to bed last night? Let me taste." And Yetta, as was her custom, kissed her son on the lips.

A pitch of colors surged through my grandfather's belly. He rose from the table without reciting the after meal benediction and ran toward the privy. On the way, he thought he saw a gleaming crescent of silver. But the flash was not silver, it was black, black as rotten tree bark. And it grew larger.

Yitzhak forgot his bellyache as he watched the streak expand across the horizon until it was one with the horizon. The sky cracked open and the roads rose into funnels of dust. Through the darkness stormed the fire colors of a cossack cavalcade. Horsemen lit the blackness, carrying the sun on their backs. Poised on black steeds whose tails swept their trembling flanks, the riders tugged their stallions' reins, pausing in their pursuit. Whips struck air as the horses pranced, rearing before falling into an agitated stillness. The whirlwind sent Yitzhak flying. Before he knew it, he was lying beside a toppled barrel of Mama's duck feathers.

It was behind that barrel that my grandfather hid for the length of the terror. Though the wings tangled his breathing and scratched his eyes, he did not cry out. Though horses kicked wells in Mama's cabbage plants and stamped David the Idiot's wheelbarrow into ribbons, he did not cry out. Though he was afraid, he did not cry out for he knew to cry out was to call the Angel of Death by name. So my grandfather sat in silence, watching streams of light fall from sabers as they struck down life as if life was only chaff. Squeezing his fists together, he shut his eyes until sparklers danced behind their lids.

"Shema!" he called with all the force of his desire to survive.

But it was too late for even silent devotion. By the time Yitzhak cried out, the Reb Gesundt had been kicked in the brain by the exhilirations of a wild stallion. The onslaught had raged through the central village during his morning walk to his Talmud Torah classroom. Exhausted by starvation and weighted down by the Midrash he held in his arms, he had heard the cavalcade's approach but had been too weak to move out of its path. Blinded by the height of the tomes in his arms and haunted by daylight visions of water balloons and slaughtering houses, he was unable to see the progressing pillage and so he was struck down.

Though his knees buckled beneath him and his pain widened like a sobbing mouth, he clutched the prayer books to his chest, not allowing them to touch ground. Even in death, the Reb Gesundt feared sinning in this world more than he feared living in the world beyond. So, clasping the handwritten Law to his breast, his soul let go of his body and rose with his ablutions to his Maker.

Meanwhile, Kishinev was lighting up like a firecracker. Women ran helter skelter, flailing carcasses and cleavers. Dissonant voices clamored a terror which Yitzhak had heard before only in dreams. Yet out of this cacaphony rose a single voice, pure and still as the mineral waters of the fabled Dukla mountain springs.

"Channah Esther," it sang, "If you won't come to me, I'll come to you!" When the voice expired, it swallowed the vagrant cries, leaving behind only the crackling of drowned fires and the hungry gurgles of the suppurative earth. Gradually, the night drew its black cape over Kishinev, drawing my grandfather into its dark skirts and heavy arms.

In the morning, Vitka Pesha discovered the Pitzkeleh. Lifting him into the air, she shook him awake.

"Get up!" she cried, sweeping matted earth from his white blouse.

Still sleepy, my grandfather Yitzhak looked around. Tar roads were pits, cracked glass sparkled in maroon pools. Slaughtered chickens hung on washing lines. Pigs from neighboring peasant farms roamed, celebrating their freedom by nosing fresh corpses. Coarse grey beards lay like codpieces besides torn trusses and ruptured boots. The Pitzkeleh Yitzhak held onto Vitka Pesha with all the force of his desire to turn time around.

"How can I wake up when I am still dreaming?" he said.

But when he pinched himself, he did not waken. Instead, the pinch settled into his flesh becoming an ache and then a sharp, hollow pain. As he walked, the pain deepened. He saw how the water had evaporated, forcing the earth to swell and crack into offal streams. Here he saw a sleeve from a cossack's tunic, there he saw Zevulun the Barber's tarnished cutting scissors. Here was Channah Esther's wig, there was Yaffa the mutt in pieces. It was hard for my grandfather to look without feeling the barber's blade scrape the sensitive part behind his left ear.

He asked Vitka Pesha where they were going.

"Home," she said, pulling her shawl tightly across her shoulders.

And there was Yitzhak's home as he had never seen it, cresting a mound of char.

The air smelled burnt and smoke soiled the horizon. The house was sealed as if Pishacts the Moneylender had come overnight to close all the openings with tar and ragged bits of lumber. Those parts of himself which had also been open also closed. He felt like he was walking into the icy enclosure of Shmulek the Butcher's meat locker.

Malka was now standing in the shade surveying flies with her slow, black eyes. Mama's chickens were now running from their wire shed, reaching for the four corners of the universe with their beaks. The tree whose berries had bled an insect liquor was torn from the sod, its roots exposed above a gaping ditch. My grandfather remembered how his father had loved to sit beneath that tree, talking about the regeneration of the spheres.

"What falls dead to earth one day returns the next as a hope," the Reb had said, tearing handfuls of grass out of the ground, "See Mama's dying flowers? See the chickens hysterical with their sense of impending slaughter? They will all return."

The thought of never having been and never being again, pinched at Yitzhak's heart.

"The Master of the Universe . . ." the Reb Gesundt had continued, ". . . is complicated. His logic does not make sense but it is time and it is fair, Pitzkeleh. Don't try to understand it, just accept it. Face what you don't understand with courage and dance to the rhythms singing within you."

Then the Reb had taken his son's hands into his own in order to show him how to make a spider silhouette with his fingers' shadows.

Yitzhak clutched Vitka Pesha as they knocked on his door. When it was opened, he beheld his mother darkened by mourning. On the kitchen table behind her, his father's body lay like an alabaster slab. Women sat on low stools basting the Reb Gesundt's marriage garment into his death shroud.

The Pitzkeleh approached the body. He ran his hands along the length of his father's hands. The nails were shorn into perfect rectangles. Curled hair freckled his fingers. Moles spotted his chest, his elbows, his feet. It was the first time Yitzhak saw his father completely naked. There was no warmth to the touch. Tateh's skin felt like melted wax hardened by an evening's chill.

"I have given birth to a new life," Yetta said as she clutched the Pitzkeleh's hair.

The worst had happened and she had survived. The edge of a drawn sabre had flecked her cheek, her wig had been tousled, her girdle reversed and she had not been struck down. Not one to taunt the causality of demons, she told her son that she had decided to leave the land of her childhood before the cossacks decided they wanted to make a second coming.

"All the rebbes are dead, my husband is dead, we have no reason to stay here, " Yetta whispered into her son's ear, "We are going on a long journey never to return. We are going to Vienna to live with your Uncle Solly." Yitzhak watched a spiral of smoke sift towards the ceiling until it broke up into webbed fragments.

Suddenly, all the motion which had raged through his body went numb. His sweet high voice returned and his pant legs relaxed. He tried to cry but he could not, he was too stopped up. His mother was calling him a man now and he was confused. Desire had been drained from him like rainwater and he was alone. He longed for his father's lap, yet now he was supposed to be a lap.

"Remember what your father said," Yetta murmured before extinguishing her son's night candle, "Even while we're standing still the earth is moving around the sun and the moon is spinning around the earth. When the spheres are in motion, God is making plans."

In the darkness, Yitzhak closed his eyes which grew moist in anticipation of his mother's lips. Waiting for the brush of her stubbled hair against his hand, his hips' ululations were stilled by the slamming of his bedroom door. A key turned in the lock which had never, as far as he could remember, been used.

"I love you," Yetta whispered into the keyhole, "But some things must come to an end, even if that ending is long beyond reason."

Racing to the door in all his confusion, Yitzhak tried to turn the knob, but found it stalwart, stiff in its rusted hinges.

"Mama!" he cried, with all the force of his desire to disappear, "I didn't do it!"

Crumbling to the floor, he sobbed with such abandon the mourners blessed his soul which they believed had been touched by an angel. Yetta heeded the warnings of those women of long ago and shut her ears to her son's shrill weeping. Denial entered the Gesundt household for the first time and Yitzhak fell asleep to the pity of his own longing, tracing in the darkness the dissolving line of his mother's smile. The line evolved into a series of boxes, each brighter than its predecessor. On the top of the last box was a golden throne and on it sat the Reb Gesundt, younger than in life, shukkling a little boy with butter-colored curls.

"Trust my singing," sang the Reb, "For I have seen the angels."

Yitzhak shut his eyes. How could he trust what he could not see?

How could he hear a voice that was not spoken out loud? Soon he
would be going to a place called Vienna. Channah Esther said Vienna
was a city of armies where *goyim* had titles and wore wigs. No one spoke
Russian there, everyone spoke German which Channah Esther said was
a *geharget* form of Yiddish. But Yitzhak had seen drawings on the back
of postal cards sent by his Uncle Solly. From these sketches he imagined
Vienna to be a city of golden palaces floating on water. Soon he would
be leaving his home for this city. Solly was the place he was going
toward even though Reb Gesundt never spoke Solly's name aloud without spitting through his fingers. Solly had been a money order, a portrait within Mama's sterling silver brooch. Solly was the threat Yetta
posed each time the Reb lost his weekly Talmud Torah salary in a game
of gin. Solly had thrown his prayer fringes into the fire and shorn his
forelocks with a knife. That knife, Yetta said, had gone through their
father's heart.

"It killed him," she wept, clutching the thin locket in her fist.

Yitzhak was confused because he knew his grandfather did not die
from heartache but from gout. It seemed to him that pain was a symptom
of longing, and death was the product of bad luck, heartburn and malaise.
And on top of that, Yetta was making less and less sense. She said that
by going to live with Solly, they were going to bring him home.

"What is still alive can still return home," she said, smiling into the
distance, "Even if home has to do the traveling. We are accomplishing a
great mitzvah by going to live with Solly. We'll bring him home," she
said, winking.

Yitzhak was not pleased. He knew home was more than an idea you
could convince someone else to believe in. He knew home to be a place
where he could walk around blindfolded and still not trip on a loose
faucet or a crumbling wall. Home was where his ancestors were buried,
where everyone knew not only his name but his nicknames. And he was
leaving his home forever.

Why is home so important, he thought, if God condemned his people, the Jews, to wander eternally in the *Yishuv,* so far away from home?
Why did God preserve the Jews alone of all the enlightened tribes of
antiquity? Where were the Pharisees in Russia? And more importantly,
why did he feel so hopeless just because he was leaving a place called
'home'?"

"*Aboyneshe Loylem in Himmel* is the unspeakable," the Reb Gesundt had said, "Because he is everything and one thing at the same time. We, on the other hand, are only people, confined to mechanical activity because of our human form. We cannot move through time and space for we are mortal. But," he continued, his eyebrows lifting until they resembled drawn bows, "What makes us the animal most like God is our minds. Though we cannot penetrate the physical spheres we can move through the eternal spheres by thinking."

"Home is in your head," Yitzhak reasoned, "so it can never be lost unless you lose your head." But itching tugged at his larynx and horses reared, nostrils flaring as they bared their teeth and gums. Soon, Yitzhak knew that he would not have a home. He would no longer be able to find himself by pushing himself against familiar landmarks.

Sometimes, he thought he saw a silver crescent slide through the moon's shadow. Sometimes he thought he heard a chorus of Tateh's gin players screaming victory. But it was always just the wind moving through the night.

So Yitzhak tried not to think about moving until the day he left Kishinev forever. By the time the day printed on Yetta's train tickets arrived, time had unfurled like a bobbin of colored ribbon. All the Gesundts' belongings had been packed into straw chests and the house had been fleshed out like a potato skin. The night before their leavetaking, Yetta hired a Klezmer band and ordered enough smoked fish to feed a cavalry of walruses. She even allowed the Pitzkeleh to drink vodka. He swallowed the liquor so fast it went down his throat like a lit coal stone. After that, the edges of absence softened. Bare walls merged and everything floated. For the first time since the massacre, Yitzhak did not see all the empty places. Instead he saw a whirling wild dancing. Limbs and scarves flew into prismatic bands of color, racing around the clarinet's revelrous melody. The whirling somersaulted, chasing the pipe's sardonic musings. Yetta parted the dervish with her scarf and Yitzhak collapsed with happiness.

"So that's what it means to return to joy," he thought before dizziness enveloped him, swallowing his stomach first.

The next morning Yitzhak looked at his mother as if for the first time. Her eyes were shadow sockets, her face, which had inspired such determined action, had fallen into depressions and valleys. Her neck was draped into folds. Yitzhak saw his mother's face as if for the first time and felt frightened.

"*Nu, mein kint,* say goodbye to your father," Yetta said as they heard Reb Schwartz' buggy clobber up the path.

When he was little, Yitzhak believed the world ended at the far side of Vitka Pesha's wheat field. Now Reb Schwartz's horse and carriage was taking him beyond the plain. Going beyond meant going beyond his imagination. Yitzhak was leaving Kishinev forever, the land of his every-thing. The past was shedding its shells, leaving him an empty vessel. Yitzhak closed his eyes and tried to remember all that the horse and buggy passed by.

"*Nu,* lazy Pitzkeleh," Yetta yelled as she knocked her son on the shoulder, "Are you getting out now or do I have to give my own son a personal invitation?"

Yitzhak opened his eyes. A timekeeper sat chewing ragweed by the window of a tall grey shack. A blue cap shrouded his curly red hair. Lit by the light of a gas lamp, his face was round and pink as an onion.

"Come help!" Yetta cried as she demonstrated for Reb Schwartz the best way to take down her straw cases without letting his back out.

Families approached the platform bearing lamps and infants on their backs. Old men, frost edging their beards, dragged rusting wheelbarrows. Parcels tied together with shredding rope formed rag mountains. Logs of cheese and bread bricks were taken from gunnysacks. One elderly man tied on the leather reins of his phylacteries. Its small boxes, placed on his forehead and right hand, anchored his prayer dance. Whirling, he defied the length of his bonds.

In the distance, Yitzhak saw a black streak. His belly seized. The black streak expanded into a ball of smoke. A whistle pierced the sky, pulling the chattering rhythms of a slowing engine. Wheels screeched and sparks flew as the railcars pulled into Kishinev station.

"Say goodbye to Kishinev forever," Yetta said as she moved behind the Pitzkeleh to escape the rising dust, "See the colors and see the shadows. See everything then forget you ever saw this place for your father, may he rest in peace, would tell you, if he were alive, that forgetting was the best kind of remembrance. So forget you ever lived here, forget you ever belonged to a people that tried to expel you from its belly."

Forget Tateh? Zevulun the Barber? *Heder*? Home? To forget was to plunge headfirst into a lake drained of water. To forget was to crack his skull open and lose the shape of himself. He could not believe what his mother asked of him. Forget? Was forgetting an act of moving forward? How could that be? To forget the past was to become nothing but an eye perceiving without comprehension.

Yet Yetta's voice was persuasive. She moved her son through repetition, pushing him beyond his will, beyond his body and his reason. His head spun as he became his vision and his senses. He was what he smelled. He wasn't the Pitzkeleh anymore, he was a new boy going on a long journey.

Jacob Gesundt of Vienna was born that moment: out of the Pitzkeleh Yitzhak and out of the locomotive's clenching brakes, out of the fireflies trapped by the engine's wheels and out of the black steam blasting from the coal chimneys. Jacob was the aroma of burned tea and spilled vodka. He was born out of the sooty air and his mother's pearl drop earrings, he emerged out of a wall of hands.

Once on the train, Yitzhak and his mother pushed to get at a window so they could wave to Reb Schwartz. Calling his name out loud, the Reb found the pair with his eyes. He had been patting his mare and feeding her a carrot. Yitzhak waved until his shoulder burned. Then the earth gave way and the car filled with the long exhalation of the train's whistle. The chugging started, sallow at first then swelling into motion. Yitzhak grasped a hanging strap and his body jerked forward, leaving his heart behind. Leaning out the window, he felt the air sweep his face. With one hand he held his mother's hands, with the other he waved goodbye to the little boy whose blonde hair curled over his skullcap's lip. He saw the little boy staring at his reflection in a pool of engine water. Jacob felt sorry for the Pitzkeleh for he was alone. He was glad the boy was not him.

Gordon Johnston

◆

PLIGHT

Some of his varsity teammates had stolen all the neighborhood roadsigns and Boogan had to climb a power pole to find Gail's house, spotting moonlight on the tin roof of the old clapboard playhouse she had told him about. He crept tree by tree across the dark yard until he reached first the shed, then the playhouse, sitting head-high on thick creosote posts in the moonlight. Boogan could find no door after walking around it or half-standing underneath, so he squatted by a piling in the shadows to wait for Gail, a hand over his mouth to keep his breath from fogging. An hour later he watched her ease the kitchen door shut and come silently over the white grass wearing her cheerleading jacket and carrying a shoebox and a thermos. She stopped a few feet away and smiled at him.

"Where's the door at?" he asked, shoulders hunched against the cold.

"That's for me to know."

Boogan grinned at her. "All right, now. Don't make me have to cut a new one." He moved squatting back under the floor, knocking between the underpinning studs.

"Hah. If it was a snake it would've bit me." He scrabbled at the dark wood, feeling from one end of the trap door to the other for a ring or knob. There wasn't one.

"Do you give up?" Gail leaned on a corner post, the shoebox under her arm with the thermos laid on top of it. He watched her.

"I reckon so." Boogan turned back to the playhouse and found the trapdoor now open before him as if the world had never been otherwise.

Gail walked innocently past him to unfold the stairs down from the door and climb into the darkness. He followed her up.

She stepped out of her sneakers and as she crossed the patch of light cast over the floorboards from the window, Boogan watched the stretch of her Achilles tendon through a hole in her right sock. The socks moving on the varnished wood whispered at the edge of his hearing and he thought of a doe he had watched walking in a backwater last fall. He didn't remember shooting it.

"Pull the door up and let that felt down over the windows." When he turned to the second window she had a kerosene lamp going. By the time he'd covered the last window she had unrolled a cotton sleeping bag cut for a child, its faded yellow cloth scattered with white-flowered petals. She sat on it in her enormous jacket and opened a notebook on her lap.

"Okay," she said. "How do we get married?"

Hetty sat rocking in the house, surrounded by the now-darkened ceramic, porcelain, colored glass, brass, and homemade things by which she dated her life and which she kept in glass-fronted cabinets and on the ornate shelves men once made for their women. She listened to the girl she had raised talking to a stranger, a boy she had never met, though she felt as he warmed from his long walk the slight swell of his feet and the sting of the lips where the boy's father had hit him. To turn your son's teeth against him: Hetty could think of nothing more despicable.

From the rocker in the living room she heard them as if through water, though they sat across a yard and beyond the barn hidden behind a curtain of felt in Gail's playhouse. She listened from a center inside herself, the words quivering from their souls like ripples in a red-lit subterranean pool that came lapping soundlessly to her out of darkness. They talked about preachers, jobs, places to live, birth control (this followed by waves as warm as bathwater from Boogan, though she didn't know his name, souls not having any). And under all the words a keening from Gail, a vibration like some spinning lure under a thin skin of water— ticking light, a bright hoop turning and, strung on it, a tiny white star. Under the boy's words hung a dark, greeny placidness, an unspoken stillness. Through the dark from both of them one word swelled into a warm

salt wave, riding on its own urging from liquid depths to solid ground:
Thursday. The wave passing seemed to deepen the element in Hetty and
as it swallowed her she found she could breathe it. Words were gone now,
replaced by a deep pulse and rising heat. Her lips opened in the dark parlor. She groped in the dark for the arm of the rocker. Her eyes opened on
the glinting things in the room, the decorations and plates from which
no one had ever eaten. The rocker had gone still and she lay slumped on
her back in it, her thighs cast open, aged peach panties muggy as a swamp
sunset. She remembered Merganser Blake and the smell of his friend's
rumble seat, how the ticking crickets had counted down her virginity out
in Mr. Harry Mack's pasture by a stock pond where the Kmart was now.

She stood, a light sweat chilling under her gown, and shuffled to the
stairs, her legs rolling in their sockets as though oiled within. She went
up, past the clock on the opposite wall, its pendulum slicing night into
precise increments, and climbed into bed. It was not her business. She
would talk to Gail and love her. She would meet the boy, she hoped,
and—if he was a good boy—perhaps have the sheriff shoot or threaten
his father. She would let Gail love how she wanted if he was a good boy.
If he wasn't—Merganser had had black eyes, sweet hairless hands with
bass fiddle wrists and fingers, a perfect thief—if this boy wasn't, Hetty
would shoot him herself.

Everything that week warned Gail not to elope with Boogan. In
Contemporary Problems Mrs. Bradshaw covered divorce on Monday,
scattering the blackboard with gritty chalk dust statistics and handing
out purple dittos on cause and effect. On Tuesday the mother of the year-
book editor came in her health department uniform and held up wrapped
condoms like suckers with the sticks pulled out. Composed, smiling, she
opened one and unrolled it, speaking in the same engaged older-sister
voice she had used in her den at the prom breakfast her son had hosted
last spring. *Over the man's penis for the* duration *of intercourse*, she said.
She didn't ignore the jokes, only singled out the boys who made them
with a tender smile, terrible in its sympathy, or said confidentially that
they *needed* to learn this. She held up IUDs, crazy voodoo shorthand
against semen that Gail recognized from *Seventeens* the other cheer-

leaders passed around. Pills, a diaphragm, the rhythm method. *Diaphragm* reminded Gail of eighth-grade chorus, when she sang with the spine of a hymn book pressed against her stomach—how badly then she had wanted Juice Newton to sing at her wedding.

Gail might have talked herself into believing she was reading too much into things if it had only been Contemporary Problems class, a course named as much for its students as for its content—hoods bragged when counselors put them in the class—and one she wouldn't be in if Mrs. Moseley hadn't miscounted her library aides. But in English Lady MacBeth walked around bloody-handed, in history Eleanor Roosevelt lived a lie, and even in chemistry pure elements came together, seared into flame, and reduced themselves to charcoal. *Discard the test tube of blackened by-product*, the manual said. *What do you smell?*

At home Aunt Hetty called her into the kitchen every evening to make biscuits, fry okra, cook rice, or make tea without letting the water come to a boil. Maybe she suspected. Gail watched her aunt potter around the kitchen, listened to her tuneless humming and familiar one-sentence warnings against over- or under-cooking. Her aunt mysteriously knew things. When Gail had been a girl and Uncle Ray had been killed by lightning, Hetty the day after the funeral had drunk one cup of coffee sitting in his chair, then risen and gone out behind the shed in her housecoat and begun to dig postholes. In a month and with no blueprint, list, or tape measure, she had finished plumb and square the playhouse Ray had planned and bought the materials for. On her last day working on it, after finishing the secret trap door that led up into the raised house and showing Gail how to open and lower the folded stairs, she showered and put on a new housecoat, then sat on the bottom step and cried.

Hetty didn't act like a suspicious parent, though. When Gail went out to walk in the evening, her aunt barely glanced up from washing potatoes or reading the paperbacks she bought indiscriminately for quarters and dimes at yard sales and Gail doubted Hetty's ability to keep knowledge that dire hidden, even if her foster daughter's future depended on it. The woman could not hold truth, good or bad; it leaked out of her. Spark put to sleep after he was run over the night before Gail's seventh birthday. The *women bleed* talk when she was in fifth grade. The long trail of presents—hair barrettes, a music box, a dress, a sweater, an AM radio with an earplug, a diary—starting after Thanksgiving and running out a few days before Christmas, when Hetty would have to go back downtown to shop in order for Gail to have anything to open Christmas morning. Her aunt always had an excuse for the early giving: Gail could wear it to the chorale concert or Penny's party or she could write in her diary tonight about her date so she wouldn't forget how things were. Hetty if she knew about Boogan would have either come downstairs with a getaway dress and an excuse flimsy as off-brand Kleenex or she would be sleeping with Uncle Ray's single barrel 20 gauge propped next to the bed.

Gail thought about Hetty, pictured herself telling her aunt about Boogan as Hetty painted over the honeysuckle on the bathroom walls. They would move around the house, have a cup of tea while the paint dried, Gail talking off and on, a rambling conversation without consequences in which Boogan's name came and went like a well-meaning neighborhood dog. As Hetty's wrists mixed the oils and then began to stroke purple pansies or thorny budding roses the size of a man's hand or English ivy onto the walls, Gail would begin to tell the deep truth: *I love him. I want him.*

Boogan moved in the same rhythms, never hurrying, wearing the expensive shirt she bought him the same way he wore his more usual flannel ones. He walked beside her in the halls, bending to hear what she said and holding doors and kissing her in one of the three places at school he had chosen as carefully as deerstands for their remoteness, invisibility, and escape routes. Her favorite was just inside the auditorium door, where they loved briefly each day between Gail's Chemistry and Government classes and Boogan's Geography and Math for Daily Living. The room was high and dim with sloping floorboards and smelled of paint, cedar sweeping compound, and dust. The auditorium was the only room of the school she had sung in or been in at night. The tall windows and heavy curtains made good kissing light.

After Chemistry she found Boogan in the hall waiting for her and, as they walked, him telling how Pettus had been sent to the principal's for deliberately mispronouncing *peninsula*, she drew him down the side hall and into the room of empty theater seats, threw her arms around his neck, and kissed him hard, open-mouthed. She pulled him to her, pressing herself against his leg as certain boys at proms and dances had tried to do to her during slow songs. Boogan kissed her back, his tongue doing laps around her open lips. He slipped a hand into her back pocket, a first for him. She slowed the kiss, drawing softly along the roof of his mouth and retreating into her own. He followed. Deeply. His other hand entered her other pocket and pressed her to him, the two of them blooming into a single warm-blooded *yes*. Eleanor Roosevelt hadn't had this from her crippled husband. Gail thought of the flairing white magnesium in chemistry: *however short it burns is long enough*, she thought. Boogan put a hand to her shirt, pressed her shallow breast gently into his palm with one long moment of pressure, then let it slip down to rest on her hip as they drew out of the deep end of the kiss.

"I love you," he said—another first.

Anywhere else the words would have been less, but they came out small, in a whisper *here*, in the dim enormous room where she had tried for and failed the good parts, receiving instead an invisible role in the mobs the drama coach wrote into each musical. His love opened shyly in the biggest room she knew of, where everybody in school could have sat at once, not quietly. Those empty, heart-carved wooden seats under the high brownstained ceiling where there could have been so many people there was only Boogan.

"Thursday," she said.

"Yes."

Thursday came and Hetty had Desirae at the Hair Haven wash, condition, and french braid her hair, though she had no appointment. Afterward she went to the Foodliner and filled a plastic basket with cheese balls, cans of mixed nuts, butter mints, table water crackers, pineapple-orange juice, gingerale, a canteloupe, strawberries, and sherbet, then ordered two small cakes at the bakery downtown. She parked in her driveway, leaving the groceries in the car, and walked across the yard to the board fence that separated the Kellers' property from hers. She propped her elbows on the top board and waited. After a few minutes Mr. Keller came around the house from the back, pushing an empty wheelbarrow.

"Hey there, Miss Hett."

"Mr. Keller. I wondered if you might do me a favor. I have a recipe calling for champagne."

He looked at her, taking off his garden gloves. "I believe you better stay on the wagon, Miss Hetty."

"Jewel. Listen to me, now. It's for a recipe."

"You reckon you could let me see it, then?"

He put his hands on the edge of the top fenceboard, looking out across her yard as if she had asked him to rake her leaves.

"All right, then. It's for Gail. I think she might announce her engagement tonight."

"Gail? She's at no age to be getting married."

"She's older than you were if I recall."

He smiled and shook his head. "So she is. All right, then. For Gail. And you can tell her congratulations for me and Sherry. Maybe send her over to see us one day soon." He turned and started toward the house.

"Jewel? Not pink."

He raised a hand and kept walking.

Hetty looked down the fence to where the back of Gail's playhouse butted against it. Hetty had built it out of what Ray had left her in the cushions of his chair, filling in the blurred parts in his spirit by looking at the barn he'd built when they bought the place or by just standing there waiting, nails between her lips and in her housecoat pockets. The week after the funeral she had picked up an old pipe of his—he'd been quit ten years by that time—and the plan for the secret door had drawn itself on the back of her eyelids. That was just like Ray, spending all that spirit on boards and nails and plumbness. Building something so it could be outgrown, just like she was doing.

Hetty waited for two hours in the kitchen, telling time by the steepness of sunlight through the windows. Gail had not come home nor would she, Hetty knew. A love that cut off other loves was serious, would not be stopped, and Gail loved this boy in that way, to not bring him to the house. How strange for Gail not to introduce Hetty and the boy one to the other for mutual admiration. Since she was six Gail had initiated select girls into the inner circle of her heart by taking them into the rooms Hetty had painted with flowers and cornfields that (Hetty knew, had heard it so from inside Gail) made the back part of her heart ache. But Gail had shown this boy nothing—not the pantry closet painted with sleeping bats and stalagmites or Hetty's bathroom with flowers copied from Georgia O'Keefe on the back of the door and Gaugin's brown-breasted island women along the walls. Her niece had left without bringing him home; it was as if the disciples had kidnapped Jesus, carrying him off to some island in the Sea of Galilee where he could feed all of them on a biscuit and a couple of shiners and love them the way they had always wanted to be loved. That was how Gail loved this boy, not as new breasts and mood-ring estrogen loved, over-ripening the heart into a soft peach, but as a woman who knew there was everything to lose now.

She took the old metal cooler from the washroom and began to load the wedding supplies into it from the refrigerator, running out of room before she got to the tub of sherbet. She went back to the washroom and fetched Ray's old styrofoam minnow bucket down from its nail. The tub fit into it perfectly. She walked briskly to her bedroom, stood with her back to the dresser mirror, and held up her mother's old hand mirror at various angles: the French braid was intact, if a bit too intricate for her personality. She turned, smoothed her dress, then put on her new flats and went back to the kitchen, reminding herself about the good spoons.

She called the preacher to tell him she was going after them, but he said he wouldn't go, that they were running from God. Hetty said she believed they thought they were running *to* Him and she guessed they would all find out for sure according to whether God supplied them somehow with a preacher who wasn't afraid of a little mess.

She wedged the cooler between the back seat and the spare tire to make sure it didn't tip and slammed the trunk. Then she walked down the pebble driveway and put one foot in the road, closing her eyes, waiting for ripples.

Gail had brought Boogan one of her Uncle Ray's ties but neither of them could knot it right. They pulled out in Pettus's mail jeep from the parking lot next to the Home Ec-Industrial Arts building with Gail still twisting and looping the silk where it fell from around her neck down between her breasts. She had told Boogan to wear the blue pinstriped shirt she'd given him and khaki slacks and had searched her uncle's closet until she found a tie that would make them look like a couple, finally having to ditch the dress she wanted to wear for a navy one with white polka dots. Gail strung and poked, crushing her chin into her throat to watch her fingers fumble at the cloth. She tried to remember Uncle Ray in front of the dresser mirror—something about a rabbit running around a tree and into its hole.

"I can't believe I'm marrying a man who can't tie his own tie," she said.

"I can't believe I'm marrying a girl'd make me wear one."

"Uh-huh. You must really be in love."

Boogan laughed. "I b'lieve I am." The sun was shining through the grimy windshield and through the steering wheel he could feel the wind wiggling the front end lightly like a fish on a line.

Gail untied the mess she had created and started over. The hiss of the knot pulling loose reminded her of what her sophomore English teacher had said about the rich people on the *Titanic*, how festive it was after they hit the iceberg—a band playing as the ship settled in the water, waiters continuing to serve drinks. Gail saw Christmas lights when she thought about it, the whole numb, cordial disaster lit by little white bulbs. Stinking rich Ben Guggenheim going to his cabin to change into a white dinner jacket, then returning to the deck to help women and babies into lifeboats. A survivor had watched him smoke at the rail, chatting with his valet as the boats pulled away.

"Can we stop at the next place that has a phone? I want to call Aunt Het."

They pulled in at a gas station. There was no answer at home.

Hetty picked up Gail's trail going north out of town toward the mountains. At first the signs were strong, love and adrenalin fresh and choppy as a motorboat wake, but as she drove on, the track calmed and cooled. She smelled Ray's aftershave, saw him talking soundlessly to a twin brother and fumbling with a tie. Ten miles later she glimpsed a man with dark, oiled hair in a white tuxedo and smelled the ocean, then a full auditorium—the right half of the audience boys wearing suits, the left half all girls in off-white veils and dresses—with the marching band playing a Juice Newton song. Twenty signless miles further down the road, worried she'd missed one of their turns, Hetty pulled over alongside a pasture of cream-colored cows, got out, and stood leaning forward in the road, listening.

She heard her phone ringing. She bowed her head and leaned against a fender.

"Has she quit on you, ma'am?"

Hetty looked across the road where the voice had come from. A man in a black suit stood with his hands clasped in front of him in the sandy yard of an unpainted cement block house no bigger than a garage.

"Nobody's quit on anybody. She stopped to call me."

"Ma'am?"

She looked at him. He stepped over the ditch to the edge of the road, his shoulders rising in the suit as he inhaled.

"I said, has your car quit on you?"

"I'm not deaf. No, it hasn't. I needed to stretch and listen a minute, that's all."

"Reckon we all need to do that every once in a while." He nodded, looking both ways down the road as if he were going to cross. He began to turn back toward the house, one hand raised. "You have a nice evening, now."

"Sir?"

He stopped, mid-turn.

"Are you a minister? I see you have a cross leaning next to the door there."

"We are all ministers, ma'am. I preach some, if that's what you mean."

"You can marry people?"

"If I wasn't already married I could."

"I mean can you conduct weddings—join couples in holy matrimony."

"Yes'm."

"Then listen, please sir. The niece I raised from a toddler is somewhere up this road with a boy. I don't know where they're at, but she wants to marry him and I want to be there for it. I need a preacher." She stopped suddenly. "You're not Catholic are you?"

"Not no more, no. Christian, pure and simple. Nothing but the blood."

They looked at each other across the road and the preacher looked off down where she had come from.

"I reckon you want me to come 'long with you, then."

"Yes. They're not far now."

"I'll need my book," he said. As he turned and walked back toward the squat house Hetty noticed his pants were a different shade from his coat. He went inside, reemerging a minute later with a tattered black Bible which he carried up the bank and across the road to the car. He got in, bringing with him a strong scent of cedar shavings and something musky, a distantly familiar corncrib smell.

Hetty rolled down the window and leaned out as if she were listening. "It's ringing again," she said. "Further off. They must have stopped again."

She started the engine and spun off with the preacher's knees pressed up against the dashboard. He looked at her as if she had eaten a frog right there in front of him.

"You got a shine." He said it like he was confirming drastic news. "Bless your heart."

From a scenic overlook Boogan saw the car glimmer in the distance as it shot the gaps between treetops, the late afternoon sun dazzling off the windshield as the car rounded the mountain below them. Gail stood out of the rocking chair and leaned against the rail over the gorge, struggling to see the car through its glare before it disappeared behind the hip of the mountain. She had been telling him about being trapped on a ski lift at Gatlinburg on a summer vacation years before and when she stopped in the middle of the story—men on the ground below her had thrown a rope with a harness on the end of it over the lift cable and were working the line down the wire to her chair—when she stopped in the middle of the story to say her aunt was coming, he knew how the child Gail had felt, suspended, bouncing mildly between the tops of the sweetgums, her stomach dangling at the end of a slinky. Football teammates had told him that their great spinejarring hits and blind, soft-fingered catches hap-

pened in slow motion. Boogan had known what they meant, but he recognized now that they were wrong, that time never slowed or changed at
all, that it was your brain searching every frame of what was happening
to find a way in or out. He stood, saying she was a mile off still, that they
could make it, come on.

But Gail had turned to look across the gorge where the sun still lit the
chest and shoulders of the mountain opposite them. Something in her
turning—her fists closing tight on the metal pipe railing, her shoulders
squaring, the way a breeze at that moment arrived from the other side—
told him this was a stand. He looked into the dim gorge, catching a gleam
of silent whitewater from its depths.

"Right here on the brink," he said. "Boogan's last stand."

Gail only put her hands out as if for balance. "Wallenda."

"What?"

"He walked across it barefooted. On a wire."

Boogan heard the gravel in the parking lot grind under tires, a growling
sound like a loose predator would make. A tightness rose up his throat
and he felt his knees bend, his fingers open. He saw Gail against the twilight, leaning over the dropoff in her dark dress, the hem of it billowing
in a slow ripple in the breath of coolness that blew up from the valley.
The dress danced, moving around her stillness as she leaned with her
thighs pressed against the rail, her arms straight and fists tight around the
iron, her oaky hair blowing. Except for the polka dots she looked like a
woman carved onto the front of a ship, leaning into wherever they were
going.

"Gail, honey."

Gail turned and Boogan with her. A small woman in a sparkling blue
dress stood on the floorboards just inside the doorless door from the parking lot. Boogan had never seen sequins before or a woman old enough to
have been his mother who was beautiful and the sudden appearance of
both in the Tallulah Gorge overlook at twilight made him sure for a second that he was dreaming. These things didn't happen. Gail didn't reply,
only flew to her aunt in a colt-legged run and hugged her.

"I tried to call . . ."

"I heard you, honey. I know."

"I'm sorry."

"No." Hetty gripped Gail's arms and pushed her a step back. "You're not sorry. You don't ever be sorry for loving. But you ought to be sorry for not bringing him to me, not knowing I'd be fair to him. When have I not let you love anything, Gail?"

She looked at Boogan, her pink lipstick going narrow around her mouth. "And you ought to be sorry, taking all a old woman's got. You've not got to be your daddy all over again."

Boogan went red. "I'm not Deddy."

"No, you're sure not. But he's in your nature."

Gail looked from one to the other. "You know Boogan?" Her eyeliner had run when she had hugged her aunt and to Boogan she looked bleakly stunned, hungry.

"Boogan," Hetty said, as if they had been introduced at a tea. She shook his still hand. "Hetty Tucker. I'm pleased to meet you. I would like to say my niece has told me a lot about you." She smiled.

"Now, Boogan, if you'll excuse us, I would like to talk to Gail in private." She saw him stiffen and step toward Gail and held up a hand. "Now wait. Let me say that I am not against anything. I only want to know the same is true for her."

"Go, Boogan."

"Gail—"

Go wait with the preacher."

"The what?"

"He's in the car."

"You brought a preacher?"

"Boogan. Just go."

Boogan found him leaning against Hetty's front fender, his arms sadly crossed, a gangly, pepper-pored man in a black suit. He looked as if he'd been stretched past full height.

"Hidy," he said.

"Hey."

"I hear you're marrying."

Boogan looked at the Pepsi machine and put a hand in his left pocket.

"Man could do worse," the preacher said.

"He could." Boogan chose Nugrape.

"They bleed you know. And cry: my first wife could cry like forty over putting too much sugar in the tea."

"You want something?"

"I just want you to know what you're doing, friend."

"I meant did you want a drink."

"I might have a sip of yours."

Boogan put in two quarters and punched Nugrape again. He handed a can to the preacher.

"Much obliged." The can sliced open with a tearing metal sound. He slurped. "Married ain't never what you think. Jesus was *the* bridegroom and look what-all his bride done to him."

"I ain't ever hit a preacher before."

"I ain't ever been hit. Look, boy, you do what you want to, what the Lord leads you to. I ain't saying you got a choice in it, not if it's a true wedding. If it's spirit-filled you got no more druthers than the man in the moon. Just you know the difference between the spirit and your pecker."

"I never yet mistook it for anything else."

"Son. You ain't got her in trouble, have you?"

"Nossir. I ain't touched her."

The preacher bent to look Boogan in the face. "You ain't touched her atall?"

"Well. We kiss some."

"But you've not touched her womb?"

Boogan rounded on the preacher, his unopened soda clenched in his right fist.

The old man lifted a hand. "I'm only a-counseling you, son. No offense." He took a hasty sip from his can. "You don't owe no man no confession. Just don't you wait too long to tell God what He already knows. Now you done said you ain't touched her, so you ain't sinned. But them balls a yours ain't full of cheap buckshot that'll rust away to nothing if you don't use it. The less you use 'em the stronger they get. Now you tell me that ain't so."

"It's so."

"Verily verily it's so. I believe they got a vote in this marriage thing, too, now ain't they?"

Boogan looked across the empty gravel of the parking lot to the shoulder of the mountain rising shingly and vertical on the other side of the road. He didn't say anything.

"You a man, boy. You can't help your flesh, the wanting in the meat. But don't you be led around by it. No, don't answer me back. You just hear what I'm a-telling you. They's fish in the world hounded to the death to go back where they's born and scatter their seed. Them fish don't settle. They want the rocks where they's born or nothing, and it don't matter what rapids or waterfalls or grizzly bears they got to beat to get there. That's love. Both of you got to be ready to make that trip alone before you can be one flesh."

"I ain't some fish flipping around in a river."

"You about to be."

The preacher leaned back over the hood, tipping the last purple slosh from the can to his mouth. The muscles seethed in his throat. Boogan looked back at the mountain, all shelving rock and clenched trees.

Hetty came through the door from the overlook, glinting.

"We need a church," she said.

"We were looking for a courthouse."

"We need a church," Hetty repeated.

She declared that Boogan had already seen too much of the bride on the day of the wedding and that he shouldn't lay eyes on Gail again until she walked down the aisle. She was to ride to the church with her aunt. Boogan bridled at this, but Gail—speaking through a knothole in the overlook wall—talked him into it, saying she would make Hetty drive no more than a car length ahead. The preacher rode with Boogan in the mail jeep.

The church was a small cinderblock house ten miles back down the highway. It squatted in a grove of cedars where enough darkness had collected for the church jalousie windows to glow yellow. They pulled to a stop behind Hetty's car in the sandy yard, Boogan not switching off his engine until the aunt had gotten out of the car and come around to the preacher's window of the mail jeep.

"You two let us go in first and get into the bathroom. Have you got a key, Reverend?"

"It ain't locked, Miss Hetty. It ain't got a bathroom neither."

Hetty looked back at her car, considering, then at the church, its plank porch resting on concrete blocks. "I suppose it's all one room, then."

"Yes ma'am. No walls between us in God's house."

Boogan and the preacher went in first. The church smelled of plywood and cedar needles and something else, a vaguely familiar musk that reminded Boogan of a sunny, rocky hillside above the creek near his father's house. There were no pews under the three hanging lightbulbs, only an assortment of battered metal and wooden chairs and benches and one row of four threadbare theater seats, all facing the emptiness where the altar should have been and where there was no dais, table, or pulpit, just bare floorboards and against the wall a box the size of a steamer trunk. An army cot leaned folded in a back corner next to a stack of folded blankets.

"We only just moved in," the preacher said, watching Boogan size the place up. "You just remember where the temple's really at."

Boogan looked at the ceiling—bare rafters with new plywood laid across them to form a kind of attic—and out the open door of the church into the twilight in the yard where the aunt leaned in the car window, her hips twitching as her hands moved inside, tucking or brushing. As if she felt his eyes, the aunt straightened and turned to look at him. She smiled.

"You turn around now," she said. He pivoted and found himself fixed in the eyes of the preacher. Boogan stared back at him as he had once stared across the line of scrimmage at receivers and tight ends before the ball was snapped.

"You hear that spirit rustling, boy? Hear her coming through them cedars to brood on this place? She's a hanging over you with her warm breast, right now. Breathing on you."

Boogan dipped his head once, nodding or bowing. He heard the car door slam, his eyes pinned to the preacher's dark, unblinking gaze.

"Feel her. Smoke of God filling them veins and arteries. Fire in your bosom. If she ain't there you can't call her in. If she ain't there don't you take this girl's little hand." The preacher closed his eyes, squinting them shut as if he were in pain.

"God gives love," he said. "All of Him we have is love."

There was a rustle from the porch. Boogan turned and watched Gail's aunt coming down the pine plank aisle, pausing between each step to compensate for the smallness of the church. She held three flowers folded from road maps in her hand. On her second step the preacher broke into "Leaning on Jesus" on a harmonica and on her fourth stride Hetty stopped not four feet from where Boogan stood with his hands clasped in front of him and sang to him, high and reedy and closer to seeing God than anybody there:

> Oh how sweet to walk
> In this pilgrim way,
> Leaning on the everlasting arms!
> Oh how bright the path
> Grows from day to day!
> Leaning on the everlasting arms!

The preacher played on and Hetty sang another verse about what a fellowship, what a joy divine, and more leaning and what a love so sweet, what a peace is mine, leaning on the everlasting arms, and then the preacher paused, letting Hetty come the rest of the way down the aisle so that Boogan saw straight down the level floor to the door where Gail stood bathed in light from the bare yellow blub screwed into the wall outside. She stood wrapped to her shoulders in white cotton, a pillbox hat tipped to her forehead and spilling a gossamer veil down over her eyes to her chin.

His heart did not swell. He didn't smile. He stood there simpler than he had ever been, reduced to the rest of his life, everything before and after this minute tiny and over already like something seen through the wrong end of a telescope. He stood there before eternity wearing someone else's crook-knotted necktie and she walked smiling toward him as the preacher played "I Surrender All." He didn't see that she was crying until she stood facing him in front of the preacher, the tears streaming like rain under the flowers woven into the veil.

The preacher finished the hymn, shook the harmonica once, and put it in his inside suit pocket. Facing the bride and groom, he reached into his other inside pocket and brought out a cornerworn black velvet box which he laid on top of his Bible. He put both hands under the dog-eared Bible as if gravity's ache for the book had suddenly doubled and looked at them, bearing grave news.

"God has brought us here to make you one," he said. He let the silence stretch until the voice of a whipoorwill floated from the twilight outside through the open door of the church. He smiled with his lips closed, as if he did not believe in baring his teeth. The girl's aunt stood to her right and a little behind her and the preacher looked at the aunt still smiling.

"Most times I would ask who brings this woman to be given to this man. But this girl has done brought her ownself. Blinded to love by love she has a-fled her home without reason. But God has restored aunt and niece, mother and child, guiding Miss Hetty's pursuit through His marvelous signs and wonders. Because God is love and works through love, though His perfect love is to us a darkening mirror." He paused, looking beyond the couple to the back of the small converted house where a moth carreered spastically around a bare lightbulb. "So I will ask who comes with this woman to witness her union?"

"I do." Hetty glittered in blue sequins, holding an origami bouquet of roadmaps. "I come with Gail."

"You're welcome, sister." He looked at the groom, a wiry young man as stiff in his collar and tie as a deer in headlights. One sleeve of his black and gold letterman's jacket was scattered with stars. "And do you come alone, friend?"

"Yessir. I reckon so."

"Then I stand with you. Do you have rings?"

The boy stood looking through the veil at his bride where she waited beside him in a dress older than his father. An anxious silence descended before he put a hand into his pocket and brought out a change purse, zipping it open to reveal a solitary diamond on a thin ring. The girl opened her own palm on a band carved with leaves and vines worn smooth.

"It was my grandfather's," she whispered to the groom.

The preacher took the rings in his fist, closed his eyes tightly, and pressed his lips to his clenched fingers.

"Pray."

They waited a polite time, heads bowed.

"God father of all come to us and burn away pride and lust and make these two one flesh. Send Your spirit among us, Lord, and fill us and fill this marriage."

The whipoorwill whispered again and, though there had been no

Amen, they opened their eyes to the Bible, light in the preacher's hand now, open to pages sprent with words dipped in the blood of God's only boy and around the other fisted hand, looped like a necklace, the snake. Light from the hanging bulbs reflected off his jeweled eyes and slipped in a fluid sheen down his bands black, yellow, and red where they wound around the preacher's wrist. The head lay watching them on the preacher's cracked knuckles.

The preacher stood like a carved saint, palms out, neither offering nor withdrawing scripture or snake. His eyes were open—the same yellowed whites and dark pupils. The groom reached out slowly, the snake's head rising to his hand until the blunt nose mildly bumped at the base of the boy's index finger.

The boy could not have said how the ring came to lie in his hand. The preacher did not open his fist, but the ring, perfect and golden, was there, the snake's dry tubular belly slipping over it in smooth, swallowing undulations as it passed from the preacher to him. He felt Gail's hand closing on his own over the ring and the snake, saw the tiny head rear from the miniature cave between her thumb (with its tender, worry-chewed nail) and forefinger. Its tongue tasted the air tentatively; it moved over and around Gail's wrist, then looped back toward the boy's arm, tracing a figure eight between their clasped hands. The preacher opened his empty fist and brought the velvet box from under his Bible. He cracked the lid and the snake slipped back over Gail's white knuckles and into its darkness. The preacher tucked the snake in its little velvet coffin back into his breast pocket.

"Look at one another. Repeat after me, Gail. I, Gail, take thee, Boogan,"—the unknown name slipping into his mouth long and unmistakable from a darkness he trusted—"to be my wedded husband."

Gail recited, feeling the words slip like ring after colored ring of snake over her skin and around her fingers and wrists, blood, sun, and darkness in a self-propelled circuit that was all one life. She ceased speaking and watched Boogan's lips form the words she had just spoken—*sickness, poorer, honor, death.* And soon after she spoke again, *plight thee my troth* and in the still room, faintly dizzy, she heard the salting shake of her old pompoms and watched a football crowd breathing steam in the cold under stadium lights, their eyes fixed on what was behind her as she led them, chanting *Plight* thee, *Plight* thee, *Plight* thee. She smiled vowing through the veil into Boogan's face. He smiled back, reddening, uneasy, happy in this strange dignity and hoarse as the preacher gave him a name for his life.

"What the spirit has brought together let no man break asunder," the preacher said. He stood there, the Bible spread on his hands, watching them as if he expected spontaneous combustion. "You can kiss her, now, boy."

They filed out between the crooked rows of folding chairs, Hetty leading, Gail on Boogan's arm squeezing down the narrow aisle after her, and behind them the preacher, playing the "Hallelujah Chorus" on the harmonica. Outside on the small porch they paused to look at the dozen-odd cows in the pasture across the road. The cows chewed placidly, knee-deep in grass, their pale caramel hides glowing in the sunset.

Hetty brought a cooler from the trunk of her car and spread a lace tablecloth on the warm, ticking hood. She arranged mixed nuts, a cheese ball, table water crackers, and two cakes—one chocolate, one white and ghostly in the twilight—along the top of the passenger-side fender. Gail watched from the porch, her eyes filling, until her aunt turned and faced them, her blue gloves placed palm-to-palm at her waist as if she prayed them come nibble. Gail hugged her and kissed her ear and said thank you, thank you, crushing the old woman to her as she had never been able to do when they were one family. Boogan felt somehow like he was the cause of the crying and looked off at the cows. But even the cows were watching the women, cuds still in their slow mouths, their eyes soft and dark as pond bottoms. Boogan felt the preacher's eyes on him.

"She'll hug ever woman she sees from here on out," the preacher said. "But that one in particular."

"I can see why."

"Yes sir, I can, too. Congratulations, boy." He stuck out his hand and Boogan took it. "You done right in spite of yourself."

"Come eat," Hetty said.

They ate sitting on the unrailed porch, enjoying the small ritual of salt and sugar. To Gail each bite bloomed in her watering mouth, baptized and significant. The cheese had been ripened by time, the cake blended from commonplace egg and flour into one sweet, leavened wholeness, and the crackers and small portions, the melted sherbet, reminded her of the Lord's Supper at church. The world was invisibly charged and flaming, full of a new ghost who had stolen like scentless smoke into the food, the cows, the glowing bugspotted porchlight, her very clothes. Her navel prickled as it did during late summer thunderstorms. She watched Boogan where he stood by the car sweetening the whang of his paper cup of champagne with spoonfuls of mushy sherbet from her uncle's ice-filled minnow bucket.

Boogan pretended not to know she was watching him. He didn't know what to say to her now that they were one flesh. The darkness deepening around the church reminded him of his father's fists on the lightless road home. Boogan worried about where he came from, about feeling his way through the dark. Her hand touched his arm and she smiled at him. She put her arms inside his letter jacket and reached around him, pressing her face into his shoulder and giving a little shiver. "It's getting cold out here."

"Here." Without pulling away from her he tugged the jacket off and threw it around her shoulders. "That ought to warm you up some."

She looked up into his face and he smelled the oldness of the dress over her familar rosey perfume. Her smile was one he hadn't seen before, slow and sleepy, like she'd just woke up. He told her she smelled good.

"All I smell are cedar trees and champagne," she answered. But she also smelled past wearings in his shirt and jacket and the woodsmoke and leafmold musk of his father's house, which she had never seen. She would wring that smell out of him, wash his arms and shoulders with a soft cloth.

He wondered how much champagne she'd had.

"We ought to go," she said.

Biographical Notes

◆

EDITORS

ALAN DAVIS, editor, is the author of *Rumors from the Lost World*, a collection of stories available from New Rivers Press. His fiction and nonfiction appear in such journals as *The Hudson Review* and *The Quarterly* and in such newspapers as *The New York Times* and *The San Francisco Chronicle*. He has received a Minnesota State Arts Board Fellowship and a Loft-McKnight Award of Distinction in Creative Prose. He grew up in Louisiana and now lives in Minnesota, where he teaches at Moorhead State University.

MICHAEL C. WHITE, associate editor, is the author of *A Brother's Blood*, a novel published by HarperCollins in the U.S. and by Viking/Penguin in England and Canada. His fiction has appeared in numerous magazines and journals, including *Redbook*, *American Way* and *New Letters*. He lives in Massachusetts and teaches at Springfield College.

ASSISTANT EDITORS

LIN ENGER, under the pen name L. L. Enger, has published six novels in collaboration with his brother Leif, including *The Sinners' League* (Otto Penzler Books, Simon and Schuster). He is a graduate of the Iowa Writers' Workshop and a former Michener Fellow whose stories appear in various literary magazines.

DEB MARQUART's work has received numerous prizes, among them the Dorothy Churchill Cappon Essay award from *New Letters* on two occasions and the Guy Owen Poetry Prize from *Southern Poetry Review*. Her book of poems, *Everything's a Verb*, is available from New Rivers Press, and her fiction, poetry and essays have been published widely. She teaches creative writing at Iowa State University.

PETER MCNAMARA, a fiction writer, manages a bookstore in New Orleans.

REEN MURPHY has served as co-editor of *Lake Region Review* and has published her work in such journals as *Plainswoman*, *Northland Quarterly*, *Loonfeather* and *Kalliope*. She is a graduate student at New Mexico State University.

MAGGIE RISK has received scholarships from the Bread Loaf Writers Conference, the Sewanee Writers Conference and the Ropewalk Writers Retreat. A graduate of the master's program in creative writing at the University of Denver, she has published stories in various magazines (one was a finalist for the Katherine Anne Porter Prize) and has taught writing at the University of Cincinnati.

AUTHORS

MICHAEL BERES has published stories in literary journals such as *Ascent, Michigan Quarterly Review* and *Missouri Review* and in mass circulation magazines such as *Cosmopolitan* and *Playboy*. He has also published two paperback mystery novels, *Sunstrike* and *Illegal Procedure*.

WILLIAM BORDEN's novel, *Superstoe*, was reissued in 1995 by Orloff Press, Berkeley; it was first published in the U.S. by Harper & Row and in England by Victor Gollancz. He has won the PEN Sydicated Fiction Award, and his fiction has appeared in numerous magazines.

CATHERINE BRADY teaches at the College of Notre Dame and in the Masters in Writing Program at the University of San Francisco. Her stories have appeared widely in magazines and anthologies, including *Redbook, I Know Some Things: Stories about Childhood by Contemporary Writers* (Faber & Faber, 1992) and *The Next Parish Over: A Collection of Irish-American Writings* (New Rivers Press, 1993).

BROCK CLARKE has worked in a fiberglass plant, as a newspaper journalist, and currently teaches English while in graduate school at the University of Rochester in New York. "The Reasons" is a part of a collection of short stories.

GARNETT KILBERG COHEN, a former fiction editor of *The Pennsylvania Review*, has published fiction and nonfiction in many journals, among them *Alaska Quarterly Review*. A collection of stories is available from the University of Missouri Press.

A. A. HEDGE COKE, with an M.F.A. from Vermont College, has a book of poetry, *Look At This Blue*, forthcoming from Coffee House Press and a chapbook, *The Year of the Rat*, forthcoming from Tender Buttons Press. She has published prose in a variety of magazines and anthologies, including *13th Moon, Caliban, Skin Deep: Women Writing about Race and Color in America* and *Reinventing the Enemy's Language*.

JENNIFER C. CORNELL won the 1994 Drue Heinz Prize for Literature for *Departures*, a collection of twelve short stories set in Northern Ireland and published by the University of Pittsburgh Press. Her work appears in the 1995 edition of *The Best American Short Stories*. She is completing a second collection and a nonfiction book on the representations of Northern Ireland in contemporary British television drama.

MISHA HOEKSTRA lives in the desert and writes in San Francisco. "The Brother" is from *The Joy of Edge Tools*, a work-in-progress.

TRACY JENNISON lives in Georgia.

GORDON JOHNSTON has a Ph.D. in American Literature and creative writing from the University of Georgia and teaches at Presbyterian College in Clinton, South Carolina. "Plight" is part of a novel-in-stories. Another story from the collection appears in *The Georgia Review*.

STEVE LATTIMORE has an M.F.A. from Iowa and is a Wallace Stegner Fellow at Stanford. His stories have appeared in various literary magazines.

DAVID MASON's narrative poem "The Country I Remember" won the Alice di Castigliona Prize, awarded by the Poetry Society of America, and is the title of his second collection of poetry from Story Line Press. His story "Pullandbedamned Point" was chosen by Anne Tyler for Third Prize in the third edition of *American Fiction*. Like that earlier story, the one herein is part of a book of interrelated stories set mostly in the Pacific Northwest.

CAMMIE MCGOVERN won the 1994 Nelson Algren Short Fiction contest sponsored by the *Chicago Tribune*. She has an M.F.A. from the University of Michigan and a Stegner Fellowship, and has been published widely.

MEGAN RANDALL grew up in Port Jefferson, New York. Her work has appeared in *The South Dakota Review* and elsewhere. She also writes on a regular basis for *The Light Journey*, an alternative newspaper.

NANCY REISMAN's fiction has appeared in various magazines, including *Glimmer Train*. She has received an M.F.A. from University of Massachusetts at Amherst and has taught at the Rhode Island School of Design. She currently lives in Madison, Wisconsin.

CHERYL PEARL SUCHER is a recipient of the 1992 John H. McGinniss Award for Fiction and a 1990 Kenyon Review Award for Literary Excellence. Her first novel is forthcoming from Scribner's.

NADJA TESICH's memoir, *Shadow Partisan*, was published to wide acclaim by New Rivers Press. She lives in New York City.